FREI KISSING

SEASON ONE

HARPER BLISS

OTHER HARPER BLISS NOVELS
Still the One
The Love We Make
A Family Affair
The Duet
And Then She Kissed Me
That Woman Next Door
About That Kiss
At Your Most Beautiful
A Breathless Place
If You Kiss Me Like That
Two Hearts Trilogy
Next in Line for Love
A Lesson in Love
Life in Bits (with T.B. Markinson)
A Swing at Love (with Caroline Bliss)
Once Upon a Princess (with Clare Lydon)
In the Distance There Is Light
The Road to You
Far from the World We Know
Seasons of Love
Release the Stars
At the Water's Edge
High Rise (The Complete Collection)

THE PINK BEAN SERIES

FRENCH KISSING: SEASON ONE

HARPER BLISS

EPISODE ONE

JULIETTE

"We haven't had sex in months." Juliette gazed out of Claire's corner office window, hesitant to look her oldest friend and business partner in the eye. In the window's reflection, she could see Claire shuffle around nervously in her seat. "Nadia, she's just… hardly there anymore. And I'm not saying it's her fault, but since she got promoted—"

"It's her time, Jules," Claire interrupted. "You had yours. Now it's her turn."

This remark made Juliette spin around instantly. "I *had* mine?" She opened her palms to the sky and made a sweeping gesture. "Past tense? Then what's all this?"

"This is what we built. Through years of hard work and spousal neglect. I'm the best example of that."

"You're just single because you're so bloody difficult and no one's ever good enough." Juliette scanned Claire's flawless face. A few laughter lines bracketed her eyes and she dyed her hair now, but she still looked a decade below her physical age.

Claire pushed herself out of her chair and walked towards

Juliette. "No need to take it out on me, dear. I may be single but I'm getting plenty."

Frustration flared beneath Juliette's skin. "As long as you stay away from the interns—"

A loud knock on the door stopped Juliette mid-insult. Steph, dressed in tight jeans and equally tight blazer, appeared in the doorway and Juliette and Claire both burst out laughing.

"What?" The puzzled look on Steph's face made it difficult to stop the giggles, but this was their place of business and, in the end, everything always stopped for business.

"We were just talking about you. That's all," Claire said.

"Glad to be the source of such gaiety." Steph always kept her cool, no matter the circumstances. It was one of the main reasons they had decided to hire her straight out of school ten years ago, despite her indiscretion with one of the bosses. "Dominique Laroche wants to meet first thing on Monday."

"She's keen," Juliette said. "We want you in that meeting, Steph. Try to wear something… politically correct."

"Sure. I just bought a really cool red tank top—"

"Don't you fucking dare. She's MRL's rising star and we want to make an impression." Juliette stared into Steph's grinning face, realising too late her friend and employee was winding her up. "Just be on time tonight."

"Is there a dress code?" Steph asked.

"Just your usual über-lesbian attire will do."

"If everybody looked the same…" Steph hummed before turning on her heels and exiting Claire's office.

Juliette checked her watch. "I'd better get going." She couldn't stifle a sigh. "Oh, and just a heads-up, even though I wasn't supposed to tell you to avoid awkwardness… Nadia has invited some doctor from the hospital she wants you to meet."

Juliette watched Claire roll her eyes. "I thought we had agreed on no more set-ups?"

"We had, but Nadia only seems to follow her own rules these days."

"Hey, cut her some slack, okay? She's put up with your workaholic habits for years. You'll find a way to make it work again."

"We have talked about, um, means to spice things up…" A blush bloomed on Juliette's cheeks. She headed towards the visitor chair opposite Claire's desk, against which Claire was still leaning, and sat down. "But this does not leave this room, yeah?"

"Of course not." Claire's eyebrows were already arched up expectantly.

"We were a bit tipsy at the time, mind you, otherwise, I mean, we would never…" Juliette knew she was rambling. She took a deep breath and continued. "We were thinking about going to Les Pêches one of these weekends with the sole purpose of picking someone up for a threesome."

Claire's face broke out in a grin. "You? Miss Control Freak? Inviting a stranger into your bed?"

"Better a stranger than someone I know."

"I'm not so sure, Jules."

Juliette ignored the smirk tugging at Claire's lips. "What? Are you volunteering?"

"Been there, done that." Claire's face was now completely split by a smile baring her impeccable white teeth.

"I'm serious." Juliette wanted nothing more than to have a giggle at it all. "My relationship is falling apart and I don't know what to do about it."

Claire scooted closer and put a hand on her knee. "It's not falling apart. You're just going through a rough patch, adjusting to changes in your life. You'll be fine. You're Juliette and Nadia for heaven's sake."

"What if we're not, though? What if we're not fine?"

Claire gave her knee a squeeze. "Don't even think about it." She looked at her watch. "Don't you have a dinner party to prepare for?"

"Yes, heaven forbid I screw that up as well."

3

"Do you need help?"

Juliette shot Claire a disdainful glare. "You'd only end up setting my kitchen on fire."

"Fair enough." Claire pulled Juliette out of her chair and pecked her on the cheek before spinning her around and gently coaxing her towards the door. "I'll see you at eight."

Juliette made a brief stop in her office next door, powered off her computer and headed home. The Barbier & Cyr office was located on a side street of the Champs-Élysées and it was a fifteen-minute downhill walk to her and Nadia's flat. Juliette pushed any negative thoughts about her relationship to the back of her mind and focused on the dish she would prepare tonight. Coq au vin with gratin dauphinois. Not that she was overcompensating.

NADIA

"What were you thinking?" Nadia tried to ignore Juliette's question. She'd been expecting it all evening, but they hadn't had a moment alone. "You couldn't have picked a less compatible person for Claire. You know what she's like."

"Honey." Nadia turned around, back against the sink. "When will you get it out of your head that the only type of woman Claire will fall for is someone exactly like you?" She painted a tight smile on her face. "People change. Tastes evolve. You may have an excellent business relationship these days, but, from what you've told me, back in the day when you were dating, it wasn't all sunshine and roses, was it?"

Nadia witnessed how Juliette's jaw dropped.

"There are so many things wrong with all of what you just said." Juliette shook her head, no sign of kindness or amusement in her eyes. "I'm going back in there, but this conversation is far from over." She spun on her heels and left the kitchen, but, just before rounding the corner, faced Nadia once more. "Claire has been my best friend for more than twenty years. I believe I know a thing or two about her." And she was gone.

Nadia, once again, wondered when they'd stopped seeing eye to eye on most matters. It used to be so easy. Now they were seriously discussing threesomes—something that would never happen, if Nadia had any say in the matter—to save what was left of their relationship.

She opened the fridge and took out the chocolate cake she'd bought rather than made herself. Another strike against her.

"Everything under control?" Steph's voice startled her.

Nadia nodded, drew her lips into a wide smile and pushed her troubles to the back of her mind. "I'll be right out with dessert."

"The doctor's nice." Steph said it with that inflection in her voice Nadia had heard so many times. *Great.* "Are you trying to set her up with Claire? Because I'm not sure that's going to work out. But you know me, always willing to pick up the slack."

"What is it with you people? You spend two hours in someone's company and your mind's made up? Has anyone even asked Claire what she thinks?" Nadia only realised after she'd uttered the words that the volume of her voice was not adjusted to the fact that the kitchen was right next to the dining room.

"Did you call for me?" Claire, all groomed to perfection, appeared in the doorway.

Still with the chocolate cake in her hands, Nadia sighed. "No."

"Oh. Sorry." She shot Nadia a quick wink and disappeared with Steph hot on her heels.

Nadia straightened her back, lifted her chin, and carried the cake into the living room. "No need for applause, I didn't bake it myself."

"But you took the time to pick it up for us," Claire said.

"Looks great, honey." Juliette's voice had that now almost

familiar undercurrent of disdain and Nadia spotted the quick exchange of glances between her and Claire.

"I'll do the cutting," Margot, the—frankly—hot surgeon Nadia had invited to dinner with her friends, offered. "It's my job after all." It was true that, unlike most French people—and Juliette especially—Margot was not in love with the sound of her own voice and didn't produce an endless stream of meaningless words just to hear it non-stop. These days, Nadia much preferred a quick, quiet lunch with Margot to one of Juliette's laboured-over suppers. Not because of romantic motivations, but mainly because Juliette, although very careful not to criticise too directly, didn't seem to have that many good things to say about Nadia anymore.

Nadia sat down and regarded her friends and partner of ten years. She usually didn't feel so deflated in their company. This was time off work, time to relax, but, in all honesty, Nadia didn't mind working overtime if this was all she had to come home to.

Steph had adopted her usual pose, incapable of sitting in a chair like an adult, with one leg drawn up under her. Claire's blonde fringe was cut so it nearly did but just didn't fall into her eyes—eyes that Nadia had seen wander to Margot in unguarded moments, no matter what the others thought. Margot was her calm self, trained to remain level-headed in every situation. Maybe it worked against her a little bit in social situations, but if it hadn't been for her co-worker's lunch time advice over the past few weeks, Nadia wasn't sure she'd still be sitting at this table.

Then there was Juliette. She'd slipped out of her business suit for the evening and looked relaxed in jeans and t-shirt. How looks could be deceiving. Juliette Barbier, the love of her life, who couldn't feel more removed from her now than if she'd been on a mission to the North Pole.

And maybe she shouldn't, but Nadia did what she had to do to numb that feeling of dread spreading in her chest. The premonition that this could not last, that the setting was false, the people present mere actors playing well-rehearsed parts. She poured herself another glass of wine.

STEPH

Nadia was drunk, Juliette sported her angry scowl in response, Claire shuffled in her chair uncomfortably, and the hot doctor was about to leave. Steph had enough decency not to flirt with Margot in front of the others, despite their levels of indifference or intoxication. Claire and Juliette had become good friends, but they were still her bosses.

"I'm heading home as well." Steph got up out of her seat and hugged the hosts and Claire, who lived just down the street from Nadia and Juliette. Steph knew full well that, in a previous life, Claire and Juliette had been lovers, but to her, her two bosses seemed more like twins, like sisters who couldn't be away from each other for more than twenty-four hours.

She followed Margot to the elevator and hopped in with her.

"To be a fly on the wall now," she joked, trying to break the ice while admiring the doctor's all-leather outfit.

Margot just gave a small smile in response, obviously not very interested in gossiping about Nadia and the people she had just met.

"Heading straight home?" Steph asked, trying to coax even a few words out of her elevator companion, not being very good at silences in confined spaces.

With pursed lips, Margot just nodded. Was she giving Steph the cold shoulder? *Heavens.* She hadn't even tried anything yet, was just making polite conversation. They exited the building in silence. Steph had a good few inches on the doctor in height, but she had to quicken her pace to keep up with Margot's swift strides. They stopped at a sporty but quite heavy motorbike. Steph's eyes grew wide.

"Very nice to meet you, Steph. I'm sure I'll see you around."

Margot produced a key from her leather jacket pocket and unfastened the helmet chained to the bike's handlebar. *Could she get any hotter?*

"Would you like to go for a night cap?" It was as if Steph's brain had stopped working. Was she really using that crappy line on this gorgeous woman? Steph wasn't that used to going after someone like this. She just had to set foot in Les Pêches and at least one person would be all over her.

"I'm driving." Margot pointed at the bike and Steph was grateful for the darkness of the night hiding the sudden blush on her cheeks. "And I'm not much of a drinker. I'm not on call but I simply never know when someone's life will be in my hands. I like to be prepared."

The simple way in which she said it and the gravitas of her words made Steph accept them immediately. Clearly, Margot was out of her league—too serious, too smart and too level-headed. *Too much of a challenge as well?*

"Besides," Margot said, her helmet already at the top of her head. "No offence, but you're a bit young for me." With that, she slipped the helmet over her head, straddled the bike, pushed it off its stand and kicked it into gear. It was the most arousing thing Steph had seen in months, maybe years. Maybe ever.

Ouch. She watched Margot speed off with a roar in the night before heading for the Métro. She briefly contemplated getting off at Saint-Paul and drop by Les Pêches to nurse her wounded ego, but that would only result in mediocre sex and a hangover.

Instead, she took the underground to her flat near Père Lachaise, fed her cat and divided her thoughts between the memory of Margot driving off and Claire's words earlier that day, just before she left work. They wanted her in the Dominique Laroche meeting on Monday. If she made the right impression, they would let her take the lead on a very important account. It had been a long time coming and Steph was ready.

She had research to do this weekend. Les Pêches would be there the next weekend, and the next. Steph was thirty-three years old and it was time to take her career to the next level.

"What do you think, Pierrot?" she asked her grey-striped cat.

"Meow," he said.

CLAIRE

Claire high-fived Steph, not a gesture she often partook in, but Steph had just landed Barbier & Cyr its first politician as a client in its fourteen-year existence. Claire had always known politics and PR were a match made in heaven, but for the first time, she would reap the rewards.

Steph had been outstanding in the meeting with Dominique Laroche, sweeping her off her feet with her boyish charm as well as with deep knowledge of the smallest events in the rising députée's career. A winning combination.

"Impressive," she said as she ushered Steph and Juliette into her office for a debriefing. "She's all yours now." Claire liked to believe that she'd taught Steph all she knew, but their once intern and now co-worker was plenty savvy herself. She simply had the instinct. And she could seduce like no other.

A sly grin on Steph's face said it all. It was the same crooked smile Claire had briefly fallen for ten years ago, in a moment of weakness. Despite scolding herself for that misstep many times, she could still see how it had come about. Glancing at Juliette, her other, more serious ex, she wondered how the three of them had made it work so well.

"I hope you're ready to work around the clock," Juliette said. "When you're on a politician's payroll, you're always on standby."

"She'll be fine." Claire didn't want Juliette to ruin Steph's moment of glory just because she'd been suffering from a skewed work-life balance the past fourteen years or, to be more precise, because Nadia was starting to show signs of being fed up with it. "Steph? Are you up for it?"

She sat up in the chair she'd been slouching in in typical Steph fashion. "Can't wait."

"This woman is ambitious." Adrenaline surged in Claire's blood. "We want to be around when it really happens for her. You have to build a relationship with her based on trust. That's the most important thing. But before you do, you'll have to dig up all her dirty laundry."

"Consider it done." Steph cleared her throat. "Speaking of which and in the spirit of full disclosure… last Friday I made a bit of a pass at Margot when we were saying our goodbyes. She blew me off. We went our separate ways."

Claire shook her head. "*Quelle surprise.*"

"I know she was meant for you—"

"She wasn't *meant* for Claire," Juliette interjected. "For heaven's sake."

"It's all good, ladies. Please." Claire raised her hands in a conciliatory gesture. There were many perks to working with your best friends, but this was one of the downsides. "Steph, I wasn't expecting anything else from you." She turned to Juliette, who'd been in a foul mood since arriving at the office, despite their big meeting. "Please thank Nadia for introducing me to Margot. She's certainly intriguing, but it was hardly love at first sight. On either side."

"If you want to thank Nadia, you can do it yourself." Juliette brought a hand to her mouth as soon as she said it. "Sorry. I shouldn't bring my personal life to work. I will fix things at home. Let's move on."

Claire gave her a slight nod of the head before turning her attention back to Steph. "She blew you off? That must have stung?"

"Maybe I've peaked and the time has come to settle down."

"And pigs will fly," Claire said absent-mindedly, thinking back to last Friday when she'd found a tight-lipped, square-jawed trauma surgeon in leather pants in Juliette and Nadia's sofa. Margot had looked as ready to slice through someone's skin as to kick someone's ass. A vibe that had, admittedly, put Claire off from the start. She had to agree with Juliette on this, as on most things, that Nadia might have made an error of judgement. And she'd had no doubt in her mind that Steph would have tried something with the *inconnue* at the dinner party.

"I'm interviewing a potential new assistant in five minutes." Juliette tapped her watch. "Can we get on with it, please?"

"I hope she's good and intuitive and brings you a better mood to be in," Claire said. "I have lunch with Renson at Le Georges. I'll give him your love."

"I'll start digging into Laroche." Steph raised her eyebrows twice in quick succession and pushed herself out of her chair.

When they'd both left her office, before shifting her focus to work, Claire closed her eyes for a minute and wondered when was the last time she'd spent some time cultivating her own love life instead of discussing that of her friends.

JULIETTE

Sybille, the girl Juliette was interviewing for the position of her new PA, was the spitting image of Nadia ten years ago. Big brown eyes, that North-African complexion that made Juliette's knees go weak, a feistiness brimming under the polite tone of her voice. Maybe it was wrong to base her decision on the turmoil her personal life was going through, but she couldn't possibly hire her. Or maybe a constant reminder of how it used to be was exactly what she needed.

Suddenly she didn't feel like asking Sybille about her strengths and weaknesses anymore—a question the girl would no doubt answer capably and even with a bit of wit thrown in. She was definitely over-qualified and surely ambitious, exactly the overachiever Juliette was looking for.

"You know what, Sybille?" She locked eyes with her and saw Nadia again. Nadia on their first date wearing that white blouse that contrasted so gloriously with her skin, it made Juliette's mouth water. "You're hired. Please see Fabio in the office next door for details. We use the standard two-month trial period. Please start as soon as possible." She stood up to shake hands. Sybille seemed undeterred, as if she'd had this in the bag from the moment she walked in. As if she'd seen it in Juliette's eyes. The guilt, the eagerness, the desperation to, for once, say yes.

"*Merci beaucoup, Madame Barbier.*" She stood tall, no trace of nervous sweat on her fingers when their hands met. "You won't regret it."

We'll see about that. Juliette's success in business was due to a good combination of gut instinct, profound analysis and a complete lack of emotion. If she didn't deal with her crumbling relationship soon, she'd be doing more than hiring assistants who looked like her wife on a whim. She'd be harming her and Claire's life's work.

After showing Sybille out, she reached for her phone and called Nadia.

"Have lunch with me," she said as soon as she heard Nadia's matter-of-fact greeting on the other end of the line.

"What? Today?" The lack of eagerness and spontaneity in Nadia's voice gripped her around the heart like a cold fist. "I can't, babe. I'm up to my ears." The same excuse Juliette had used for years, meaning she had no defence against it.

"Please. We need to talk." If neither one of them ever insisted, how could they ever work it out? If all they did about their current impasse was instigate half-hearted conversations after too much wine—usually resulting in a flaming fight because they both couldn't control their temper very well when under the influence—how could they possibly find a way out?

"I know, but can't it wait? The most I could possibly spare

you for lunch is half an hour." Nadia sighed. "We deserve more than that."

Juliette could hardly argue with that. "Tonight?"

"I'll be home at eight. I promise." A sweetness had crept into Nadia's voice. Juliette didn't want to hang up now.

"I'll cook." She realised she'd been overcompensating in the kitchen of late.

"Why don't you relax. Open a nice bottle of wine. I'll take care of dinner."

"Sounds perfect, babe. I love you." It was so easy to say, and certainly no lie, but what if it wasn't enough? What if their love had developed into something different over the years. Something more pragmatic and less romantic.

"Love you too. Got to run."

Juliette sagged against the leather back rest of her chair. They'd had all weekend to talk, but Nadia had had a nasty hangover to nurse on Saturday and Juliette had been so angry, so frustrated and utterly unwilling to talk anything through. On Saturday evening Juliette had attended a ghastly play with Claire courtesy of a good client—attendance not optional.

On Sunday, just like every Sunday for the past six months it seemed, Nadia had had to deal with an emergency at the hospital, keeping her away from home for the better part of the day. Juliette had been so tired, so emotionally exhausted, she'd barely made it out of bed at all. Resentment was a heavy burden to bear, not just resentment for Nadia's job which had transformed her into someone Juliette wasn't sure she particularly liked—possibly because that new person emerging reminded her a bit too much of herself for comfort—but, mostly, resentment for how the whole situation made her feel so helpless, so dependent on someone else's availability and time for her.

Juliette wasn't used to playing second fiddle, but Claire was right. Maybe it was Nadia's time to shine professionally. But where did that leave her, if not in the shadows?

NADIA

Nadia scooped the noodles into a bowl, mostly to enhance the impression they were about to indulge in a home-cooked meal instead of another takeaway dinner. The days when she prepared fresh dishes for herself and Juliette almost every night seemed long gone.

It was difficult to not immediately be on the defence when she sat down opposite her partner of ten years. And this time she couldn't even blame Juliette, who looked relaxed in the jeans and t-shirt she liked to wear at home—slipping out of work mode and clothes as soon as she set foot in the apartment.

Juliette poured them each a generous helping of wine and the sound of the liquid meeting the glass at least untied some knots in her stomach. Raised by second-generation immigrants, Nadia hadn't grown up to drink wine like water, but she sure was making up for that in her forties.

"Did Margot say anything?" Juliette asked. "Apparently Steph couldn't help hitting on her in the street after they both left last Friday."

"Not a word. She's not really one for small talk."

"It's hardly small talk after you've been invited to a colleague's house to meet one of Paris's most eligible bache-lorettes and end up being propositioned by Les Pêches's resident heartbreaker."

Nadia swallowed a large gulp of wine before speaking. "At least Steph showed some initiative and interest. You and Claire are always so quick to judge. So Margot doesn't speak a mile a minute like you PR people do for a living, but she's smart, considerate, thoughtful, and bloody hot."

Nadia witnessed Juliette's lips tighten into a forced smile. "So you think she's hot?"

Jealousy was better than nothing at all. "You don't?"

"Sure, objectively speaking, but she's not really my type, you know that." Juliette's wavy straw-blonde hair bounced off her shoulders as she got more agitated. What gave her away more, though, was the way the left curve of her upper lip—the slightly uneven, ultra-sexy one—twitched when she started to feel as if she was losing control. Nadia knew her so well, could read her like an open book.

"What *is* your type these days?"

"You didn't answer my question." Juliette put her fork down and reached for her glass.

Here we go again. The endless going around in circles, the taunting, the reproachful remarks that kept them from really addressing the issue. They hadn't had nearly enough wine for that. Nadia pushed her glass away and looked Juliette in the eye. "What the hell does it matter? It doesn't. Nothing matters but the thoughts in our heads, all the assumptions we make about each other all day long and bring home at night and let fester because we don't talk to each other anymore. We seem to have lost the ability to communicate entirely and I know you probably think it's my fault and yes, I readily admit I fall into the trap of blaming you, but tell me, where will that get us if not split up within months and never talking to each other again?"

Juliette took a deep breath and sucked her bottom lip into her mouth. "I don't know anymore, babe. What is happening to us?"

Nadia wanted to get up, rush over to her and hold her. Tell her everything would be all right. But it wouldn't. "You resent the fact that I work more hours than you now, that I'm not there for you twenty-four seven like I used to be. That I stopped putting your happiness before mine."

"That's simply not true." Juliette pushed a strand of hair away from her cheek. "I want nothing more than for you to be happy, but the fact that you work such long hours can only mean one thing to me. Whatever the source of your happiness, it most certainly isn't me."

"If only, just once, just for a single second, you could admit that what you look for most in a partner is a doting housewife."

15

Nadia ogled her glass of wine. "And you can't deal with me not being here for you all the time." She braced herself for Juliette's reaction.

"You've never been a housewife. You've always worked."

"But I've always put you first."

"I just—you make me feel as if I'm not important to you anymore. Or at least less important than I used to be."

"And how do you think I felt every time you called me to say you were working late just as I finished cooking your bloody dinner?"

"But you knew it would be like that. You knew Claire and I were building our business—"

"You mean you expected me to resign myself to the fact that the agency and Claire would always come first? Like a good housewife, despite working a full-time job myself."

"No, of course not. I always believed we complemented each other so well on that front."

"Because it worked out so well for you."

Juliette shoved her chair back, its feet screeching on the hardwood floor. "Why now? Why are you telling me all of this after so many years? If it made you so miserable, then why didn't you say anything?"

"Because… circumstances change. I've changed. My job is just as important as yours, only, you don't seem to think so."

Juliette stood up and placed her hands on the back of the chair. Nadia watched her knuckles turn white as she squeezed the leather upholstering in frustration. "In all the years we've been together I can count the times you've yelled at me on the fingers of one hand. You don't scream at people, babe. That's not you. Have you looked in the mirror recently? Because when I look at you, I hardly recognise you."

Tears welled behind Nadia's eyes as despair gripped her. "And you know what your problem is, *honey*? No matter the volume of my voice, you never bloody listen to me. Thank you for this delightful conversation." She grabbed her glass of wine, emptied it in one long gulp, stood up, and made for the door.

"Where are you going?" It was hard not to notice the despair in Juliette's voice, and Nadia was just as guilty as her partner of sabotaging their relationship, but she had to get out before too much damage was done.

"To the hospital." With a dry click the door fell in the lock while Nadia furiously stabbed the elevator call button.

STEPH

Steph suffered from a case of unexpected nerves as she waited outside of Dominique Laroche's office in the building housing the *Assemblée nationale*. Not just because of the grandeur of her surroundings, but because of the topic she was about to discuss with her new client.

"Mademoiselle Mathis?" A perfectly coiffed lady in her fifties appeared in the waiting area, which consisted of a row of two chairs perched together in the hallway. "Madame Laroche will see you now. Please make it brief, she doesn't have a lot of time today."

She'd better make time for this. Following the woman, Steph glanced at her impeccable attire and suddenly realised she'd forgotten to dress to impress. She looked more like a perpetual college student in her velvet blazer and faded jeans and didn't quite fit the Palais Bourbon. She made a quick mental note to dress more career-oriented from now on and swap the jeans for something more appropriate.

"Bonjour." Dominique leaned against a majestic oakwood desk with one hip, a stack of papers in one hand and a pen in the other.

"Can we speak in private, please?" Polite but to the point. Just like Claire and Juliette had taught her. Don't waste anyone's time, especially your own.

"Bien sûr." She nodded at the older lady who took the

papers from Dominique with a nod and strutted out of the office, closing the door behind her. "What's on your mind?" Dominique remained at the front of her desk, hips slanting against the edge.

Steph didn't know whether to sit or stand, so she remained upright. "If we're going to make this work, I will need complete honesty, not just what you decide to tell me."

"Of course, that's what we agreed upon."

For a split second, Steph felt as if she were a detective about to nail the prime suspect. "So, would you care to tell me who Murielle Fontaine is?"

Dominique pursed her lips together into a pensive pout. "Maybe you should sit down." She straightened herself and headed to the other side of her desk.

"I'm here to help, not to judge." Steph held her hands up. "But I need to know these things."

"What... I mean, how did you find out?"

"I'm well-connected." Steph knew full well that anyone else at any other agency could never have dug up this particular nugget of information on Dominique Laroche. Her lifestyle had many an advantage, but this had been a rather unexpected perk.

"You must be." At last, Dominique allowed herself to sit down. "She was the only one and it happened when I was at uni. You know what it's like."

Steph chuckled. "Sure." She didn't say anything else, hoping her silence would coax a bit more information out of Dominique.

They sat in quiet stand-off mode for a few seconds. Dominique spoke first. "We swore to never tell anyone. We haven't really been in touch since then and we're both married with children now. It really isn't such a big deal."

Preaching to the choir. "It may be a big deal once you become a minister in a conservative right-wing cabinet."

"Seriously though, who told you?" Dominique ignored Steph's statement and tapped the tips of her nails on her desk.

"Let's just say Murielle hasn't stayed on the straight and narrow as well as you have." Steph leaned forward in her chair. "People talk, Madame Laroche. It's only in our nature."

"Please, call me Dominique." She rested her eyes on Steph for a few long seconds. "What do you suggest we do?"

"There's no reason to assume this will come out at all." Steph gave a small smile. "No pun intended." She eased back into her chair. "All that needs to happen is for you to be completely honest with me."

Dominique nodded. "Of course." She seemed to consider Steph's statement for an instant, drawing her eyes into narrow slits. Shifting her glance to her computer screen, she said, "Are you free for dinner... tomorrow night?"

Steph wasn't expecting that. "That much to tell, huh?"

Dominique shot her a harsh glare over the edge of her screen. Her eyes were greenish grey and piercing. "Just arrange for somewhere discreet where we can meet and call me on my private number to set it up. I'm blocking two hours for this."

"Well worth it in the end, I hope." Steph couldn't help but wonder what kind of secrets her first politician client was keeping. She couldn't wait to find out. This was far more exciting than drawing up positive press releases for software companies.

"See you tomorrow." Dominique rose and extended her hand. Steph did the same. When their palms touched, Steph detected the slightest hint of sweat on Dominique's skin.

CLAIRE

For once, Claire didn't have anywhere to go after work. Tuesday evenings were particularly popular for networking events in the PR industry, but tonight was all hers. She sat nursing a cosmopolitan at the bar of Le Comptoir, located halfway between Barbier & Cyr and her empty apartment, angled so she had a clear view of the door, when a dark-haired woman all dressed in leather walked in.

It took a split second to register her features and realise it was the same woman she had sat across from all night last Friday. She looked at Margot as she scanned the bar. Was she meeting Nadia here? This was more her and Juliette's kind of place, a spot to unwind after work and discuss matters away from the office.

"Looking for someone or is this just a coincidence?"

Margot's eyes briefly widened as she turned to Claire. She approached and leaned against the black marble countertop of the bar.

"I'm looking for Juliette, actually." She sighed and ran a finger over her lips before continuing. "I know it's not my business but Nadia is my friend and, believe me, I wouldn't be here if I didn't think I needed to be." She eyed Claire's drink. "I stopped at their flat but no one was home and Nadia told me she comes here often after work."

"She does, but she's still in the office, I'm afraid." Not that she needed to be, not tonight, but clearly Juliette didn't have the slightest interest in going home today. "Can I help?"

"Nadia asked if she could stay with me for a while."

No wonder Juliette had been in a dark mood all day. Claire knew better than to push on days like that. Besides, she'd had three client meetings, a strategic planning session with the web team, and not a minute to herself all day. And Juliette knew where to find her if she wanted to talk. She signalled Tony, the bartender, who came straight over.

"Another cosmo for me and whatever the lady is having."

Hesitation crossed Margot's face but after a few seconds she relaxed her shoulders and dragged a bar stool close. "A small Stella, please."

Claire waited until Margot had taken off her jacket and settled down next to her. "Are you sure you want to get involved in Nadia and Juliette's mid-life crisis?" She lifted her glass a fraction of an inch off the counter and tilted it in the direction of Margot's beer glass.

"God no." Margot stared into the golden liquid in her glass, as if the answers lay buried there. "Meddling is not my style, but the state Nadia's in... I'm not sure Juliette even realises how bad it is."

Claire was very familiar with the ins-and-outs of her friends' relationship, possibly too familiar, but Juliette was her best friend, had been for twenty years. She knew better than to stick her nose in by now.

"She does and she doesn't."

Margot looked up at her and smiled. "Could you be more specific, please?"

Claire reciprocated the smile and concluded that, although the doctor wore a stern frown well, the small laughter lines crinkling around her temples added an irresistible warmness to her face. "She knows that what they're going through at the moment could be fatal, and that the circumstances are very much against them, but she's in denial because she's scared to death of losing Nadia." She took a sip of her drink before continuing. "I know you mean well, but some people can't be told. They need to feel it. Need to experience the shock of impending heartbreak. Juliette is very much one of them."

"I just, huh, wouldn't want her to think it has anything to do with me because I'm letting her crash at mine. I found Nadia in a right state this morning in the on call room. I had to take her somewhere and she didn't want to go home."

The utter stoicism Margot had displayed last Friday stood in stark contrast to the worry apparent on her face tonight. Claire decided she liked this side of the doctor much better. "I'm sure Nadia's in capable hands with you." She shot her the crooked grin she usually reserved for flirting. "Don't worry about Juliette. I'll talk to her."

"Thanks." Margot downed her beer in a few long gulps. "I'd better get back to Nadia. I think she might have gone off on a cooking frenzy." She was already slipping off the bar stool.

"One more?" Claire didn't feel like emptying the rest of her drink on her own. "You came all this way…"

"She does manage a hospital, I suppose I can trust her not to set my never-used kitchen on fire." A smile again. She waved at the bartender. "A cranberry-soda, please." She looked back at Claire. "I'm riding my bike home. Would you like another?"

"Why the hell not?" Claire swiftly downed her cosmo and presented Tony with the empty glass.

After Margot had sat down on her stool again, stirring her straw in her drink, she surprised Claire by saying, "No matter how much I try to stay away from lesbian drama, it always manages to find me in the end."

"That explains—" Claire was interrupted by someone barging into the bar with lots of airs and graces. *Juliette.* "Here comes trouble…"

Without exchanging niceties or noticing the company Claire was in, Juliette launched into a wounded tirade.

JULIETTE

"I can't fucking believe it! She's staying with that uptight doctor she tried to set you up with last week. If they're having an—"

"Calm down, Juliette!" Claire pointed at the person sitting next to her, who had her back to Juliette, tilting her head in the stranger's direction. *Oh fuck.* Could this day get any worse?

The doctor rose from the bar stool she'd been perched on. "I think I'd better go."

"I'm so sorry." Staring into Margot's face and finding unexpected compassion etched in the lines of it, sent Juliette over the edge. She'd been holding on for days, weeks and months even, and now stood face to face with someone who made her realise most of her accusations had been solely based on her own frustrations. "I shouldn't have said that." Juliette brought a hand to her chest. "I'm really sorry."

Margot scanned her from head to toe. "I have a spare helmet. I'll take you to her." She reached for a leather jacket hanging from the next bar stool. "Good thing you're wearing trousers."

"W-what?" Juliette had trouble processing Margot's words. *What was that about a helmet and trousers?*

"Just go with her, Jules." Claire's hand rested against her bicep, squeezing gently, before addressing the doctor. "Merci."

Before she had a chance to think things through, Juliette found herself outside of Le Comptoir with a musty helmet on her head, staring at a black-and-red motorbike with great fear. "There's no way," she said.

"Do you want to see Nadia?" Margot fastened her own helmet under her chin, visor still open.

Juliette swallowed and nodded. Margot snapped her visor shut and then Juliette's. No more words were spoken. Juliette's fear of losing Nadia was far greater than getting on a motorbike with a virtual stranger—and at least she was a doctor. After watching Margot mount the bike, she followed suit and swung her leg over, then hesitantly placed her hands on Margot's sides. Instantly, Margot gripped her wrists and pulled her arms all the way around her middle.

They set off into the Paris evening. The streets were almost dark and when the bike first roared to life, anxiety rose in Juliette's stomach, but Margot was a careful and considerate driver and manoeuvred them effortlessly through back alleys instead of the big, jammed-up boulevards. Juliette would never even have considered riding a motorbike in a city like Paris, but in a way it made sense. Parking was easier. Traffic could be dodged.

She pulled up in front of a classic building just off the Boulevard Saint-Germain. When Juliette dismounted from the bike, her legs were shaking like leaves in the wind. She was also rather impressed by the location of Margot's home, but not in the mood for talk like that.

Margot fastened the bike to a steel bike stand and covered it with a canopy she kept in the storage space under the seat. She held out her hand and Juliette gave her the helmet. They rode the elevator in silence, nerves gnawing at Juliette's insides.

When they reached the front door, Margot turned to her. "I'll let her know you're here first, okay? Then I'll go to the café on the corner of the street to give you some privacy."

Juliette nodded. She couldn't believe she had actually considered that Margot might play a negative part in their relationship crisis. She waited outside the closed door, too jittery to take in her surroundings well. She hadn't smoked in years, but her hands were itching to hold a cigarette. It took long minutes before Margot re-emerged and let her in.

"Just go through there. You know where to find me." With that, she zipped up her leather jacket and headed back to the elevator. Maybe she could be a good match for Claire, after all. Maybe Nadia hadn't been that far off. *Nadia.*

Her heart thumping furiously beneath her chest, Juliette made her way into Margot's apartment. She found Nadia perched in the corner of a large beige sofa, legs drawn up under her, looking much more relaxed than Juliette had expected.

"Hey," she said. The smell of Tunisian spices hung heavy in the air, reminding Juliette that she hadn't had a single bite to eat all day.

"Salut." Nadia's tone sounded anything but conciliatory.

Juliette bit back the anger that so easily flared these days. Was it really all her fault? *Stop thinking like that.* "Can I sit?"

"Sure." Nadia seemed to want to retreat even deeper into the sofa, but she'd already reached its corner.

Juliette kept her distance. If only she knew what to say. She spun stories for a living, turned bad news into good, negatives into positives. "I realise I've taken you for granted for a long time. That I haven't given nearly as much as I've received. I'll do whatever it takes. Just tell me, and I'll do it."

She was met with a disdainful huff from Nadia. "Oh, so you need me to tell you. I'll tell you one thing, Juliette, your head is so far up your own ass you only see yourself anymore. And if you've come here to ask me to go home with you, you've come for nothing. I'm staying here until you figure out what to do. I can't—I simply can't be with you now. I need some space."

"I—" Juliette tried to reply, but Nadia hadn't finished yet.

"You say you don't recognise me anymore, well, the same goes for me. I feel so far away from you, as though we have absolutely nothing in common, which is a very strange thing to feel when you've been with someone for a decade."

Nadia appeared calm and collected, as if she'd thought this through, as opposed to Juliette, who had received a simple text message an hour ago saying, *Not coming home tonight. Staying with Margot. Need to be alone.* It might as well have said that Nadia was leaving her for Margot.

"I'm a workaholic and we've grown apart because of that. But we've always said—"

Nadia interrupted her again. "I meant what I said, Juliette. I need to be away from you for a while. I need a break from the stifling atmosphere in our flat. Nothing you say now will make any difference. I appreciate you coming here, but I'm going to ask you to leave now."

Juliette's heart broke into a million pieces. She looked at the woman she loved and felt utterly powerless. Defeated, she obeyed Nadia's wish and left without looking back, not because she didn't want to but because she couldn't.

NADIA

Maybe Juliette believed it was easier for Nadia to say she wanted her to leave than to pull her close and try—once more— to just cuddle it all away. She couldn't have been more wrong if she did. Nadia sat frozen in her seat for a long while, etching the memory of Juliette's hurt face into her memory. How she'd gone from standing in front of her regally, with that tall and lanky posture Nadia liked so much, to a crumpled mess in the sofa. Nadia could tell she was trying, grasping at straws, but what chance did they really have if she just brushed it all under the carpet again? If they just continued and pretended like nothing had happened until the next fight—always bigger and more hurtful than the last.

She waited for Margot to return to the flat, immobile in her spot in the sofa, unable to move. Her mind was too busy absorbing the after-shock of actually having sent Juliette away to allow her muscles to do much work.

The door fell into the lock fifteen minutes later and before Margot even took off her jacket, she presented Nadia with a tumbler of brandy.

"Drink this." She shrugged the leather off and neatly hung it over the back of a chair.

"I appreciate you going to find her and I don't want to impose on your hospitality, but I can't go home yet."

"I'm not the greatest with guests, but you can stay here as long as you like." Margot reached for the bottle. "I need a drink." She poured herself a stiff one and crashed down next to Nadia in the sofa. "I take it it didn't go very well."

Nadia sipped from the glass. She wasn't much of a brandy fan, only turning to it in times of great emotional distress, and the liquor burned her throat. The warmth of it spread through her veins and the worst of her nerves died down with the hot glow of the booze. "I just, for once, need her to feel how I feel." Nadia looked at Margot over the rim of her glass. "Or is that a terrible thing to say?"

Margot let out a huff. "You're asking the wrong woman. I don't have a clue what it's like to be in a long-term relationship."

Nadia pursed her lips together, contemplating Margot's love

life. She'd joined the hospital just as Nadia had been made administrator eight months ago, just as things with Juliette had started going downhill. She'd seen it before. The more ambitious the doctors, the worse state their affairs of the heart were in. "What's your longest?" Nadia felt a blush of shame creep up her cheeks because she hadn't asked before, but Margot was far from the talkative kind. Nadia did know about Margot's last girlfriend Inez though, how she had left and broken her heart.

Margot averted her eyes before answering. "Seventeen months."

Nadia had to strain to hear the words coming from her co-worker's mouth. She took another sip of her brandy. She hadn't exactly told Margot she was setting her up with Claire when she'd invited her to last Friday's dinner party, expecting a certain refusal if she had.

"I have night shifts and weekends when I'm on call and I basically live for my job, it doesn't leave a lot of room for another person." She managed a tight smile before continuing. "But I appreciate you introducing me to Claire. That was very subtle." She paused to drink. "I ran into her at Le Comptoir earlier when I went looking for Juliette."

There was nothing like some juicy lesbian gossip to take Nadia's mind off her troubles, if even for a few seconds. "And?" Her toe approached Margot's leather-clad thigh and she gave her a light shove.

"She's certainly stunning and quite possibly way out of my league."

Nadia shook her head. She straightened her posture to better get her point across. "Doctor de Hay, please. Have you looked in the mirror? Do you not notice how Sylvie and Emma go quiet or burst out into giggles every time you even approach the nurses station? Please don't tell me you're one of those people convinced of their own unattractiveness because you are gorgeous. And if so, I'll send you to the eighth floor for a consultation with Doctor Bailly, who, by the way, also has the hots for you." Nadia ended her speech with a smug grin. It felt good to experience a flicker of joy, even at the expense of her friend. But clearly Margot needed a talking-to.

"You're crazy, really, I think that brandy must have gone to your head." The words exiting Margot's mouth didn't match the coyness with which she expressed them.

"Give me your phone." Nadia held out her hand. "Come on. I know you always have it in your pocket and it's always switched on. Give it to me."

"No! Why?" Margot put her hand over her pocket. "You're not the boss of me in my home."

"You're someone who needs coaxing in the right direction. I'm your friend and I will happily oblige."

"I don't think I'm her type and I try to avoid situations—"

"Give me your bloody phone, Margot." Nadia prodded Margot's hand with her bare toes. "You have to at least take a chance."

"I refuse. I'm old enough to arrange my own dates." She cupped her fingers tighter around the bulge her phone created in her pocket.

"You might be old enough, but clearly that's not sufficient to present you with a multitude of satisfying date nights… but suit yourself." Nadia reached for her purse on the rug and dug out her own phone. "I don't need your permission for this." Before Margot had the time to protest, Nadia typed a message and sent it to Claire.

"What did you send her?" The mock indignation on Margot's face was the perfect cure for the heaviness in Nadia's heart. Maybe the demise of her own relationship would instigate another.

"Just that you thought it was fun to run into her, despite the circumstances. That's all. Let me just send her your number and then the ball's in her court." Nadia quickly took care of that. "And believe me, Claire Cyr is not shy like you."

Knowing Claire, and Nadia had known her as long as she'd

known Juliette, she was probably giving Juliette a piece of her mind right now. Nadia's heart sank at the thought. No amount of setting up other people could undo the knots in her stomach and the tightness in her chest.

CLAIRE

"What are you grinning at?" Juliette peered at Claire over the rim of her glasses. They'd both been pretending to watch the ten o'clock news while lost in thought, when Claire's phone beeped.

Claire had predicted, if Juliette and Nadia couldn't figure things out quickly, that Juliette would turn up on her doorstep after her visit to Margot's apartment.

"You'd better not be sexting while sharing the sofa with me."

Claire burst out laughing. "Sexting? I'm a little too old for that, *chérie*. It's just a friend."

"I'm your friend and I bet I don't make you smile like that when I text you."

Claire was glad the evening was taking a lighter turn, after all the drama of the hours before. "A bit more than a friend then, I guess. A friend with benefits." She waited for Juliette's reaction.

"You have a friend with benefits?" Juliette straightened her posture. "You're seeing someone?" Her eyes grew wide.

"She's a pilot based in Hong Kong. She flies to Paris once or twice a month. It's very casual and, erm, mutually beneficial. She'll be in town tomorrow."

"What? How long has this been going on?" Juliette reached for her wine glass. "Talk about a dirty little secret."

Claire could see how Juliette was racking her brain. She waited patiently.

"Wait… is she the one you met that night at Les Pêches? The one you had a one-night stand with months ago?"

Even if Juliette believed there were secrets between them,

there weren't. They shared everything, even a bed at one point in their lives. "Yep."

"I didn't know you'd kept in touch." Juliette whistled through her teeth. "She was hot."

"It's hardly a regular thing and certainly not something with a future, it's just… fun."

"Fun, huh? Well, I'll make sure to make myself scarce tomorrow."

"No need. I'll go to her hotel." Claire couldn't help but smile at the prospect of seeing Jennifer again. Tall, dark, handsome Jennifer who always made sure to greet her in her uniform, cap included. Her phone beeped again. She picked it up eagerly, expecting it to be Jennifer to double confirm their date. It wasn't. It was Nadia.

Margot says it was a nice surprise to run into you tonight. Do call her some time if interested. N. xo

A second text quickly followed containing a phone number.

"What?" Juliette asked, no doubt able to read the bewilderment on her face. Against her better judgment, but too perplexed to spare Juliette's feelings, she showed her the screen of her phone.

"Jesus christ!" Juliette went off. "First of all, I can't believe she's still trying to set you up with that woman, and secondly, you'd think she'd have other matters on her mind." Juliette's face sagged into a wounded scowl. "I just don't get it. If I did, I wouldn't be here, I guess." She sighed. "I didn't cheat. I don't have feelings for anyone else. All I want is for us to get out of this rut, but I'm afraid that Nadia is just so utterly and totally sick of me. That she's just had enough. That she has changed and I haven't and I can't keep up. That she's fallen out of love with me."

Tears dangled from Juliette's eyelashes. Claire inched closer to hug her, because she had no more words. She'd said them all, over and over again.

"If I'm the cause of all of this, how come I have absolutely no idea how to fix it?" Juliette sobbed in her arms, letting it all out.

"Take tomorrow off." She reached for Juliette's wine glass and handed it to her. "Take the time to think and—"

"Are you crazy? We've just taken on Laroche and I have meetings—"

"I'll handle it. Steph will handle Laroche. Take the day. I mean it. Just one day, Jules. One day of the year. See it as compensation for all the weekends you worked, and the evenings you spent cozying up to potential clients while all you really wanted was to be at home with Nadia. Do it for her."

"I'll go nuts. I swear. When I have nothing to do, all these thoughts start swirling in my head."

"That's the point." Claire grabbed her own glass off the coffee table. "When was the last time you went for a run in the Bois de Boulogne? When was the last time you really put yourself first?"

Juliette shrugged. "According to Nadia, I do nothing but put myself first."

"Not everything Nadia says is true, Jules. She's hurt. You're hurt. You've been hurting each other. Take the time to fix it."

"And a run in the park is going to accomplish that?"

"No, but at least you'll have made a start." Claire patted Juliette on the knee. "Go to the market and invite her to a home-cooked meal. Show her you're willing to make an effort. Don't put too much distance between the two of you."

"She's made it abundantly clear that she doesn't want to see me for a while."

"Then let her know in no uncertain terms that you don't agree. That to make it work, you'll have to get through it instead of ignoring it."

"If only I knew what *it* was."

"I think you do. Deep down, you know."

Claire took Juliette's subsequent silence as agreement and briefly let her mind wander to the last text she received. *The doctor liked her.* She had it in writing. And she had her number. She also had a date tomorrow—more of a booty call, really.

"I think you should call her." Juliette's voice startled her.

"What?"

"I think you should call Margot. Maybe I was too hard on her."

"We'll see." Claire let her body fall against the back of the sofa, suddenly exhausted. Her day job was draining enough, and all this relationship drama wasn't helping. "I'll sleep on it."

STEPH

"When did Barbier & Cyr turn into the centre of lesbian drama in Paris? I know this is the city of love and all that, but seriously, aren't we supposed to be professionals?" Steph sat opposite Claire in her office with the intention of briefing her boss on what she'd dug up on Dominique Laroche but getting the story of everything that happened to her friends the night before instead.

"We are professionals, which is why Juliette had to take the day off. I have full confidence that you can handle Laroche on your own."

"Oh, I can." Steph couldn't suppress a grin. "She's more like us than you'd expect at first glance."

"What do you mean?" Claire arched up her perfectly-sculpted eyebrows.

A knock on the door prevented Steph from dishing the dirt.

Claire's PA, Fred, appeared in the doorway. "Juliette's new assistant Sybille is supposed to start today, only Juliette's not here."

Steph turned around and winked at Fred. They often hung

out together after work, heading to Le Marais for a few drinks and some 'catch of the day' as they called it.

"*Merde.* I'd forgotten about that." Claire slapped a palm against her forehead.

"Is she hot?" Steph joked.

"Oh yeah," Fred quickly responded, as if they were sitting outside of l'Univers chit-chatting and looking at passers-by instead of in their boss's office.

"I'll take care of her." Steph shot Fred a sly grin.

"No funny business, Steph. I mean it." Claire's face clearly showed the struggle raging inside of her. She had no authority when it came to demanding of Steph that she not fool around with co-workers, seeing their history together. But Steph never crossed the line. No matter the impression she gave, her job was far more important to her than the hottest bedfellow. She loved to flirt—and tease Claire while doing so—but, at work, she never took it further than that.

"My bosses are women of the greatest integrity and I want nothing more than to act in their image." Steph rose from her seat.

"Get out already." Claire made a dismissive gesture with her hand.

"A thank-you would be nice." Steph joined Fred in the door-way. "Oh, and boss, call the doctor." With a nod, she exited Claire's office, taking Fred with her, and closing the door behind them.

She didn't have time to engage in a lot of banter with Fred, as he swiftly presented Steph to Juliette's brand new assistant. It was impossible to miss why Juliette had hired her. She couldn't have looked more like a younger version of Nadia than her own kin.

"Enchantée." She took the girl's hand and was surprised by the firm squeeze Sybille subjected her palm to. *Ambition. Excellent.* "Stéphanie Mathis, but do call me Steph."

"Nice to meet you, Steph." Sybille held Steph's gaze a fraction of a second longer than necessary and that, combined with finely-honed natural instincts, was how Steph knew. *Not another. There's enough drama going around already.*

She decided to keep a close eye on Sybille, especially now that Juliette was in an emotionally weakened state, and working alongside the spitting image of her estranged partner could mean trouble. "You have the distinct pleasure of starting your career at Barbier & Cyr by acclimatising for the day. No one else here was ever given that privilege." She put her hand on Sybille's back and guided her along the corridor. "I'll quickly introduce you to everyone and then Fred will take over to show you the ropes."

Not interested in flirting with Sybille, despite the girl's incli-nation, Steph's mind drifted off to tonight's meeting with Dominique Laroche. Her client had asked for a discreet place to meet and the only truly secluded spot Steph had been able to think of was her own flat.

JULIETTE

Nadia's words kept ringing in Juliette's ears. *I need to be away from you for a while.* Juliette aimlessly wandered around the market, feeling out of place in between the housewives and grandparents buying sweets for their grandchildren. The cheese looked good, but buying a few humps of goat's cheese and Tomme, Nadia's favourites, hardly constituted preparing a meal. Juliette enjoyed cooking, but she just didn't have the energy today.

The run Claire had suggested she'd go on to clear her head had been dismissed as ludicrous as soon as she'd woken up with a slightly heavy head. Instead, she'd made her way from Claire's place to her and Nadia's flat and, despite Nadia only having left two days earlier, the complete absence of her had made her flee instantly.

She wasn't even sure Nadia would come. It felt odd, to say

the least, that for a woman who spent a good part of her day talking to people on the phone, persuading them this way and that, she was afraid to dial her own partner's number. What if she spoke the same words again? *I need to be away from you for a while.* Juliette wasn't sure she could take it again. Even though she had trouble pinpointing exactly what she had done wrong, she knew instinctively that the initiative for any sort of progress had to come from her.

She stepped away from the crowds, finding shelter around the corner of a building not a lot of people passed by. When she dug her phone out of her jeans pocket, her heart thudded with fear. When the dial tone rang in her ear, she was afraid her heart may jump out of her chest altogether.

"Allo." Nadia's greeting didn't give away anything about her state of mind, but at least she had picked up.

"Hey. It's me." Juliette felt a drop of sweat make its way down her spine. "Would you have dinner with me tonight, please? I'll cook."

Silence on the other end of the line. *Unbearable silence.*

"Please," she repeated. "I'll make your favourite."

"You don't have time for that."

Juliette racked her brain for Nadia's favourite meal. "I do. I have all day." She didn't need a poker face over the phone.

"All right. I'll be home at seven."

Excitement had taken over from fear, which didn't make any difference to the rate at which her heart hammered away beneath her ribs. "Merci."

"We'll see." With that, Nadia hung up.

Juliette walked back to the market square. Her eyes scanned the many vegetable stalls and the meat stall a bit further and she knew. If she was going to make Boeuf Bourguignon the way her grandfather had taught her, she'd better get a move on.

With a renewed spring in her step, she breezed through the required shopping and walked home. *Their home.*

CLAIRE

A woman dressed in a pair of pressed navy-blue trousers, a white bra and a pilot's cap opened the door for Claire.

"New uniform?" She asked, entering the room, always a little insecure at first.

"I tweak it for booty calls." Jennifer's voice was husky, her shoulder-length black hair falling from under the cap. She winked and offered Claire a tiny glass of champagne. A small popped bottle sat on top of the minibar.

They clinked rims and sipped while their eyes met, and for the first time since hooking up with the pilot, Claire wondered if this was all there was to her love life now. Sporadic meetings in hotel rooms. Text messages from miles away. Waiting for a plane to land.

"Do you have a girl in every city?" She held Jennifer's gaze.

Jennifer smiled. "I don't do girls." She took a step closer. "Only sophisticated, accomplished women like you." She was so close Claire could smell her perfume.

Did it really matter? This monthly fling would always end with Claire walking out of the room, until she decided never to return. Until she decided she deserved more than this.

Claire hadn't been as lucky as Juliette. She hadn't found a woman like Nadia who seemed to meet Juliette's needs so perfectly—until she started wanting a little more for herself as well. She'd gone from non-committal fling to fling, and sometimes a relationship grew out of it, but something always went wrong sooner rather than later.

At one point, just when Juliette and Nadia had decided to move in together, Claire had even found herself in bed with the young, hot, new intern. She'd been secretly jealous of Juliette's domestic bliss and Steph had made it very easy on her. *How that could have backfired.*

"You seem distracted." Jennifer's voice brought her back to reality.

Claire sighed. A gorgeous woman stood right in front of her, available and, by the look of things, extremely willing. "I'm not sure I can do this anymore."

"Have you come to break up with me?" The smile still didn't disappear from Jennifer's face. She probably believed Claire was playing hard to get. She inched closer. "Or do you want to go steady?"

It was exactly what Claire wanted. But not with a pilot who only flew into town once a month, twice if she was lucky. A woman she barely knew, who evaded any question that got a bit too personal a bit too expertly.

"I'm sorry." Claire took a step back. "I really am. I shouldn't have come."

"You're serious." Jennifer walked backwards to the bed and crashed down on it.

"I'm afraid I am." She crossed to the bed and sat down next to Jennifer. "If you lived in Paris, I would definitely date you, but I'll be forty-five years old next year and I want more than one night every few weeks."

"Have you met someone?"

The question threw Claire off guard. *Maybe she had.*

"Maybe. I don't know." She turned to Jennifer. "I'm sorry to spoil our night like this."

"Hey…" Jennifer grabbed Claire's hand. "No false promises, no heartbreak. That was the deal from the start."

"No hard feelings?"

Jennifer shook her head before planting a gentle kiss on Claire's cheek.

"I'd better go." She gave Jennifer's hand a soft squeeze.

They both rose from the bed and fell into a tender hug. Gosh, it felt good to feel another woman so near. Just to feel another person's body heat radiate onto her skin. "Goodbye, Captain." Claire looked Jennifer in the eyes and kissed her on the lips.

Jennifer didn't say anything when Claire headed for the

door and closed it softly behind her. The first thing she did when she stood in the empty hallway was unearth her phone from her bag and scroll to Nadia's message with Margot's number. It was her call. Was she ready to make it?

She waited until she was outside of the hotel, with its memories of satisfying but emotionally empty sex, to dial the number. Margot picked up after the first ring.

"Doctor de Hay speaking." Her voice was firm, her tone clipped.

"Hey. Hi." Claire found herself stuttering. "This is Claire Cyr. Nadia gave me your number." She hadn't exactly prepared for this conversation. "Are you free to grab a coffee this weekend?" Maybe she should have started with a polite 'How are you?' instead.

"I'm working all weekend, starting Friday evening."

"Oh." The adrenalin of actually dialling Margot's number was wearing off and swiftly being replaced by sullenness.

"How about tomorrow after work?" Margot's voice sounded hopeful over the phone, so hopeful Claire was suddenly eager to forget about her own schedule, which she couldn't remember anyway—but she probably had some cocktail party to attend, she always had.

"Sounds good. At Le Comptoir?"

"Not really my thing. Do you know Le Coin des Chats in Saint-Germain-des-Prés?"

"No, but it sounds delightful." Claire couldn't suppress a chuckle.

"I'll text you the address."

They rang off and Claire decided that a two-minute phone conversation with someone promising was much more worthwhile than a romp in an anonymous hotel with someone merely passing through.

NADIA

"Did you hear?" Nadia asked Juliette after kissing her awkwardly on the cheek. She felt like a guest in her own home.

"Hear what?" Juliette seemed to have trouble letting go of her.

"Claire and Margot have a date tomorrow night." Nadia couldn't hide the triumphant tone in her voice. Setting them up had been another one of her so-called ludicrous ideas Juliette had shot down without giving it any more thought. She'd barely given Margot a chance, sizing her up and writing her off as soon as she had entered their flat.

"Really?" Juliette deposited the bottle of wine Nadia had brought on the table. "I did tell Claire to call her."

Nadia rolled her eyes but decided it wasn't worth arguing over. They already had enough ammunition to last them several weeks of fighting.

"Smells great." The scent of beef that had stewed for hours wafted into the living room from the kitchen. Juliette really had made an effort. "Did you knock off work early?"

"I took a personal day."

This made Nadia stop dead in her tracks. "You? You didn't go into work at all?"

"How could I when the woman I love is on the cusp of leaving me?" Juliette couldn't meet Nadia's gaze. "Nothing is more important than trying to make you stay."

Another one of those surprise statements and Nadia feared she might suffer a heart attack. The guard she'd put up two nights earlier when she'd stormed off started to come down a bit. Juliette Barbier was a woman of many words, but hardly ever words like these.

Nadia sat down in her favourite spot in the sofa. "I'm not leaving you. I just need you to make some changes." She looked idly around for a glass of wine, but Juliette hadn't had the chance to pour her one. "And I need you to understand some hard truths about us."

"I do and I will." As if reading her mind, or perhaps to win time, Juliette reached for the bottle of red and the opener on the tray next to the coffee table. Her fingers trembled when she tried to fit the opening of the bottle opener around the neck of the bottle.

Nadia held out her hands. "I'll do it." She could clearly see that Juliette was in a right state, but she still needed to hear the words, without having to put them in Juliette's mouth herself.

"I, uh, I just need to stir the meat. I'll be right back."

Nadia watched her partner flee into the kitchen. She wore day-off clothes. Jeans and a black turtleneck sweater. No shoes or socks. Her bare feet slapped onto the hardwood floor. Her reddish blonde hair was pushed up into a loose bun at the back of her head. No matter how fragile the state of her heart, Juliette Barbier always looked to die for. But Nadia had made enough sacrifices.

She served them both a large glass of Cabernet and waited for Juliette to return from the kitchen. At least she had remembered what her favourite dish was, despite not having made the time to prepare it for her in years.

Juliette sat down in the one-seater opposite from where Nadia was sitting. "I turned off the stove. It should be ready."

"Let's talk first." Nadia appreciated the fact that Juliette had spent hours in the kitchen, but she was hardly hungry. Her stomach was in knots, not just because their relationship was in such a rocky place, but also because of the emotional distress displayed on Juliette's face. Juliette, who was always in control and always knew what to say. It was hard seeing her that way. Hard, but necessary.

Juliette nodded. "I know I attach too much importance to my work and I've neglected our relationship. And you." Her right index finger frantically rubbed against her left thumb while she spoke. "I know I need to make changes, but if you could just, huh, make a few suggestions so I know I'm on the right track."

Nadia shook her head. "No. I'm not going to tell you what to do and have it come back to bite me in the ass later. That's not how this is going to work."

"I'll work less hours. I'll cook—"

"How?" Nadia could see Juliette's frustration levels rise dangerously high. "How will you work less hours? What is your concrete plan?"

"I don't know. I—"

"You're desperate, Jules. You'd say anything right now, but you haven't thought it through. Not really. You're just vaguely telling me what you think I want to hear. It's not enough. It's not change. It's just more words. I've had enough of false promises."

"Of course I'm desperate. You said you didn't want to see me for a while. You left home. You left me here all alone without a clue of what to do or what it possibly could be that I did so wrong all of a sudden."

The tightness was back in Nadia's chest. She wondered how many times they would go on this merry-go-round. She could leave Juliette to stew on her own a bit more, but clearly she would never reach the extremely logical conclusion—from Nadia's point of view—by herself.

"My job is important too. We save lives, for heaven's sake. We heal sick people. All you and Claire do is make companies look better than they are."

Juliette leaned forward in her seat, her eyes drawn into slits. "You keep hinting that this is about our jobs. And yes, you're busier than before, and sure, I should make an effort to be here for you more, but I refuse to believe that it's our professional lives driving us apart." She tapped a finger to her chest. "The despair I feel in here. The pure dread that has settled in my heart, it's not *because* we've been avoiding each other, it's *why*."

Nadia had seldom seen Juliette so emotional. Her stomach tightened, but Juliette wasn't finished yet.

"I'm not saying you stopped loving me, but your love is different. You've found something else to care for, hundreds of other people. I don't come first anymore." Juliette's voice broke, and with it, Nadia's heart in a thousand pieces.

"You're wrong, babe. You're so wrong." Nadia shot up out of the sofa and hurried to Juliette's side. The first contact of their skin lodged itself like an electric current in her flesh, coursing through it so swiftly it made Nadia dizzy.

Nadia had made mistakes, but she'd never stopped loving Juliette.

JULIETTE

"I miss you." Juliette couldn't keep the trembling in her legs under control. They shook next to Nadia's, who put a hand on her knee and changed everything, just for a split second.

Juliette turned to face her partner and she saw the love, the years of commitment and companionship. Their life, together. She stared into Nadia's dark eyes and suddenly the anguish in the pit of her stomach was eclipsed by a surge of pure lust.

Perhaps, when words failed, this was what they needed.

Eyes wide open, she inched closer, slanting her head. Her heart thudded frantically out of fear Nadia would pull back. If she did, what then? Juliette erased the possibility from her mind and pressed her lips to Nadia's. To her relief, they opened instantly, inviting Juliette in.

They hadn't touched like this in such a long time, it almost felt new to Juliette. Her hands disappeared in Nadia's voluptuous mane of hair as she drew her near, as close as she could possibly get.

"Fuck me," Nadia whispered in her ear.

"What?" Juliette pulled back slightly.

"Fuck me." Nadia's lips were parted, her breath ragged.

"You never say that. I mean, this is not—"

Nadia gripped Juliette's cheeks between her palms. "Stop thinking, just do it." If they could have, her eyes would have blazed fire.

Nadia was always the more intuitive one, the one to go with the flow. She was also—always—the one on top. *Not tonight then.*

Something new started glowing beneath Juliette's skin. She pushed Nadia down into the sofa, their gazes firmly locked. Before straddling her, Juliette pulled her jumper over her head and tossed it aside. When Nadia's cupped palms reached for her breasts, she swatted them away.

"You asked for it." A grin curved on her lips. "You're going to get it."

Juliette unclasped her bra and hurtled it somewhere onto the floor of their living room. She rested her hands on the back seat of the sofa, behind Nadia's head, so her chest was inches away from Nadia's mouth. Her nipples perked up instantly at the thought of her lover's lips so close by.

"Don't you dare touch me." She was merely giving Nadia a taste of her own medicine, seeing as she was usually the one playing games like this.

"I won't." Nadia's voice came out a hoarse whisper.

Juliette angled her body so her nipples ran across Nadia's cheeks, leaving her gasping for air. She'd felt so out of control in their relationship of late, that she wanted nothing more than to take control now. Even if, in the bedroom, control was more Nadia's domain.

Juliette leaned back and started to unbutton Nadia's beige linen blouse. She'd bought it for her last year, before things had started to go sour.

Running her fingers over Nadia's bra-clad breasts, at first, she almost felt as if she needed to re-familiarise herself with them. They'd gone from sleeping stark naked through the seasons, to gradually covering themselves in more and more sleep wear in the past six months. Juliette should have paid more attention, should have seen the small changes as significant enough to question them.

She curved her arms around Nadia's back and undid the lock of her bra, quickly following the action by guiding Nadia's blouse and bra off her torso. Nadia's breasts were heavy and dark-nippled, made for worshipping. In the beginning of their affair, back in the day when Juliette still ran regular 10K races, Nadia always refused to go jogging with her. "Not with these," she'd say, pointing at her large bosom. So she stayed behind and cooked for Juliette, who ran so fast—and soon after stopped altogether—just so she could rest her head on Nadia's chest sooner.

Nadia's flesh was soft and inviting, then and now, and Juliette ran the back of her fingers over her breasts, trapping her nipples, coaxing a guttural groan from her partner's mouth, before pushing herself off the sofa. Hooking her hands behind Nadia's knees, she pulled her down. With two fingers, she unbuttoned Nadia's trousers and yanked them down.

"Stretch out on the sofa." Juliette barely recognised her own voice. While Nadia obeyed her order, she slipped out of her jeans, leaving them a crumpled mess on the floor.

The sofa was wide enough for Juliette to be able to flank Nadia. She lay down next to her, pressing her pale flesh into Nadia's warm curves. She hadn't felt so at home in a long time.

Her fingers stole over Nadia's skin, lightly skimming, until they stopped at her nipples. With the tip of her index finger, Juliette circled Nadia's pert nipple, teasing gently.

"This is not what you want, is it?" She whispered in Nadia's ear, her nose hidden in her thick black hair. In a flash, she pinched Nadia's nipple hard between her thumb and previously teasing index finger. "*This* is what you want."

Nadia cupped Juliette's fingers with her hand, squeezing tight. She turned her head so their eyes met. "Fuck me." Even when she didn't appear in charge, she was. "Now." She guided

Juliette's hand from her breast, over her belly, to her panties. Her eyes sparkled, the determination in them impossible to ignore.

Juliette had missed Nadia's commands—silent and other ones. So in control of every second of her life in the light of day, she needed someone like Nadia to balance her out at night. To take the reins and bring her back.

Juliette briefly toyed with the idea of defying Nadia's order, but, even if, somewhere in the depths of her soul, she wanted to, she couldn't. That's not how it worked between them.

She slid her fingers under the waistband of Nadia's knickers, meeting her wiry, curly hairs there, and lower, until she reached the velvet heat of her pussy.

"I'm so wet for you, babe." The severity in Nadia's eyes had made way for longing. Nadia started tugging her panties off and Juliette gladly helped her. As soon as their hands hovered over Nadia's body again, Nadia grabbed hold of Juliette's wrist and steered her hand between her legs.

Juliette bent down to kiss Nadia full on the lips as the tip of her finger slipped between her moist folds. Nadia let go of Juliette's hand as her muscles tensed with anticipation.

Damp heat enveloped Juliette's finger as she thrust deep. The groans escaping Nadia's mouth and the way she curled one arm around her neck was all she needed to feel whole again. She quickly added another finger while keeping a rhythm of slow, deep thrusts.

"Oh, chérie," Nadia hummed. "More. Harder." The stamina and patience she displayed when fucking Juliette always seemed to go out of the window as soon as Juliette slipped a finger inside. As if they always only had a certain amount of time and ninety percent of it had to be spent on Juliette, Nadia's climax always coming quick and hard—and last.

Juliette added another finger, spreading Nadia wide, feeling her from the inside, loving her. Every time she went deep, she let her thumb flick over Nadia's engorged clit, a little more urgently with every stroke.

She kissed Nadia again as she felt the walls of her pussy starting to contract around her fingers, so hard it squeezed them together tightly. She breathed her in as she came on her fingers, trapped her moans in her mouth as Nadia gave herself up to Juliette's touch.

She hadn't expected the tears. The soft sobbing as Juliette slid her fingers out and covered Nadia with as much of her body as she could, that quickly transformed into a stuttering heave.

"I'm sorry," Nadia said, her cheeks wet against Juliette's. "I'm so sorry."

STEPH

"How cozy," Dominique Laroche said, looking around Steph's shoebox-sized studio. "Definitely discreet."

Maybe it hadn't been the best idea to invite Dominique to her flat, but what with the recent discovery of certain events from the députée's past, Steph didn't feel at ease inviting her to a restaurant. Mostly because, and she'd never considered this to become a problem in her professional life, she had a bit of a reputation herself.

"Do you cook here?" Dominique's eyes rested on the tiny corner kitchenette that barely had room for a microwave oven.

"Dinner will be served soon." Steph gestured at the Ikea sofa she'd had for ten years and suddenly felt self-conscious about everything. Bringing back someone half-tipsy to her place in the middle of the night was an entirely different affair from inviting in one of the country's most promising politicians. "Please, sit. Can I offer you a glass of wine first?"

"Sure, any red will do." Dominique sat down with an amused smile on her face. "What's that sound?" She looked around, her eyes landing on the door separating the bathroom from the kitchen.

"Oh, that's my cat. I thought it best to lock him in there while—"

"Nonsense." She got up and strutted towards the bathroom, which was only two steps away from the living area. "May I?"

Steph nodded, relieved to set Pierrot free from his prison.

As soon as Dominique opened the door only an inch, he slipped out, let out a disgruntled meow, and rubbed himself against her calves. He'd found his saviour.

"What an adorable little thing. We have one just like this at home, and a ginger as well." Dominique squatted next to Pierrot and scratched him behind the ear.

Friends for life already.

Steph had just deposited two glasses of wine on the small coffee table when the intercom buzzed. "That must be dinner."

While Dominique settled in the sofa, a glass of wine in her hand and Pierrot in her lap, Steph paid the pizza guy and presented her with a slice of pepperoni.

"I hope that little dalliance in your past hasn't left you a vegetarian." If Dominique didn't eat meat, she would have known, having spent the better part of the past week familiarising herself with every detail of her life she could find.

"Classy." The grin on Dominique's face betrayed that she didn't mind the student-like vibe of the evening too much. "I love pepperoni."

"Who doesn't?" Steph handed her a plate and a napkin and they sat munching in silence for a few minutes.

"So," Dominique said after a while. "You know about my past, now let's talk about the present." She found Steph's eyes. "And the future, I hope."

"Tell me everything." Steph leaned back, unprepared for the bombshell Dominique Laroche was about to drop on her.

"My husband is having an affair. He claims to love her. I want a divorce."

47

A million thoughts collided in Steph's brain. She wanted to call Claire. Should she offer a shoulder to cry on? So that was why the politician had hired an expensive PR agency.

"Okay." Steph had to swallow before she could continue. "Well, thank you for being so straightforward." *You could have said so in that first meeting we had at Barbier & Cyr.*

"I know I should have told you sooner, but—and you can blame the political side of me—I wanted to feel you out a bit first. See what you were made of. You pleasantly surprised me yesterday. Now all my cards are on the table."

"That's it? No more secrets?"

"Isn't that enough for you?" Delivering the news had wiped most of Dominique's killer smile off her face.

"Oh yes." Steph had trouble staying calm. "I'm going to need the details, no matter how painful for you. I'm sorry."

"You're the first person I've told. It didn't come as a surprise. I'd been suspecting for a while, but I confronted him three weeks ago. He didn't even bother denying it."

Steph considered the PR nightmare this could become, especially in light of next year's elections. Dominique's cheating husband really couldn't have picked a worse time. "Will this be an amicable separation?"

"It has to be. We have two children."

"Of course." Steph dreaded asking the next question. "What about the other woman?"

"A colleague. A fellow architect. She's a professional woman, not out to get me." She interjected with a deep sigh. "Just my husband."

"Are you all right?" Steph's mind had been so bombarded with questions, she had forgotten to ask the only one that mattered.

"Ever since my popularity surged after the last election, a rift has been growing." She let her head fall back against the back rest of the sofa, seemingly drained of any fighting spirit. "Not a lot of men can handle having a successful politician as a wife. I thought Philippe was different, but clearly, he's not that special."

Steph scooted a little closer, unsure whether to give Dominique's knee a consoling pat or not. "We don't have to talk about all the details now. How about some more wine?"

"Splendid idea."

Steph grabbed the bottle and refilled their half-empty glasses. "I will have to tell my bosses about this, if we want to come up with the best strategy possible."

"I know. I just couldn't bear waltzing into your office last Monday and telling everyone my husband had found someone better."

"I'll take care of it and report back to you."

With a limp wrist, Dominique brought her glass to Steph's and clinked rims. "I knew I could trust you."

CLAIRE

"She's the hottest, most exciting politician this country has had in decades and her husband is cheating on her?" Claire had been in an excellent mood this morning, with the prospect of a rare date with a hot woman in her immediate future, and Juliette seemed to have patched things up with Nadia judging by the grin on her face when she had walked in earlier. Things were looking up, until this meeting.

"A politician through and through." Juliette sat shaking her head. "It explains a lot."

"What do you mean?" Steph asked.

"Open your eyes, Steph. She must have known much longer than she let on. She has planned this and she wants to use this to her full advantage."

"How can she have planned her husband's affair?" Steph's voice shot up.

Claire was with Juliette on this one. She'd been in this business long enough. "She didn't plot that. She's just making sure she's turning this setback into an advantage. We all know her story. Old money. Lots of it. Her father a confidant of Chirac. Conservative wing of the MRL. Model husband on her arm. Two adorable children who photograph exceptionally well. The Socialists are not doing well and MRL is expected to win the next election. Laroche is their poster child."

"The woman sitting in my sofa last night was not a calculated ambitious bitch with a hidden agenda—"

"Your sofa?" Claire gripped the edge of her desk tightly between her fingers. "What was she doing in your sofa?"

"Telling me about this. She asked for a discreet place to meet."

"And you chose your flat?"

"Well, yes—"

"Be careful, Steph. She's a client first, a smart one who knows exactly what she wants, not your friend."

Steph bit her lower lip but didn't reply, just nodded.

"Is there anything else we should know?" Juliette asked.

"No." Steph met Juliette's eyes defiantly. Maybe she was fooling her, but she wasn't fooling Claire.

"My day is packed absolutely full. Can we have a strategy meeting about this tonight?" Her heart sank while she made the proposition.

"No way." Juliette rose from her chair and hovered over Claire's desk. "No politician's crumbling marriage is going to keep you from that date tonight."

"Date?" Steph whistled through her teeth. "A real date? You?" She arched up her eyebrows. "With who?"

"The hot doc," Juliette said, as if Claire wasn't even in the room.

"Oh."

Claire would have told Steph in person, if only she'd been given the chance.

"Cancel something else. If I work late tonight, I won't be

able to see Nadia." Juliette's tone was firm. "We really have to start paying more attention to a better work-life balance."

Now it was Claire's turn to paint a quizzical expression on her face. Nevertheless, she was loathe to postpone her date, especially because Margot would be working all weekend. "Fine. I'll arrange it. Fred will let you know."

"Your new assistant started yesterday, by the way, Jules," Steph said.

Claire didn't understand the grin accompanying that statement.

"Oh shoot. I forgot about Sybille."

"Don't worry, I took good care of her." Steph rose from her chair and elbowed Juliette in the bicep. "Let me know when the strategy meeting is scheduled." She exited Claire's office, always the place where they touched base first thing in the morning, and let the door fall shut behind her.

"What was that all about?" Claire asked.

"Search me." Juliette headed for the door.

Why did Claire feel as if everyone was hiding something from her? Having enough on her plate already, she decided to drop it. "I take it your home-cooked meal was a success?"

"Let's just say it didn't involve eating a lot of the meat I prepared." The smile on Juliette's face beamed.

"I'm happy for you, Jules."

————

Claire adjusted her hair in the reflecting window of the bar. She'd wanted to stop at home for a quick shower after a work, but she would never have made it to Saint-Germain-des-Prés on time if she had. And she had an inkling Margot would not be fond of a date arriving late.

The bar was small, even by Parisian standards, but, unlike most cafés in this city, the few tables inside were spaced out enough to allow for a little intimacy without the people perched

around the next table being able to hear what you were saying
—or what your chat-up line was.

Excellent choice.

Margot occupied a corner table next to the counter, an open
bottle of white wine and two empty glasses in front of her.
Would the doctor be consuming copious amounts of alcohol tonight?
She rose when she spotted Claire. She'd dressed down in jeans
and a light-pink blouse tucked tightly into the waistband of her
trousers, open at the throat and bringing out the ochre of her
skin. Without her leathers, she looked more petite, perhaps even
a bit less intimidating, but still very much intriguing.

"Ça va?" She smelled of honey and flowers when she
pecked Claire briefly on the cheek.

"You look relaxed." Claire felt a bit overdressed in her stiff
business suit.

"Day off." She grabbed the bottle of wine and presented it to
Claire so she could read the label. "Is white okay?"

"Perfect." Claire couldn't remember the last time she'd been
on a date. Truth be told, she wasn't sure if women her age actually went on dates.

"Nadia and Juliette are talking again," Margot said after
she'd poured them both a glass.

"Do you think they'll be all right?" Claire sipped from the
wine. A bit too fruity to her taste, but she wasn't going to say
that out loud.

"I honestly have no idea, but at least they made a start."

Talking about mutual friends was a great way to break the
ice, but Claire had had enough of her friends' dramas. She
wanted to talk about Margot, get to know her better. She stared
at the doctor a bit too long, lost in thoughts of how to start the
real conversation between them.

"What?" A small smile played on Margot's lips.

"I was just wondering if you were born here."

"Might as well get that out of the way." The smile didn't
fade from Margot's lips. She seemed in an agreeable mood,

much more so than the first time they'd met. "My sister and I were both born in Korea. We were adopted as babies. I've lived in Paris all my life."

"Concise and precise." Claire sipped from her wine again before meeting Margot's ink-black eyes.

"It's the training." Margot shrugged. "How about you?"

"Born and bred in—" The loud beeping of Margot's phone, shamelessly deposited next to the bottle of wine on the table, interrupted Claire.

"Sorry, I have to take this." Margot had already answered the phone and pressed it to her ear. "Oui, oui," she said a few times, followed by the dreaded words, "I'll be right there."

"Work?" Claire asked when Margot rang off.

"Worse." Margot sighed. "My mother."

"Oh." Claire waited for an explanation.

"My parents are not so young anymore. Apparently my dad took a nasty fall. I'm so sorry, but I'm afraid I have to go."

"Gosh, I hope he's all right." Claire tried to hide the disappointment coursing through her. They'd barely had five minutes.

"That's what I need to find out." Margot's forehead wrinkled with worry. "I will make this up to you."

"But not this weekend."

"I'm sorry." Margot reached into her bag and dug up her wallet.

"It's fine. I'll get it." Claire waved away the twenty euro note she wanted to leave on the table. "You can buy next time."

"Deal." Margot rose and plucked a brown leather jacket from the back of her chair. "I'll call you." She quickly planted a clumsy kiss on Claire's cheek and strutted out of the bar.

Claire fully understood why the sexy surgeon was single. She also wondered if Jennifer was still in town.

STEPH

Steph had no idea what she was doing in this luxurious apartment on Avenue Foch on a Sunday afternoon. Barbier & Cyr paid her to advise Dominique Laroche on public relations affairs and to come up with the best strategy to preserve her image for the coming elections, but frankly, she had a hangover, and the phone number of a desirable woman she met last night burning a hole in her pocket.

"I have a few other secrets, I guess." Dominique leaned against the marble mantle. "This place, for example. I inherited it from my grandfather when he passed away ten years ago." A coy smile split her lips. "His mistress lived here before he got too old to satisfy most of her needs and she left him." Steph scanned the living room. It was decorated in the colours of bourgeoisie, salmon pink and broken white and lots of flower patterns. "Being his only grandchild had its advantages."

Steph didn't know if she was expected to contribute to the conversation or if this was a monologue, and if it was, what the point of it was.

Dominique crossed to a cabinet in the corner of the room and lowered the front panel. A vast collection of hard liquor appeared. Steph's stomach protested at the mere sight of it.

"Would you like a drink?"

Steph was well aware that the fee Barbier & Cyr charged the politician included politeness at all times, so she nodded, a queasy feeling rising in her gut. She watched Dominique pour two whiskies with a steady hand.

When she handed Steph the glass, she remained in her personal space a fraction too long. "I thought this would be a better place to meet than your studio, no offence."

"None taken." Steph pretended to sip the liquor but just the smell of it was enough to make her knees go weak. "Nice place." She shuffled in her seat before continuing. "You know I'm at your disposal at, huh, most times, but I have a family dinner on the other side of town I need to get to in an hour." She looked at her watch ostentatiously.

"Not a hot date then?" Dominique sat down next to her. "I asked around about you. After you dug up that intel on Murielle, I was intrigued. You have quite the studly reputation."

Steph tilted her head and her face broke out into a smile, as if she couldn't help herself. "All lies."

"I'm sure." Dominique nodded with pursed lips. "Philippe is introducing the children to Angelique this afternoon. Not as his girlfriend just yet, but he's taken them to some open house thing in Neuilly his firm has organised. She'll be there. At least he had the courtesy to tell me beforehand."

"I'm sorry. It must be difficult." Steph was convinced Claire and Juliette had Dominique all wrong. She wasn't naive when it came to human nature, but she saw the pain on Dominique's face, the loneliness in her eyes.

"The only thing that makes me feel marginally better about this ordeal is talking to you." She gave a small chuckle. "Does that make you uncomfortable?"

"PR is more psychology than anything else." Steph deposited her glass on the coffee table, tired of the smell in her nose. "That's what I'm here for."

"It means a lot." She drank again. "We've decided I shouldn't postpone telling my father about the divorce. I'm seeing him later tonight."

"The mighty Xavier Laroche. I imagine you're not looking forward to that." Maybe this was all going over Steph's head a bit.

"Just going through the motions. I can easily predict what he's going to say and *suggest*. It's not that I disagree, it's more that I feel as if my life is being lived for me. That everything is planned and I just have to show up."

Steph reached for her glass and took a big gulp. "I can stay a while longer." The whiskey burned its way down her throat.

"Do you know what I would want to do if I really had the choice. If I didn't have an entire nation watching my every move and an entire Socialist party—and half of my own party—waiting for me to screw up?"

Amused, Steph shook her head.

"I'd want you to take me to the biggest lesbian club in Paris. I'd dance the night away, and wait for you to take me home when I was all partied out."

Steph was grateful she hadn't just taken a sip of her drink, or every last drop would have landed on the expensive rug below their feet. She wondered how much Dominique had drunk before she arrived. "We have booze." She fished inside her jeans pocket for her phone. "And we have this. We can have our own private party right here." *But not the kind you have in mind.*

Dominique stared at Steph's phone with wide eyes.

"It plays music, you know. What do you like?"

"Anything they play at the clubs these days."

"Really?" It was Steph's turn to look surprised.

"I honestly don't care. Just put on something. I'll pour us some more whiskey."

Steph opened the Spotify app and searched for an eighties playlist. She wasn't going to subject Dominique to the beats she danced to at Les Pêches. It wouldn't work in a place like this.

She watched Dominique as she returned with the bottle of booze. She was definitely good-looking, which played a large part in her popularity, with piercing green eyes and long salt-and-pepper hair, but she was hardly the type Steph would go for. Let alone the fact that she'd surely get fired for even thinking about it. So what on earth was she doing?

"One hell of a party." Dominique raised her glass. "To the men ruining my life."

So that's what it's all about. Steph relaxed a bit. She could deal with that.

"Don't you have a family dinner to go to?" Dominique asked as she added more whiskey to Steph's glass.

"Don't you have to go see daddy?" It sometimes slipped her mind that she was sitting opposite the rising star of the MRL. The circumstances didn't exactly enhance a professional atmosphere either.

To Steph's relief, Dominique burst out laughing. Big gurgles of laughter bubbling up from her belly, creasing the skin around her eyes and mouth. She looked relaxed, maybe even obliviously happy for a split second. She raised her glass. "To you and me, Stéphanie. We'll show them."

NADIA

"I wasn't expecting you here tonight," Margot said as soon as Nadia entered the living room of Margot's flat.

It was eleven p.m. on a Sunday night and she'd wanted to stay at her and Juliette's place but, just because their physical relationship had magically reignited again, she didn't want to give the wrong impression that all their problems had been solved because of it.

"You're probably not the only one." She heeled off her shoes and sank down into what had become her spot in Margot's sofa. "The look on Juliette's face when I told her I wasn't staying... that lopsided curve in her upper lip, it starts quivering a bit when she's upset but she doesn't want to say." Nadia sighed. "It would be so easy to just go back, but I didn't move out for nothing. If I go back now, the next time I leave, it may be for good."

"Baby steps." Margot was her usual talkative self. Truth be told, the fact that she never said more words than strictly necessary was one of the main reasons why Nadia enjoyed her company so much.

Nadia nodded. "Rough shift?"

"Nothing too unusual, but knackering as always." Margot looked exhausted. Strands of hair had come loose from her usually tight ponytail and dark circles gleamed underneath her eyes.

It hit Nadia that she'd left the hospital on Friday before Margot had arrived and hadn't had an opportunity to ask. "Hey, how was your date?"

Margot expelled a puff of heavy air while shaking her head. "I'm afraid I screwed it up."

"Why?"

"We'd barely sat down when my mother called. My father fell down in the shower and since his surgery we're always worried about his hip, so I rushed home, leaving Claire with a full bottle of wine." She leaned back in the sofa, intertwining her fingers behind her head.

"And?"

"And… my father barely had a scratch and a promising date was ruined."

"I'm sure Claire understands. Have you spoken to her since?"

"I texted her on Friday to let her know dad was all right and we exchanged a few messages over the weekend. I—I, huh, I don't know."

"Tell me." Nadia knew Margot well enough to know she wouldn't be stuttering if she didn't really like Claire.

"Well, I'm hardly ideal dating material, am I? At least one weekend shift a month, on call for another weekend, which seriously limits the activities I can engage in. Irregular shifts during the week. Plus, I'm not sure it's all worth it in the end."

Nadia also knew fear when she saw it. "What happened with Inez was not your fault. She left."

"She chose the job over me. It's what we do."

"Either way, if that's what you're worried about, Claire should be a good fit. She works just as many hours as Juliette. She has unexpected meetings and drinks in the evenings, not even mentioning client emergencies. Trust me, she understands, or at least she should."

Nadia fully understood the irony of the situation. She was telling the woman she was temporarily staying with because, amongst other things, her partner worked too hard, to take a chance on a woman who was exactly like Juliette—probably even worse, since Claire hadn't had a real relationship in a very long time. Still, she didn't stop. Nadia could picture them together. Maybe she was the only one, but she could.

"You have tomorrow off. Invite her to lunch. Take her to dinner. Don't just sit here and assume it's over before it has even begun." She stood up and picked up Margot's phone from the coffee table. "In fact, call her now. Claire Cyr does not go to bed before midnight ever, except when she gets a better offer, if you know what I mean." Nadia winked at Margot. She was getting a bit caught up in the excitement of their early courtship, something she herself hadn't experienced in ten years.

She searched for Claire's number, dialled it and handed the phone to Margot, leaving her no choice.

Juliette was right, she really was the bossy one.

JULIETTE

"The sex is earth-shattering." Juliette sat at the bar of Le Comptoir with Claire for a quick one after work before Claire's date with Margot. "It hasn't been like this in years, or maybe I just forgot." She looked sideways at her friend. "Are you listening to me at all?"

"As riveting as the stories of your sex life are to me, I believe I've just been stood up again."

Juliette scrunched up her eyebrows. "What now?"

Claire showed her the screen of her phone.

So sorry. Work emergency. Call after.

59

"Jesus Christ." She shook her head. "But who are we to pass judgement?"

"I believe I'm beginning to understand how your significant other has been feeling all these years every time you called her to say you were working late."

"This probably means I won't get to see Nadia tonight either, if they're calling in Margot on her day off." Juliette signalled Tony to give them the same again. "I know it's Monday, but let's get wasted."

"I can't believe I left work early for this. I just wanted one drink to take the edge off, but yes, I think I may have several now."

"Are you texting her back?"

"It would be the polite thing to do." Claire polished off her half-empty cosmopolitan as soon as Tony deposited the next one in front of her. "But I'll let her stew for a while."

"Do you like her enough to get stood up on what looks like regular occasions?" Juliette had warmed up to Margot considerably since she had driven her to see Nadia on the back of her motorbike, but when push came to shove, Nadia was still living with her and that could hardly sit well with Juliette.

"She's got that silent, tough girl act going on, which isn't really my thing, but I am intrigued. But honestly, we haven't had a conversation lasting longer than fifteen minutes, so it really is too early to tell."

"But you'll give her another chance?"

"Depends how she plays it. If we actually manage to go on a date, she'd better make it a spectacular one." Claire toyed with her phone. "I'd better text her back."

Juliette sipped from her daiquiri while Claire composed and sent the message. They both jumped when a phone beeped loudly behind them just as Claire pressed 'send'. Without exchanging words, they turned around on their bar stools and looked into a leather-clad doctor's smug face.

So she did have a sense of humour.

"Surprise," Margot said. "My horse awaits outside. If the lady would care to join me."

Juliette expected her to end with a little curtsey, but Margot wasn't the type to take it that far. Well-played, though.

"I, um, I—" Claire was hardly ever at a loss for words, but she was now.

Juliette was grateful she was there to witness it so she could use it against her friend when she needed to. A warmth spread through her flesh at the sight of them, and at the sudden thought that, if there wasn't an emergency at the hospital, she could ask Nadia to come over.

"Get out of here, you two," she said. "I'd confiscate both your cell phones so as to avoid any interruptions, but I shall remain realistic."

"See you tomorrow." Claire gathered her affairs and followed Margot out of the door.

Inspired by Margot's romantic gesture, Juliette quickly paid the bill and took a taxi to Saint-Germain-des-Prés, where she hoped to find Nadia in Margot's apartment. She wanted to ask her something.

CLAIRE

It wasn't easy straddling the back of a motorcycle when wearing a pencil skirt, but Claire took it in her stride. Margot hadn't said where she was taking her, but judging by the route she took, it wasn't to the restaurant where they had agreed to meet.

Curling her arms around Margot's waist—holding on for dear life, really—and feeling her hard stomach through the leather of her jacket was exhilarating though, as was this ride at dusk through their beautiful city.

The bike rumbled beneath her, the twitches of Margot's muscles against her body indicated she was in complete control, the wind whipped through the strands of her hair not covered by the helmet and Claire wondered if what she was feeling in her stomach was just excitement or something else.

Margot slowed down in a street just off the Champs de Mars. She was agile enough to get off the bike quickly—displaying amazing flexibility in doing so—before Claire had a chance to climb down. Margot helped Claire so she could dismount in the least embarrassing way possible and while Claire pulled her skirt back over her knees, Margot popped open the storage of the bike and took out a bottle of wine.

"Could you hold this, please?" She handed the wine to Claire while she took her helmet and attached it to the lock that fastened the front wheel of the bike to a concrete structure in the ground.

She grabbed a folded plastic bag from the storage and added plastic cups, a baguette—broken in two to fit the small space underneath the seat of the bike—a tupperware container with cheese and salami, a knife, a cutting board and a blanket.

Claire wanted to whistle in admiration, but stopped herself, not wanting to spoil the moment with irony of any sort. She was quite perplexed by Margot's display of spontaneity and, frankly, her desire to woo Claire with a picnic with full view of the Eiffel Tower.

Margot put her own helmet in the now empty storage space, locked it and turned to Claire. "All good to go."

They'd barely exchanged any words since Margot had turned up at Le Comptoir, but, Claire suspected, as far as setting the mood went, Margot was doing a better job than she ever could with words. She followed Margot onto the lawn as the last of the sun dipped behind the horizon.

Despite growing up in Paris, she'd never come here at night. When you live in Paris, you tend to avoid the most obvious tourist traps, but the spot Margot had chosen, just far enough from a lamp post to not be too lit up, but close enough to allow them to see each other and the magnificently lit-up tower, was perfect.

They spread out the blanket and sat down, and once again Claire cursed the choice in clothing she'd made that morning. She'd dressed to impress in a restaurant and possibly a bar after, not to ride a motorcycle and sit on a blanket. She had to hike up her skirt a bit higher than made her feel comfortable, but she could hardly complain about the setting, Margot's manoeuvre and how things had played out. It beat listening to more tales of Nadia and Juliette at Le Comptoir.

Margot poured them a cup of wine. A Bordeaux from a good year she believed, but Claire wasn't really paying attention to that.

"To our first real date," Margot said, and clinked the plastic rim of her cup against Claire's.

"You had me fooled for a moment." Claire couldn't help but smile from ear to ear.

"That was the idea." Margot had tossed her leather jacket aside and wore a simple white t-shirt underneath. It was the first time Claire noticed her arms and the gentle swell of her biceps. It stirred something in the area covered by her propped-up skirt.

"Can't say I saw that one coming."

"How could you." Margot took a sip and locked eyes with Claire over the rim of her cup. "You don't know me very well yet."

STEPH

Steph's temples throbbed when she arrived home from the office at well past nine p.m. All she wanted was to soak in a hot, soothing bath, but she only had a shower at her disposal in her tiny flat.

She'd ordered a pizza on her way home and crashed down on her sofa with Pierrot while she waited for its delivery. She was surprised when her intercom buzzed because Pizza Italia's delivery service wasn't usually that fast. She buzzed them in without asking who it was, too tired to pay much attention to anomalies.

She dug out some cash from her wallet and waited for the doorbell to chime. Instead of the out-of-tune ding-dong that her bell produced, someone knocked on the door—another something her usual pizza guy never did. Maybe he had been replaced or had a day off.

Steph opened the door and found herself face-to-face with someone holding a bottle of wine instead of a pizza.

"Thank goodness you're home," Dominique said. "I really didn't want to drink this all by myself."

Steph stood with her mouth wide open for an instant, her heart hammering away in her chest. She recovered quickly. "Seriously? You want to drink again tonight after we killed that bottle of whiskey last night?"

"Depends… are you going to invite me in?" Dominique had that triumphant smile on her face, the one she used for posters and other election promotion material.

"Well, I'm kind of contractually obliged, I guess." Steph opened the door wide, scooping up Pierrot before he could make a dash down the stairs.

"You're no such thing. Unless I didn't read the clause that stipulates you need to drink with me whenever I demand it."

It's not as if I can kick you out. Steph didn't say it out loud. She didn't mean it, either. Last night was a bit of a blur. She didn't remember much after the second glass of whiskey—which was really not the type of liquor Steph excelled in drinking. There was a lot of ranting by Dominique, a lot of cursing at her husband and her father and the party leader, who was just a front with a younger face—according to Dominique—because everybody knew Xavier Laroche was still the one pulling the strings and setting the course—as right-wing as possible.

"You're very welcome in my humble crib. Truth be told, I hadn't expected you to show up here again. Not posh enough for you." Steph deposited her cat on the sofa and took

Dominique's coat. It smelled of her perfume, a scent she'd gotten quite used to over the past week. That wasn't in the contract either.

She fetched two wine glasses from the kitchenette and held them out so Dominique could fill them. She looked at Dominique while she uncorked the bottle with a corkscrew that somehow always remained on her coffee table. PR was an alcoholic business, as much inside as outside the home.

"I have my reasons for being here," Dominique said while filling their glasses. Steph sat down next to her. She would have vacuumed if she'd known she'd have company.

"I'm sure you have." Steph arched up her eyebrows, waiting for some sort of revelation.

"I've come to realise I was very rude to you yesterday. I must admit I had a few, even before you arrived, and I kept banging on about myself without even once stopping to ask about you. That's why I've come." She said it as if she was giving a speech in parliament, confident and totally convinced of her own justness.

"You've come to ask how I'm doing?" Steph looked into Dominique's green winner's eyes.

"To even out the balance." Dominique drank some more wine. "There are two other people on this planet who know what you know about me and you're the only one I'm on speaking terms with." She narrowed her eyelids. "Unless you've told your bosses."

Steph shook her head, glad she hadn't had the chance to tell Claire and Juliette when she was about to. "I haven't. You can trust me."

"I know I can." Dominique put a hand on her thigh and Steph felt the impact shoot all the way through her. She didn't remove it. "Tell me about you, Steph. I take it you don't have a girlfriend?"

Steph sucked her bottom lip into her mouth, caught between a rock and a hard place. She decided she might as well play.

After all, most nights when she went to Les Pêches, she felt as if she had invented this game herself. "I don't. I guess I haven't met that one person yet who can sway me into domesticity."

"If there's one thing that's overrated." Dominique squeezed Steph just above the knee before withdrawing her hand. She gulped down the rest of her wine and set her glass on the table. "That's really all I needed to know."

"Does that mean you're leaving already?" Steph sat up a little straighter, holding her wine glass in both hands in front of her chest.

"No. I wouldn't dream of it now." Dominique held her gaze, her full-wattage smile dimmed to a crooked grin. "I wish I had more time to dedicate to this, but I am an incredibly busy woman, so I'm just going to come out and say it." She reached out her arm and, without asking, took Steph's wine glass out of her hands, depositing it on the table next to hers. "I'm very attracted to you, Steph, and let's just say I'm hardly in two minds about wanting to kiss you right now."

NADIA

Nadia had half-expected Juliette to turn up. What she didn't see coming was the way Juliette shoved her against the front door the instant she closed it behind her and kissed her with such intensity it seemed her life depended on it.

This is what they did now. Instead of talking about their problems and attempting to find a way out, they tried to fuck them away. Nadia didn't want to say it out loud, but it was typical of Juliette. The mere thought of a real confrontation, of having to face an emotional, intimate issue head on, made her clam up. Or kiss her as if they'd just met, hormones still unsettling their blood.

Nadia was hardly brave herself, and she reciprocated Juliette's kiss with a desperation unknown to her, as if clinging on to something she knew she stood to lose.

"We have to talk, babe," she tried, when they came up for air. Before she had a chance to say more, Juliette pressed her swollen lips against hers again, ignoring Nadia's plea.

"I know you're home alone," Juliette hissed in her ear. "I have plans for you." She planted her palms on the door next to Nadia's head, her arms stretched along Nadia's cheeks. At least this was new. Different.

Nadia used the opportunity to take in the image of her estranged partner. She was still in her work outfit. Stark white blouse, pitch black pants suit. Nadia had always preferred her in jeans and a t-shirt. Maybe it was symbolical.

"What do you have in mind?"

"You'll see." Juliette took her by the hand and led her to the guest bedroom, as if she owned the place.

Nadia followed. She didn't mind Juliette pretending to take control like this, but she knew it wouldn't last, knew it was just a front. Something Juliette had basically made a career out of.

Juliette kicked off her shoes—as if finally allowing herself to sink to Nadia's barefoot level—and cupped the back of Nadia's head in her palms. "We'll talk later. I promise."

The promises Juliette had made her over the years and never kept. Nadia could still pinpoint the exact moment she'd decided to start holding them against her. The day it had all become too much and what she'd done in response. The secret she'd been keeping.

"Okay, baby," she said, wrecked with guilt, finding Juliette's hands with her own in her hair. "But let's do it my way."

Nadia gave. It's what she did. But in giving, she also took. Juliette knew that and that was why their relationship had worked so well, until Nadia had decided to change her boundaries.

She stripped Juliette of her blazer slowly, mindfully, wanting to counter the mad physical frenzy they'd fallen into of late—as if it could somehow undo the previous months of emptiness between them. Her blouse was next to go and, no matter what had happened, no matter how ignorant Juliette had been and how reckless Nadia had acted, seeing her lover stand in front of her like that, as good as stripped bare, still felt like home.

Nadia willed herself to push the regret from her brain and started on Juliette's trousers.

JULIETTE

Nadia's fingers undoing the button of her pants made Juliette shiver in her skin. She wondered if Nadia knew this was the only way she could feel as if they were on the same page, as if they were in synch with each other the way they had been effortlessly for years, before it had all started to unravel. Slowly, almost imperceptibly—at least to Juliette.

It's not that she didn't understand, but it was hard to admit. It was failure. And this, the way Nadia's hands roamed across her skin, this was so much easier.

In the end, all it did was prove that lack of passion was not the real reason they'd drifted apart. That it was just another symptom.

Juliette watched Nadia take off her own clothes. She'd dressed in white linen slacks, comfortable and homely attire, which meant she was somehow starting to feel at home in Margot's flat. Juliette wouldn't let it happen. Not if she could help it. But first, Nadia's naked skin. The sight of it. The coconut scent of it. It represented the best years of Juliette's life.

Nadia took a step closer and pressed her warm flesh against Juliette's. She curved her arms around Juliette's waist and held her so close, the only way she could be closer was inside of her. She let her hands trail up Juliette's back, until they found the lock of her bra and undid it.

This was a practiced routine, executed thousands of times before, but this was not their bedroom, and afterwards Juliette would ask Nadia to come home. She'd beg her if she had to.

The actions were the same, but the sentiment lurking behind them much more powerful.

Clad only in panties, Nadia pushed Juliette onto the bed. As soon as her back hit the mattress, Nadia hooked her fingers under the waistband of Juliette's knickers and tore them down. It was always a statement before they really got stuck in, Nadia's way of showing what she had in store for her.

Before she joined Juliette on the bed, Nadia stepped out of her own panties. Her dark nipples stiffened and Juliette salivated at the prospect of taking them into her mouth, if Nadia would let her.

Nadia lowered her body onto Juliette's, the meeting of their skin familiar and exhilarating, and for a little while, it all fell away. The quiet insults. The growing rift. The distance that had gathered between them. It wasn't there anymore when Nadia kissed Juliette beneath the ear, it evaporated with the silent sighs already escaping from Juliette's mouth.

Juliette ran her nails over Nadia's back, she wanted to dig deep, brand her as hers, but this was enough. They didn't need marks for that. Ten years together was enough. This was a rough patch, a minor glitch in their long history together. She'd ask her to come home. The first step to recovery.

Nadia's lips suckled a moist path down Juliette's neck, stopping at her collarbones to plant some gentle kisses there. Juliette kept her eyes on Nadia in case she looked up, so she could catch a glimpse of the storm in her eyes. Something in her glance always changed when they ended up in bed, a delicious darkness took hold, a magnetism drawing Juliette in and keeping her there.

With her knee, Nadia pushed Juliette's legs apart, before positioning her pelvis so their pussy lips touched. Her weight rested on her arms and a fire raged in her eyes while she ground herself against Juliette. It wasn't the sensation between her legs, which was subtle at best, that turned Juliette's skin into gooseflesh, it was the look in Nadia's eyes. The way she prepared herself for what was to come by crashing her hips into Juliette's—as if already claiming her.

Apart from the sound of their skin slapping together and the ragged puffs of their breath, the room was silent. Nadia bent her arms and kissed Juliette full on the mouth, her tongue crashing through the gap between her lips with full force. That's how Juliette knew playtime was over. She grabbed Nadia by the back of the head and pulled her closer.

The things she wanted to say, everything she couldn't say when they sat opposite each other ready for 'the talk' bubbled to the surface, but Nadia freed herself from Juliette's hold and made her way down. Wet pecks led the way, only interrupted when Nadia took Juliette's nipple between her teeth and bit down—always much harder than Juliette expected, even after all these years.

Juliette was still wincing at the torturous delight when Nadia's lips had already reached her belly button and then the edge of her pubic hair. Nadia slowed the pace of her kisses, making them more deliberate.

Juliette regarded Nadia's big mass of hair, how it bounced up and down while she was busy between her legs, how the tone of their skin contrasted where Nadia's arms curved over her thighs. She drew up her knees, exposing herself completely, as Nadia settled between her upper thighs. For a brief moment, there was nothing. Only breath being expelled at a quickening pace and Juliette's fingers digging into the sheet with anticipation. Nadia looked up once, just a fraction of a second, but long enough to lock her eyes with Juliette and make her press her fingernails deeper into the mattress.

Then, the tip of Nadia's tongue started dancing, an onslaught of light licks being unleashed on Juliette's lips and clit in a steady rhythm.

"Aah," Juliette moaned. "Aah, baby. Yes."

Nadia wrapped her lips around Juliette's clit, sucking it into her mouth, before letting her tongue circle around it at a more determined pace. Juliette stretched out her arms, trying to find a few strands of Nadia's hair to wrap her fingers around, craving the connection.

Nadia's tongue appeared to be everywhere at once, slithering along her lips, delving inside, circling her clit. Her fingers dented the fleshy part of Juliette's thighs, keeping away from her pussy. This was tongue only, the way Nadia liked to start things off.

Juliette let her head fall back into the pillows and closed her eyes, their history displayed on the back of her eyelids. The day they met. That first, hesitant kiss. The first time Nadia had pushed her down onto the bed and told her to stay there. The images followed in quick succession now, to the rhythm of Nadia's tongue on her clit, demanding climax.

With a deep shudder in her muscles, Juliette came, everything compressed in that moment. Waves of love and obliterating, freeing lust.

After relaxing her limbs and swallowing away the beginning of a tear, Juliette couldn't pull Nadia to her chest fast enough.

"This is who we are, babe," she said. "Who we used to be. This connection, it made us."

Nadia wrapped her arms tightly around Juliette's torso, as if never wanting to let go. She pressed her lips against the swell of Juliette's breast.

"Come here." Juliette brought her hand underneath Nadia's chin. "Look at me." Her heart hammered away, the finger guiding Nadia's head towards her trembling. "Please come home. I need you there."

Silence, followed by a single tear falling down Nadia's cheek. "Not yet. I can't."

"Please, babe. This push and pull. The distance between us and then this, it's hard to take. It's hard going home to an empty flat after this."

"If you want me to come home, we need to start talking instead of ending up in bed every time we meet."

"I agree, but at least the fact we're doing it must mean something." Juliette pushed herself up, the blissful post-orgasmic vibes soon leaving her. "I can't stand that you're away. That we're not together. It's not right. How can more distance possibly fix us?"

"It's not distance we need, it's perspective." Nadia didn't say any more and for the first time, after months of feeling as if all the blame for their crumbling affair was being heaped solely on her, Juliette got an inkling that there was more to it. That maybe, it wasn't all her fault.

CLAIRE

"You're a difficult woman to read," Margot said. She sat with her legs stretched in front of her and her body weight resting on her elbows.

Claire nearly choked on her wine. She'd polished off most of the bottle by herself because Margot was driving. "That's a good one coming from you."

Margot looked into the distance for an instant before replying. "I do admit that I've always been more focused on work and improving myself instead of developing my conversational skills, but I wasn't always this withdrawn."

"What happened?" As far as first dates went, an indulgence Claire hadn't allowed herself for quite some time, this one appeared to be going quite well.

"A case of severe heartbreak." Margot looked away again. Claire didn't know if it was because of the lingering pain of the breakup or because she couldn't look her in the eye when divulging something personal. This was by far the most intimate statement Margot had made all night.

Claire didn't say anything, allowing Margot to continue at her own pace. In the few moments of stretching silence that lay between them, Claire came to the harrowing conclusion that she'd never fallen hard enough for someone to end up with a broken heart.

"We were together for a year and a half when she got the chance to work with Médecins Sans Frontières in Rwanda, something she had always wanted to do. It was just around the time my dad started doing poorly and I couldn't leave my parents. We tried long-distance for a while until she met someone else and, well, the rest is history."

"When did this happen?"

"Almost a year ago. She's in India now." Margot sighed. "She's doing important work so I can hardly hold it against her."

Claire was not big on giving advice, or even commenting on matters of the heart. "It must have hurt," she tried.

"Not anymore." Margot eyed what was left of the wine in the bottle a bit too eagerly.

"Why don't we go back to that café near you, so you can have a proper drink."

Margot reached for the bottle and poured the remainder in her cup. "I'll just leave the bike here and we can walk."

Claire furrowed her brow. "Not in these shoes."

Margot's eyes wandered from Claire's face to her exposed legs and the high-heeled shoes resting next to them. "Oh that's right, you're dainty." The grin on Margot's face surprised Claire.

"I'm no such thing," Claire quickly said. "I'm dressed for dinner in one of the many fine restaurants this city has to offer, not a ride on the back of a motorcycle and a picnic in the grass."

"Complaints?" Margot drained her cup, her biceps bulging ever so slightly when she bent her arm.

"Not at all." Claire tossed her empty cup to the side and inched a little closer. "This has been really lovely. Thank you."

The Eiffel Tower twinkled to the left of them, stars above them. She had the taste of excellent wine in her mouth, and her eyes rested on the most intriguing woman she had met in a long time. Although this was technically their first date, they had a connection already, something that drew them to each other.

"What did you think of me after that dinner at Nadia and Juliette's?" Margot asked, her legs now tucked underneath her, her upper body slanted towards Claire.

"I thought you were most likely someone who preferred listening to others than to the sound of your own voice."

"How diplomatic. You must work in PR."

"It has its perks." Claire shuffled a little closer. "What did you think of me?" Her heart started beating a little faster as she waited for the reply.

"Frankly, the whole atmosphere of the evening threw me off somewhat, but that being said…" She discarded the plastic cup she'd been twirling around between her fingers. "I thought you were probably a bit too posh for me, maybe somewhat out of my league. I felt a bit out of place, I guess."

"And then Steph hit on you."

"She told you?"

Claire nodded. *Out of her league? In which universe?* "Let me show you how out of your league I think I am." Claire pushed herself up on her knees, tilted her head sideways and looked into Margot's ink black eyes. Margot met her halfway, her head canted in the opposite direction.

Their lips barely brushed against each other at the first attempt, forcing a smile to form on Claire's face, which in turn made it harder to purse her lips. She pulled herself together, revelling in the pure romance of the moment, and leaned in again. This time, Margot didn't leave anything to chance and cupped the back of Claire's head in the palms of her hands. She pulled her close and let the tip of her tongue slip between Claire's lips.

STEPH

Steph knew this couldn't happen, but the odds were not in her favour as she stared the forbidden fruit straight in the face.

"But it's really up to you," Dominique whispered, suddenly looking vulnerable.

Steph was hardly the type to mull everything over before going in for some action. She'd slept with married women, she'd landed in bed with girls wanting to make someone else jealous, she'd even had a one-night stand with Claire, and she'd always considered the ramifications the other person's problem. This was different.

"It's not that I don't want to. It's more a question of ethics." The words came out reluctantly. Steph had considered the notion—and she'd received the hints loud and clear—but theory and practice were always two very different things. She compared it to presenting Pierrot with a saucer of milk and then asking him not to drink it. Then again, Pierrot was an animal and he didn't have a job and bosses to consider. Claire and Juliette were her friends but their friendship would not extend to the workplace if they ever found out about this. "I could lose my job."

"Same here, I guess." Dominique inched closer, her drawn up knee pressing into Steph's thigh. "No one has to know." Her hand was back on Steph's knee, already boldly traveling upwards. "Our secret." She slanted her head so her lips could find Steph's ear. "Our deliciously dirty, little secret."

"You politicians think you can talk people into anything." Steph straightened her posture but kept her gaze on Dominique. "But you can't fool me." She turned and shifted her weight until she could swing one leg over Dominique's lap. "I know why you want me. I'm easy and available and I don't do seconds very often. I'm safe and a little dangerous at the same time. The perfect calculated risk." She straddled Dominique, trapping her underneath her body, looking deep into her green-grey eyes.

"I'm bloody lonely and you're incredibly sexy. Is that an honest enough reason for you?" Dominique's voice had grown hoarse.

Steph bent down and pressed her lips to Dominque's ear. "Can't you tell? I'm already sitting on top of you."

"Then what are you waiting for?" Dominique's eyes sparkled with the intensity of someone knowing they were about to get what they came for.

"You're good. Really good. I can see why so many people would vote for you." Steph bent her elbows so her face was a mere inch away from Dominique's. "Because they want to fuck you."

"I bet you didn't vote for me." Dominique's fingers found Steph's thighs.

"Correct, but I *am* about to fuck you." Steph narrowed her eyes. The face below her would be on posters plastered all around the country soon.

"Let's keep it civil and start with a kiss." In a flash, Dominique's hands cradled her neck and pulled her in. The first touch of their lips was electric, much more so than Steph had anticipated. It set her free of all inhibitions and reservations. If this was to be their secret, she really wanted to make it as dirty as possible.

While their tongues met, and burst after burst of lust ripped through Steph—no doubt fuelled by the position the person she was kissing held in society—she started fumbling with the buttons of the politician's immaculately starched blouse, careful not to accidentally tear one off.

When she had Dominique half-naked from the waist up, exposing a surprisingly racy black bra with lace trimming along the edges, Steph pushed herself up, hoisted her top over her head, and gently pulled Dominique down by her legs and twisted and draped her body so she was stretched out on the sofa. She made light work of disposing of Dominique's trousers, slipped out of her own—no longer the familiar pair of jeans she comfortably wore to the office before they started representing politicians—and lowered herself onto the sofa next to Dominique.

"Such efficiency." Dominique said it with a sultry sigh and Steph quickly kissed the words away. *She'd show her efficiency.*

The more intensely their tongues crashed together, the higher Dominique pushed her pelvis against Steph's thigh. The politician was nothing if not frisky—judging by the state of her love life, it had probably been a while. Unless she was playing games like this with other aides. If she was and she hadn't told Steph about them, she'd be in serious trouble.

"I wanted you from that time you came into my office and told me how well-connected you were," Dominique whispered in Steph's ear while Steph kissed her collarbone. How predictable that she wouldn't be able to keep her mouth shut during sex. "My panties were drenched by the time you left, and you were only there for five minutes." She briefly stopped to pant when Steph sunk her teeth into the soft flesh of her upper breast. "Imagine what they're like right now."

Steph replied by trailing her fingers along Dominique's flank, skimming the waistband of her panties, and dipping under slowly to measure the effects she had on her. Her fingers met wetness straight away. "Politicians do sometimes keep their promises," she hissed, not wanting to let on how turned on she was by the free flow of Dominique's juices.

"It's about time you kept yours." Dominique brought one hand down and started tugging her panties down. "Fuck me."

A bossy bottom. Nothing Steph hadn't dealt with a million times before. She climbed off, found Dominique's eyes and tore down her panties. They were soaked beyond salvation.

She draped herself next to Dominique's body as best as her narrow sofa allowed before pulling down the cups of her black bra. Her nipples stood pertly, dark-pink pebbles in a sea of pale gooseflesh. Steph wrapped her lips around one while her hand skimmed down, barely touching Dominique's skin until she reached her pubes. She drew a quick circle around Dominique's clit, just to gauge the effect it would have. Dominique's muscles tensed beneath her, her body going rigid for a split second. Steph would have smiled if her lips weren't busy elsewhere.

She tore her lips away from Dominique's nipple because she needed to see her face when she entered, needed to see the surrender in her eyes. Dominique drew up her knee closest to the back rest, giving Steph better access. The wetness had spread to her upper thighs, creating a velvety feel no matter the direction Steph's fingers roamed in. They only had one destination left now. Inside.

Slowly, Steph inserted two fingers, causing Dominique to go limp beneath her instantly. She stroked deep and slow, allowing Dominique the time to get used to them inside of her. Steph scanned her face, saw how she tried to keep her eyes open, the green of them already obscured by half-closing eyelids.

Intensifying the pace while curling her fingers, Steph craned her neck and sucked Dominique's nipple between her lips. She added another finger, feeling the rim of Dominique's pussy strain around them, and started brushing her clit with her thumb with every stroke.

"Oh," Dominique moaned. "Oh yes, fuck me." Her nails dug deep into the flesh of Steph's back, surely leaving marks. "Harder." Her pelvis bucked up, meeting Steph's thrusts, setting the pace. "Oh yes, oh yes."

With a surprisingly limp whimper, Dominique climaxed on Steph's fingers, pulling Steph's head up to kiss her deeply.

"I can't believe I waited more than twenty-five years to do this again," she whispered in Steph's ear.

"And we've only just started." An unexpected tenderness swept over Steph. It caught her by surprise and she pushed it away immediately, pretended it wasn't there. "Can you stay or do you need to get home?"

"I can stay, after all, I have unfinished business." In between their sweating bodies, Dominique's hand travelled down, to the panel of Steph's drenched panties. "If there's one thing politics teaches you, it's to give as good as you get." With her other hand, she pushed Steph up. Displaying an impressive amount of core strength by sitting upright without the support of her arms, Dominique toppled Steph on her back on the other end of the sofa, untangled their legs, curled her fingers under the hem of her panties and yanked them down as swiftly as Steph had done to hers earlier. "Let me show you what right-wing conservatives can do with their tongue." Dominique's face disappeared between Steph's legs and before she had a chance to consider what was happening, her tongue made contact with Steph's clit.

One night, she thought, most times it means nothing and sometimes, it can change your life. Then all thoughts fled her brain.

EPISODE TWO

STEPH

Steph woke to the sound of someone rumbling around in her bedroom, which wasn't technically a room, but an area cordoned off from the living room by a curtain hanging from the ceiling.

"Morning." Dominique's voice triggered memories of what had happened the night before. The unexpected visit. The wine. The dirty little secret they had created. *Oh fuck.*

"Hey." Steph, normally not an easy riser, shot up from under the duvet, only to realise she was stark naked. She clumsily covered her torso with her arms.

"Nothing I haven't seen before." Dominique, already half-dressed, crashed down next to her, making the mattress dip.

"What time is it?" A rush of adrenalin chased the last remnants of sleep from Steph's brain. The first light of dawn already made its way beneath the curtains.

"Six. Sorry I can't stay for breakfast." Dominique sat stock-still for an instant regarding Steph, that million-dollar-smile on her lips.

Steph didn't know whether to touch her, or to run away. She leaned towards the latter, but she had nowhere to go.

"I'm really rather sorry we can't do this again." Dominique inched closer until her lips hovered over Steph's. "But that would really be breaking all the rules." She pecked Steph lightly on the mouth. "I'm not sure whose rules exactly, but either way, we can't have that." She leaned in again, this time for a lingering kiss, the tip of her tongue slipping in between Steph's lips. She broke off the intimate contact abruptly, leaving Steph wanting more. "Good thing you don't do seconds."

Steph was too stunned to speak. Too stunned by Dominique's effortless power over her, mostly.

"I have to go." Dominique rose and looked around for her trousers.

"We have a meeting tomorrow at Barbier & Cyr."

Dominique turned around and faced her, staring into her eyes. "I look forward to it already." She winked and disappeared behind the other side of the curtain.

Steph tried to wrap the duvet around her, but it was too heavy and big, so she dashed behind Dominique naked, suddenly desperate to see her out.

"Hey, um…" She watched Dominique as she fumbled with a button of her blouse. She looked so on top of everything. Steph felt strangely privileged to have seen her with her head tilted back and all of her exposed. "I really enjoyed last night." She tried the crooked grin she used for flirting, but somehow, it felt more like a lame grimace.

"Yeah." Dominique just nodded and made for the door, scooping up her bag in the process. "See you."

Steph stood looking at the door for long minutes after it had fallen into the lock, Pierrot rubbing himself against her shins with mounting effort. She ducked down to pet him.

"Some ladies have something special, don't they, little man?" She picked him up and deposited him on the bed before curling back up under the covers for a while. Dominique's presence had filled her tiny studio with some sort of magnetic force she couldn't explain. She'd come here to get what she wanted, and she had received. And given. Now all Steph had to do was keep her mouth shut, which wasn't that much of a problem for her.

The real issue was that, just like Dominique, she felt sorry they couldn't do it again. What would the consequences be if they did?

No. No. No.

Steph forced her way of thinking into a different direction and started summing up all the reasons why they couldn't. It helped for a little while.

She also knew that one of the main reasons for wanting Dominique back in her bed was that it absolutely couldn't happen.

———

"Morning sunshine," Fred craned his head into the open door to her office. "Are we still on for lunch?" He arched up his eyebrows and quickly closed the door behind him. "Oh my." He sat down in the visitor chair, crossing one leg over the other. "You have that tired too-many-orgasms-too-little-sleep glow going on, sweetie. Do tell."

Was she really that much of a giveaway? "You're just projecting, dear. Just because you found love in the Raidd of all places doesn't mean you have to come rub it in."

"Ooh, going on the defensive, are we? You must like her then." He rose from his chair. "I'll take you somewhere special and discreet for lunch." He blew her a kiss and exited her office.

Steph could deal with Fred. What was harder to deal with was his mention of the word 'discreet' and how inviting Dominique to the discreet place that was her home had probably started all of this.

Steph rubbed her temples and focused on the screen in front

of her. On it flickered a blank document which had to become the action plan to safeguard Dominique's image during and after her divorce.

It was all well and good picking someone up at Les Pêches and only risking a run-in with them on the weekend when off work, but this, this having to face a one-night stand at the office, and soon on TV and any other possible media outlet, was something Steph had entirely forgotten to take into account.

CLAIRE

Claire's thoughts started drifting towards her first kiss with Margot again when a knock on the door interrupted her. Before she had a chance to respond, Juliette barged in.

"So?" Juliette stood with her legs slightly apart, her arms crossed over her chest—full interrogation mode.

Claire eased herself against the back of her chair, a big grin pulling on her lips. "How was *your* night, Jules?"

"Not nearly as good as yours if that smirk on your face is anything to go by."

"Let's just say the doctor really surprised me."

Juliette shuffled closer, resting her palms on the back of the chair opposite Claire's desk. "Details, please."

Claire grinned and shook her head lightly. "Do you know how long it has been since we've had a conversation like this?"

"Months? Years? I lost track." Juliette marched to the front of the chair she'd been leaning on and sat down. "So don't keep me in suspense."

Claire remembered the flex of Margot's biceps as she'd brought the bottle of wine to her mouth. "It was lovely. Really lovely."

"Just lovely?"

Claire contemplated the question for a moment. "Thoroughly lovely. I mean, it's not every day someone surprises me with a motorcycle ride through Paris, a picnic at le Champs de Mars and a kiss beneath the Eiffel Tower."

Juliette whistled through her teeth. "You've been wooed."

"I believe I have and it feels so good."

"Anything else? What happened after the kiss?" The impatience in Juliette's voice was a good reflection of how Claire felt.

"We talked some more. She drove me home. We kissed again. I woke up with a bit of a hangover because I drank most of the wine, but I didn't care, because, well, she's a really good kisser."

"Did you invite her up?"

"We both agreed it would be better not to." Even if Claire hadn't been looking directly at Juliette, she could have predicted the quizzical look on her face.

"Any particular reason?"

"I think this could be something. We have chemistry and I want to do it right. I want to take it slowly." Claire rubbed two fingers over her chin. "She also doesn't strike me as the type to dive into bed with someone on the first date."

"Fair enough." Juliette painted a big smile on her face. "I'm happy for you, Claire. I hope it works out."

"Thanks." Claire briefly eyed the wall clock above the door. She had a few minutes to spare. "How was your night? More earth-shattering sex?"

"Yes, but apparently this has now become a problem as well." The smile quickly faded from Juliette's face. "I asked her to come home and she refused. I just—" Juliette hesitated for an instant. "I know we need to talk more, but I get the feeling there's more going on. That there's something she's not telling me."

"Like what?" Claire leaned forward, placing her elbows on the desk. The sad state her friend's relationship appeared to be in was not exactly the best advertisement for long-term affairs.

"I have no idea." Juliette shook her head.

"Have you asked her?"

"It's a bit difficult when you don't know what you're asking for and are simultaneously scared to death of the possible response."

"Maybe you should go on holiday. Just the two of you for a few days—"

A knock on the door reminded Claire that they were still at work and not at Le Comptoir having another difficult conversation over a cosmopolitan—which would probably be the case tonight if Juliette was going home to an empty apartment.

"Oui," Claire said. Juliette's brand new assistant Sybille appeared in the door frame.

"Sorry for interrupting." Sybille really was a stunner, her intelligent eyes staring into Claire's briefly before landing on Juliette. Claire made a mental note to keep an eye on the newcomer. "Madame Du Bois is here for you, Juliette. She's early. I've put her in the conference room."

Juliette stood up and headed for the door. "Best get some work done," she said before leaving with Sybille and closing the door behind her.

Claire wondered if, soon, they'd have to start coming into the office even earlier to get their ever lengthening personal conversations out of the way before starting the work day.

She allowed herself another brief moment of remembering the soft touch of Margot's lips against hers before dialling Steph's direct number for an update on Dominique Laroche.

NADIA

"A holiday?" Nadia sat across from Juliette at a tiny table at La Grande Bouffe, their favourite restaurant, still recovering from the shock that Juliette had invited her here after she'd refused to come home.

"You know, little getaways people go on to relax." Nadia picked up easily on the frustration in Juliette's tone.

"I'm open to the idea." She put her fork over her plate, indi-

cating she was done with her only half-finished meal of esca-
lope de veau and green beans. "Can you take time off work?"

"In case you missed it, I own half of the company and am
my own boss. It's not as if I need to ask someone for
permission."

Nadia swallowed the snide remark she could have made. It
wasn't difficult to deduce that Juliette was upset about Nadia's
refusal to move back home. Still, Nadia was impressed by her
partner's continued efforts to reconcile their differences—even
going as far as suggesting they take time off work to go on
holiday together.

"It would give us the time and opportunity we need to talk
things through." Juliette's tone grew milder again. "I was
thinking of Barcelona."

Nadia couldn't suppress a smile. Their first real holiday
together had been in Barcelona. Ten years ago. They'd barely
been together for two months but she'd already known that it
was serious—the real deal. Barcelona would always remind her
of that. "Quatorze Juillet is a Monday. If we take the Friday
before off, we can go for four days."

The expression on Juliette's face mellowed even more, her
eyes narrowing and sparkling at the same time. "I'll arrange
everything first thing tomorrow. Do you want to stay in the
same guesthouse as last time?"

Up until about five years ago, they'd returned to Barcelona
frequently after that first time, always staying in the same
decent but very reasonably priced hotel. "I could see the
romance in that, but I think we can do better now."

"Thank god." Juliette sighed, a relaxed smile taking hold of
her face—a smile that melted Nadia's heart and racked her with
a fresh onslaught of guilt. "I'll book something near the beach.
Haven't seen you in a bikini in way too long."

Nadia wanted to ask for the bill there and then. The smouldering glare in Juliette's eyes was enough to make her knees go
weak, but she couldn't ignore the distance between them.

Despite their physical re-connection, emotionally, they were still far removed from each other. She remembered Margot's words. *Baby steps.*

And then there were the things she hadn't told Juliette yet. If she ever did.

"I look forward to it already." Nadia snaked her fingers across the table in search of Juliette's hand. "I really do."

"What we're doing now, is it sort of like dating each other again?" Juliette trapped Nadia's fingers with hers.

"No, babe. I already know you through and through." Nadia gazed into Juliette's blue eyes. *Did she, though?* Did she still know her? And did Juliette still know her?

"Let's do something this weekend. Something we haven't done in a long time."

Nadia giggled. "I'd love that."

Juliette's eyes lit up. "Let's pretend we're still in our early thirties and go dancing. We'll ask Steph and Claire, maybe even Margot, and go to Les Pêches."

It wasn't exactly what Nadia was expecting as a suggestion. She was thinking more along the lines of something romantic like roller skating or a visit to the Musee d'Orsay—both activities that belonged to their past—but she was at a point where she'd say yes to everything Juliette suggested. "Sure. I still have moves."

"There's no doubt in my mind." Juliette bit her bottom lip. She looked as if she were about to start salivating at the mere thought of Nadia swaying her hips.

"Not sure about Margot's attendance, though. Maybe she and Claire will want to go somewhere a bit more quiet," Nadia said.

"You can persuade her. You're good at that." Juliette squeezed Nadia's palm between her fingers. "I'll work on Claire, and Steph practically lives there during the weekend so that shouldn't be a problem."

"Let's ask them to do it for us." *And hope it doesn't turn into a disaster like last time we were all together.*

"Claire really likes her, you know. Have you spoken to Margot today?"

"Briefly, but you don't need to have made her acquaintance long ago to know she's hardly an open book. I'll ask her all about it tonight when I get home, though." As she spoke the words, the atmosphere changed instantly, all the carefully built-up good vibes deflating all around them.

Juliette let go of Nadia's hand and called for the waiter.

Baby steps.

JULIETTE

Despite barely coping with the constant collision of hope and disappointment in the process of rekindling her relationship with Nadia, and having the distinct feeling she was making all the effort and Nadia was deciding to go along with it or not on a whim, Juliette contacted her travel agent and booked a trip for the two of them to Barcelona first thing in the morning. If she didn't do it now, Nadia may still change her mind—and Juliette needed something to cling to.

She had come into the office early, unable to stay in bed any longer after another night of tossing and turning. Only Fabio in HR was already there, but he was on some special seven-to-four timetable Juliette had never really agreed to. In this instance, Claire had somehow managed to put her foot down.

A knock on the door surprised her. Before she had the chance to reply, Sybille entered carrying a double espresso.

"Bonjour, Madame Barbier."

A headache, caused by sleep deprivation and an all-encompassing feeling of discontent with her life in general, throbbed behind her temples. "I appreciate you knocking, but please wait for my reply before coming in." Juliette's tone of voice sounded much harsher than she had intended.

"Sorry." Sybille looked her straight in the eyes, gaze unwavering. She always did that. Not that Juliette expected her assistant to be demure and humble, but a little respect always went a long way.

"Gosh, no *I'm* sorry. I shouldn't have snapped."

Sybille deposited the cup of coffee on Juliette's desk. "Rough night?"

"Something like that." The scent of coffee hit Juliette's nose and had a positive effect on her mood. "Thanks. You're in early."

"I always arrive before eight, just in case. This is the first day you beat me to it." Sybille stood leaning against the visitor chair, her hips slanted against the arm rest.

"Oh." Juliette had been too preoccupied of late to pay much attention to her new assistant's habits. "Sit down for a minute, will you?"

"Bien sûr." Sybille, dressed as if she were running the place in a tailored light-grey pencil skirt and matching blazer, sat down opposite Juliette, crossing one particularly smooth leg over the other, thus pushing the hem of her skirt up over what looked like rather toned thighs. *Nothing like Nadia in that department then.* Juliette immediately regretted the thought.

"Are there any rumours going around about me in the office?" Juliette thought it was about time to test where Sybille's loyalties lay. Somehow, though, she suspected Sybille would always be firmly in her camp.

"Some." Sybille rested her dark eyes on Juliette. She didn't blink once.

"Please elaborate." Juliette sipped from her coffee. "I'm not interested in who's doing the talking, I just want to get the gist of what's being said."

"Well," Sybille said, pulling the hem of her skirt down just a fraction of an inch—but not nearly as much as she could have with some real effort. "I am the new girl so certain people feel the need to bring me up to speed on things." She flashed Juliette a cunning smile. "I hear your relationship is on the brink. Your partner moved out and it's turning you into a bit of a bitch. Although, I must add, I haven't had that experience."

Maybe because you only arrived after it all went to hell. "That's very frank, Sybille."

"That's what I'm here for, right? Being your eyes and ears where you can't be…"

It wasn't exactly in the job description, but Juliette certainly appreciated the initiative. "Nadia and I will work it out." Juliette said it more to convince herself, but the words sounded hollow and weak.

"I'm sure you will, boss." Sybille's voice grew a bit hoarser when she pronounced the word 'boss', or maybe it was just Juliette's imagination—or the lack of sleep again.

"Speaking of which, I'll be taking the Friday before the Quatorze off. Please reschedule anything I may have had on the books for that day."

"Certainly." Sybille stood up and, this time, pulled her skirt all the way down. "Anything else?"

Juliette shook her head. "No, thanks."

"Just a quick reminder, Dominique Laroche will be here in an hour."

Dealing with someone else's divorce was not something Juliette looked forward to, and she hoped Steph had things firmly under control on that front. Juliette nodded, emptied the cup of coffee and handed it back to her assistant.

She couldn't help sneaking a peek at her swaying hips as Sybille exited her office, and couldn't shake the feeling that a sway that lush was not purely accidental.

STEPH

"I'd like to speak to Stéphanie in private if that's all right," Dominique said, her gaze firmly planted on Steph.

Steph had kept a straight face throughout the meeting,

admiring Dominique's matter-of-factness about it all, but now her nerve was crumbling.

"She's all yours," Juliette said, a wide smile glued to her lips. Obviously, she didn't have a clue. Claire knew Steph better, and in a more intimate way, though. Steph glared at her from under her lashes.

Claire shot her a quick glance, her face expressionless, but didn't say anything. She just shook Dominique's hand and exited the conference room, hurrying to her next meeting.

"Shall we go to your office?" Dominique directed her attention back to Steph before turning to Juliette and offering her hand. "Thank you for all your help, Madame Barbier."

"Our pleasure." Juliette stood there beaming for a while.

"Stéphanie has been such a delight through all of this. Her support has been invaluable."

"Glad to hear it." As Juliette made for the door, she shot Steph a quick wink.

"Shall we?" Dominique held the door open for Steph, as if she was the one working at Barbier & Cyr and inviting Steph into *her* office.

They walked to Steph's broom closet of an office—a far cry from Claire and Juliette's corner offices with magnificent views —in silence. Steph felt as if all the other employees were looking at her as they walked past, suspecting, their stare burning into her flesh, branding her as the person who, no matter what the stakes, simply couldn't keep it in her pants.

"Almost as fancy as your flat," Dominique said with a smirk, closing the door behind her.

"With the accounts I've been getting lately, I believe I may be on my way up." *But not if anyone ever finds out.* Steph leaned against the side of her desk.

"I have a problem." Dominique stayed glued with her back against the door, keeping her distance from Steph.

You're not the only one. "What's that?"

"I can't seem to get you out of my head." The expression on Dominique's face didn't change.

"Oh," Steph said, her heart thundering beneath her chest.

"I guess what I'm saying is…" Dominique's voice had dropped an octave. "I wouldn't say no to doing *that* again."

"Really?" The throbbing in Steph's chest seemed to be travelling downwards.

"I'll be at l'Avenue Foch after nine tonight." She inched even closer. "You know where to find me if you want an encore."

"But, I thought the whole point—"

Dominique was so close to Steph she could put a finger on her lips. "Shht." She shook her head. "Let's not talk about it." She pressed her finger into the flesh of Steph's lips and dragged it down.

Steph squeezed her fingers around the edge of her desk, holding on tightly for support. She had to swallow before she could speak. "I—"

Dominique kissed her gently on the lips. "Shht," she repeated. After one last stare into Steph's eyes, she turned on her heels and was out of the door.

Steph stood leaning against her desk for long seconds after. She'd only just held it together to make it through that meeting with her bosses. This account had such potential to make her career. Was she really willing to give that up for another romp, no matter how good, with a totally unavailable woman?

If only she could ask someone—anyone—for advice. She dug out her phone from her blazer jacket and called Nadia.

NADIA

Nadia met Steph on a park bench just outside the hospital, half-expecting a speech on how badly she was treating Juliette, despite that not being Steph's style at all. Then again, nothing was how it was supposed to be these days.

"What's going on?" It wasn't even lunch time yet, and she already longed for a glass of wine.

"I don't even know where to begin, but you're the only one I can talk to about this."

Relieved this wasn't about her, Nadia straightened her spine and regarded Steph expectantly. "I'm all ears."

"I seem to have developed feelings for the one person in the world I shouldn't have feelings for."

"Feelings? You?" Nadia joked, but soon pulled her face back into a serious expression when she noticed the utter despair in Steph's eyes—not something she'd witnessed many times before.

"We have this client. Very high-profile, and they're letting me take the lead. She came on to me and I went with it and then… oh fuck. What a mess." Steph buried her head in her hands.

"Hey, hey…" Nadia put a hand on her friend's back. "Slow down. Start again." Nadia had never been very involved in Juliette's work and, especially lately, she had no idea who was on Barbier & Cyr's client's list.

"This stays between us. You have to promise me." Steph looked up at her.

"I swear." Nadia grabbed Steph's hands and held them in hers.

"It's Dominique Laroche. We slept together on Monday night and I can't stop bloody thinking about her. We decided it had to be a one-off, but then this morning, she propositioned me again."

"Jesus fucking christ." Nadia's eyes grew to the size of saucers. Utterly speechless, she just shook her head. "No way," she managed to say after a while.

"This could cost me everything and, instead of walking away, something you know I usually have no problem with, I'm so attracted to her I just can't…" Steph shook her head.

"But, Steph, she's married. Not to mention the poster child for a political party dead set against gay marriage."

"She's getting a divorce."

Nadia tried to process all the information as quickly as possible. "But still."

"I know. I know." Steph squeezed Nadia's hands so hard, she was afraid she may leave them bruised.

"Look at me, Steph." If she had come to Nadia to have some sense talked into her, she'd come to the right person. "Are you sure you're not falling for her just because it's so impossible? Something illicit can be very exciting, until it comes out and you find there was really nothing to it, but you've only gone and lost everything you worked so hard for in the process."

"You're probably right."

Nadia couldn't remember a single time in the years of their friendship she'd seen Steph so dejected—hurt almost—over another woman. "You've come for my advice, I take it?"

"Yes." Steph looked at her with so much hope sparkling in her eyes.

"Reject her advances. Don't give her this power over you. Keep it professional." Nadia realised it was easier said than done.

"I'm sorry to lay this on you. I don't want this to come between you and Juliette, especially now…"

"Don't worry about Juliette. This stays between us." *What's another secret?* "But if you decide to break it off now, and I sincerely hope you do, Steph, don't tell Claire and Juliette about it. There's no need for them to know."

"What if Dominique blabs?"

"She has much more interest in keeping this quiet than you. End it now, before it's too late."

"She invited me to her place tonight."

"Don't go." Nadia wondered when she had become the voice of reason. "It may be difficult and tempting, but is it really worth it? What else does she have to offer but a few orgasms?"

Steph feigned a chuckle. "Of all the women in Paris…"

"We all make bad judgement calls, Steph. It's how you clean up your mess that matters most."

"Don't take this the wrong way, but you and Juliette always made it look so easy, but now, even you two are barely holding on…"

"It's complicated." Nadia knew she was hiding behind a silly cliché, knew it all too well.

"Why, Nadz? Why is it suddenly so complicated? She's in pieces, you know. You moving out, that hit her hard."

Sadness bunched in the back of Nadia's throat. "I—" All the tension of the past months, and especially the last two weeks, seemed to transform into tears. Inspired by Steph's candour and trust in her, and before she had the chance to realise fully what she was doing, tears streaming down her cheeks, Nadia launched into her own confession, saying the words out loud for the very first time. "I cheated on her."

Steph's skin tone was naturally pale, but she seemed to grow even paler. "What?"

"A one-night stand with a visiting consultant from Belgium. She's long gone now. It meant nothing and left me feeling utterly devastated and empty, but the worst of it was that Juliette didn't have a clue. She was too busy, too ignorant to notice any change in me at all. Ironically, it was only *after* I slept with someone else that our relationship really started to deteriorate. She just doesn't have a clue. Never even bothered to ask me if something was up. I mean, how do you *not* notice? She knows me through and through…"

"Shit." Steph pursed her lips together. "When did this happen?"

"A few months ago, when she was spending even more time at the office than usual… not that that's an excuse, I just, I wanted to be noticed."

"Probably when we lost the ICM account, one of Juliette's major clients." Steph, the most promiscuous person Nadia knew, had trouble looking her in the eye. "I presume Juliette doesn't know."

"God no."

"Are you going to tell her?"

"I fear it may totally destroy us if I do, but how can I not?"

"Shit," Steph said, again.

"Oh yeah." This was hardly the lunch break Nadia had imagined when she came into work that morning, but, in a way, she was glad to at least have gotten it off her chest. Not that it changed much.

CLAIRE

"Are you sure me being here is okay?" Claire asked. She didn't really care, what with Margot's dark eyes staring back at her the way they did.

"I'm on call and I want to see you…" Margot shrugged. "What was I going to do?"

"You know, you are much less uptight than I thought you were."

"Is that a compliment?" Margot sipped from the coffee Claire had brought her, black and large. It was gruelling sitting next to her in the on call room and not being able to kiss her.

"I can't really imagine giving you anything but." Inwardly, Claire cringed a bit at the cheesiness of her comment, but the look on Margot's face more than made up for that.

"Just to be clear, and to avoid further disappointment, this is not a date and I can get called away at any moment." Margot's blue scrubs were tight around her shoulders, the sleeves cutting off just at that delicious hint of bicep.

"I suppose I'd better get used to that." Claire was distracted and began to suspect quite the toned body was hiding underneath Margot's clothes.

Margot downed some more coffee. "You're looking at me in a funny way."

"Do you work out?" Claire knew she sounded like a middle-aged cliché. She felt like one as well.

"Of course I do. Kickboxing at least twice a week. You don't?" Margot made it sound as if it could be a punishable offence to not belong to a gym or at least own a pair of decent trainers.

"Erm, between work and social obligations, I can't really seem to find the time." A reply so inadequate, it almost made Claire blush—and she was not the blushing type. She was also starting to feel self-conscious about her body.

"You seem to have time for cosmopolitans at Le Comptoir though." There was not a hint of reproach in Margot's voice, just amusement.

"Touché." Claire sagged against the backrest of her chair. "I was just wondering, you know, where those biceps came from. If you've always had them or started working on them to impress me."

Margot was so pretty when she smiled, the naturally more stern expression dissolving from her face completely. "You should come with me some time. I take morning classes at a little boxing club near your office."

"Oh god," Claire groaned. "Next you'll be telling me you practice yoga at sunrise every day and only drink green tea."

Margot held up her coffee cup. "And I'm only drinking this out of politeness."

"Or because you're smitten." Claire chuckled.

"Clearly," Margot leaned over the small formica table that separated them, "I have other ways of impressing you." With one hand she pulled the sleeve covering her right upper arm all the way over her shoulder while flexing her bicep.

"Clearly." It was all Claire could muster.

Margot leaned back in her chair and let her sleeve fall back over her arm, muscles relaxed. "If I were to ask you on a morning kickboxing date, would you make a counter offer?"

"Hell yes." It was Claire's turn to lean forward, staring into

FRENCH KISSING: SEASON ONE

Margot's eyes while doing so. "Dinner at my place this Friday. I can't cook but I'll figure something out."

Margot broke out in the cutest giggle. "Gosh, you just made that sound very tempting."

Claire arched up her eyebrows expectantly. "I'll take that as a yes."

"How can I possibly resist?" The playful tone in Margot's voice awoke more than one butterfly in Claire's stomach.

Claire sucked her bottom lip between her teeth and sat staring at the doctor silently for a few seconds. There was something so pure and direct about Margot, so simple and irresistible. She could kick herself for missing it the first time they had met.

"What?" Margot asked.

"Did you really think I was out of your league?" Claire couldn't wait until Friday, when she was planning to make a move. On home turf, in the privacy of her flat.

"You're so glamourous. I guess your lipstick was so sparkly it blurred my vision."

"You're a kickboxing surgeon who rides a motorcycle. If anyone should have been intimidated, it should have been me."

"Who said anything about being intimidated?" Margot narrowed her eyes and twirled a finger around a loose strand of her glossy black hair.

The excitement rushing through Claire's blood was a sensation she hadn't felt for a long time. *This could really be something.*

A device clipped to the waistband of Margot's trousers started beeping, signalling the end of their impromptu non-date.

Margot scrunched her lips together in a pout, one eyebrow raised. "Got to go."

They rose from their chairs simultaneously and before Margot had a chance to take a step, Claire grabbed her by the wrist and pulled her near.

"We should do this again some time," she whispered in

Margot's ear. Standing so close to her made Claire's tummy go funny again.

"Soon." Margot stared up into Claire's eyes for a split second before leaning in for a soft, quick kiss on the lips.

A huge smile spread on Claire's face as she watched Margot dash off into the corridor.

JULIETTE

"Is this about that threesome you hinted at a few weeks ago?" Claire asked.

Steph nearly spit out the beer she had just sipped. "What?"

The three of them sat at one of the high-top tables outside of Le Comptoir for a drink after work. Steph and Claire opposite Juliette, both drinking beer—Steph's usual tipple but uncharacteristic for Claire.

"Nadia and I just want a night out with our friends, for old time's sake. That's all." Juliette looked at Steph. "You practically live there, so I figured we could count on you."

"Sure, but what was that about a threesome?" Steph's face was hidden behind her pint glass.

"Nothing. We don't want a threesome. We're fine and I told you that in confidence." Juliette shifted her gaze to Claire who sipped from her beer uncomfortably. "What the hell are you drinking that for, anyway?"

"Can't you tell?" Steph said. "She's in love."

"Margot is fond of a beer now and then, so I thought I'd give it a go," Claire said without qualms. Her crush on Margot seemed to have taken thirty years off her mental age, the way she was behaving.

"Will you come with us to Les Pêches or not?" Juliette couldn't help but feel a little bit jealous of the early stages of romance her best friend found herself in.

"It will have to be on Saturday night. I have a hot date on Friday."

"Ooh, planning on playing doctor and nurse, are you?" Steph cooed.

"If I have my way, oh yes." The love-sick smile on Claire's face was more than enough to rack Juliette with guilt about the current sorry state of her own relationship.

"I thought I'd find you here," a familiar voice beamed from behind Juliette.

Juliette noticed how Steph tensed in her seat, but ignored it, happily surprised to have Nadia joining them unexpectedly. She turned around and looked at her partner, who had that relaxed, nonchalant air about her Juliette loved so much. Nadia was a summer child, someone who blossomed in time with the leaves on the trees.

Nadia kissed her on the lips, a lingering, sweet kiss, and for an instant, it was as if they were transported back in time to a year ago. When meeting after work like this was a regular occurrence, the four of them sitting on a terrace and engaging in the most relaxing banter, before she and Juliette would go home and sag in the sofa together, content with the day and each other.

"I just convinced them to go out with us this weekend," Juliette said as Nadia sat down in the chair next to her.

"It took a whole lot of arm twisting," Steph said, her demeanour casual again.

"I'm still working on Margot," Nadia said. "Clubbing is not quite her thing." They both looked at Claire expectantly.

"No guarantees," Claire said. "Margot is not like us. She does things differently, which is why I like her so much. What a breath of fresh air."

"Oh, thanks," Steph said. "Sorry to be such predictable bores." Juliette noticed how she exchanged a glance with Nadia she didn't understand.

"Hey, Nadz…" Claire tried a sip of beer again before continuing to address Nadia. "Have you seen her? Has she, you know, said anything?" Juliette really had trouble recognising her best friend. She'd seen Claire in love, in lust, in pain, but hardly ever in a state of bewildered madness like this.

"Margot is not one to wear her heart on her sleeve, but she does seem a lot more mellow these days… must be because of that new kickboxing instructor they hired at her gym."

Juliette watched Claire's face fall for an instant before the joke registered. "You're evil, Nadia," Claire said. "God, I need something else to drink." She got up to place the order. "What will it be for Queen Mean," she asked Nadia.

"Dry white, please. This weather is just asking for it." Nadia patted Claire on the thigh amicably before she sauntered off inside.

The four of them like this, sitting around on a beautiful summer evening, felt like old times, but not quite.

Nadia would not be going home with Juliette tonight, and even if she did briefly, she wouldn't be staying.

STEPH

Steph was blessed with an excellent pokerface, but sitting across from Juliette and Nadia like this, after what Nadia had confided in her, was not easy. Then there was the small matter of the dozens of messages from Dominique on her phone—a mobile provided by Barbier & Cyr. The messages were neutral enough to appear innocent to someone not in the know, but Steph knew very well what they meant. Truth be told, she'd been rather perplexed at Dominique's tenacity to get her into bed again.

The fact that, out of all the women she'd bedded in the last years and had walked away from so easily—not always without tears from the other party—she couldn't stop thinking about this one, was an irony that didn't escape her.

But she knew Nadia was right on this matter, despite apparently not always making the best choices herself. Steph, hardly the image of virtue and monogamy herself, had been truly shell-shocked after Nadia's confession. So perplexed that she'd found it, in that moment, easier than expected to brush off Dominique with a quick, business-like text after her proposal to stop by the Avenue Foch flat last night. Instead, she'd found herself nursing a solitary drink in a bar she'd never set foot in before, contemplating all the reasons why relationships were just not worth it in the end.

Steph knew Juliette through and through, not just because they were friends, but more so because they'd been working together for ten years. There's no better way to acquaint yourself thoroughly with someone's personality than spending eight hours a day beside them. Steph knew that, if Nadia told Juliette, it could well be the final straw.

"Earth to Stéphanie. Earth to Stéphanie," Claire said, her elbow jabbing into Steph's ribcage. "What's up with you?"

Steph avoided looking at Nadia directly and, instead, swivelled in her seat to face Claire. Frankly, a much better view than the crumbling relationship on the other side of her, despite the front they were putting up. The way the four of them sat there, cosily around that table, elbows perched so they almost touched, implied an intimacy that didn't tolerate secrets. *Fat chance.*

"Nothing." Steph painted a care-free smile on her face. "Just imagining what it will be like to take three old birds to my stomping ground."

"As if you'll notice us at all." Claire raised her glass for a toast. "But I'm looking forward to a night out with my besties."

"Gosh, you really do have it good," Juliette interjected, "if you're now breaking out into spontaneous sentimentality."

Lucky her. Steph wasn't one to fall in love easily, choosing to protect herself from heartache and all the other complications she believed to be inherent to relationships—as if it was a choice at all. Still, here she sat, jealous of her friend and boss, for quite simply being able to vocalise her feelings. To have it out in the open and be teased about it. Such a simple, profound joy.

They clinked rims as if it was just another ordinary summer

evening in the city of love, when Steph's phone buzzed again. She dug it out of her pocket and shielded the screen from view.

Do I really need to send you a picture of my cleavage?

Steph couldn't help but smile at Dominique's audacity. She probably wasn't used to the word 'No' that much either.

"One of your many admirers?" Juliette asked and reached out her hand playfully, as if wanting to snatch her phone to inspect the message.

"Don't," Nadia said, in a tone much harsher than the light atmosphere of the evening warranted.

"I'm just joking," Juliette said, undercurrents of hurt playing in her voice.

Steph's heart skipped a beat. Close calls like this were exactly the reason why this had to end. She ignored the message, a tinge of sadness creeping into her soul, and pocketed her phone.

"It was nothing." She downed her beer in a few long gulps. "Next round's on me." She got up and headed inside, away from the questioning looks her friends shot her, two of them ignorantly and playfully, the third one knowing everything. It was that look she could bear the least.

NADIA

Nadia stared at the résumé as if it was the first time she laid eyes on it, despite having studied it for the past ten minutes. The photocopied black-and-white picture at the top right of the page was of poor quality, but Inez Larue still managed to look gorgeous after being xeroxed a few times. *Shit.*

Her hands were tied, the board had made sure of that. So much for autonomy. She had to hire the pretty ER doctor, fresh from a stint with Médecins Sans Frontières in Rwanda and India. Not only would Inez be starting a job at the same hospital as her ex-girlfriend Margot, but they'd end up working together on a daily basis as well.

Inez would only be joining them in a few weeks and Nadia decided to hold off telling Margot for now, at least until after the weekend. A weekend that would see them all going out together. Not that Nadia didn't trust Steph to keep a secret, but, despite the brief relief telling another person had offered her, sharing her indiscretion with Steph had caused her more stress than she had expected. She'd sat across from Steph long enough the night before to notice that hint of disappointment in her eyes, the unease that came with knowing, the awkwardness of furtive, shared glances under the noses of the people they loved.

It was as if, by telling Steph, the burden of what she had done had multiplied. She'd been unable to go home with Juliette after the drinks at Le Comptoir. Both of them had been quite light-headed and unsteady on their feet, but Nadia had been afraid to face Juliette alone. Because, however meaningless the actual act of sleeping with someone else had been at the time, the repercussions told another story. The reason why she'd gone that far and the rage she'd fallen into after, had blurred most of the guilt for months. But not anymore.

Nadia stared at the e-mail from Juliette blinking on her screen, at the flight details for their trip to Barcelona. *Je t'aime*, it said at the bottom.

She picked up her mobile from her desk and dialled Steph's personal number.

"Allo," Steph's voice sounded as if she'd just come back from the dead.

"Are you all right?" Nadia wanted to cut straight to the chase, but she was worried about Steph. She had issues of her own to deal with.

"We drink too much."

I wonder why. "I know," Nadia agreed. "Can you talk?"

"Yes." Steph didn't sound very convinced, possibly because she could predict what was coming next.

"Should I tell her?"

Silence on the other end of the line.

"Steph?" Nadia knew it was unfair—so much seemed to be these days—but she had to talk to someone.

"Look, Nadz, it's not really my place to say."

"I know I'm asking a lot of you, but I need another perspective on this. You know Juliette, you know what she's like. I need your opinion on this."

Steph cleared her throat. "I think it will destroy her."

Tears burned behind Nadia's eyes. Her throat was too closed up to speak.

"All the blame of whatever happened to your relationship will automatically fall on you, no matter what reason you give." Silence again. Nadia waited. "But how can you possibly try to make things work again while keeping it from her?"

"I don't know." It was exactly the same conclusion Nadia had drawn herself many times. She'd had the distance between them to hide behind, and the fact that she'd started blaming Juliette for what had happened, souring their relationship even further. "Thanks, Steph."

"I didn't go see her," Steph said, her voice suddenly smaller. "She's not making it easy on me, though."

Juliette would explode if she only had an inkling of what was going on behind her back, at home and at work. "Good for you. I mean it."

They rang off and Nadia sat staring at her screen a while longer, none the wiser than before. Still, she knew it had to be done—she had known it all along.

———

Nadia slipped her key in the lock of the door to their flat, her stomach in knots and her resolve already crumbling to bits.

How do you tell someone the last thing they want to hear? How could she possibly make her partner understand the total emptiness of that night, and how utterly lonely it had made her feel in the end?

"Hey, babe," Juliette said, while greeting her with a peck on the cheek. "Here's your wine." She offered Nadia a glass of red, and it was as if they'd just stepped back a decade in time.

There was no way in hell Nadia could tell her tonight.

CLAIRE

Claire tried to remember the last time she'd invited a serious love interest to her place. She drew a blank. *How utterly pathetic.*

She sat across from Margot at her woefully underused dining table, trying to squeeze as much information out of her as possible. It wasn't often she wanted to find out everything she could about another woman.

"How long were you and Juliette together?" Margot beat her to it.

"Two years, we'd both just started at university. She was my first, I wasn't hers."

"Two years with your first girlfriend? Intense." Margot sipped her wine with more abandon than usual. She'd taken a taxi, which Claire had taken as an excellent sign of things to come.

"She broke my heart, you know, and look at us now."

"I guess time does heal all wounds." Margot pasted a silly smirk on her face.

"Said the doctor…" Claire shoved her plate to the side. "Additionally, most lesbians have the remarkable ability to transform heartbreak into friendship. I've never really under-stood that, despite having done it myself."

"It's fairly safe to say that's an ability I, myself, do not possess." Margot confirmed her statement with a jerky nod of the head. "When it's over, it's over. No looking back."

"No friendly exes in your life, then?" Claire gently prodded.

"When Inez and I finally broke up, I was so relieved that she was in Africa. I couldn't bear running into her. I haven't seen her. She must come back from time to time, I presume, but I really couldn't care less. Not anymore."

"Tell me about her. What was she like?"

"Really? You want to hear about my ex?" Margot arched up her eyebrows before taking another sip of wine. "Is that really why you invited me to your fancy bachelorette pad tonight?"

God no. "I just want to get to know you better." Claire felt put on the spot, an unfamiliar flush rising to her cheeks.

"Then ask me a better question." Margot narrowed her eyes, creasing the skin around her temples.

"Have you been with anyone else since Inez?" *If they were being direct…*

"No. I have zero interest in being intimate with someone I don't care about emotionally. It's so hollow, so meaningless. A waste of my time, to be honest."

"So you haven't… in the last year?"

"Had sex?" Margot shook her head. "No." She locked her black eyes on Claire's. "You must go without for long stretches, or do you have fuck buddies?"

It sounded so ridiculous when Margot said it like that. "Well, no, not exactly, I just…"

"Am I making you blush?" Margot leaned over the table, studying Claire's face. "How cute." This only made Claire's cheeks burn brighter. "Do go on…" She shot Claire a sexy half-smile.

Claire wondered how she'd lost grip of the conversation so easily, and what this woman was doing to her. She had nothing to be ashamed of. She was a single woman with healthy urges. There was nothing wrong with that. "I get by," she murmured.

"I know most people don't think the way I do. I'm not judging you. I'm sorry if I made it seem that way." The kindness was back in Margot's features.

"When I met you, I had a 'friend with benefits'," Claire curled her fingers into air quotes, "but I ended it."

"Oh, really. Why's that?" It was Margot's turn to sport a little blush. *Not such an ice queen after all.*

"Why do you think?"

"You really have to stop answering my questions with another question."

"Who's going to make me?" Claire grinned, enjoying the innuendo.

"Have you seen these biceps?" Margot wore a no-frills sleeveless blouse and Claire had, quite possibly, been staring at her toned upper arms for the better part of the evening. She flexed them only a little, but more than enough for the sight of them to make the heat return to Claire's cheeks.

"Be my guest." Claire, quite used to taking the initiative, was happy to toss the ball into Margot's court, what with the clear statement she'd made earlier.

Margot just smiled, took another sip of her wine, and addressed Claire with an unexpected serious expression on her face. "I want it too." She scratched her bicep nervously, only drawing more attention to it. "I do, but it's too soon for me."

Oddly, it was more than enough for Claire. She was in no rush. She stretched out her arm and reached for Margot's hand across the table. "There's nothing like a good dose of abstinence to build up the tension," she joked. "And some French kissing."

"Come here." Margot pulled at her arm and slanted her torso over the table. Claire followed suit and met Margot half-way, her lips already parting for a delicious kiss.

JULIETTE

Juliette hadn't been to Les Pêches in ages, but tonight she wanted to dance, and, even more so, she wanted to watch Nadia dance. She wanted to leer at her as she swayed her hips to the beat, put her arms around her shoulders, and claim her as hers in front of all the baby dykes surrounding them—not that they looked as if they cared one iota about the old-timers that had just walked in. Most of them did have eyes for Steph though, a few of them even turning their heads for Margot who, against all odds, had decided to join. *She must really be fond of Claire.*

The five of them stood by the bar, downing shots like people half their age. The more Juliette drank, the more bearable the incessant thud of the beat became. She turned to Claire and found her ear.

"How was your hot date last night?" she shouted over the music.

"Wonderful but frustrating," Claire yelled back into her ear. "The more I see her, the more I want to rip those leathers off of her, but we're still taking it slow."

Juliette's mind wandered to last night and how Nadia had barely taken the time to greet her, her mouth immediately too busy elsewhere. *And she was the one who had insisted they'd talk more.*

"I can see it now, you know. We should have given her a fair chance from the start." Juliette eyed Margot, who stood with her back against the bar, one knee drawn up. She had one of the most impressive shoulder lines Juliette had laid eyes on. "And she's smoking hot."

Claire nodded. "And the best part is that she doesn't even know it."

"Come on," Nadia interrupted their conversation. "We came here to dance, didn't we?" She tugged at Juliette's arms, dragging her towards the dance floor. Juliette hadn't downed enough tequila to overcome most of her self-consciousness, but followed Nadia nevertheless, making eyes at Claire in the process, urging her to come along. She was fairly certain Margot wasn't the dancing type. Then again, she'd misjudged her before.

Juliette wasn't much for matching beats with her body

either, but ten years ago, when she and Nadia still came here at least once every weekend, it was her favourite moment of the week. The music was different back then—less aggressive—and people weren't dressed as if they'd be ready for a catwalk moment any minute, but either way, none of these memories compared to the first time she'd witnessed Nadia find her groove. It was as if the music moved through her, lived in her muscles and pulsed in her blood.

Juliette was always too preoccupied with enjoying Nadia's moves to care much about her own clumsy attempts at bopping to the music. On the dance floor, she would always be in Nadia's shadow—exactly where she wanted to be.

Just like so many pleasures of their early days, dancing had taken a back seat. Life got in the way. They became too old for clubbing, chose wine-laden dinners over dance floors with beats that throbbed in their ears for hours after leaving. Coming here tonight, was like stepping back in time.

Nadia was already at it, twisting her hips this way and that, turning heads in the younger crowd, because nothing on this world was sexier than a woman in her forties finding a missing piece of herself again. Juliette could tell by the look on Nadia's face, the way her features relaxed and her lips naturally curved up into a smile, her eyes half-closed. In that moment, they were both happy.

When Nadia beckoned Juliette to come closer, to dance right next to her, hips glued together, a shudder of lust ran up her spine. She realised that with the frantic love-making they'd embarked on of late, foreplay had become a thing of the past. Until now. This was foreplay of the sexiest, most enticing kind.

Juliette wouldn't last long.

She ground her hips against Nadia's backside, not the way teenagers did on TV these days, but slow and sensual and with all the right emotions lurking behind the action. With one hand she grabbed Nadia by the shoulder, while the other scooped the hair away from her neck and ear. Juliette leaned forward, hips still rolling, and whispered, "Come outside with me."

Nadia turned around, bliss portrayed in every line of her face, her eyes sparkling in the disco lights. "One more song."

It was a tune Juliette had never heard before, with staccato female vocals, maybe a bit too high-pitched, but it didn't matter because Nadia was grooving again. The mesmerising appeal of it didn't lie so much in her movements or the way she tilted her head back, but in the complete effortlessness and supreme confidence she displayed.

Gulps of hot, wet anticipation already unleashed between Juliette's thighs, but she waited patiently, ogling Nadia, not having eyes for anyone else. It was just the two of them. The way it should be.

"Come on," Nadia whispered, the sultriness of her movements leaking into her voice. "Let's get some air."

NADIA

Nadia knew nothing turned Juliette on more than watching her dance. She'd be like putty in her hands the instant they found that secluded spot in the alley, with a glimpse of the Seine, just behind the club. She was tipsy enough to forget what she had done for now, the thoughts in her head blurred into almost not being there anymore. It was easy to ignore that nagging little voice coming at her from the back of her mind when she was on the dance floor, a thrill she'd, seemingly, so easily forgotten about.

It was early and the alley was deserted, something that would surely change over the course of the night as more women succumbed to the call of too much alcohol, pheromones and dance floor seductions.

Nadia stopped and turned to face Juliette, their fingers still intertwined. About to take the initiative, as usual, she was surprised when instead, Juliette pushed her against the coarse brick wall—possibly the first time in her life Nadia had felt the roughness of this particular, well-used wall against her barely protected skin.

The alley was scarcely lit, mostly shadows with a bit of fractured light coming from a street lamp on the corner, but Juliette's eyes burned so brightly it simultaneously ignited a fire in the pit of Nadia's stomach and racked her with icy, inescapable guilt. Nadia had no choice but to let the moment seize her, to fall into Juliette's arms—no commands, no control—and let her be who she wanted to be then. The woman on top, the one in charge, the person telling her when to come, and how.

The night turned to liquid around her as Juliette hoisted up her dress—a flowy, deep red one that was as flimsy as the breeze catching it. Juliette's lips were on her neck, moist, sucking hard, and then on her collar bone, kissing their way down. *Surely she wouldn't expose her breasts?* No? Yes. She scooped them out of the low-cut top of the dress, baring them to the night, her lips already wrapping themselves around a hard nipple. The early summer air swept over her skin, leaving it in goosebumps. Juliette's other hand made its way under her dress, fumbling with the panel of her panties, pushing it aside.

There were no words, only sounds. Chatter from the street. Cars humming in the distance. Their breath caught in their throats as Juliette entered with one finger, brusque in its swiftness but tender in intent. Nadia opened her eyes to the sky—no stars, only diffused summer darkness—and felt Juliette inside of her. This was different, almost new. In this alley, on this night, after a dance of seduction as well as rekindling. It was love and lust and sadness and memories all colliding and melting into a burst of energy in her blood.

It wasn't how Juliette added more fingers, increased the pace, and sucked the nipple between her teeth harder, that made Nadia's knees buckle. In the moment of surrender, when she gave herself up to Juliette for that brief instant of nothingness and everything at the same time, Nadia knew they would make it. She knew because they had love, they had this, would always have it.

Her muscles trembled as she stood panting against the wall. "Jesus christ, who are you and what have you done to my partner?"

Juliette's eyes were glazed over, as if she didn't know what had just happened, what had come over her. It took a while before she could speak. "We should go dancing more often." She regarded her fingers—the ones she'd used on Nadia.

"If you call this dancing." Nadia grabbed Juliette's hand and wrapped her lips around her fingers, sucking off her own juices, her eyes locked on Juliette's.

Juliette curled the fingers of her other hand around Nadia's wrist and gripped tight. "Come home with me tonight."

Nadia let Juliette's fingers slip from her mouth and, with the scent of herself on her lips, said, "Okay."

Juliette's eyes grew and the joy reflected in them ignited that twang of guilt inside of Nadia again. She took Nadia's hand and coaxed her out of the alley. "Then I'll wait my turn."

STEPH

Nadia and Juliette were fucking away their differences some-where outside and Claire and Margot only had eyes for each other. *So much for a night out amongst friends.* Not that Steph minded that much. She came to Les Pêches on her own almost every weekend. It was the place where she felt most at home—its damp, sweaty air like pure oxygen in her lungs.

She knew all the bouncers by name, and Melanie behind the bar, who slipped her lemon drops until her eyes burned and she could barely walk straight.

An extremely attractive couple had been ogling her for the past fifteen minutes, making no secret of their intent. Steph had seen them around before, but had always ignored their advances. She believed that, by definition, amongst lesbians, threesomes were *always* messy and she didn't want to get caught in the middle—both literally and figuratively. But tonight, her head overflowing with tales of Nadia's betrayal and Dominique's seductive messages, she decided not to care. Maybe in the middle was exactly where she should be.

The woman doing all the heavy lifting—the eye contact at regular intervals, the strategically placed hand on her girl-friend's bare shoulder—was tall and blonde and tom-boyish and definitely something Steph could go for. Her partner had dark, curly hair falling to her shoulders in waves, her lips painted a peculiar, almost purple colour. Both dressed in the lesbian clubbing uniform of jeans and tank top, they displayed enough arm porn between them to take Steph's mind off Dominique Laroche. At least it was worth a try.

She made her way through a throng of high femmes by the bar and headed for the ladies room, passing through the couple's personal space just enough to let them know she was considering their offer. Her mind only half on it—the image of the delicious glint in Dominique's eyes just before she was about to go down on her still too lodged in her memory—she wasn't going home with anyone tonight before some serious vetting.

When Steph exited the stall, after a short but enraging debate with herself whether to check the messages on her phone or not, and ultimately deciding not to, the couple awaited her just outside the hallway leading to the washrooms.

"Hey," Blondie said. She was so tall, she almost towered over Steph. "I got us some lemon drops." Obviously, she'd done this before. Offering Steph the shot glass, she let her finger linger on her knuckles a fraction longer than necessary. She sported a sideways cut fringe that covered half her face, but when she tilted her head back to drink, her green eyes and high cheekbones exposed, another flashback dashed its way through Steph's mind. Dominique's bare throat as she drank, the confi-dence in her eyes when they landed back on Steph.

Steph knocked back the shot and was eager for another. The woman appeared to possess the power of prediction because as soon as Steph set down the glass, she handed her another. Or maybe she needed some liquid courage herself.

The liquor boosted Steph's self-confidence. She looked at the two women and, usually, in a situation like this, when she was drinking with someone she was interested in going home with, the booze would blur her mind in a way that she could see it already. A film projecting the outcome of the night would play in her mind's eye, uncensored. She'd see herself taking off the other person's clothes, visualised the bounce of their breasts as they were freed from undergarments. Only this time, she didn't see it.

All she could see, as the alcohol did its work and clouded her blood and her judgement, was Dominique, sat in her sofa, prying a glass of wine from Steph's hands. Steph had been seduced many times, but this was different. She had no clue why. Maybe it was the chemistry women's magazines she didn't read, kept mentioning. That elusive spark that she'd encountered many times but had never managed to trap for much longer than a few dates, the fire already dimming by the second meeting.

She let her eyes wander around the club, her gaze landing on Claire and Margot whispering in each other's ear, the very picture of two people falling in love. It warmed and broke her heart at the same time. She was happy for them, but, simultaneously, a sense of hurt, of being denied something very basic and necessary, clung to her. If this was what falling in love really felt like, she'd ignore it happily. But how could she fool herself when, apparently, the simplest of pecks of Claire's lips on Margot's cheek could make the doctor burst out into such a wide smile?

"Thanks for the drink," Steph said. "I'm very sorry, but I'm afraid I have to go."

L'Avenue Foch was miles away from Les Pêches, but Steph

needed the walk. Maybe she'd sober up before she got there, but she doubted it.

CLAIRE

"I think everyone has ditched us," Margot said, scanning the dance floor.

"Do you want to get out of here?" Somehow, the fact that they were surrounded by dozens of other women, but hunched so close together, made Claire feel even friskier than she had been the previous night, when she'd kissed Margot goodbye in her doorframe, staring at the elevator for a long time after its doors had slid shut behind her.

"Sure," Margot whispered in her ear, her lips lingering just below. Claire could feel her heartbeat pulse between her legs. "Let's go somewhere more quiet." Claire fervently hoped Margot meant her place, which wasn't that far from the club.

If Nadia and Juliette had hoped for some nostalgic night out, the five of them going crazy on the dance floor, they'd ruined any chance of that when they left barely an hour after they'd arrived.

"Where's Steph?" Nadia's voice suddenly sounded from behind them.

Claire turned to face Nadia, whose dress looked dishevelled enough to give away what they'd been up to—not that Claire didn't already know. Between them and Steph disappearing, she felt like a granny amongst a bunch of teenagers.

"Who knows?" She shrugged. Juliette had the biggest grin on her face. *If everyone was getting some, then so was she.* "We're heading out."

Juliette nodded, indicating she understood. Nadia was already making eyes at the dance floor again, ready for round two. They kissed each other goodbye and Claire and Margot exited the club.

"Where to?" Claire asked as they stood on the kerb, a mild breeze whipping up Margot's hair.

"Shall we walk to mine?" Margot curled her arm into Claire's. "It's such a gorgeous night."

Yes please. "Sure," Claire said, trying to sound casual, but mentally high-fiving herself. Come to think of it, her behaviour was starting to resemble a hormonal teenager's as well. "I'm betting Nadia won't make it home tonight."

"We'll see," Margot, still the voice of reason, said. "No matter where she sleeps tonight, she'll be at the club for the next few hours."

Claire wasn't sure what to make of that, if it meant Margot was starting to 'feel ready' or if it was her way of saying Claire shouldn't expect an invitation to stay the night.

But the night air was mild, the Boulevard Saint-Germain quiet, and, if she squinted and used a bit of imagination, she could spot some stars in the sky. Claire straightened the arm Margot had hooked hers through and found her hand. It felt good against hers, cool and steady, its fingers strong. All the blood in Claire's veins seemed to rush to one place again. She needed to focus on something else if she wasn't to slam Margot against the nearest wall and thrust herself upon those fingers.

"Where do you get those leathers?" It was the first subject that sprang to Claire's tipsy, one-track mind.

Margot chuckled, her giggles echoing faintly in the darkness. "Why? Would you like a pair?"

Until she'd met Margot, Claire had never really been a leather kind of girl. "No, I don't know, you wear them so well, I was just wondering if you have them tailor-made?" Any trace of keeping her cool slid away from her like an oily fish would from her hands.

Margot squeezed Claire's fingers before replying, indicating —she hoped—that she understood she was babbling, and the reason why. "I get them from a shop in Bastille. I'll take you some time. I bet you'd look hot in a pair of leather trousers."

She squeezed Claire's hand again, not helping with that rush of blood.

They approached the side street on which Margot's building was located. Despite not having been there yet herself, Claire had gotten the details from Juliette—including the whereabouts of its exclusive location.

"This is me." Margot stopped abruptly.

"Am I just walking you home or are you inviting me up for a nightcap?" For a split second, Claire was afraid of Margot's reply.

"Not that you haven't had enough, but I can't leave you in the street like that." She punched in the code and opened the door. Claire followed, anticipation building by the second.

Once upstairs, Claire, despite being mildly drunk, was thoroughly impressed by Margot's flat. Possibly because of the state she'd been in when she first visited, Juliette hadn't relayed any information about the size of the place, and its, frankly quite unexpected, plush and cosy interior.

Claire whistled through her teeth. "Do you rent or own?" This was Paris and real estate conversations were never out of order.

"I own, but I'm not as well-off as that makes me sound." Margot kicked off her shoes and put them in what looked like their designated spot by the door. "My parents got it for me and my sister. I bought her half when she got married. She's more the suburban type."

"How generous of them." *Meeting the parents would surely be interesting.* Without thinking, Claire heeled off her shoes as well and left them by the door.

"Mm," was all Margot said, and then, there they stood. Alone in Margot's flat. Claire wondered if Margot suffered from the same flush of heat building beneath her skin.

"Would you like some water?" She flicked a switch and a bank of soft lamps hidden behind a beam in the ceiling lit up, bathing them in dim, yellow light.

"No, not really." Claire reached for Margot's wrist and pulled her close. They stared into each other eyes for an instant, wordless, before the first kiss.

The fire stealing through Claire's flesh this time was much fiercer, much more insistent, than any other time she'd kissed Margot. It shot from her belly to her groin, to every little tip of her fingers. She let her hands roam across Margot's biceps.

There was no chasteness about this kiss, no room for doubt about where it was headed, their lips crashing together with a hunger that had been building for days. Until Margot pulled back.

"What?" The word exited Claire's mouth without thinking, her guard down completely.

"I need you to be sober for this."

"Are you joking?" Claire pulled Margot closer.

Margot shook her head. "It's our first time. I want us to be fully present."

"Look, I know we had a few, but we're hardly off our heads—"

"You'll thank me later." Margot pressed her lips to Claire's cheekbone.

Yeah right. "Do you want me to go?" Claire's heart sank.

"No, silly." Margot looked her in the eyes. "You can sleep it off in my bed, but keep your hands to yourself."

Fat chance. Claire bit down hard on her bottom lip to keep herself from uttering the words in her head. "Lead the way to your boudoir." Claire could only hope that Juliette and Nadia were about to truly patch things up, as she didn't want Nadia arriving at Margot's place at any time of the day tomorrow. Waiting was good, but her patience was about to run out—especially if she was supposed to sleep next to the hot doctor.

She was beginning to suspect Margot was more a fan of mind games than prudent abstinence.

STEPH

Steph fumbled with her phone, trying to find the door code Dominique had sent her when she'd first summoned her to the Avenue Foch. She was tired and thirsty—having seriously underestimated the distance from Les Pêches in her drunken state of mind. It was late and the effect of the shots was starting to wear off. *What was she doing?*

She stared at the message with the four-lettered code for an instant before turning to the keypad next to the massive, blue door.

"Looking for someone?" Seemingly out of nowhere, Dominique appeared on the sidewalk beside her. Only then did Steph spot a taxi driving off.

"You're out late."

Dominique looked stunning in a knee-length navy summer dress, a pensive smile painted on her lips. "I didn't know I had a curfew." Dominique stepped closer, keyed in the code quickly and held the door open for Steph. "Come in." Her heels came down hard on the tiles in the quiet hallway.

They rode the elevator in silence, Steph's heart beating frantically beneath her flimsy, clubbing t-shirt. She caught a whiff of Dominique's scent, the same perfume as always, weakened by the hours since it was applied, and faint notes of whiskey on her breath.

Dominique shut the door of her flat behind them, dumped her keys on the cabinet by the door and stepped out of her high heels. "I take it you're not here for a meaningful, late-night conversation."

"I'm tipsy and I may regret this in the morning, but fuck, I want you." Her voice sounded hoarse and low, like when she was going in for the kill after picking someone up.

"Let me make sure you don't regret it then." Dominique curled her arms behind her back and Steph could hear the distinct sound of a zipper being lowered. She couldn't imagine a sexier noise. A blink of her eyes, and Dominique stood before her in a set of matching blue bra and knickers. *Right-wing party colours all the way.*

Steph swallowed the dryness out of her throat. She'd tried to push any sexual thoughts of Dominique out of her head since her conversation with Nadia, but they'd crept up on her when she least expected it. On the Métro, in the shower—as soon as she woke up in the morning.

This wasn't a matter of thoughts anymore. Dominique approached wearing only lingerie and everything inside of Steph went mellow, any remaining sliver of resistance melting with the rest of her. If she didn't know any better—if she allowed herself silly thoughts like that—she'd believe she was falling in love.

"What's the matter, Stéphanie?" Steph felt Dominique's hot breath on the skin of her cheeks. "I do hope the cat didn't get your tongue."

Steph's only reply was to pull Dominique near and flash the tip of her tongue between her lips. The heat coming off Dominique's half-naked body radiated through Steph's t-shirt, and, only breaking their lip lock for a split second, she pulled it over her head, needing to feel Dominique's warm skin on hers.

"I missed you," Dominique whispered in Steph's ear, and it was so much more powerful than any clever quip or even the dirtiest word.

Despite knowing full well this had no future, no chance of being more than a string of fleeting moments like this, Steph felt the warmth of Dominique's words close around her heart. She could brace herself for heartache, or she could pull Dominique's knickers down and feel the wetness gathered there for her. It wasn't really a choice at all.

Dominique pulled at the buttons of Steph's jeans and let her hand slide in while Steph's fingers found their way into Dominique's panties. The touch of a finger on her clit made Steph's muscles twitch momentarily, but the moist heat between

Dominique's legs roused her to action. She had no trouble slipping in deep—just like that, as if the entire week had only led up to this moment—and coaxing a low moan from Dominique's throat.

Dominique steadied herself against the door with her other hand, her eyes firmly locked on Steph's. As if she could read her mind, Dominique slid two fingers between Steph's throbbing pussy lips, her wrist curving into Steph's open jeans.

They found a rhythm, going deep while the other pulled back, to and fro, the pace growing faster, their breaths becoming more ragged. Hands frantic, eyes glazing over, Steph felt it crash in to her. She didn't close her eyes when the walls of her pussy contracted around Dominique's fingers. Instead, she lost herself in Dominique's green gaze while her body surrendered.

Steph had the presence of mind to finish her task, thrusting deep until Dominique's eyes narrowed—as if wanting to mirror the spasms of her pussy—and her body thundered down on top of hers.

"Now that we've gotten that out of the way," Dominique whispered after catching her breath, "can I offer you a drink?"

JULIETTE

Juliette waited until the light coming through the drapes was strong enough to wake Nadia up naturally. She'd been awake for a while, revelling in the fact that Nadia was back in their bed. They'd danced for hours—Nadia moving, Juliette watching at first, until she'd drunk enough to get her limbs limbered up. Too tired for anything else, they'd fallen into bed, a deep, dreamless sleep seizing Juliette instantly.

She could make out the vague symptoms of a hangover, but it wasn't enough to spoil the gloriousness of the moment. Nadia was back. It was Sunday. They'd had such fun the night before. Actually, Juliette briefly wondered if it was, in fact, real and she wasn't dreaming.

Nadia opened her eyes, a smile immediately lighting up her crumpled face. She pushed a strand of hair from her forehead and the simple gesture almost roused a tear from Juliette's eyes —as if it had been lodged there for days, waiting for a reason to break free.

"Morning," Juliette whispered, her voice half-gone.

"Hey stranger." Nadia's skin stood out against the white sheets and Juliette had missed the sight of it so much, the tear now made its way down her cheek.

"What's the matter?" Worry suppressed the smile on Nadia's face. She brought her thumb to Juliette's cheekbone and brushed away the tear.

"Absolutely nothing." Juliette trapped Nadia's hand against her skin, letting the sleepy warmth of it penetrate her flesh. "Just so happy you're here." Juliette pressed her lips against the heel of Nadia's hand, her eyes fixed on Nadia's. She kissed her hand again, and again, remembering their romp outside the club last night. She pecked her way up Nadia's arm, her bare shoulder, the gooseflesh on her neck and, finally, her lips.

They could have a quickie outside against a concrete wall, in the sofa, or in Margot's guest room, but nothing could compete with the intimate history of their own bed.

Nadia's skin was still warm with sleep, and soft—always so soft—and inviting. Juliette pushed herself up so half her body landed on top of Nadia's, running her toes over her smooth shins and her knee along Nadia's thigh.

Nadia cradled Juliette in her arms, reciprocating the kiss, but her body remained rigid, not yielding just yet.

Nadia broke the lip lock and found Juliette's ear. "You know I'm not a morning person, babe."

And sure, Juliette knew, but she hardly thought it mattered in these circumstances, and believed Nadia would make an effort after last night. *Clearly not.*

Juliette planted her palms next to Nadia's head, stretching her arms and looking down at her. "We have all day." It wasn't just that Nadia wasn't one for a morning rumble, though, Juliette could see that in the unexpected—and rather hurtful—dullness in her eyes and in the way the corners of her mouth stretched almost dutifully into a smile, as opposed to the real one she'd woken up with.

"Are you coming this afternoon? It's okay if you don't feel up to it."

Juliette searched her brain. "Where to?" The dim throb in her temples seemed to launch itself into a full-blown headache, possibly enhanced by the sting of rejection.

"My dad's birthday."

"I thought that was next week?" And just like that, the moment had passed. Juliette let herself fall back onto the mattress, staring at the ceiling of which she knew every little hairline crack.

"It is, but they're going on this last minute trip to Tunis, so we're celebrating early." Nadia made no effort to find Juliette's gaze, or to apologise further. "You don't have to come. I'll tell them you have a work thing."

An afternoon with the Abadi family was the last thing Juliette felt like, but she was Nadia's partner and it was her duty. "Do you want me to come?" Juliette rolled onto her side, facing Nadia, already running a finger over her belly again, unable to not touch her. *Didn't she feel this?*

"Of course." Nadia shuffled her body so she lay on her side as well. "You know they adore you."

It wasn't Nadia's parents' adoration Juliette was after. "Sure."

"Thanks, babe," Nadia said. "Last night was fun." She pushed herself forward to plant a kiss on Juliette's forehead. "Maybe we should try to get a bit more sleep before setting off to Saint-Denis."

"I think I'll get up, but you should get back to sleep." *If that's what you want.* Juliette turned away from Nadia and slipped out of their bed, in search of a double dose of pain killers and a tall glass of water.

CLAIRE

Claire had slept in fits, unable to relax with Margot lying next to her in a shoulder-line enhancing tank top and a pair of flimsy boy shorts. Subconsciously, she kept listening for the door to fall in the lock, waiting to see if Nadia would make it home—because with her and Juliette these days, you just never knew.

She'd dozed off as the morning light was starting to throw shadows through the windows, her hands buried underneath the pillow and her body so exhausted with the sheer force of unanswered desire, it just gave up.

Through half-lidded eyes, she noticed Margot shift. It was warm in the bedroom, and Margot had shaken off the duvet. Her tank top had ridden up her stomach, displaying the impressive abs Claire had always suspected were hiding underneath her layers of clothing. If she'd still been sleep-drunk an instant before, Claire was now wide awake. She felt a deep throb spread from beneath the moist panel of her panties to every extremity of her body.

If Margot wasn't on the same page as her now, surely she'd have to flee and tend to herself, such was the level of her arousal. Claire was sober. They'd bided their time. Their affection for each other could hardly still be questioned. Claire fully respected that Margot needed time. She understood. But surely, they'd waited long enough.

"I know exactly what you're thinking." Margot's voice surprised her, its gravelly morning rasp cutting through the silence. "I suggest that, if you need the washroom, you go now because you're about to be tied up here for a while."

"Good morning to you too," Claire said, countering Margot's matter-of-factness with a soft kiss on her bicep. Her words had caused the wetness between her legs to multiply, though.

"Hey." The smile that broke on Margot's face lit Claire's skin on fire. She understood the virtues of waiting even more now. "How are you feeling?"

"Ready." Claire shuffled closer, inhaling the sleepy, comforting scent of Margot's skin.

Margot held out her arm and Claire nestled in the crook of her shoulder. "I mean it, though."

"What? About me using the loo or you tying me up?"

"Both." There wasn't a trace of irony in Margot's voice.

Claire pushed herself up, away from Margot's body. "Are you serious?"

"Deadly." She detected only a hint of a smile on Margot's face.

"Don't you, erm, have to ask for my consent first or something?" A tingling sensation took root in Claire's stomach.

"What do you think I'm going to do to you while you're tied up?"

Claire was momentarily at a loss for words at such a display of determination and confidence this early on a Sunday morning. Maybe Margot had been holding off until *Claire* was ready. "Can't wait to find out now," she said, injecting as much bravado into her voice as she could muster.

"Good." Margot sat up and, in one swift movement, toppled Claire onto her back. "Don't worry, I'll go slow," she said as she straddled Claire, her nipples poking hard through the fabric of her tank top. The grin on her lips faded as her face approached Claire's for a kiss, soft at first, exploratory and gentle, until Claire, still with full control of her hands, pulled Margot close and let her tongue roam free in her mouth.

Claire was afraid that, even if Margot only inadvertently brushed against her knickers with her knee, she'd come on the spot. But Margot's knees were firmly planted on either side of Claire's thighs, pushing her legs close together, while the intensity of their kiss grew and Claire could clearly feel moisture trickle through the back of her panties, down the sensitive flesh there.

Claire's hands travelled down from Margot's hair, down her strong back, searching for the swell of her biceps. She figured she'd cop a good feel now that she still could. The tingle in her belly increased when Margot rose from the bent-over position she'd been in and locked her dark, mysterious gaze on Claire's.

Without saying a word, she hoisted her tank top over her head, exposing her breasts and nipples as hard as pebbles. Claire only seemed to have eyes for her abs, which stood out spectacularly in the position she was sitting in.

Instead of discarding the tank top, she briefly deposited it on Claire's torso while taking her wrists in her hands. She tied the tank top around Claire's wrists and brought her arms over her head, hooking the fabric over something Claire hadn't noticed before—because she'd had no reason to—on the bed frame behind her.

A devilish grin took hold of Margot's face. *Told you*, it seemed to say.

Claire was stuck under Margot's muscled, strong body, her arms tied above her head. Not exactly how she had expected things to turn out. She'd slept in a t-shirt Margot had lent her, which Margot was now slowly pulling upwards, until her chest was bare, the fabric of the t-shirt bunched up under her chin.

Claire guessed the slight slant of Margot's head was as close to a nod of approval as she was going to get. She wanted to ask —and in normal circumstances would have—if she liked what she saw, but her throat was so dry with anticipation, any questions remained mute and confined to her mind.

Claire felt her nipples reach skyward violently, eager for some relief. The darkness in Margot's eyes shimmered with mischief as she leaned over and took one in her mouth. It couldn't have had more effect on Claire if Margot had wrapped her lips directly around Claire's clit.

"Ooh," she moaned, two weeks of pent-up arousal escaping from her lips. Her breasts jutted out, pressed together by the upward curve of her arms, seemingly begging for Margot to lavish all her attention on them.

Margot kissed a moist path down Claire's breasts, biting at the skin stretched over her belly, and, at last, dipping her tongue underneath the waistband of Claire's drenched panties. Her long black hair floated across Claire's nipples, leaving them just as erect as when Margot's lips had been locked around them.

Margot shuffled down, over Claire's legs, freeing them. "Let's get this off you," she said more to herself than to Claire, already hooking her fingers under her panties, taking them down.

Arms tied, t-shirt rolled up over her breasts, knickers off and at the mercy of Margot, unable to roll Margot's nipples between her fingers or even reach for them with her lips, Claire spread her legs. Whatever Margot had in store next, climax was imminent.

Margot took position between Claire's legs, staying immobile for an instant, locking her eyes on Claire's.

"Oh god, please." Claire couldn't take it any longer. "Please just—" The words died in her throat as Margot averted her gaze and peeked down between her legs, her glance as smouldering as any touch could have been. Being on display had never aroused Claire as much as now.

"Looks like I'll need to teach you some patience." The zen in Margot's voice was long gone, her excitement shining through.

She planted her palms next to Claire's thighs, their skin barely brushing together, and kissed Claire's belly. Slowly, she pecked down, but nowhere near enough to where Claire needed it most.

In response, Claire bucked up her pelvis, trying to meet Margot's lips, which had now reached the wetness of her inner thighs, subjecting them to the same slow torture.

When Margot flicked the tip of her tongue once over Claire's clit, a ball of fire burst in her stomach, but Margot didn't indulge her just yet. Instead, she circled her tongue in wide ellipses around Claire's nub of pleasure.

Margot slid her tongue over Claire's engorged nether lips, briefly brushing her clit on the way up. More fireworks exploded in Claire's veins. Then, nothing but faint puffs of hot breath. Claire looked down, straight into Margot's narrowed eyes. They stared at each other for another moment, Claire's flesh simmering under Margot's breath.

At last, she sucked Claire's clit between her lips, once, twice, before touching her tongue to it in rapid-fire flicks. A sigh of relief exited Claire's lungs, expelling all the lust that had built up, all the tension coiled inside of her. She curled her fingers around the fabric of the tank top as best as she could as the first wave crashed through, so much more forceful than she could have imagined.

She heard someone shriek loudly, but was too far gone to realise it was her own voice losing control. When Margot sucked her clit into her mouth again while simultaneously slipping a finger inside her pussy, Claire believed she would pass out with pleasure. The second wave left her slightly more aware of what was happening, bursts of relief engulfing her, prickling on her skin.

"Jesus," she yelled, when Margot thrust mercilessly inside of her, not letting go of her clit. She had nowhere to go but under, her hands in place and her legs—and heart—wide open.

Her muscles shook when she came down and Margot quickly untied her, massaging her wrists and pouring her body over hers. Unable to speak, she lunged for Margot's head and pulled her in for a long kiss. Now that her hands were free, she let them roam over Margot's body, pushing her up so she could run them over her breasts.

"Straddle me," Claire said.

A soft willingness glimmered in Margot's eyes as she threw

her thigh over Claire's belly. Before inching close enough for contact, she looked down.

"Please, don't break my heart," she said, before Claire's tongue connected with her pussy.

STEPH

Steph woke to the loud jangling of a ringtone that wasn't hers.

"Fuck," Dominique said, rubbing the sleep from her eyes in the bed beside her. She scrambled for her phone. "Oui," she said, her voice still deep with sleep. "What?" She shot up, the sheets falling off her naked torso. "Now?" She looked over at Steph in a panic. "Okay." She rang off and threw the phone onto the bed. "My kids are here."

"What?" Steph, only half-awake, didn't understand, although the message was loud and clear.

"I'm taking them to Disneyland today." Dominique got up and started looking around the room. "They can't see you. You'll have to hide in the en-suite."

"What?" Steph felt like a toy monkey that could only say one word.

"I'm sorry. They're at the door. I overslept. Just, please, do this for me." She wrapped herself in a bathrobe and headed for the door, shaking her head. "Mother of the bloody year," she muttered as she exited Steph's field of vision, closing the door behind her.

Stunned, Steph located her clothes and shut herself in the bathroom. Muffled voices came from the adjacent living room. Footsteps, approaching but then ebbing away again. Children's cheers. When, at last, it all registered, Steph felt like hiding her face in her hands and breaking out into a good sob. *What the hell had she gotten herself into?* Not only was Dominique out of bounds because of their working relationship and her job as a career politician belonging to a party that shared none of Steph's beliefs, but she had two children in the age bracket that

—judging from the sounds coming from the living room—still very much enjoyed going to theme parks.

On top of that, she was hiding in someone's bathroom, being invisible. Pretending not to exist.

As glorious as last night had been, round after round of groping at each other, never getting enough—resulting in grossly oversleeping—it surely couldn't be worth this. This humiliation. This flagrantly being asked to erase herself.

But it wasn't as if she hadn't known in advance, or she had anyone else to blame. It wasn't even an error of judgement anymore and, perhaps, that was the worst of all. She hadn't come here just for sex. If she'd wanted that, she could have easily gotten it at Les Pêches. She'd come for Dominique Laroche. Pretty, photogenic, unavailable Dominique Laroche.

Before Steph had the chance to start feeling even more sorry for herself, Dominique barged back into the bedroom, locking the door behind her. "I could die of shame," she said.

Although Steph could recognise this situation was probably a lot harder on her, *she* was the one ensconced in the bathroom, hiding from view. She also fully realised that the only reason she failed to see the humour in this, was because she'd, some-how, gotten way too close.

"I can quietly tip-toe through the hallway while you shower. The noise will distract them." Steph heard blaring cartoon voices coming from the living room. "And if they're anything like my nephews, nothing will tear their gaze away from that television."

"No." Dominique stood in front of her, bathrobe half-open, arms crossed over her chest. "It's too risky. I'm really sorry. The quicker you let me shower, the quicker we can leave." She sighed and brought her hands to Steph's upper arms for a comforting squeeze.

"I don't suppose there's any chance of me joining you in there?" Steph eyed the shower cabin.

Dominique just shook her head, disrobed and opened the glass door.

"This has got to end, you know," Steph murmured, but the water falling down onto the tiles drowned out her voice.

She had no choice but to wait, trying to not make too much noise as she studied Dominique's lotions and creams. She sprayed some of Dominique's perfume on her wrist, as if a pleasant scent could undo the bitterness that clung to this morning's events.

"That was fast." Steph handed Dominique a towel.

"Once you have children, you automatically spend less time on yourself." Dominique covered her body with the towel—a blue one, of course.

For the first time, Steph sensed the pressure Dominique was under. She wanted to hold her, but the moment couldn't have been more wrong for a sentimental gesture. Fast as lightning, Dominique brushed her teeth, and slipped into jeans and a navy shirt—a good look on her. She pulled a comb through her hair and arranged it in a loose bun on the back of her head, looking nothing like, but at the same time being every inch, the politician she was.

"I can't apologise enough." She turned to Steph one last time. "I won't forget this." She kissed her on the cheek. "Feel free to shower and stay as long as you like. Just let the door fall into the lock when you leave." With that, she was gone.

Steph waited until the rustling in the living room died down and a loud bang of the door announced their departure. As if glued to the floor, she remained in the bathroom a little longer, stunned by what had happened—and the unmistakable message it sent.

NADIA

Nadia watched Juliette as she effortlessly engaged in small talk with her father, possessing the gift of being able to talk to anybody about any subject—even football.

"Give me a hand?" her mother asked, collecting the plates from the table.

Nadia stood up, gestured at Juliette to stay seated, and followed her mother into the kitchen, carrying a bowl of left-over couscous.

"What's going on?" her mother whispered as soon as they were alone.

"What are you talking about?" Nadia turned her back, digging into a drawer for cling film.

"You're my only daughter, sweetie, I know when something's not right." *If it was that obvious to her mother, why didn't Juliette notice?*

Nadia steadied herself with her hands against the sink. "It's nothing, just a bit of a rough patch. We'll be fine. We're going to Barcelona for the Quatorze."

"You can always talk to me. You know that, right?" Her mother put a hand on her shoulder, a gesture so sweet and comforting, it touched her to the core.

"Mamy, je t'aime," she spun around to face her mother, "but some things are better left unsaid."

"That bad, huh?" Her mother drew her near for a hug. At forty-one, it still reduced Nadia to a girl who could only ever find comfort in her mother's arms. She could feel the secrets well up inside of her, trying to find a way out. Not just the sword of Damocles hanging above her and Juliette's head, but also Steph's indiscretion and the news she'd soon have to deliver to Margot. It was too much. So much so, that she'd had no choice but to reject Juliette earlier that day. The hope in her eyes had been too devastating.

Nadia pushed back the tears. This was not the time, nor place. But the inevitable was looming—the moment of truth she'd been dreading. A small teardrop fell from the corner of her eye onto her mother's scarf. Nadia bit back the rest of the tears gathering behind her eyes and pulled herself together.

Breaking free from her mother's hug, she said, "It's a bit of a mess, but I'll sort it." *How, though?* She rubbed her eyes. "Let's go back in."

"Hey." Her mother grabbed her by the wrist. "No matter what happens, you've got me."

"I know." Nadia could barely still look her mother in the eye. How could she possibly tell her about what she'd done?

They walked back in together. Juliette, lit up from behind by the light coming through the window, looked like an angel, a vision that would soon blur away.

"Your phone's vibrating," Juliette said, her voice flat. They both knew what that could mean on a Sunday afternoon.

"Oh." Nadia was so tired of coming to her own defence. She picked up her phone from where she had left it on the table, surprised to find a message from Steph.

Can you talk?

"The hospital?" Juliette asked sharply, probably trying to make a point to her parents.

"It's nothing. It's just Steph." Nadia started typing a dismissive reply.

"Steph? What does she want?" Genuine surprise clung to Juliette's voice.

"Just apologising for disappearing last night." *Another day, another lie.* Nadia didn't have to think very hard to figure out where Steph had ended up after she had left the club.

"Okay." Visibly relieved that Nadia wasn't being called away on an emergency, Juliette resumed her conversation with Nadia's dad. Nadia thanked the heavens that they were at her parents' house and Juliette didn't inquire any further.

When she looked up, she caught her mother's worried

glance. Anguish lodged itself in the pit of her stomach. After this, after they went home, she'd have to tell Juliette.

"Do you have more wine, Mamy?" Nadia asked.

―――――

"Getting wasted at your parents now?" Juliette asked as their taxi reached the périphérique.

Nadia gazed out of the window, at the glaring city lights in the distance. "I'm not wasted," she whispered.

"It would help if you looked at me when you spoke." A cattiness had crept in Juliette's voice. For once, Nadia couldn't blame her.

Nadia turned her head to face her partner. "We need to talk."

"No kidding."

"Tonight, as soon as we get home." Despite the glass of wine too many she'd had, mainly to calm her nerves, Nadia's heart hammered beneath her ribs.

As the taxi pulled up to the kerb of their building, Juliette received a text message. She paid the driver and got out first before checking her phone. Her eyes went wide, her mouth forming an 'o' but no words coming out.

"What's wrong?" Nadia asked.

"Oh, Steph." Juliette shook her head. "I should have known she couldn't be trusted."

A whole new set of nerves settled in Nadia's stomach as Juliette lifted her phone towards her to show her the screen. On it, a blurry picture of Steph was displayed, looking disheveled, in a street Nadia didn't immediately recognise.

"And?" Nadia asked. As far as she could tell, it was just an innocent image of Steph.

"Read the message," Juliette instructed. She scrolled down and showed Nadia.

Guess whose flat she's fleeing, S.

"Who's S?" Nadia asked, panic gripping her.

"That's your question?" Juliette arched her eyebrows up high. "Jesus Christ." She shook her head, scanned the street for a taxi, holding up her arm. "I have to go, because, apparently Steph is shagging the députée."

"What? How do you know?"

"I know Steph, that's how I bloody know." Juliette started dialling a number. The person on the other end of the line picked up immediately. "Meet me at the office as soon as possible," she barked into the receiver. "I'm sorry. Our talk will have to wait." Juliette got into the taxi, leaving Nadia flabbergasted on the sidewalk.

As soon as she found her bearings, Nadia texted Steph.

I don't know how, but Juliette knows about you and DL. Someone just sent her a picture.

JULIETTE

"I live in the building where Dominique Laroche has her pied-à-terre. She's been staying there on and off since she separated from her husband," Sybille said, her voice steady, her demeanour not showing any signs of stress or excitement. *What a pro.* "I was crossing the road when I spotted someone coming out of the building. I saw it was Stéphanie. She didn't notice me. Instinctively, I took a picture, because I know Dominique lives in the building and, well, it was nine-thirty on a Sunday morning and she was hardly dressed for a business meeting."

"Jesus Christ." This was all Juliette needed after the day she'd just had. "I'm calling in Claire. Please, delete that picture."

"I'm sorry I didn't send it to you as soon as I took it." Sybille leaned against Juliette's desk as if she owned it. "I didn't want to get her into trouble, but there's no way this can ever be a good thing for Barbier & Cyr if it comes out."

"It's fine," Juliette said while waiting for Claire to pick up the phone. There could only be one reason why she didn't after the first ring. She dialled again, letting it ring and ring, until, at last, Claire answered. Juliette beat her to an exasperated greeting.

"Come into the office now. Big emergency. It can't wait."

"What is it?" Claire asked. "It's kind of a bad time—"

"Not over the phone." Juliette hung up before Claire had a chance to protest. She eyed Sybille. "You live on the Avenue Foch? That's fancy for a twenty-something."

A hint of redness bloomed on Sybille's cheeks. "My partner lives there. I moved in about a month ago."

Juliette whistled through her teeth. "Some partner. What does she do?"

The blush beneath Sybille's cheekbones intensified. "I—I never said it was a woman."

"No need to. I always presumed that was one of the reasons you wanted to work here, because we're so open about these things, which today, I've actually come to regret for the first time in all these years." Juliette sighed. "I'm beginning to think there's so much more to Laroche hiring Barbier & Cyr. That woman is one sly fox. I almost feel sorry for Steph." The reality of the situation hit her again. "Almost, but not quite." She found Sybille's eyes. "So?"

"What?" Sybille seemed distracted, caught off guard.

"What does your partner do?" Juliette crashed down into her office chair, not the seat she'd expected to be in that late on a Sunday evening—then again, maybe, in a way, it was better than another gruelling conversation with Nadia.

"Nothing much. She just has a lot of money. Trust fund, you know."

Juliette didn't know, but nodded anyway. "Listen, Sybille. I know it probably goes without saying, but once Claire arrives, this information does not leave this room. Ever."

"Of course."

"We need to know we can trust you." Juliette fixed her eyes on Sybille.

"Unlike other people in this firm, you mean?"

Juliette pursed her lips together and nodded slightly, her chin moving of its own accord.

"What's going to happen to her?" Sybille asked.

"I don't know. We'll need to get her side of the story." Shrugging, Juliette leaned back in her chair. "This may get complicated."

———

After Claire had uttered enough expletives to put an Australian to shame, she asked, "What now?"

Juliette looked at her watch. "Do we call her in now? If we wait until tomorrow morning, when everyone is here, it may get ugly."

"Hold on." Claire turned to Sybille. "We greatly appreciate you bringing this to us, but we'll need to discuss this in private. I hope you understand."

"Of course." Sybille straightened her posture. "See you bright and early."

"Thanks," Juliette walked towards her and put a hand on her shoulder. "You may have saved us a lot of trouble and we won't forget this."

They waited until Sybille exited her office. Juliette sat down in her chair, facing Claire.

"Why doesn't this surprise me as much as it should?" Claire bit her bottom lip. "You know, I was having the best weekend I've had in," she shook her head, "as long as I can bloody well remember, and then this happens."

"We can't discuss this behind her back. I'm calling her." Juliette reached for her phone, the damaging picture still displayed on the screen.

STEPH

By the time Juliette called her, Steph's brain had gone into full-on damage control mode. At least she had the advantage of knowing they knew before Juliette and Claire confronted her. She considered calling Dominique, but after the awkwardness of this morning, she decided not to.

When push came to shove, though, there wasn't much she could do—and she was dying to find out who had sent the ominous picture Nadia had spoken of in her text. It definitely wasn't Dominique. They'd been careful—Steph had been hiding in the bathroom for the better part of an hour this morning just to make sure.

When she arrived at the Barbier & Cyr office and pushed the heavy front door open, she wondered if this would be her last visit to the building.

She walked past the empty offices, dimly lit by the fading light outside, until she reached Juliette's door. Before knocking, she took a deep breath—ready for execution.

Over the phone, Juliette hadn't told her this emergency was Dominique-related. Steph tried to keep a clear head, her face neutral, when she walked in.

"Hey," she said, a hint of a smile on her face. "What's up?"

"You slept with Laroche." Claire was the first to speak. "The one person, Steph, the only one in this city of millions you had to stay away from."

Despite expecting the statement, and not being able to deny its accuracy, a rush of shame made its way from Steph's gut to her face, leaving her cheeks flushed. She felt like a teenager being called into the principal's office—for something far worse than smoking outside the gates.

"How do you know?" Against her better judgement, Steph went on the offensive.

"So you don't deny it?" Juliette asked, hunched over, her elbows leaning on her desk.

"In order to defend myself, I'll need the facts." Steph's confidence was quickly wavering.

"You were seen exiting her home this morning." Juliette fumbled with her phone before sliding it to the edge of her desk.

Steph picked it up and stared at a blurry image of her on Avenue Foch. "Shit." Panic coiled in her stomach. She looked up at Juliette. "Press?" If it was, Dominique's life was about to turn into hell, and it was all Steph's fault. It didn't matter that she could have been at Dominique's flat for various reasons, a picture like this always looked bad and implied the worst.

"Luckily for us and our client," Claire said. "No."

"Thank god." Steph's muscles relaxed a fraction. "Then who?"

"Sybille lives in the same building. She saw you—"

"And she took a bloody picture of me instead of addressing me?" Rage flared in Steph's veins. From the beginning, she'd known there was something untrustworthy about Juliette's new assistant—the unflinchingness in her gaze and that calculated stare.

Juliette shook her head. "That's hardly the point here, Steph."

Steph, still standing close to the door—ready to make a quick exit—padded to the closest chair and sat down. "I know how this looks, but this doesn't really prove anything." Steph couldn't actually believe she'd just said that. Juliette and Claire were her bosses but also her friends. They knew.

Their response of crushing silence was the worst.

"I'm sorry," Steph started again. "I—I think—" She stopped herself before saying something really silly, like admitting to her feelings for Dominique out loud. "It happened twice. It ended this morning."

"Twice?" Claire looked genuinely shocked, as if it was such an impossibility in her perception of Steph's world.

"What were you thinking, Steph? Really? That it would just be your dirty little secret?"

Steph remembered Dominique's words, that first time at her studio. It would have been if she hadn't gone back last night, if she'd been strong and hadn't given in to that nagging feeling in her gut—that feeling of what? Love? As if that was ever good for something.

She could put up a fight, tell them how strongly Dominique had come on to her, how she'd kept sending her seductive texts, but the fact of the matter remained that she should have been above that. But the worst of it all, topping the shame and the guilt and the very real prospect of losing her job, was that, now that it was out in the open, now that Juliette and Claire knew, even the tiniest sliver of hope—the one that had been nagging her inexplicably since that first time—of her and Dominique ever taking it beyond two nights, was dead and buried. Gone.

"I'm sorry. You should probably get on with it and sack me. I, really, um, don't have anything else to say." Tears were not something Stéphanie Mathis indulged in regularly—possibly ever—but now, she felt them burn behind her eyes. Not because of the job, not even because of her friends losing all respect for her, but because of a woman she couldn't have. And it was the first one she'd desperately wanted in a very long time.

"Steph," Claire urged. "Look at me."

Reluctantly, Steph looked up, her eyes stinging and her hands shaking, unable to meet Claire's gaze fully.

"Are you?" Claire bunched her eyebrows together. "Are you in love with her?"

"What the fuck does it matter?" She exploded. "It's impossible." She shot out of her chair. "Look, nobody knows. Just keep Sybille in check. Handle the account yourself. I'll clear out my desk tomorrow." Steph reached the door, practically falling against it, the wood cold against her forehead, breaking out in sobs. She wanted to storm out, but she couldn't move.

"Hey," Juliette said, her voice trembling. "Come on." Steph heard her footsteps approach. "Let's not be so drastic." She curled an arm around Steph's shoulders, which only made her cry more. "Turn around."

With great difficulty, Steph found the strength to swivel her body around. "Fuck, I'm so sorry." Her voice sounded broken, as broken as her soul.

"Let's all go home. Sleep on this. We'll come up with a strategy first thing tomorrow." Juliette pulled her close for a hug. "Come on, I'll take you."

CLAIRE

"The client is king, or, in my case, queen," Dominique said. "If you want to keep my business, Stéphanie stays on as my account manager."

Bloody hell. The feeling is mutual. Earlier that day, they'd decided to inform Dominique that Claire would be handling her affairs personally, not mentioning the reason why, but expecting that it would be silently understood and easily agreed upon.

Claire and Juliette sat across from the députée, in visitor chairs on the other side of her impressive oakwood desk.

"She is still working for you, I presume?" Dominique asked.

The nerve this woman had. Claire supposed it was necessary to survive—and thrive—in a political party full of conservative, entitled men.

"Yes, of course, but under the circumstances I do believe it would be better—" Claire tried again. They had also decided that firing Steph would do more harm than good. Over the years, they really had become friends first and co-workers second.

"I'm sorry to be so blunt, Madame Cyr, but what I do in my bedroom is none of your business." Dominique said it as if it was the most normal thing in the world that she was sleeping with another woman—one more than ten years her junior—a mere week after she'd announced the separation from her husband, less than a year before an election that could make or break her.

"With all due respect, Madame députée, but that's where you're wrong." Claire had had about enough of pussy-footing around the issue and if Laroche was too smitten to get it, then tough luck for her.

Dominique rose from her chair. "It's very simple, ladies. Do you want my business or not?"

"Of course we do," Juliette replied before Claire had the chance.

"Then deal with it. It's what I pay you for." Claire could almost feel Dominique's green eyes pierce through her skull. "Handsomely as well, I believe." She reached out her hand. "Do we have a deal?"

Juliette shot out of her chair to shake it. "Deal," she said, with a voice like dripping honey. Did she not realise this could be their firm's downfall?

Claire didn't have much choice but to stand up as well. "Of course," she said, while taking Dominique's hand in hers, feeling quite dirty while doing so.

"And Stéphanie stays?" Dominique gave Claire's hand an extra squeeze, emphasising her point—that she was in charge.

"Oui." She couldn't suppress a slight disdainful chuckle. Politicians were all the same. It really only was about power and sex.

"Merci." Dominique waited to sit down until they'd exited her office.

Once they were outside of the Palais Bourbon, Claire broke out into the rage she'd been holding in for the past fifteen minutes. "We should have dropped her as a client, Jules. This is not right."

"They're consenting adults. Nothing unethical is taking place here." Juliette still sounded convinced, but Claire had known her long enough to know what that slight quiver of her lip meant.

"She's not even divorced yet. She has children. She just treated us like dirt in there, and, as the icing on the cake, we both know how she will vote when gay marriage comes up in the Assemblée. The hypocrisy of it all is just too much."

"Welcome to politics, my friend."

"We were doing just fine before we started working for Dominique Laroche and I certainly don't feel a moral obligation to help her. I agree with none of her party's standpoints. Zero."

"Maybe not her party's, but she's a woman fighting an uphill battle. She's crushing all these old farts that used to run the MLR as if nothing could touch them. You have to respect that."

"So we have to support her just because she's a woman? You were there just now, weren't you? The way she spoke to me—"

"She was defending Steph, which frankly, I had not seen coming at all."

"So now they're going to be together and live happily ever after?" Claire let out a loud chuckle. "You know Steph just as well as I do. The only reason she thinks she likes Laroche is because she's so utterly unavailable. It's going to crash and burn. They won't be able to work together anymore and we'll have to pick up the slack and hope this whole affair doesn't blow up in our faces."

"Oh and you have a crystal ball, do you?" Juliette stopped to look at her. "Look, we decided to enter the big leagues together and go after politicians. We caught the biggest fish possible with Laroche. We roll with the punches, it's what we do. And if we do it well, we can retire in ten years. How does that sound?"

Claire's eyes grew to saucers. "I thought we were in this

business because we loved it, not for the money." In all the years since they'd started the firm, they'd never had an argument like this one—one that addressed their core values.

"Of course we love it, but let's not be naive, Claire. We're hardly in the business of making the world a better place." She looked at her watch. "I'd love to continue this delightful discussion, but I need to get home." Juliette sighed. "Long overdue conversation with Nadia."

Claire stood around for a bit after Juliette had caught a taxi, glancing at the Palais Bourbon, where Dominique and the likes of her ruled the country. She decided she needed a long walk to Saint-Germain-des-Prés where, hopefully, she'd find Margot at home.

NADIA

Nadia poured herself another glass of wine, even though she knew that liquid courage would not help her much tonight. Even though she was expecting her, she jumped when she heard Juliette turn the key in the lock. After filling another glass with wine, she went to meet her in the hallway.

"I thought you might like this." She offered Juliette, who was heeling off her shoes, the glass.

Juliette looked far from relaxed enough for the conversation they were about to have. *If she was already half-boiling with rage now...*

"How did it go?" Nadia enquired.

"Claire strongly believes we should ditch Laroche as a client." Juliette accepted the drink. "This would never have happened if Steph had kept it in her pants." She took a sip. "Now, it feels as though everything is turning to shit."

"Come inside, babe. Sit down." Relief began to spread in Nadia's chest. It was only a temporary, cowardly stay-of-execution sort of relief, but nonetheless, she couldn't possibly tell Juliette what she'd done if she had all of that on her mind. That would just be cruel.

"Look, babe, huh, Steph came to me with this early last week. She begged me not to tell you and I honoured her wish, but now that it's all out in the open…"

Juliette deposited her glass of wine on the coffee table and sat down in the sofa. "You knew?"

"Only briefly before you found out and I urged her to end it. I mean, this is Steph, I didn't think it would be that much of a problem, but clearly, well, something more is going on."

Juliette sank into the sofa, half her body disappearing into the cushions. "The worst part about all of this is that I'm genuinely starting to believe that Steph might have feelings for her."

"That's the impression she gave me as well. She would never have come to me if she didn't." Nadia sat down next to Juliette. "What I still can't wrap my head around though, is how it all came out."

"My new assistant Sybille, she's already proven her worth, I'll tell you that. Only two weeks on the job—"

"Isn't it a very big coincidence?"

"Maybe, but a very lucky one for us." Juliette turned to face Nadia. "Would you have told me about it if it hadn't come out?"

Guilt and shame fought for the upper-hand in the mess of Nadia's emotions. "She came to me in confidence, Jules."

"I understand that, but I'm your partner and Steph's boss and her actions had a direct impact on the business Claire and I have worked so hard to build."

"Do *you* think I should have told you?" It was the best defence Nadia could come up with.

"I don't know." Juliette surprised her. "The state we're in…" Deep melancholy had taken hold of her voice. "So, about that talk…"

Fear ran through Nadia's veins like an icy liquid replacing her blood. "It can wait, really."

"Really?" Juliette reached for her wine glass again. "Come on, now that we're sharing."

Nadia's mouth went as dry as the desert. She took a long gulp of her wine before speaking. "It's not just one thing." She heard the words coming out of her mouth, but she couldn't really imagine it was her saying them. "This thing with Steph has been bugging me and I have this other conflict of interest at work." Nadia looked at Juliette expectantly, hoping she'd pick up on her last statement—granting her more reprieve before dropping the big one.

"What sort of conflict?" Juliette took the bait, genuine interest displayed in her eyes.

Aside from everything—and the real purpose of this talk—it felt so good to just have what felt like a normal conversation. The first one in months.

"Margot's ex, who is a doctor with Médecins Sans Frontières, and broke her heart pretty badly when she left, is coming back. The board gave me no choice. She's related to one of the members and she has excellent credentials. But I suspect Margot will not be taking it very well. Inez is an ER doctor and Margot a trauma surgeon, which means they'll probably end up working together on a daily basis."

"Oh fuck." Juliette shook her head. "Poor Claire, she really likes Margot. I haven't seen her this smitten in years."

"I know, the timing is a bit off." Nadia drank again. "But it doesn't have to be the end of them."

"Looks like you've been sitting on a lot of secrets of late." Juliette spared her a small smile.

You have no idea. "Hence my preoccupation this weekend. It was all a bit much."

Juliette reached out her hand and touched Nadia's knee. "I'm sorry I haven't been here."

"I'm sorry too, and you have plenty of problems of your own."

"Are you staying?" Juliette's hand travelled higher, caressing Nadia's thigh. "We could just order take-out and watch crappy TV."

Nadia was up for the lazy TV dinner, but the way Juliette's hand made swift progress up her leg, betrayed other desires—desires she couldn't possibly meet. Not with the one secret she hadn't shared still wreaking havoc on her soul.

"Indian?" she tried, cupping Juliette's hand with hers, stopping its flight up her thigh.

"I'll have some Tunisian first," Juliette murmured, her voice already in the lower, bedroom register.

Nadia had to choose between giving in to her partner's advances or telling her why she couldn't possibly be intimate with her.

STEPH

So many questions crowded Steph's brain. The only one that mattered to her, though, was if she would see Dominique again. After Juliette had dropped her off at home last night, she'd been in such a daze, such a depressed funk, she'd swallowed half a sleeping pill and fallen into a dreamless sleep. Only to wake up to a world that was still the same—still falling to pieces.

After Claire and Juliette had informed her that she wouldn't be fired—a direct consequence of their friendship, Steph was certain—and they'd be handling Laroche personally from now on, Steph had hidden in her office, avoiding Sybille's knowing glare. She'd obeyed her bosses' orders for once and hadn't contacted Dominique. What would have been the point anyway?

Mostly, Steph had felt ashamed because of her outburst in Juliette's office the night before. Because of having needed her boss to take her home. Because of feeling so broken over something that was never meant to be.

She sat in her cheap Ikea sofa, tainted forever by what had happened on it that first night with Dominique, nursing a beer, toying with her phone. *To call or not to call.*

"What do you think, Pierrot?" She scratched him behind the ear and he just purred louder.

While she was staring at the screen of her phone, it lit up, displaying a message from Dominique.

I'm coming over. Be there in ten.

"That's that conundrum solved," she said. Pierrot still didn't care.

She sat waiting, finishing her beer, thinking back to the time Dominique had showed up uninvited, bottle of wine in hand, and how, in a way, it had always seemed inevitable.

Steph hadn't seen or talked to Dominique since she'd left her in the en-suite of her bedroom at Avenue Foch. Knots formed in the pit of her stomach. *When had her life become this complicated when all she ever did was try to avoid a mess like this?*

Pierrot's head shot up when they heard a soft knock on the door—someone must have let her in downstairs. Probably not a good development either.

Steph let Dominique in, not knowing what to expect. Someone on the war path, ready to drink blood? For all Steph knew, Dominique could be convinced that she had spilled the beans.

"Hey," she said, her features soft—against all expectations—when she walked in. Pierrot greeted her with a rub against the calves and she briefly bent down to pet him. "How are you?"

Steph could have broken down there and then—the tension she'd been carrying with her all day dissolving with Dominique's display of kindness—but she stood tall, because, what other choice did she really have? "Fine. I'm so sorry about all of this though. I didn't—"

"I know you didn't tell them, Stéphanie." Dominique moved towards the sofa. Steph had a flashback to that time Dominique's face disappeared between her legs on it. "Tell me what you know."

Steph explained about Sybille, last night's emergency meeting at Barbier & Cyr, and the photo.

Dominique shook her head. "I know everyone in that building and no girl in her twenties named Sybille lives there. This is an old money building. You don't get in that easily." She grabbed her phone out of her purse. "Spell that name for me, please. I'll make inquiries."

"What are you thinking?" Steph had found it quite implausible as well that Sybille happened to live in the same building —especially one like that on the Avenue Foch. "Were we being followed?"

"She works for your firm." Dominique shrugged. "Maybe someone asked her to."

"She's Juliette's PA, but I'm a hundred percent certain Juliette didn't ask her." Steph racked her brain. "Could this be political?"

Dominique giggled uncomfortably. "A socialist conspiracy to bring me down?"

Steph knew it sounded silly. "She did start at Barbier & Cyr right after you became our client. Your enemies might have gotten wind of the fact that you were talking to us…"

"My enemies?" Dominique broke out into a full-on chuckle. "French politics, just like any other country's, are dirty, but this is a bit too far-fetched." Pierrot jumped on Dominique's lap. "Besides, if she were really spying on me, why would she give the evidence to your bosses instead of who she's supposedly working for?" Dominique shot her a smile. "But I do admire your active imagination."

Maybe it was personal then. Steph would be keeping an eye on Sybille, and would be doing some digging of her own.

"I made them keep you on as my account manager."

"Really?" Steph didn't know if she should be flattered or worried about this. "Is that wise?"

"Oh yes." Dominique's hand found Steph's on the back rest of the sofa. "And if not, at least it's extremely exciting."

"You know, sometimes, I think you don't give a fuck about the elections." Steph interlaced her fingers with Dominique's. Pierrot eyed the tiny movements of their hands with interest.

"I do, but if you knew what I know and you'd seen what I have seen, you'd allow yourself a little indulgence now and then—even if you were in my position." Dominique lifted their hands towards her mouth.

"But aren't politicians supposed to be above scrutiny, you know, better than the ordinary man."

Dominique's lips were hidden by their hands in front of them. "Oh yes, but the truth is, we are far worse than anyone." Her eyes narrowed as she planted a kiss on the top side of Steph's hand before turning it so she could slip one of her fingers between her lips. She sucked it hard, turning Steph's blood into liquid fire. "What do you say, Stéphanie?" she asked after letting Steph's finger fall from her mouth. "Do you want to be bad with me?"

It hit Steph that what she liked most about the politician seducing her in her sofa—and not for the first time—was the lack of respect they shared for the rules.

"Fuck yeah." Steph inched closer and, her torso bending over Pierrot's curled-up body in Dominique's lap, leaned in for a kiss.

CLAIRE

"Hey you," Margot said, and the sight of her, dressed in her leather motorcycle outfit, was enough to rid Claire of most of the anguish that had been building in her gut all day. Claire had been waiting for her at Le Coin des Chats, drinking half a bottle of red by herself. "Shall we take that to go?" She winked at Claire, sauntered to the bar, exchanged a few words with the bartender and settled the bill. Claire had seldom felt so taken care of. Margot wrapped an arm around Claire's shoulders, pulling her close. "Rough day?"

"You have no idea." Claire had wanted to go on a rant, to let out all the frustrations of the day, but now that Margot was here, she revelled in the calm her mere presence inspired.

They rode the elevator together, both visibly relieved to find Nadia wasn't there. Claire imagined Juliette was in dire need of some partner therapy as well.

"Do you want to talk about it or forget about it?" Margot asked, while shouldering off her jacket.

"Depends on your definition of forgetting about it." Claire stepped closer, curling her arms around Margot's waist. "Does it involve tying me to a bed post?"

Margot drew her eyes into slits. "Only if you want it to."

The memory of Margot's face when she'd started wrapping the fabric of her tank top around her wrists, hit Claire in a very pleasant way—a funny feeling beneath her ribcage and a more defined one between her legs. "Maybe," she said, meaning yes.

"I'll see what I can do." Margot kissed Claire on the nose before planting a gentle peck on her lips. "How about I cook us dinner first?"

"I'm not, um, intruding, am I?" Claire suddenly felt very lesbian, spending all of her free time at Margot's already.

"I know an emergency when I see one." Margot smiled reassuringly. "When I play doctor," she brought her lips to Claire's ear, "it's for real."

"Forget dinner," Claire whispered back. "Fix me now." She dragged her fingernails over the skin of Margot's bare arms, looking deep into her eyes before leaning in for another kiss. As she did, it felt as if she'd known Margot forever—as if she'd always been the best cure for her pain.

Margot responded by fastening her grip on Claire's waist, pulling her closer.

Claire's brain flashed back to the previous morning, to the moment when Margot had begged her not to break her heart. As Margot's lips landed on hers over and over again, their tongues meeting, their breath catching, Claire considered the notion inconceivable. She was falling in love and nothing else mattered. Not Juliette, nor Steph or Nadia, and definitely not Dominique Laroche.

Overwhelmed by the intensity of her emotions, she hoisted Margot's top up—another one of her vast collection of white t-shirts, Claire had seen a pile of them in Margot's wardrobe when she'd dressed yesterday. Somehow, she doubted she'd end up tied to the bed frame tonight.

"I want you," she hissed, overcome by a desire so sudden and strong, she had no choice but to push Margot against the nearest free wall and made a play for the button of her trousers. And if she'd ever wanted anything or anyone else, she couldn't remember because from then on, it was all Margot de Hay, the quiet, confident doctor who, frankly, hadn't needed to do much to knock Claire off her feet.

Claire's gaze found Margot's dark eyes. "You have me," Margot said, and it felt as intoxicating, as maddeningly exhila-rating, as when she'd taken off her top the day before while straddling Claire, gazing deep into her eyes and knowing instinctively what she wanted, without Claire knowing it herself.

Claire's hand disappeared in Margot's trousers, easily slip-ping in. Margot pushed them down anyway—always one to pay attention to practical matters, it seemed—giving Claire better access. Claire teased Margot's clit through the fabric of her boy shorts—an extensive and colourful collection had also caught Claire's eye the day before. She'd chuckled at the fact that the doctor preferred to hide her true colours beneath the black leather of her trousers.

Claire was hungry for so much more though. She'd had plenty of time to imagine their first time, and this frenzy was much closer to how it had played out in her head—mostly because she'd never expected to get cuffed to the bed with a crumpled, sleep-worn tank top.

Always busy, always on the go, Claire was more inclined to quick satisfaction against the wall than a strung-out, tender love-making session. She still had to find out if Margot shared that preference, although she had a strong inkling that Margot would probably change her mind about that too.

Claire broke free for an instant to yank her blouse off her frame, tossing it to the floor—the last reminder of a disastrous day at work. She bent down and manoeuvred Margot's trousers off her legs—not that easy when dealing with leather—but she wanted her to spread wide. Claire wanted to kneel between her legs, lick her, taste her essence.

Margot's hands were in Claire's hair, twirling strands of it around her fingers, spurring her on. Because the most delicious fact about this infatuation that Claire was in the middle of, was that it appeared to be completely mutual.

Claire inhaled Margot before kissing her between the legs. This was as much about getting off, about dealing with the crazy hormones occupying their bloodstream, as it was about acquainting themselves with each other's most intimate details.

"Ooh." Margot's voice seemed to break at the first contact, her body going limp against the wall. The doctor had quite possibly done some daydreaming as well. "Oh, fuck." Her nails drove into Claire's skull—luckily, being a surgeon, she kept them short.

Claire didn't have it in her to tease, her resolve no match for such heartfelt lust, such quietly but efficiently vocalised desire. She lapped at Margot's pussy as if it offered the first fluids she'd drunk in days. Circling, digging, twirling, until Margot gripped her head hard between her palms, her pelvis spasming against Claire's lips. Soon, the hands clasping her head pulled her up. Claire looked at Margot, at the sated grin on her face, and ostentatiously wiped her mouth with the back of her hand.

"I think we ought to skip dinner altogether and go to bed now," Margot said, lust glinting in her eyes. She grabbed Claire's hand—the one she'd used for rubbing—kissed it and curled her fingers around Claire's wrist, pulling her into the hallway, in the direction of the bedroom.

JULIETTE

Juliette's hand crept under the fabric of Nadia's blouse. She knew Nadia wanted to talk, but she'd done enough of that for one day. The touch of Nadia's warm skin would do for now—it was already relaxing her.

"Stop," Nadia said. "I—I just can't. Not anymore."

She might as well have dumped a bucket of ice-cold water on Juliette's head.

"What?" Not that Juliette felt as if she was owed—it didn't work that way—but she had given Nadia exactly what she wanted against the wall outside of Les Pêches on Saturday night and all she'd gotten in return was a cold shoulder—twice.

"There's something else." Nadia spoke in a voice that Juliette had seldom heard—raw, trembling, insecure.

Juliette pulled her hand away and sat up, worried. "What is it, babe? Whatever it is, we can talk about it?" They were just words of consolation, as much for herself as for Nadia, while fear and hopelessness collided in her brain. *Was this it? Was Nadia finally leaving her?*

"I don't know how to say this." It was as if Nadia had shrunk to a shadow of herself in mere seconds. "I—" She buried her head in her hands briefly, inhaling deeply.

Juliette was really starting to fear the worst now. She wanted to encourage her partner by, perhaps, putting a hand on her knee, but the pure fear of what she might say was too big. It paralysed her, chained her, immobile, to her seat in the sofa.

"I'm so sorry." Nadia looked her in the eye for a fraction of a second before averting her gaze again.

And before she could say the words, in that instant before they came out of her mouth, Juliette knew. She saw it in the guilt displayed on Nadia's face, in the pure shame etched in every line of it.

"I slept with someone else." The tears came, dripping one by one across Nadia's cheeks at first, quickly transforming her face into a wet mess, as a cold hand seemed to reach into Juliette's chest and squeeze tightly.

Was this worse than she had expected? Was this better than Nadia telling her she was leaving her? Juliette didn't know. All she knew was that she'd been cheated on and lied to. That Nadia had stepped into their bed after she'd shared someone else's. Juliette felt nothing but complete and utter betrayal.

"It happened months ago," Nadia started rambling, her words barely registering with Juliette at the moment—although they would echo in her mind for long, lonely nights to come. "It meant absolutely nothing. She was a visiting consultant and you and I were doing badly and—" She stopped to sniffle and wipe her nose with the back of her hand. "I'm not making excuses because there are none. I know that I should have come to you instead of giving in to some stranger's advances like that. I know all of that too well and it's been driving me insane."

A stoic calmness descended upon Juliette. "So, what you're saying is that, just two weeks ago, when you were sitting in that very spot and you basically told me it was my fault our relationship was faltering, you were covering up for yourself."

Nadia shook her head. "I never said that. I never said it was your fault."

Juliette huffed out some air. "I was working too much, blah blah blah. But hey, at least now it makes sense why you were spending so much time at the hospital. Such excellent service you offer in that place."

Nadia's eyes narrowed. "I knew you would react like this, which is exactly why I didn't tell you before."

"Oh, so now that's my fault as well, is it?" The previous calmness was about to desert Juliette. "And next you'll tell me you did it because you felt neglected by me. Boo fucking hoo, *babe*."

"I think I'd better go. There's no talking to you when you're like this." Nadia rose. "And that has *always* been the problem."

"Don't you dare leave and turn this around on me." Juliette broke out into a fury, white noise crackling in her brain. "Don't you fucking dare tell me you cheated on me and leave me to deal with it on my own." Tears that had been rising from the back of her throat started to find their way out. The magnitude of what Nadia had just confessed hit her with full force.

"You didn't have a clue, Jules," Nadia said with a small voice. "You didn't even notice. I might as well not have been here most of the time in the past months. I could have carried on a full-blown affair and you still wouldn't have known."

"Who was she?" Juliette stared at Nadia, who, truth be told, now as much as any other time in the past year, might as well have been a stranger standing in their flat.

"Do you really want to know?" Nadia sat down on the armrest of the sofa.

All Juliette could do was nod, through the tears and the anguish knotting in her stomach, through the knowledge that, now that it was all coming out, their relationship was far from strong enough to make it through this.

"Her name was Marie. She works in a hospital in Brussels. My predecessor had contracted her services before for—"

"Don't tell me that. Tell me how it happened." Defeated, Juliette leaned back against the soft cushions. "Tell me how my partner of ten years came to sleep with another woman." Juliette heard her own voice bounce back nasally in her head—her nose bunched up from too much tears at once. "How did it make you feel? Avenged?"

"Empty. Disgusted. Devastated. Utterly alone." Nadia blinked away another tear.

"And now here we are," Juliette put a cool hand to her overheated cheek, "both feeling that way."

Silence fell, only interrupted by sniffles from both sides, and in that silence, Juliette knew it was over. Regardless of whose fault it was and whose actions had caused what, she'd never felt so far away from Nadia—and she had no desire to be close to her again.

"Maybe you should go now," she said after a while.

"Yes." Nadia stood up without protest, only emptiness in her eyes, and headed for the door. "I'm sorry," she said, one last time.

Juliette nodded, almost absent-mindedly. "Yeah, me too."

EPISODE THREE

CLAIRE

Claire was about to reach another climax, Margot's fingers buried deep inside of her while her own hands were, once again, tied behind her head—seemingly multiplying the effect of even the smallest caress—when the doorbell rang.

"Don't stop now," she pleaded, but the moment was gone, her approaching climax dissolved with the chime of the bell.

"I'm sorry." Margot still had her fingers inside of Claire. "It's probably just Nadia being polite. I'll be right back." She slipped her digits out, winked at Claire and jumped off the bed. "Don't move a muscle."

"You can't leave me here like this," Claire protested, the arousal that had fled her moments ago already returning.

"Looks like I can." The smirk on Margot's face didn't help. She threw on a robe, sauntered to the bedroom door and closed it behind her.

Claire had a perfectly comfortable apartment of her own a few Métro stops away—and she didn't share it with one half of a couple on the brink. Why did they always end up here? She made a mental note to invite Margot to hers next time.

The ongoing stumbling—and was that sniffling?—in the hallway made her feel extremely self-conscious, being tied up like that with nothing whatsoever covering her naked skin. The padded handcuffs Margot had used on her, unlike the loosely-knotted tank top she had employed the first time, were impossible to unlock on her own—which was, of course, the whole point of them.

The door opened to a crack. "I'm very sorry." Margot rushed to the bedpost to which Claire's hands were tied. "Nadia's in quite a state. I'm afraid we'll have to postpone."

Claire uttered some choice curse words under her breath until her hands were freed. Rubbing her wrists, she asked, "What's going on?"

"I don't know. I've poured her a brandy and sat her down." Margot pecked Claire on the cheek. "Let's find out." Margot looked her in the eyes earnestly, seemingly quite undeterred by Nadia's arrival. "Best put some clothes on."

With regret, Claire ogled Margot's covered up skin. She looked around for her clothes and realised her blouse was still somewhere on the living room floor, discarded after a hellish day at work.

As if reading her mind, Margot tossed her a t-shirt and a pair of sweatpants from her wardrobe. "I'm not sure they'll fit, but they'll have to do." She said it with such a wicked grin on her face, Claire could hardly hold it against her. Margot was at least two inches shorter than her, and their waistline wasn't exactly the same size either.

Claire manoeuvred her long limbs into the clothes, still feeling quite exposed afterwards, and followed Margot into the living room.

Nadia looked as if she'd been crying all the way over there, her face blotched, her eyes red, her trembling fingers curled around the tumbler of brandy.

"Oh god, I'm so sorry for interrupting—" She started to say when she spotted Claire.

"Don't worry about it." Margot kneeled next to her. "What happened?"

"I fucked up. Royally." Nadia sipped from the brandy and pulled a face when it made its way down her throat. It didn't stop her from sipping again.

Claire sat down in the sofa opposite her and wondered what state Juliette was in. She'd call her in a second, but wanted to hear Nadia's side of the story first.

Margot patted Nadia on the knee. "You don't have to say, if it's too difficult."

"I cheated on her. Months ago. Once. I told her tonight; she didn't take it well."

Oh fuck. Claire could predict exactly how Juliette would have taken news like that—by kicking Nadia out.

"Do you remember Doctor Dievart? The neurosurgeon we got to come over from Belgium a few months ago to consult on that little girl with the brain tumour. It was her." Nadia shook her head. "I know it was a mistake. I know that."

"I remember," Margot nodded. "She couldn't help Camille either. You were upset."

"Hardly an excuse." Nadia's eyes landed on Claire. "You should probably check in with Jules. She's, well, you know." Nadia couldn't continue, tears preventing her from speaking. She buried her face in her palms.

"I'll take care of Juliette." Claire rose. "I'll go over there right now." She found her blouse crumpled next to a standing lamp in the corner closest to the hallway.

"You've been together ten years, Nadz," she heard Margot say to Nadia. "This will not be the end of you."

Claire slipped into her wrinkled clothing and made her way to Juliette.

NADIA

"I'm so sorry, Margot." As if she didn't feel bad enough, Nadia was mortified to have, quite obviously, disturbed Claire and Margot right in the middle of the act.

"Don't mention it. Seriously," Margot said, but she couldn't hide the look of longing she shot at the door Claire had just walked out of. "You're always welcome here." Margot rose from her crouched position next to the sofa Nadia was perched in and sat down in the spot Claire had been sitting in minutes ago. "Do you want to talk or just sit here? I'm fine with either."

"She kept asking me to move back in. We even booked a holiday." Nadia shook her head again. "I had to tell her. She had to know before I decided to go back. She truly believed we were on the mend, and we were, we were doing a little bit better, but I just, I couldn't keep it to myself anymore. And maybe that's selfish and maybe it's all gone now, but I couldn't... I just couldn't."

————

Nadia thought back to that fateful night she had ended up at a bar near the hospital with Doctor Marie Dievart. She had been upset and she had known full well that Juliette, who practically slept at Barbier & Cyr then, trying to hold on to one of her biggest clients, wouldn't be home to offer support.

Marie was dashing, stylish, a little older, with pale green eyes that seemed to look right through her defences. She had the right words to offer. They had shared a bottle of wine.

"Outside of that hospital," she had said, pointing her thumb to the door of the bar, "there is no one who understands what you're going through right now." But Marie understood. They had shared another bottle of wine. And it was more comfort than anything else. The deep desire to be with someone who knew what it was like to be in the business of saving lives and being so helpless at the same time.

After a quick bout of mindless, tipsy sex in Marie's hotel room, Nadia had fallen asleep, tired from too many emotions and too much wine. She'd woken up in the middle of the night, in a panic, scrambled for her clothes, and taken a taxi home to find Juliette fast asleep in their bed. The next morning at break-fast, which Nadia had sat through with a throbbing headache and no appetite whatsoever, Juliette had just asked what time she got in.

"Late," Nadia had said. And that was the end of it. No further questions. Not even the tiniest display of interest as to why Nadia had stayed out so late. Juliette's eyes had been fixed purposefully on the screen of her smartphone, reading e-mails that had come in during the night.

They might as well have ended it there and then.

Marie had gone back to Belgium the day after, which was a flimsy border away and sometimes, when Nadia was feeling extra-paranoid, she looked out for her in the streets, afraid to run into her by chance. But Paris was a big city, and the hospital hadn't contracted her services again. Nadia hadn't told anyone until Steph had opened up to her about Dominique Laroche. And maybe she should have told Juliette straight away, but, quite honestly, she had no idea when she should have done that, the way Juliette's focus was single-mindedly aimed at work, and then the moment had just passed. She had buried the secret and let it fester. And now here they were and, of course, in Juliette's eyes, it was all Nadia's fault.

———

"Looks like I'll be staying here for a bit," Nadia said, after a while, staring blankly at Margot.

"Of course." Margot refilled Nadia's glass of brandy. "As long as you need."

"Thank you." The kindness in Margot's words struck a chord. Claire was a lucky woman—but for how long? Nadia was holding on to another piece of news, one she hadn't had the heart to deliver to her favourite co-worker just yet. She downed the brandy. It eased her shot-through nerves, calmed her down. "I think I'll go to bed. See what good news tomorrow brings."

JULIETTE

Juliette opened the door to Claire, relieved to see a friendly face.

"It's over," was the first thing she said. "There's no way she's coming back here after what she did. And the lies. How could she lie to me for such a long time?" Maybe it was overly dramatic, and drastic, but it was how she felt.

"Jules, you need to calm down." Claire pushed her way into the living room. "You can't just throw your partner of ten years to the kerb because of one mistake."

"Have you seen her?" Juliette asked. "Did she ask you to come?" The thought of Nadia was simply too much to bear at the moment. All Juliette saw on the back of her eyelids was a faceless woman slipping her fingers into Nadia. Although, knowing her partner, it had probably been the other way around.

"She's at Margot's." Claire walked to the cabinet where they kept the wine glasses, took one out, and poured herself a generous glass from the bottle Juliette had opened earlier. "I understand you're upset and shocked, but let's not make any rash decisions."

"She cheated on me, Claire." Just saying the words caused bile to rise from Juliette's stomach. She swallowed it away with another gulp of wine.

"I know what she did." Claire sat down next to her, throwing an arm around Juliette's shoulders. "And I know you'll need time to let it sink in and get over it, but this is not the end of the world."

"Easy for you to say, Miss Lovebird." Juliette let her head fall back onto Claire's arm. "Your world didn't just come crashing down."

Juliette heard Claire sigh. "Did it really?" she asked. "Because from where I'm sitting, this very much looks like a crash you should have seen coming from a mile away, provided you were paying attention."

Juliette's muscles tensed and she shot up, shrugging Claire's arm off her. "What's that supposed to mean?"

"Come on, Jules. You're hardly the only victim here."

Perhaps her friend was right, but Juliette had expected her to have saved the hard truths until tomorrow. "What has Nadia told you?"

"Nothing. I left as soon as she arrived and told us what she'd told you, but I have eyes in my head and I'm not stupid. Neither are you." Claire's voice remained calm, but not calm enough to stop Juliette from shooting daggers at her.

"What? So it's my fault for not suspecting sooner that she was cheating on me?" It felt as if her own best friend was turning against her.

"No, but it's not just about that." Claire tried putting a hand on Juliette's shoulder again. "Look, I know this hurts, Jules. I know this was the last thing you expected and wanted to hear and it's hard. And I'm not saying you should just forgive and forget, but nothing is a one-way street."

"If you've come here still pissed about that business with Laroche, to work out that grudge on me now, you've come at a really bad time." Juliette half-knew that Claire was right, but she had her pride and, at the moment, it was spectacularly wounded, and all she wanted was a little support, a little understanding from the other person who knew her best—seeing as she'd already lost Nadia.

"I'm here for you, Jules. I always have been. You know that."

"Yeah, well, you have a really crappy way of showing it."

"Do you want me to stay tonight?" Claire shuffled a little

closer. "It's going to take a lot more abuse to get me out of here, is what I'm saying."

Juliette was touched by Claire's words and they wormed their way into her broken heart. "I'm sorry. I—" She leaned her frame against Claire's in the sofa. "It's such a bloody mess and I've no fucking clue what to do about it."

"I hear swearing helps." Claire chuckled. "Remember when you'd just met Nadia and you were so blown away by her?"

"And you were so jealous." Juliette turned to face Claire.

"The hell I was." The smile on her face betrayed the lie she just told.

"You were so jealous you slept with Steph just to get back at me."

Claire put her hand on Juliette's forehead. "I think I'll call Margot. You must have a fever, the way you're rambling."

Juliette grabbed Claire's hand and pressed it to her chest. "Thanks for being here. I know I'm not always an easy person to be around."

"But you're worth it in the end." Claire nudged Juliette in the ribs lightly with her elbow. "And Nadia knows that, too."

The tears that Juliette had held back since Claire's arrival started coming, tracing thick tracks down her cheeks.

STEPH

Steph was on the warpath when she arrived at work the next day. Dominique had heard back from the manager of the building at Avenue Foch and no one fitting Sybille's description, or name for that matter, lived in the building. She knew Sybille arrived early every day, before most people—probably to snoop. The plan was to corner her well before Juliette arrived.

"Hey," she said, leaning against the flimsy wall of Sybille's cubicle. "I bet you're surprised to still see me around."

To her credit, Sybille didn't flinch. "Of course not, Stéphanie. And good morning to you too."

"Cut the niceties and stop following me." Rage boiled in Steph's blood. "Whatever you're up to, it ends now."

"Oh, but I wasn't following you." She waved her hand as if Steph had said the most ludicrous thing ever. "I live there, you see."

"No you bloody don't." It was impossible for Steph not to raise her voice.

"What's going on?" Juliette's voice beamed from behind her. *What was she doing here so early?*

"Nothing I can't handle, Madame Barbier." Sybille rose from her desk and shot Juliette the most calculated, saccharine smile Steph had ever seen. *Surely Juliette would see through it?*

"Steph, my office, now." *Clearly, she didn't.*

Steph followed Juliette, who looked a bit worse for wear. Steph had hoped she would have processed the business with Dominique by now, not because it was all her fault, but because that's what she was used to from her boss.

"Close the door." Juliette's tone was decidedly unfriendly.

Steph did as she was told and leaned against one of the visitor chairs instead of sitting down, not wanting to stay in the office for too long. She decided against launching into a tirade against Sybille straight away. Juliette didn't look as if she would open-mindedly listen to anyone's opinion today.

"Leave Sybille alone. I mean it." Juliette crashed down in her chair with a loud sigh, but not less authoritatively.

"But—" Steph started.

"I don't want to hear it, Steph. She has done nothing wrong, except blab about you and, in the process, done us all an enormous favour. Wouldn't you think so?"

The aggressive approach clearly wouldn't work. Steph shuffled to the front of the chair and sat down. "No offence, Jules, but you look like shit. What happened?"

"Couldn't sleep." She sighed, deeper and sounding more desperate this time. "It's all gone to hell." She avoided Steph's gaze. "Nadia cheated on me and, the worst part is, I think it's my own damn fault."

Oh shit. That cat was out of the bag, too. "I'm so sorry, Jules." A twinge of relief lodged itself in the back of Steph's brain. One more secret she didn't have to keep.

"And now what?" Juliette lifted her hands up in a desperate gesture. "How the hell do we get past that?"

Was she really asking Steph? She might as well have posed the question to the bookcase lining the wall.

But Juliette didn't wait for her to reply. She was merely venting, shaking her head in disbelief, until she was interrupted by the beeping of the telephone on her desk.

"Oui, Sybille." Juliette picked up instantly, probably happy with the distraction.

That little minx, Steph thought. *That sly fox, interrupting my private conversation with Juliette.* Steph wouldn't be surprised if she'd been listening on the other end of the door, her ear glued to the wood.

"Look, Steph, I'd better get to work," Juliette said after recradling the receiver. "I forgot to tell Sybille to come in here for a second. Could you ask her, please?"

"Sure." Steph rose and thought it better to display goodwill until she'd gathered some hard evidence against Juliette's new assistant. Either way, Juliette was in ruins, and now was not the time. "You know where I am if you need me."

"Thanks." Juliette looked as if she were about to burst into tears. Steph briefly considered going over to her side of the desk and hugging her, but she knew Juliette better than that.

Steph exited, coldly told Sybille Juliette was waiting for her, ignored the smug smirk on her face, and walked to her office.

She thought about Nadia and the conversation they'd had. A thought that brought her mind back to Dominique, and last night, and when she'd see her again. "Maybe this weekend," she'd said. "Depends on the kids." Steph tried to make up her mind if this was a good or a bad thing.

NADIA

Nadia hadn't slept, and she was in no mood to have this conversation, but it was no longer fair to Margot to postpone it. She'd left her office door open, and even the slightest shadow made her pulse pick up pace. She looked at the résumé on her desk again. She hadn't even met Inez yet—that would happen tomorrow, another reason to get this difficult conversation out of the way.

"Hey." Margot knocked on the door frame. "You wanted to see me?"

"Please sit." Nadia didn't want to ask her to close the door behind her as well, out of fear that would sound too ominous.

"You sound very formal," Margot joked. "Am I getting the sack?"

Nadia took a deep breath and slid Inez' résumé over her desk in Margot's direction. "Guess who's back from saving the world." She studied Margot's face, waiting for a reaction, but none came. "I tried to fight this, Margot. Please believe me. When I got this job I was promised autonomy, but we both know that, when it comes to certain matters, it's just a meaning-less word. She's Leclerq's niece, and that's the end of it."

As if the news only just then registered with Margot, her eyebrows shot up, making her face look more comical than worried. "Inez is coming here?" She looked Nadia straight in the eyes. "When?"

"She starts in two weeks. After the Quatorze." This reminded Nadia of the holiday Juliette had booked for them. She doubted they'd ever make it to Barcelona again.

"Of all the hospitals in Paris, she's coming here." Margot's voice was neutral, matter-of-fact, injected with the calmness she used to deliver a difficult diagnosis.

"I'm sorry. Leclerq said she had her heart set on it."

Margot nodded, as if she understood. "Because I'm here," she said. She found Nadia's eyes again. "What are my options?"

171

"What do you mean?" A flash of panic fluttered in Nadia's chest.

"She'll be working in the ER, I presume. I doubt she has changed specialties in the third world." Margot flicked the piece of paper away from her with her fingertips. "Which means we'll be working closely together." She pursed her lips before continuing. "Not something I look forward to."

Nadia should have tried harder, but she had no real arguments. She knew that Margot would never have wanted her to use any personal information to persuade the board otherwise, being much too discreet and professional for that. "I'm sorry, Margot. There's really nothing I can do for you."

"I know." Margot pushed her chair back and stood up. "I can handle it." She turned her head away briefly before looking at Nadia again. "How are you holding up?"

"I'm in a facility full of doctors and nurses but none of them can heal a broken heart."

"Full marks for melodrama." Margot shot her a half-smile. "I'll be home tonight if you want to talk."

"I'll be fine. Please, go be with Claire. I don't want to stand in the way—"

"Claire knows this and you know it as well." Margot planted her palms on Nadia's desk. "Heartache always comes first." She leaned in a little closer. "And I don't take no for an answer easily." Her half-smile had transformed into a full-on grin.

Nadia actually chuckled, an action she hadn't thought she'd be partaking in today.

"And when you see Inez, you can tell her that if she chose this hospital because I work here, she picked it for the wrong reason." Margot pushed herself up from the desk. "Show her a picture of Claire while you're at it."

"You can count on it." Nadia scanned Margot's face, unsure if it was a pokerface or if she genuinely didn't care. She feared the former.

"See you later." Margot turned on her heels and exited Nadia's office. Nadia sat staring at the résumé a while longer, at the xeroxed picture of the striking woman in the top right corner of it, and didn't have a good feeling about it.

CLAIRE

"Can you meet for lunch?" Margot's invitation startled Claire.

"Depends, can we meet somewhere private?" She played it cool. And she hadn't forgotten about the previous night's coitus interruptus.

"Can you come to the hospital, please? I need to tell you something and I'd rather do it face-to-face."

Claire sat upright in her chair, definitely startled now. "That sounds serious."

"It's not, I just want to tell you as soon as possible. That's all." A strange urgency clung to Margot's voice.

"I'll be there." Claire checked her watch. "I'll leave now. I'll call you when I get there."

"Thanks." With a dry click, Margot hung up.

A nervous curiosity settled in Claire's stomach, but, truth be told, what with all that was going on at Barbier & Cyr of late—and she hadn't forgotten about the argument she'd had with Juliette the day before, despite it being swept under the carpet because of Nadia's revelation—she couldn't wait to get out of the office for a bit. And seeing Margot was always a treat.

"Hey boss." Steph appeared in her doorframe, just as Claire was getting up to gather her affairs. "Fred told me you're free for lunch. I'll buy." The way she stood there, leaning against the frame, one leg crossed over the other, oozing confidence no matter what had happened and how bad the consequences of her actions could have been, Claire could see why Dominique had made a pass at Steph. She was the kind of person emanating a magnetic attraction that could persuade a homophobic nun to give up her life-long beliefs, and all in the blink of a long-lashed eye.

"My plans have just changed, so I'll have to take a rain check."

"Oh, okay." Steph straightened her posture a bit. "Can we talk later, please? It's sort of urgent."

"Personal or business?" Claire cursed herself, and the way she ran the company lately, for even having to ask.

"A bit of both, I guess."

The reply didn't please Claire and she vowed to run a tighter ship, not that that would be possible as long as Steph was handling Laroche personally. "Set it up with Fred for this afternoon."

———

Claire's heart beat a little faster when Margot sat down opposite her in the hospital cafeteria. She'd gotten them both a salad, but Claire was too worked-up to even pick at it. She didn't want to come across as an impatient teenager either, so she sipped from her tea to hide her concerns.

"Sorry for dragging you all the way out here," Margot said. "And thanks for coming."

"Anything to get a glimpse of you." Despite her nerves, Claire always seemed to go into automatic flirting mode when facing Margot.

Margot smiled. "I know I owe you."

Claire wished they had agreed to meet somewhere privately. It wasn't just the early stages of infatuation that diluted her blood with hormones. There was something so irresistible about Margot, an inner strength and beauty she'd rarely come across. It only made the frantic throbbing of her pulse descend all the way down to between her legs.

"Is that what you wanted to tell me?" Claire's curiosity won out in the end, despite the unflinching gaze Margot regarded her with, and the promises it held.

"Sadly, no." Margot looked away. "My ex is coming back. Nadia just told me she'll be joining our hospital in two weeks. We won't be able to avoid each other."

"What? Nadia? Uh—" Claire didn't know what to say. "Inez? The one we talked about?"

Margot nodded. "Look." She briefly reached out her hand over the table, giving Claire's fingers a quick squeeze. "This doesn't change anything. Once I'm through with someone, I really am done with them, but I'm all for complete and total honesty and I wanted you to know."

Alarm bells rang in Claire's head, although she couldn't immediately tell why. Maybe because, despite claiming it was no big deal, Margot had called her over to give her the news immediately and in person. Or, perhaps, because of how Margot's voice had cracked slightly when she'd first told Claire about Inez. "Okay." Ultimately, Claire was not afraid of a ghost from Margot's past. She knew what she had to offer and what was blooming between her and Margot was going in the right direction. "I appreciate your candour."

"I'm not someone who looks back often. You have nothing to worry about." Margot served her the same smile she'd greeted Claire with after surprising her at Le Comptoir—that debonair got-you smirk Claire adored.

"Okay," Claire repeated, realising she was at a loss for words. *But who was convincing who?*

JULIETTE

"Just because I'm working late, doesn't mean you have to stay." Juliette addressed Sybille, who was toying with her phone behind her desk outside of Juliette's office. It was after eight. Sybille had been in the office before eight that morning—before Juliette had arrived herself—getting an earful from Steph.

"Trust me, you don't want to follow my example. It *will* wreak havoc on your relationship."

"That bad?" Sybille looked up at her.

Juliette just nodded. Something shimmered in Sybille's glance and Juliette didn't know if it was just compassion or something else.

"Do you want to go for a drink?" Sybille gave her that unwavering stare—the one so assured of itself, it didn't take no for an answer.

"Don't you have a partner to go home to?" *And talk to about all the dramatic shenanigans going on at your work place.* They really didn't pay Sybille enough to keep their secrets.

"She's away, staying at her aunt's place in the south." Sybille pocketed her phone and rose. "Come on, boss. Just the one."

Shy of better offers, Juliette acquiesced. "Why not?"

Ten minutes later, they faced each other across a high table outside of Le Comptoir, a bottle of chilled white wine between them.

"What's new on the rumour mill today? Any chatter about your tired old boss?"

"You're hardly old, Madame—"

Juliette held up her hands. "If we're drinking together, you'll have to call me Juliette."

"Gladly." Sybille sipped from her wine without taking her eyes off Juliette.

"So? Spill," Juliette urged. "Is the news out yet?"

"What news?" Sybille genuinely looked as if she didn't know.

Juliette sighed, reminded of the utter hopelessness of the situation again. "It's hardly official yet, but Nadia's moving out." Juliette's phone beeped and she looked at the screen. "Speak of the devil."

Can we talk, please?

No, Juliette said to herself, not ready for a new confrontation by a long shot, put her mobile on silent mode and slid it into her bag, out of view.

"Do you want to talk about it?" Sybille appeared to have dug up her best therapeutic voice. Juliette couldn't remember that clichéd phrase ever sounding so inviting.

She shook her head. "No. I'm done talking about it. Let's talk about you. Tell me something funny. And that's an order." She looked straight into Sybille's face and smiled. Her eyes were wide and dark brown, like Nadia's, giving her features that inexplicably deep but caring vibe. Sybille appeared so young and innocent next to the thought of Nadia, so unspoiled.

"You're putting me on the spot, boss." A playfulness had crept into Sybille's voice.

"I think you're up to it. Otherwise I wouldn't have hired you." Juliette was surprised that smile stayed so plastered on her lips.

"All right." It seemed as if, like in a cartoon, a little twinkling star appeared in the corner of Sybille's left eye. "Why can't blondes eat bananas?" she asked.

Juliette shrugged, well aware of the colour of her hair—more a reddish high blonde than platinum, but still, unlike Claire's, it was her natural colour. *The nerve this girl had.*

"Because they—"

"This looks cozy." Seemingly out of nowhere—Juliette hadn't really been paying attention to her surroundings—Claire appeared on the sidewalk. She eyed Juliette. "I've been calling you."

"Oh, sorry." Juliette reached for her bag. "I've been avoiding my phone."

"I thought you could use some company."

"Great minds and all that," Sybille interjected, clearing her belongings off the chair next to hers. "Would you like to sit? I'll get you a glass."

Tony, the bartender, had already clocked Claire, one of his

most loyal customers, and was on his way out with an extra wine glass. Claire sat down. The setting reminded Juliette of last week's, when she'd occupied this same table with Nadia, Claire and Steph. It felt like months ago.

"No hot date tonight?" Juliette teased.

"Not tonight." Claire's reply was curt. Obviously, she had objections to Juliette enjoying after-work drinks with her assistant.

"Please excuse me." Sybille rose. "I'll be right back." She headed for the washrooms inside, head held high, gait steady, hips swaying like they always did—not too much but enough to invite a sideways glance nonetheless. She was smart, ballsy and could read an awkward situation and respond to it gracefully. Juliette was impressed.

"Does she know?" Claire asked.

"I just told her Nadia's moving out. She's my assistant, she was bound to find out sooner rather than later."

Claire scanned the rest of the terrace. "Steph voiced some suspicions about Sybille. Just, you know, be careful."

Juliette shook her head. "Well, what did you expect? That Sybille would be her favourite person? Frankly, I'm disappointed in Steph, the way she's going after her. And all the while Sybille hasn't said a word out of turn."

"She did bring you the picture."

"Exactly." Juliette eyed the door to make sure Sybille wasn't on her way back to the table. "I don't expect Steph to share my judgement, but I have a really good feeling about Sybille. I trust her."

"Just keep an eye out, that's all I'm asking." Claire poured herself a glass of wine and topped up Juliette's. "Have you heard from Nadia?"

"She keeps texting me, which is why I've hidden my phone."

Claire hesitated before speaking again. "Are there any messages you'd like me to pass on."

"Yeah." Juliette nodded, a small movement of the head that in no way reflected the utter turmoil in her soul. "Tell her the holiday is off."

STEPH

There was no way in hell Steph could go home after a day like that, sit in her sofa with Pierrot and wait for a message from Dominique. Instead, she enjoyed the summer weather and walked through le Jardin de Tuileries to Le Marais, where she was fairly certain to find the degree of distraction she was looking for.

She understood Juliette's reluctance to cast suspicion on Sybille and she regretted flying off the handle the way she had in front of her. At least Claire had been more susceptible to her doubts about Juliette's new assistant. Steph scanned the people around her, abruptly turning around, just to make sure she wasn't being followed—and felt like a total idiot for doing so.

If anyone was after dirt on Dominique Laroche, they wouldn't find it tonight anyway. And Steph was about ready to stop thinking about the députée every waking moment. Having a crush, a condition she had determined she suffered from— against her better judgement—was so exhausting and compli- cated, especially in this case. She needed something to take the edge off, and she wasn't thinking about a gin and tonic. Not even a batch of lemon drops would do. Tonight, Steph was looking for that other means of distraction, the one she'd turned to for years after that first, devastating bout of heartbreak, and she knew exactly where to find it.

She was sober tonight, her clarity of mind not compromised by too much alcohol. She wasn't pining for Dominique the way she was at Les Pêches last Saturday, a weakness which had, in Steph's very strong-minded opinion, only been caused by having been exposed to one too many lovey-dovey couples and, quite simply, too much booze. She didn't really get people who drank to forget because, in her case, it only ever seemed to make matters worse.

Steph picked up the pace and made her way out of the park and followed the Rue de Rivoli with a decided spring in her step, until she took a side street, and another, and, on the outskirts of Le Marais, reached Paris' best kept secret.

It wasn't exactly a dark room for women, which was a bit too much of a contradiction, but it came close enough. It offered the kind of nameless, faceless and, more than anything, brainless relief Steph was after. From the outside, it looked like a private members club, but you definitely didn't need to be a member to enter. Unadvertised and too intimidating for most women to inquire, you had to have heard about it through word of mouth to know of its existence, and Steph had been made privy to Le Noir by one of its owners herself, a woman in her sixties with a three hundred euro haircut and a feminist past.

She rang the bell and was buzzed in. Inside, she paid the fee with the smell of chlorine in her nose—a bit like going to the swimming pool, really—and was handed a large white towel. She noticed the bulky bouncer skulking in a dark corner and gave her a small nod. The woman didn't show any signs of recognising her, keeping her features even and unmoved. Steph progressed to the changing area and, tension coiling in her tummy, undressed quickly and methodically. The thrill of this moment, before anything happened, was unrivalled, but, of course, it didn't exist without what was to follow.

Wrapped in the towel, her bare feet slapping on the cold tiles, she made her way from the still sufficiently lit changing rooms to the ever darkening area beyond. Soft instrumental jazzy music played from small speakers in the ceiling.

Steph had been here on week nights before, but never so early, and never so in need to just get it over with—to quench that thirst that Dominique, being so physically unavailable, couldn't. Nevertheless, this wasn't about needing it so badly she couldn't wait until Dominique granted her the privilege of her time. It was about taking control, about not being chained to anyone for matters like this, about supreme independence and not belonging to anyone— ever. And maybe also, a little bit, about forgetting that hunger gnawing at her core, that desire to walk in le Jardin des Tuileries hand in hand with her lover like she'd just seen countless couples do, and not having to hide in the bathroom on a Sunday morning.

"Hey," a low voice whispered. "Ici." *Here.*

Steph squinted against the darkness, her eyes getting used to it now, and entered a room dressed entirely in burgundy velvet. This was not a poor woman's club and the decor reflected that. The entrance fee was steep, but it assured anonymity and other priceless things, like no questions asked, security and the highest level of hygiene one could expect in a place like this.

A woman lay with her head tossed back on a bench, her legs spread wide, her fingers where it mattered. Another woman, short cropped hair, eyes on fire, looked directly at Steph. "Venez."

It happened that, in daily life, Steph crossed paths with a woman who looked vaguely familiar. But the way people were in here, undressed, free of everything that shackled them on the outside, was so far removed from their every day persona, that it was never more than an inkling of recognition that passed as soon as they exited each other's field of vision. People didn't come to Le Noir to fall in love. On the contrary.

The woman held out her hand. Steph took it and allowed herself to be pulled closer. The arrival of a new person in the room didn't seem to deter the other woman from her actions, by which Steph was already quite mesmerised. With one hand she pulled her pussy lips apart while stroking her clit with the index finger of the other. Her moans easily eclipsed the jazz notes coming from the speakers and Steph felt the familiar throb between her legs, that rush of blood away from her brain, down to her pussy. And that was all she was then. A pulsing cunt with its own one-track mind.

The woman who'd pulled her close took position behind Steph, pushing her hard nipples into the towel in which Steph was still wrapped. She relaxed her grip on it and let it drop to the floor, not caring where it landed or if she'd find it again later. If you couldn't deal with things like that, this wasn't the place for you.

"Qu'est-ce que tu veux?" the woman whispered in her ear, her voice sounding as moist as Steph's pussy felt.

"Fuck me," Steph said without taking her eyes off the masturbating woman—something she never said outside of these walls.

"Mais oui," the woman softly said, her fingers already travelling along Steph's skin, leaving a trail of goosebumps in their wake. Steph could feel her bush against the cheeks of her bottom, coarse and soft at the same time. And it wasn't as if she wasn't thinking of Dominique while all of this was happening, it wasn't as if she was so easy to forget about—even for a few minutes—but this moment was hers and hers alone.

The woman's arms curled around her, one hand around her waist, the other cupping a breast, then pinching a nipple. Steph's moan coincided with one of the masturbating woman's groans and, together, they echoed back and forth in the room, amplifying the pleasure being had in it.

A finger brushed over her clit, basically ignoring it, and ducked straight for her pussy. Steph spread her legs and leaned into the body pressed against her back. A film of sweat formed between their skin and Steph's knees buckled when a finger dipped inside.

The woman on the bench opened her eyes and locked gazes with Steph and although they were a few feet away from each other, it felt as if Steph was being caressed by two women.

"Harder," Steph hissed, because she hadn't come here for softness or foreplay—or to stay for hours. The fingers burrowed deeper inside of her and the panting in her ear grew quicker, more ragged.

Steph focused her glance on the fingers of the woman pleasuring herself, on the increased speed of them now that she was being watched so intently, on the agility of the hand in front of her and the way its movements seemed mimicked between her own legs.

When she came it was quick and empty and soulless—exactly how she wanted it. Without casting another glance at the other two women, Steph picked up her towel from the floor and hurried towards the changing rooms. She quickly rinsed off under a scalding hot shower and pushed every thought from her brain until she stood outside, in the Paris dusk.

Her phone beeped in her pocket. There was no doubt in her mind who the message was from.

My next meeting is in one hour. Any chance of meeting me at le PB between now and ten minutes?

Summoned. Again. *I'll be there,* Steph typed and headed to the main road to find a taxi, all she'd just done erased from her soul.

NADIA

The woman sitting across from Nadia was a million times more beautiful than the photocopied picture she'd seen of her, and much more charming than Nadia had imagined as well—but then again, all she really knew about her, apart from her impressive professional credentials, was that she'd broken Margot's heart. She oozed an effortless sort of charisma that enhanced the allure of the freckles around her nose instead of taking away from it, and the sparkle glinting in her eyes didn't really invite the stern line of questioning Nadia had wanted to use on her.

Instead, in a sickly sweet voice, she heard herself ask, "Why did you come back to France, Doctor Larue?"

"It eats away at your soul," Inez said, her sea blue eyes sincere, "even though we're supposed to be trained to block out the misery." She shook her head. "I'm not proud of it, but I simply couldn't stand it anymore. Sleepless nights, constant worry about patients… in the end, I had to ask myself if me being there was still a good thing for anyone involved." When she sighed, Nadia could sense how torn up about it she was. "After ten months in Rwanda I transferred to India, to Mumbai, to see if moving to a different country would re-energise me. It only took me a month to come to the final conclusion that I'm not cut out for the work that's done in these areas." She looked away briefly. "I see it as a great personal failure on my part." She tilted her head sideways a bit. "But hey, here I am."

"If you don't mind me asking." Nadia shuffled in her seat, but she owed Margot this question. "Why did you choose Saint-Vincent?"

"Purely selfish reasons, I guess." She twirled a strand of curly ginger hair around a finger. "I know people here and I need familiar faces. After being away, in dire circumstances like that, I just couldn't imagine going through a whole process of —"

Semi-honesty was better than nothing. Nadia felt the protective side of her take the upper hand, now that she was starting to get used to Inez' dazzle. "I know about your history with Doctor de Hay. I hope this is not going to be a problem." Margot would give her the silent treatment for at least a week if she had any idea Nadia had just said this.

"Of course not." Inez blinked three times in rapid succession. "It's not as if we parted on such bad terms."

Nadia needed her best pokerface to counter that statement. "Well then." Not the best liar by nature—although circumstance had sort of made her one of late—Nadia had trouble keeping her voice level. "Welcome to Saint-Vincent." She stood up and extended her hand. Inez followed suit.

"If you were to need me earlier, I am free to start next week." Inez' hand met hers. "I just need—want to work."

Nadia hoped Inez wouldn't be taking up this request with her uncle who was on the board. She figured Inez would be trouble enough and the later she started, the better. "That's very kind of you to offer, but it's best to keep things as they are." Nadia meant it in more ways than one.

Inez nodded, her arm falling to her side. "Say hello to Margot for me, will you please?" She reached for her purse on the floor. "Can't wait to see her again."

Nadia watched her exit, unable to shake the impression that Doctor Larue wasn't telling her everything. Obviously, she had a heartfelt story at the ready explaining her return, and Nadia didn't doubt its sincerity as much as its completeness. Something else was going on. Margot had spoken of another doctor Inez had met in Africa, and Nadia couldn't shake the feeling that, perhaps, she could also have played a part in Inez' transfer to India and her subsequent return to France.

Then there was that nagging feeling in her gut making her aware that she was watching a train wreck waiting to happen, in slow-motion, totally unable to change the train's course—or the people standing in its way.

There was one thing in her life she *could* do something about, although not very easily, but at least something could be done. She sat down, focused her eyes on her computer screen, opened an e-mail to Juliette, and started typing.

JULIETTE

With a massive headache pulsing in her temples, Juliette read Nadia's e-mail. It didn't contain any new information. Nadia had still cheated. Maybe there were mitigating circumstances, but that didn't mean Juliette could just turn it into something trivial, something that had happened and should now be overlooked because of the bigger picture. What would actually help was the name of the woman Nadia had slept with, so Juliette could google her and see for herself who'd gotten her hands on *her* partner. What kind of doctor was that anyway? The kind that hit on unavailable women. Or perhaps Nadia hadn't made clear that she was in a long-term relationship. Maybe she had even instigated it.

For every question that burned in her mind, her skull seemed to contract and expand with another throb of pain. One bottle of wine had turned into two. Claire had left after the first one. She and Sybille, who looked as if she'd gone for an energising run this morning, a double espresso at the ready when Juliette had arrived, had easily polished off the second bottle. It didn't feel so easy now.

Juliette clicked reply and let her fingers hover over the keyboard for an instant.

It's about time you gave me details instead of apologies. I want to know everything. Who was she? How did it happen?

Juliette wasn't sure she wanted to know, but if she didn't find out, she'd always be wondering. Maybe if she knew what she was up against—and perhaps if she could, hopefully, brush the other woman off as someone to compete with easily—she could eventually see it for what it was. Because it was easy for Claire to say that she should give Nadia a break, even after what she had done, but she didn't realise how utterly spoiled everything about their relationship now felt. How impure and soiled, spat upon by a stranger.

The comfort Juliette had found in Nadia's body the past weeks, the hope the warm glow of her skin against hers had given her, had all but evaporated because that same body had been touched so intimately by someone else. At least, for a short amount of time, they'd had that intimacy again—Nadia had allowed them to have it despite having done what she'd done—and now even that, even that glimmer of hope, had turned into a lie.

Juliette hit 'send' and rubbed her fingers along her forehead. She had back-to-back meetings after lunch. After longingly eyeing the sofa she never used in the far corner of her office for a few minutes, she stood up, and opened the door.

"No interruptions in the next hour, Sybille." How could she look so fresh? The moment they'd said their goodbyes the night before sprang to mind again. Sybille pecking her hesitantly on the cheek, lingering, imprinting her scent onto Juliette's nostrils. The warmth of her body and how Juliette had just wanted to hug her, just because it was another body close to hers—just for comfort before going home alone to an empty apartment. "Wake me if I'm not up in an hour."

Juliette no longer had the luxury of youth that allowed for a pain-free day after a bender. She shut the door, sauntered to the leather sofa, which didn't look that comfortable for a nap, and lay down, her arms wrapped around herself, closing her eyes against the drilling in her head.

———

"Juliette… Juliette." Still half-asleep, Juliette felt warm fingers against her cheek, stroking gently, lovingly, and in that short stretch of time before fully waking—that instant in which reality hadn't come back fully yet—she believed it was Nadia. "Wake up."

When she opened her eyes, she stared into Sybille's face, her lips curved into the kindest smile.

"Sorry," Sybille said, retracting her fingers, "I didn't want to scare you."

"That's all right." Juliette stared into Sybille's eyes, they were the same colour but a shade lighter than Nadia's. "What time is it?"

"Lunch time." Sybille pointed at a paper bag on the coffee table next to the sofa. "I got you a baguette with brie from Chez Patrick."

The warmth that had spread from Sybille's fingers onto Juliette's cheek didn't seem to leave her. It lingered even longer when Juliette looked into Sybille's eyes again. A thought crossed her mind, briefly, but Juliette pushed it away instantly.

"You're a life saver." She sat up and straightened her blouse. "Thanks," she said, avoiding Sybille's glance.

CLAIRE

Claire wondered if she'd gone completely crazy. She stood outside the hospital, torn between going in and walking away. *It's not because you surprise her that you have to give it to her.* She took a step closer and the automatic doors opened. Making her way through the wide hallway, she breathed deeply to calm her nerves. It was too soon. What the hell was she doing? Claire stopped in her tracks and turned around, quickening her pace.

"Claire?" Margot's voice sounded surprised, but still had an instantly calming effect on her. "Do you have an emergency?"

Claire spun on her heels and looked into Margot's face, eyes brimming with happiness. "I think it's called phantom pain." She rubbed her fingers over her wrists. "I seem to be missing something around here."

"Come with me." Margot grabbed her by the wrist. "I can help."

Claire's heart beat in her throat and she felt her panties drench as Margot dragged her along, their feet quick on the linoleum floor, sounding, Claire imagined, as they would if this were a real emergency.

Margot shoved open a door to what seemed to be a supply room, not much bigger than a closet. She pushed Claire's back against the door and pressed a kiss on her lips. "That should help with the pain."

"It's a start," Claire said, grinning from ear to ear.

"To what do I owe this pleasure?" Margot's body was still pressed against hers, her nipples poking easily through the fabric of her scrubs.

"Just wondering what you were doing after work."

"You could have called."

"True," Claire brought her lips to Margot's neck. "But then I wouldn't have been able to do this." She sank her teeth into the sensitive skin just above Margot's collarbone.

"Against hospital regulations," Margot said, with a chuckle. "Were you on your way out?"

"Yes, I mean no." The nerves that had momentarily left her, hit Claire with full force again, the object she had come to hand over seemingly burning a hole in her blazer pocket.

"What?" Margot regarded her with narrowed eyelids, as if seeing right through her.

"Nothing," Claire tried, leaning forward to nip at Margot's skin again.

"You can't fool me, I'm a doctor," Margot sighed into her ear, before pulling away and locking her gaze on Claire's. "Tell me."

"Erm, I don't mean to go all lesbian on you, but what with the situation with Nadia and her staying with you and, well, we're seeing each other and, um, well…" *What a disaster.*

Margot's smile transformed into a skeptical, lopsided grin. "Yes?"

Claire dug her hand into her blazer pocket and presented Margot with a spare key to her front door.

Margot's eyes went wide, her lips opening up, perhaps to speak. If they were, nothing came out.

Claire shook her head. "I know it's too soon, but I just want you to have a place to go to, you know, after a night shift, if you'd feel like coming over, I thought it would be easier…" She was rambling like a maniac again.

"Is this because of what I told you yesterday? About Inez?"

"What? No, no, of course not," Claire lied. After she'd left

Juliette and Sybille with another bottle of wine last night—perhaps not the best of decisions either—she'd gone home and turned to Google.

It wasn't hard to find a doctor named Inez who'd volunteered with MSF and who was also a lesbian who'd lived in Paris before. The internet seemed to be filled to the brim with model-like pictures of this highly evolved human specimen displaying both incredible looks, an amazing brain and oodles of compassion for her fellow man. How could Claire, when it came down to it, possibly rival that?

"You're right, though. It is too soon." Margot put some distance between them, taking a step back. "You must know how I feel about you, Claire, and it's quite obvious how you feel about me. Can't we just let this take its natural course?"

With the air that Claire let escape through her nose, tension fled her body, leaving her feeling as deflated as when she'd first laid eyes on a picture of Inez Larue. "I'm sorry. I knew it was a mistake, which is why I was leaving without giving it to you."

"Without saying hello?" The stern expression on Margot's face broke into something kinder. "That's not very nice, is it?"

"You do know this is all your fault, right?" Claire grabbed a handful of fabric of Margot's scrubs and yanked her near. "You drive me crazy." She looked into her eyes. "You literally make me lose my mind."

"Shall I take you to the psychiatric ward? They can have a look at you."

The beeper clipped to the waistband of Margot's trousers started making noise just as her lips met Claire's. Claire felt Margot's muscles tense against her and she wondered what it was like to always have to be so alert, always ready, always prepared for the worst.

"I have to go." Margot quickly pecked her on the cheek. "I'll come by tonight after my shift." She drew her lips into that smirk again. "I'll ring the bell."

Claire put the key back in her pocket and made her way out of the hospital.

STEPH

Steph sat waiting for Dominique, who had, obviously falsely, claimed to not have any time to spare for Steph this week. Steph was happy to see her, but she wasn't used to being at someone's beck and call like that. She had her own life and if Dominique kept springing unexpected 'appointments' on her the way she'd been doing all week, there wouldn't be much left of it.

As soon as Steph let her in, Dominique let her briefcase fall to the floor and lunged for Steph.

"This is becoming a problem," she hissed into Steph's ear. "I can't stop thinking about you. I think it's affecting my work."

"I feel so sorry for your lovely constituents. All, without a doubt, salt of the earth people with their heart in the right place."

Dominique had just left a bite mark in the flesh of Steph's neck, but retreated quickly. "Are you confusing me with someone else or are you just picking a fight?" She regarded Steph with that piercing green-eyed stare that lit a fire underneath her skin.

"I appreciate you stood up for me with my bosses, as well as, huh, the sentiment behind it, but you can't just drop in or summon me to your office—or ask me to hide in your bathroom, for that matter—when it suits you. I don't live like that." Steph wondered if the reason why these words were coming out of her mouth had as much to do with how she felt inside as with how she expected Dominique would react—like the politician she was, always attacking and never backing down.

"Well." Dominique took another step back. "If you want to talk, you should just say so." She sat down in Steph's sofa. "Come on." She patted the seat, beckoning Steph over, like a naughty child whose punishment needed to be discussed. This appalled Steph as much as it aroused her.

She stayed standing, leaning against the bookshelf Dominique had pushed her up against.

"I don't want to have a big discussion about where this is going and blah blah blah. I know what this is, *and* its limits, but—"

"What do you want from me, Stéphanie?" It also simultaneously made Steph's blood boil with rage and sizzle with want when Dominique used her full name. Dominique gazed into her eyes, her glance saying it all.

"Look…" Steph was backing down already and it was this power, this supreme, unflinching control that Dominique seemed to exert over her, that made her surrender. Steph's natural instinct was to fight it, but her mind was already starting to wander to the moment when Dominique would slip her fingers inside, that exact same look in her eyes.

Dominique rose from the sofa, silencing Steph in the process. "I know what this is about." Everything was quiet in the flat, their breath the only sound. "You have feelings for me and you have no clue what to do with them."

Steph shook her head, lying to herself and this woman who had, somehow, wormed her way into her heart.

Dominique inched closer and grabbed Steph's hand, bringing it to her own chest. "I feel it too, Stéphanie." She cupped Steph's hand with her own and squeezed it tight around her breast. "And you mustn't think this is easy for me." Steph felt Dominique's nipple stiffen against the palm of her hand.

"I didn't expect to feel this way." To her horror, Steph's voice cracked a little when she said it. The soft expression that melted Dominique's face only made matters worse. Steph wasn't going to say it out loud, but they were falling in love. Maybe it was time to follow her instinct, the only thing that had ever protected her from silly situations like this.

"Neither did I, sweetheart." Dominique's lips landed on her earlobe. "This desire I feel for you, however complicated it is, I'm certain it makes me a better human being, it makes me more aware of what's important, it even makes me a better representative for my lovely constituents."

And every defence Steph had previously relied on crumbled when Dominique sank her teeth into her earlobe, biting down so softly but so determinedly at the same time. Steph felt her pussy open itself up for her already.

"If you don't mind," Dominique said, "I think I'll stay the night." Her hand found its way into Steph's pants, always going straight for the prize. "Should I call the fire brigade, Stéphanie? We seem to have a bit of a flood going on down here."

JULIETTE

Please, meet me tonight and I'll answer every single one of your questions. No exceptions. Nadia's reply to her e-mail had been much shorter than Juliette had wanted, but also very different from what she had expected: another long e-mail drenched in apologies.

When she opened the door and set eyes on Nadia, who seemed to have aged ten years since Juliette had last seen her, her heart sank and a wave of compassion washed over her. But then the image came back to her—the picture in her mind of a faceless woman moving inside of Nadia, giving her pleasure. The image that would stand between them forever if she didn't get more of an explanation. Compassion was instantly replaced by frustration and anger because, while Juliette had believed their sex life was going through a bit of a slump, Nadia had been getting it elsewhere. It may have only been once, but once was more than enough to add to Juliette's mounting feeling of inadequacy.

"Bonsoir," Nadia said, her voice sounding as broken as her body looked.

Juliette had prepared the wine, their usual day-to-day bottle of Cabernet, because neither one of them would make it through this conversation without plenty of it.

They didn't kiss each other hello and the omission of that simple gesture alone was like a neon sign flickering on the wall: *Beware. Dying relationship. Possibly already dead.*

After they sat down and the wine had been poured, Juliette stared at her partner—or was it ex-partner now?—for a few seconds before launching the questions she'd prepared in her head. *Ten years,* she thought, *ten years and then this.*

"What was her name?" Juliette broke the silence that had settled around them.

"Marie Dievart." Nadia said it like a witness on the stand on the TV shows they used to watch together—another thing of the past.

"Did she instigate or did you?" Juliette had to keep her tone harsh in order to ask these questions, to mask how uttering every single word of them made her die a little inside.

"It, erm, just happened. It wasn't really a question of who instigated what…"

But Juliette knew Nadia, knew she wasn't one to be seduced just like that—which was, most likely, what hurt the most. "I don't believe you." Juliette vividly remembered the first time she'd met Nadia, and especially the aggressive way she'd come after her. Nadia was a hunter and she always would be.

Nadia sucked her bottom lip into her mouth before speaking again. "I know you don't believe me, but it's the truth."

"What? No one said anything and you just magically ended up in bed together? And then what? Did she fuck you? Did you let her?" Juliette lost control of her voice and a deep sob escaped her throat. Had she really believed this would be a good idea?

"Jules, come on, it's not really about that and we both know it."

"No," Juliette spat through the tears. "Maybe for you it's not about that, but for me it bloody well is." She wiped most of the wetness from her cheeks. "And I'm sick and tired of you telling me what it is and isn't about." She wanted to gulp down the wine in her glass but was afraid she'd break it with the sheer force of the rage trembling in her fingers. "Instead of confronting me, instead of slamming me against the wall and telling me what it was all about, which is, let's be honest, totally your style, you chose to fuck another woman."

Anger had pushed away the deflated look Nadia had walked in with. "If you really want to know, she offered me the comfort my own partner couldn't give me when I needed it most. I let her seduce me and yes, I let her fuck me." Nadia stood up. "At least, between the two of us, I know I made a mistake, which is much more than can be said of you."

Juliette knew she should say something, but Nadia's words crushed her, wounded her more than any knife stabbed deep into her gut could. She knew she had to fight, but the pain paralysed her, made her mouth go dry and the words die in her throat.

"I think we're done here." Nadia made for the door, her footsteps sounding determined, as if she would never come back.

Juliette still couldn't speak. The neon sign glittered: *Dead*. And all she could see was a woman named Marie Dievart kissing Nadia's lips, fucking her, and she knew that, as long as she couldn't get past that, any further conversation was useless.

The front door slamming into the lock woke Juliette from her daze. Nadia was gone. The flat empty again. Automatically, she reached for her phone and scrolled to Claire's number. Before her thumb could move again, the tears came, much more forceful this time, oceans of regret and pain raining from her eyes, loud howls coming from her mouth, as if someone was really wielding a knife to her gut.

CLAIRE

As Claire lay in her sofa waiting for Margot to ring the bell, watching nothing in particular on TV because the late night news had passed and she really wanted to go to bed, she reasoned that offering Margot the key had really been much more a practical matter than a romantic one. Perhaps she should have tried a different approach, and maybe her timing was off, but Margot was not leaving this apartment without her own key to it. Then again, perhaps it wasn't really about the key so much as about the insecurity nagging inside Claire's mind since Margot had told her about her ex's imminent return. As if a tiny piece of metal could change that.

Ding-dong. Claire jumped up, happy to have her train of thought interrupted, and even happier to see Margot.

"House call," Margot said as she entered. "Please take off your top and lie flat on your back with your hands above your head."

"I love the sort of medicine you practice." Claire drew her near, planting a quick kiss on Margot's lips.

"Only for you, though." Margot looked up into her eyes, her glance unexpectedly stern. "You do know that, don't you?"

And Claire knew, all the doubts dissolving in the heavy, sexy air that hung between them—at least for a little while.

"Sorry I'm a little late," Margot said, pushing Claire into the bedroom. "I had to make a detour to pick something up."

"Did you get me a present?" Claire noticed how the glimmer in Margot's eyes changed from mischievous to downright bossy.

"Oh yes." She shrugged off her leather jacket and, very uncharacteristically, just let it drop to the floor, next to her bag, which she had carried into the bedroom. Next, she came for Claire, tugging her top over her head and getting rid of her bra in the process.

"What is it?" It wasn't just curiosity that burned beneath Claire's skin.

"It's your lucky day." Margot pushed Claire down onto the bed before reaching for her bag. "Because I have not one, but two presents for you."

Claire watched Margot as she crouched down and opened the bag.

"Number one." She produced a set of fur-lined handcuffs. "Let's start with that."

"Rather predictable," Claire teased, and pulled Margot down on top of her.

"Don't make the mistake of underestimating me," Margot whispered in her ear, her voice low and a little bit threatening. "Now hold on to the railing."

After she'd fastened Claire's hands to the bed, Margot stripped quickly—much too quickly to Claire's taste—and unearthed another something from the bag and put it on the nightstand outside of Claire's field of vision.

The not knowing soaked Claire's panties to such an extent she feared for another lost pair—she'd had a lot of those since meeting Margot.

"Let me examine you first," Margot said as she climbed onto the bed again. She hoisted down Claire's pyjama bottoms and knickers in one go.

"Not wasting anytime tonight then."

"Why spend time on foreplay if you're already so wet?"

Claire lay naked on her bed, chained to the frame again, her clit throbbing between her legs. She wondered since when she'd been able to be reduced to such a hot mess in a matter of minutes and with just a few words.

Margot poured her warm body on top of her, careful not to touch any bits that would set Claire off too quickly, and kissed her softly on the mouth. Claire wondered what was waiting for her on the night stand. Nipple clamps? A blindfold maybe? Margot was still such a mystery, it could be anything.

"Let me know if you don't like it." Margot pushed herself up and reached for the night stand. She presented Claire with a medium-sized pastel-pink dildo.

The mere thought of Margot using it on her sent a jolt of lightning straight to Claire's clit. "I love it," she croaked, her voice so hoarse it only produced whispers.

"I thought you would." Margot stroked Claire's nipple with the tip of the dildo. It felt soft against her skin, much softer than any other of these toys she'd ever encountered. Margot trailed it slowly across Claire's skin, finding her other nipple, and lingering there before tracing it upward, over her collarbones and neck until it reached her lips. "Better lubricate," Margot said, and dragged the tip of the dildo along Claire's mouth.

Claire saw something shimmer in Margot's glare, something she hadn't seen before—an unmet need, a flash of darkness. In that moment, Margot's eyes pinned on hers while she eased the dildo slowly into Claire's mouth, the sight of it, the unspoken desire it expressed, made Claire's blood melt even more for her.

Claire was completely at Margot's mercy and she trusted her. Even if she didn't want her key and even if her ex came back to work alongside her every day of the week, she trusted Margot with her life the way she trusted her with the dildo in her mouth.

Claire sucked the toy between her lips, the soft outer coating of it sizzling against the inside of her mouth. She twirled her tongue around the tip, as if licking an extension of Margot, while keeping her eyes firmly locked on Margot's. Juices oozed from between her legs and when Margot let the toy slip from her mouth, Claire was ready to beg.

There was no need because, eyes still locked on hers, Margot seemed to read her mind. She bent over to kiss Claire on the lips while her hand travelled downward with the toy clasped between her fingers.

She dropped it between Claire's legs briefly to run a finger over her soaked pussy. She didn't say anything, just shot Claire a small, approving smile after breaking free from the kiss.

All of Claire's energy seemed to have focused in one place, all of her blood pooling in her pulsing pussy lips and clit.

"Ready?" Margot asked, but it wasn't really a question, more a word of warning.

The dildo slid in easily, welcomed by Claire's copious juices. She couldn't remember ever having felt so wet, so saturated with desire.

Margot slipped it in further, filling Claire in a way she hadn't been in a while. There was no agileness of fingers, no subtleness, just the trust that Margot knew what she was doing, and the sensation of a foreign object inside of her, moving in her, that felt like a part of both of them.

As Margot started wielding the dildo with more purpose, Claire started to feel more and more in tune with her body. She was nothing but a toy being thrust inside of her, nothing but Margot's burning, smouldering stare locked on her face.

She heard someone shriek but it couldn't possibly be her. Claire didn't produce noises like that, no matter how satisfactory the actions being performed on her. She held Margot's gaze. Her face was focused, determined, her eyes turning an even darker shade of black.

Claire was nothing but a sensory mass, every cell in her body overcome with pure joy, her skin a pincushion of delight. She couldn't move her hands, but her pelvis shot up violently with every one of Margot's thrusts inside of her, meeting her, wanting, needing more.

"Oh, oh, oh," that woman shrieked again, and Claire realised it *was* her, and then she shrieked some more, because it felt so good and so right and the wave that crashed over her first, already so strong, was just a warning sign, a warm-up for the next one, that seemed to take every last ounce of her energy.

She closed her eyes against Margot's stare because it was too much, she was too far gone, and the waves kept breaking over her, washing over her, every new one heavier than the previous one, until they subsided and, out of breath, Claire came up for air.

Unable to speak, she found Margot's eyes. Margot didn't retract the dildo, she kept it inside of Claire, holding it immobile, but not releasing her. They stared into each other's eyes for a few seconds, wordless, just breath and hot air between them, until Margot started moving it inside of Claire again. Tiny, minute movements that multiplied through Claire's sensitive flesh.

Claire understood. Margot wanted her to come again. She wanted her completely spent—although Claire thought she already was.

But Margot kept shifting the toy inside of her, so slowly at first, so gently, until she bent over and the closer her face came to Claire's, the deeper she started thrusting.

"Come for me again," she whispered in Claire's ear, her breath like fire on Claire's skin. "Do it for me." It sounded like a plea, almost a cry for help, and Claire felt it was nothing less than her duty to please Margot.

Then, as if a beast inside of her had been unshackled by saying the words, Margot's hand seemed to take on a life of its own, pounding away inside of Claire, no signs of the earlier subtlety, just brute, powerful ramming. Despite Claire having already reached her peak earlier, this uncontrolled thrusting, as if Margot had let go of something important, brought her there again and then beyond it. Beyond reason, and beyond what she thought her body was capable of. The fire beneath her skin swelled from a low flicker to a blazing riot in a matter of seconds, as if fuelled by a new batch of gasoline. *Woosh*, it seemed to go inside Claire's flesh, tearing through her skin, melting her blood until it was all she felt. Just fire and the sensation of being touched in a place that only someone special could reach.

She came again, with a deep tremor inside her belly,

Margot's lips on the delicate skin of her neck. A sob, and then another. Claire couldn't check her own cheeks for wetness, but she knew she wasn't the one doing the crying.

She couldn't move even if she wanted to. Her muscles had given out after all the contractions and her legs seemed to be sinking into the mattress. Margot lay half on top of her, breathing heavily, as if she was the one who…

"Oh my god," Claire said, without thinking. "Did you?"

Margot pushed herself up and looked into her eyes, all signs of darkness gone. At last, she let the dildo slip from Claire's pussy, and Claire folded one leg over Margot's lower body. Margot just nodded.

Claire shook her wrists, reminding Margot that they were still bound and she was the only one with the key. *How ironic.*

"Oh, sorry," Margot said, suddenly flushed. She grabbed the key off the nightstand and uncuffed Claire, rubbing her thumbs over her wrists.

"Come here." Claire drew her near. "I can honestly say that was the best sex of my life." Because if Claire had ever felt more satisfied and closer to someone in bed, she couldn't remember.

"I think I'm falling in love with you." Margot's voice was muffled by her hair that kept her mouth from kissing Claire's neck fully, but Claire had heard it loud and clear.

NADIA

Nadia didn't have anything better to do than to give the new doctor a tour of the hospital on a Sunday afternoon. Any communication between her and Juliette had been firmly halted after their last meeting. They hadn't exactly said the words yet, but Nadia was starting to prepare for them, although she had no real idea how. How could it possibly be over between them? Would it really end like this? With fighting, endless reproach and nothing but bitterness between them?

"Madame Abadi?" Inez knocked on her doorframe. "Thank you so much for agreeing to see me."

"I thought it better to show you around during the weekend. Not so hectic." Nadia stood up to greet Inez. She held out her hand. "And please, call me Nadia."

A cool hand met hers. "I prefer Doctor Larue." Inez kept her facial expression neutral for a few seconds before breaking out into a wide smile. "Just kidding." She let her fingers slip from Nadia's grasp. "When you've stitched people up in the jungle, formalities become less important."

"I bet." Nadia couldn't help but grin back. "Shall we." She led the way down the corridor, thinking about the other reasons why she had agreed to meet Inez today. Next weekend, she'd be on holiday. Via Claire, Juliette had let Nadia know that she was 'welcome' to go to Barcelona alone, and frankly, Nadia needed to get away. She needed to leave this city where her world consisted of work and Juliette. She needed time to think, to let her mind go blank before conjuring up a miracle. And it was all booked and paid for, anyway. If they cancelled now, they'd just end up losing the money—and they'd lost enough already.

The other reason was walking towards them now. Nadia had given Margot ample warning and they'd both concluded that this would be the best way for her and Inez to meet again— as opposed to running into each other in the middle of an emergency when on the job. Margot had the weekend shift and this way, she'd have Nadia around to coax Inez away after a few minutes.

Margot held her head high as they approached her, looking way above feigning surprise.

Inez stopped in her tracks and let Margot come to her. From out of nowhere, the thought crossed Nadia's mind that it had somehow always been that way. Inez clasped her hands in front of her mouth for a brief second before throwing her arms wide. "Margot!"

"Don't act so surprised," Margot said in a flat voice. "It's not as if you didn't know I worked here."

Undeterred, Inez took a step closer and curved her arms around Margot, who stood motionless in the embrace. "It's been so long."

Nadia studied Margot, feeling a bit ill at ease witnessing this moment. Margot wore her mask of steel, hiding any discomfort deeply underneath it.

After releasing Margot from the awkward hug, Inez looked her over and said, "You look good. We should catch up before I start here officially."

"I don't think that will be necessary." Margot eyed her beeper, as if willing it to go off. "I'll see you on the fifteenth." A grimace crossed her face. Her armour was all the way up and she had retreated far inside it.

"Sure." Even Inez, with all her effortless charm, couldn't keep up the charade in the face of such indifference. "I look forward to it."

"Okay." Margot nodded at Nadia and proceeded in the opposite direction.

Nadia didn't know what to think. This was not the Margot she'd come to know and appreciate so much.

"That went well," Inez said, giving a nervous chuckle. "You and Margot are friends, right?"

"We are." Nadia already wasn't liking where this was headed, but if she had a chance to warn Inez off in any way, she'd gladly take it.

"I don't mean to pry, but I'm just curious." Inez seemed to have found her confidence again. "Is she seeing anyone?"

Nadia knew it wasn't her place to say and, in any other circumstance she would have told her colleague off for asking untoward questions, but, as Margot's friend, she couldn't let the opportunity pass. "Yes, she is. A good friend of mine, to be precise."

"Oh, good for her." Nadia felt Inez' eyes on her as they walked side by side. "Is it serious?"

The audacity. "Yes, it is." Nadia stopped just before they reached the nurses station.

"I'd love to meet her some day. I'm glad Margot found someone." She shot Nadia one of her camera smiles again. She could see why MSF would have been keen to hire her, such a poster child.

Nadia couldn't help but doubt the sincerity of her statement, but, if they were all going to be working together, she had to give Inez the benefit of the doubt.

After she had introduced Inez to the ER nurses on duty, her mind drifted to that beach in Barcelona, and how empty it would feel without Juliette.

JULIETTE

Somehow, ever since they'd shared a bottle of wine too many the week before, it had become a habit for Juliette and Sybille to have an early morning chat when Sybille brought in her coffee. Juliette found herself looking forward to it. Sybille was easy to talk to and they worked together so effortlessly. Juliette couldn't remember ever having such a comfortable relationship with an assistant. Then again, she'd had a whole slew of them after her very first assistant Madame 'I will absolutely not address you by your first name' Bouffious had retired three years ago, never seeming to find that perfect match again, until now.

The only issue with Sybille, as far as Juliette could see, was that she was obviously very ambitious and after a higher-up job at the firm. If she kept proving herself the way she did on a daily basis, it wouldn't take long, and Juliette would be without an assistant again.

"What's wrong with your shoulder?" Sybille asked, prompting Juliette out of her reverie.

"Must have slept on it wrong." Juliette wasn't aware she'd

been massaging it. "Still getting used to sleeping alone, I guess." Certainly, Juliette would never have had a conversation like this with Madame Bouffious.

"I know an excellent chiropractor. Shall I book you an appointment?" Sybille sat in the chair opposite her desk, impeccably dressed as usual. Maybe they should promote her already, before Juliette got too used to her excellent care, exceeding her job description far and beyond.

"That's okay. It'll pass." Juliette rubbed her shoulder again with one hand while she held her coffee mug in the other. She felt a pang of disappointment when Sybille stood up. Usually, she stayed longer, waiting for Juliette to let her know it was time to get to work.

"Let me see what I can do then." To Juliette's surprise, Sybille crossed to her side of the desk and put her hands on Juliette's shoulders. Her skin broke out in goosebumps at the unexpected contact, her muscles momentarily contracting. "If that's all right?" Sybille asked, a little too late after the fact. Her thumbs were already driving into the tight muscles in Juliette's shoulders and the tension they released from Juliette's body felt so good, she just grunted.

"A little lower," Juliette instructed, not wanting Sybille's hands to leave her shoulders all day. The girl clearly had many talents.

Sybille kneaded her flesh and, though it was innocent enough, it felt like such a relief to be touched by another person.

"Just so you know, boss." Sybille hit a particularly painful spot just next to Juliette's right shoulder blade. "I'm available for anything you want, any time you want it." With that, the kneading action seemed to transform into a caress, soft fingers flying across her back, trailing towards the bare skin of Juliette's neck.

Juliette was stunned and her muscles tensed, instantly undoing the effects of the impromptu massage. A knock on the door startled her further and she blurted out 'come in' before she had a chance to consider how this set-up would look to anyone walking in.

"Juliette, I just wanted to—" Steph entered, stopping dead in her tracks when she noticed Sybille's hand slipping off Juliette's shoulder just a fraction of a second too late.

"Sorry," she said, her voice stern and reproaching, "I didn't know you had company."

"That's all right," Sybille said before Juliette had the chance to say anything. "I was just leaving." She picked the coffee mug off of Juliette's desk and swaggered out of Juliette's office.

"Just a second." Steph held up a finger and sauntered after Sybille, closing the door behind her.

Jesus Christ. Juliette let the back of her head crash against the leather of her chair. She could have really used that Barcelona getaway, with or without Nadia.

STEPH

"What do you think you're doing?" Steph tried to keep her voice down, but it was hard while looking into Sybille's smug face. *Did nobody else notice? Really?* "You stay the fuck away from Juliette."

"Or what?" Sybille crossed one leg over the other, looking relaxed and totally in control. "What are you going to do, Stéphanie?" She painted a sly grin on her face. "Maybe it would be better for *you* to stay away from Juliette." She picked up her phone and dangled it in between them. "Don't forget what I have and what I can do with it."

"You," seething with anger, Steph planted her palms on Sybille's desk and looked her straight in the eyes, "have nothing and you know nothing. I'm on to you and it's only a matter of time before Claire *and* Juliette catch up. They weren't born yesterday, like you."

"Having some anger management issues, Stéphanie?" Sybille slanted her torso over her desk until her face was mere inches away from Steph's. "It mustn't be easy being a right-wing politician's secret lesbian lover."

"That's enough," a voice behind them beamed. "You wanted to see me, Steph?"

Steph drew a deep breath, hoping Juliette had caught that last remark. She straightened her posture and averted her gaze from Sybille, unable to look at her treacherous face any longer. "Yes." She followed Juliette into her office and closed the door behind them with a loud thud.

She had no choice but to pipe down in front of Juliette, who had obviously been quite taken with Sybille since she'd brought her 'the news', and—especially—after the events of the past week. Steph had to at least show some gratitude for not getting the sack, and openly accusing Sybille now was simply not an option.

She needed evidence, and she needed it fast.

"I understand she's not your favourite person, Steph. I do." Juliette looked tired and was unable to hide the sadness oozing from every pore of her skin. "But please, I'm literally begging you here." She tapped her hand to her chest. "Don't make me deal with this feud on top of everything else."

Juliette's request would have appeared over-the-top in any other circumstance, but not today. Dull despair emanated from every laboured gesture of her hands. She'd lost her sparkle and, clearly, Sybille had picked up on that, preying and waiting for the right moment to make her move.

Steph held up her hands in a gesture of surrender. "It's forgotten." *As if.* "But I care about you deeply, Jules." She stepped a little closer. "And I wouldn't want you to make silly mistakes because you're hurting."

After what she had done, Steph felt ludicrous launching into a speech like that. Luckily, Juliette didn't appear to have the energy for further arguments today.

"Whatever you think you saw, it was nothing." Juliette

reached for her shoulder again. "I just have this pain here that won't go away."

I'm sure you do. "Have you talked to Nadia?"

"Not since last Wednesday. She's at Margot's." The deflated look Juliette shot her felt more like a blow to the stomach. "It's going to take time and, well, I don't know what else. Let's just say we're currently at an impasse and neither one of us has any idea how to get out of it."

Having completely forgotten what she'd come to ask Juliette in the first place, Steph sat down in the chair opposite her. Not that she had any clue what to say. She wasn't exactly an expert on matters like this. "I know how much Nadia loves you, Jules. I know what she did seems like this insurmountable obstacle right now, but in time, I hope you can see the big picture again."

Juliette looked away from her and directed her attention to her computer screen. She typed a few words and turned the screen towards Steph. "This is the only picture I see in my head these days."

A slightly pixelated image of a woman flickered on the screen in front of Steph. She looked in her late forties, distinguished, with high cheekbones, wide lips and pale green eyes. *Not bad.* Then it registered.

"Is that—"

"Doctor Marie Dievart. Neurosurgeon no less." Juliette shook her head.

"You really shouldn't torture yourself like that. It was a one-night stand. I know it sounds like a cliché, but these things happen all the time. Looking her up online will not make you feel any better."

"Yeah well," Juliette turned the screen away from Steph, "it would have made me feel better if she was ugly."

"That picture is probably photoshopped." Steph tried a grin.

"Nadia's going to Barcelona on her own next weekend." Juliette ignored her remark.

"Well, then you're coming out with me." Steph pinned her gaze on Juliette. "I'll arrange—"

"What? A secret date with you and Dominique Laroche?" A hint of a smile crept along Juliette's lips. "Not the threesome I had in mind."

Steph pondered the approaching weekend that she'd probably spend waiting for Dominique again. The kids were off school and their father was taking them on vacation, but Dominique would have work and party obligations because of the national holiday. Steph couldn't believe this was what her world consisted of now. Children. Waiting. Hiding. She didn't even have a quip to counter Juliette's joke with, just drew a blank.

"Shall we get to work." Juliette straightened her posture in her chair and tried to paint on a professional smile. It almost worked—she was good like that.

"I forgot what I came for." Steph stood up. "Anything you need. You know where to find me. But just in case you need reminding, I make for an excellent drinking buddy." She shot Juliette a wink before heading for the door. Once she shut the door of Juliette's office behind her, she walked past Sybille's desk as if she wasn't there.

CLAIRE

"I'll take that key," Margot said. She'd granted Claire the rare pleasure of visiting her at the Barbier & Cyr office, bringing her lunch.

"Oh really." Just from staring into her dark eyes—and remembering what shone in them every time Margot tied her to the bed—made Claire's clit throb wildly beneath her stiff office attire. "For someone who likes to take things slowly, you're suddenly moving fast."

"Are you calling me fickle?" Margot was dressed in running

tights and a black tank top. "Because you could just choose to call me adaptable instead."

"Just wondering what changed your mind." Claire didn't really care that much, she just wanted Margot to have that key.

"You were right. With Nadia staying with me, I will probably end up spending more time at your place." Margot rested her eyes on Claire. "And with my irregular shifts I just thought it would be advantageous for both of us."

Usually, Claire hung on every word Margot said, but today she was terribly distracted by her outfit and how it enhanced all her best features. "Great."

"I was expecting a little more enthusiasm." Margot drew her lips into a pout, but they both knew she was hardly the pouting type.

"Why are you dressed like that?" Claire narrowed her eyes, focusing on the swell of Margot's chest just above the hem of her tank top.

"Because it's my day off, the sun is shining and I'm going for a run after this."

"Oh really. A run." Claire leaned back in her chair, well aware that she was leering at her girlfriend—were they girlfriends yet? "Are you sure you will have the energy for that?"

"Why would I not?" Margot pretended not to catch her drift.

Claire reached for her phone, wanting to tell Fred to hold all calls and not let in any unexpected visitors.

"He's gone to lunch," Margot said, reading her mind. "Besides, it will be more fun like this."

The words alone were enough to send a bolt of lightning up Claire's spine. She'd never done anything like that in her office before. "At least let me lock the door."

"No." Margot crossed one leg over the other. "Let's live dangerously for five minutes."

"But—" Claire protested.

"It's okay. No one will see. I won't be touching you."

Margot's voice dropped a little, the darkness Claire was just thinking about reappearing in her eyes. "Hike up your skirt."

Without giving it any second thought, because that was what Margot's stare did to her, Claire complied. She hoisted up her skirt as high as it would go given the position she was sitting in.

"You'll be doing all the touching." Margot's eyes started blazing fire. "And don't worry, from where I'm sitting, I can't see anything. The desk covers you. Okay?"

Claire nodded.

"Put your hand in your panties and touch yourself the way you do when you masturbate."

Claire didn't know what was more exciting. The instructions Margot was giving her or the complete contradiction between the stern, emotionless expression on her face and the desire glinting in her eyes. She spread her legs as far as she could and slid her fingers under the waistband of her knickers.

"I'll talk you through it," Margot said. "Try to keep your eyes on me."

It was difficult to focus her gaze on Margot when her fingers met the wetness in her panties. Her clit was already so engorged Claire was convinced she wouldn't even last a minute.

"Imagine that's my tongue on your clit," Margot continued, her voice breathy when she said the word 'clit'. "And imagine that the waistband of your panties pushing against your wrist is a tank top I tied around it."

Claire's eyes wandered to the tank top Margot was presently wearing, to the complete stillness of her muscles and how that stood in stark contrast to how they twitched when she moved in her.

A muffled noise outside the door startled Claire. It only seemed to transport more blood to her throbbing pussy lips.

"Ignore that," Margot said, her voice an oasis of calm. "Focus on me." She brought her left hand behind her neck and leaned back a bit, while her other hand slowly pulled up her tank top.

Claire couldn't suppress a whimper at the sight of Margot's abs and how her biceps flexed above her head. *I was never like this before*, she thought. *Never this easy.*

But it wasn't just the sight of Margot's abs that had her rapidly approaching orgasm, it was the whole of Margot, sitting in front of her, telling her to do it.

"Come for me," Margot said, hoisting her tank top all the way over her bra.

Claire didn't stare at her exposed skin when the waves came crashing over her; she looked straight into Margot's eyes.

"Oh god," she moaned, the climax as forceful as if Margot had administered it herself, as if it was her finger on her clit, flicking left and right.

Margot smoothed her tank top back over her chest and sat in the chair as if nothing had happened.

Claire caught her breath, removed her hand from her panties and yanked her skirt down. "Jesus christ," she said, "I'm beginning to believe no one does any work anymore in this firm."

NADIA

Nadia met Steph for a round of after-work drinks at a bar in Le Marais. They sat outside, perched around a miniature table on the narrow sidewalk, sipping rosé, because it was that time of year.

"You don't, by any chance, want to join me on a romantic trip to Barcelona, do you?" she asked Steph who looked as if she needed cheering up as much as Nadia did when she examined herself in the mirror.

"I would if I could take Friday off, but with everything going on at Barbier & Cyr these days, I feel as if I have to be there every minute of every day." Steph smirked, at last showing that she wasn't taking Nadia's request too seriously.

"And then there's my own miserable love life to take into consideration."

"That bad, eh?" It could never be as bad as the sorry state of Nadia's relationship, if it even still qualified as one.

"I know everyone thinks Dominique and I are doomed and perhaps that's how part of me feels as well, but the other part just can't get enough of her." Steph sighed. "And then there's that business with Sybille." Steph eyed Nadia with unexpected intensity. "Have you met her?"

"No." Nadia shook her head. She'd heard Juliette mention her name and she knew she was the one who'd sent Juliette the picture of Steph's Sunday morning exit from Laroche's flat, but recent events had taken her mind far off that subject. "What's going on?"

"She can't be trusted, only, Juliette seems to believe she walks on water or something, and earlier today…" Steph hesitated. "I'm not sure I should be telling you this, Nadz."

"Well, you have to tell me now." Anxiety rose inside of Nadia.

"This morning," Steph lowered her voice to a conspiratorial whisper, "I walked into her office and Sybille was massaging Juliette's shoulders." She slanted her body over the table. "I'm not saying it meant anything and I'm definitely not claiming something untoward is going on… yet."

Despite the soft tone with which Steph delivered the news, it still came as a blow to Nadia, a slap straight across her face.

"Juliette is vulnerable right now and Sybille knows it," Steph continued. "And she's definitely one to take advantage."

Perhaps, for the first time, Nadia understood how Juliette really felt. The mere mention of her long-term partner considering touching a stranger instantly made her feel hollow and powerless, and rendered her speechless.

"I've got my eye on her. We've had a few altercations and, obviously, Juliette believes I can't stand her because she blabbed about me, and that has something to do with it of course, but that girl is after something and I believe it may well be my job."

Nadia refilled their glasses from the bottle in the ice bucket. "You think she's after Juliette *and* your job?"

"Think about it, Nadz." Steph started fiddling with her fingers nervously. "The minute she shows up, everything turns to shit. And her explanation for taking that picture doesn't add up either."

"Wow, she's really got you backed into a corner." Nadia drank some more.

"I know I sound paranoid, but she still has that picture of me leaving Dominique's building on her phone and she has threatened me with it. It's not just me or you she can hurt, Nadz, she can do serious damage to Dominique as well."

Nadia's mind was too focused on Sybille trying to get Juliette into bed to pay much attention to Steph's conspiracy theory. "I'd speak to Juliette, but I doubt she'll listen to me." Deep despair descended upon Nadia again. "Your only hope right now is Claire."

Steph exhaled deeply. "Claire's mind is elsewhere as well, plus I know she and Juliette are in serious disagreement about having kept Dominique on as a client." She bent over the table again. "I'm good friends with Claire's assistant Fred and he told me that earlier today, when Margot paid an unexpected visit to Claire, he could have sworn they were, you know, doing it in Claire's office."

Giggles rose like bubbles through Nadia's body. "Oh god," she said. "What happened to Barbier & Cyr?" Laughter convulsed in her belly. "I always believed it was such a respectable place."

Steph laughed with her, because, really, what other option did they have than to just have a good chuckle at their own expense.

After the dire reality of it all came back to her and the laughter subsided as quickly as it had sprung up on them,

Nadia said, "You keep an eye on that…" She didn't want to say the word. It wasn't her style.

"Bitch?" Steph drummed her fingertips on the table. "Oh, I will."

If Juliette started something with her assistant, there'd be even less chance of them patching things up, and they already had such a long road to go.

"I'm going to ask her again if she won't change her mind." Nadia slipped her phone out of her purse and, without giving it any further thought, dialled Juliette's number. It rang and rang, but no one picked up. Whereas at first, she'd just had hurt and self-pity coursing through her whenever Juliette ignored her calls, now there was the added sensation of paranoia. Had they ended up in bed already?

Nadia stared at Steph, despair tightening her muscles.

"I think she had a work do tonight," Steph said, probably catching the fear in Nadia's eyes.

"I'll send her a message instead."

"I have a better idea." Steph's voice shot up. "Why don't you come to the office tomorrow and ask her in person.

Obviously she wanted Nadia to meet Sybille, and Nadia had become quite curious about her as well.

"Maybe I will," Nadia said, and put her phone down.

JULIETTE

Darkness was already falling outside, but Juliette was still in her office, thinking of ways to manage the crisis when Dominique Laroche's secret came out. She had insisted on continuing to represent the politician's PR interests and she wanted to be ready, just in case.

She knew that, just outside her office door, Sybille was waiting for her to leave, despite Juliette's insistence that she'd go home.

"There's always work for me to do, Juliette," she had said

half an hour earlier, when Juliette had craned her head outside of the door and commanded her to go home. "And I'm happy to stay. You never know, right?"

Juliette had seen it then, that eagerness to please above anything else. It was ridiculous that a junior assistant would still be in the office on a gorgeous summer evening after nine p.m., but she couldn't claim to not appreciate it, or enjoy the attention.

Because, yes, there was always work to be done, but they both knew it was as much flirting as anything else. Harmless flirting, as far as Juliette was concerned, because she wouldn't stoop to Steph's—and even Claire's—level and sleep with clients or employees. But those brief moments of someone expressing interest in her, and making it absolutely clear that she would have her back no matter what happened, was all she had. Besides that, all that was left was an empty flat to go home to and long hours of not sleeping and being torn between calling Nadia and that dreadful, devouring feeling of having lost everything.

A knock on the door startled her. "Oui, Sybille," she said, already happy with the brief distraction she would offer.

The door opened and, to Juliette's utter surprise, Nadia appeared in her office. Maybe she should have taken one of her incessant calls or replied to her messages.

"It's me," Nadia said.

Juliette nodded to Sybille, who stood behind Nadia, indicating she should close the door. The resemblance between them hit her again. She noticed how Nadia eyed Sybille curiously.

"I went by the flat and Le Comptoir, so I figured you'd still be here."

"Summer's not supposed to be this busy, but here I am." Juliette was unprepared to face Nadia and felt strangely put on the spot.

"Can I sit?" Nadia asked.

Juliette gestured at a chair, her palm open. "Please."

"I don't mean to ambush you, but I just really wanted to see you, to ask you something." Nadia appeared nervous. Juliette felt a mixture of nerves, anxiety and despair play tricks on her stomach as well. Nadia seemed more like a stranger than her partner of ten years.

"It's okay." Then it was just plain sadness crushing Juliette's soul. There they sat, opposite each other in her office, as if in a business meeting, exchanging niceties.

"Would you please reconsider coming to Barcelona with me?" Nadia's voice was small.

As a matter of self-preservation, Juliette had already erased that trip from her brain, ignoring the possibility of joining completely. Automatically, she shook her head. "No. That's out of the question."

"Please, babe." Nadia's voice cracked. "We need to do something. We can't stay in this limbo."

Juliette's mind flashed back to the evening she'd proposed the trip to Nadia, when everything was still hopeful and untainted by secret one-night stands. Rage flared inside of her again and there was no way she could take all the frustration and agony that had been building inside of her on a four-day trip with Nadia.

"I can't. We can't. Look at us." Exasperated, she let her upper body fall against the back of her chair. "There's nothing left between us except disappointment and hurt and this dreadful sadness here." She tapped her chest.

"So what are you saying?" Tears sprang up in the corners of Nadia's eyes, the overhead lamp in Juliette's office catching them. "That it's over? That we're beyond repair?"

Juliette looked away because keeping her gaze on Nadia was too painful. "I don't know," she mumbled. "You tell me."

"I refuse to believe that." A sudden power rose in Nadia's voice. "Look at me, Jules."

Juliette glanced at Nadia, unable to ignore the command in her tone.

"We are so much more than this and I will fight for you." But it wasn't enough. Once, that tone had set Juliette's blood on fire, while now, she could only wonder if Nadia had used it on Marie Dievart and how the neurosurgeon had reacted to it.

"From where I'm sitting, there's not a lot left to fight for." Juliette straightened her posture. "No matter how you twist or turn it, you cheated on me and lied about it, by omission, for months. I don't trust you and, truth be told, I'm disgusted by you." Even Juliette was taken aback by the harshness of her words.

Defeated, Nadia stood up. "I understand if you need more time, but don't give up on us." All the zest had left her voice and it sounded flat and broken. "I won't." Juliette watched how she swallowed hard, wiped a few tears away from her cheeks, before turning to leave.

"It's a little fucking late for that," Juliette mumbled to the closed door of her office after Nadia had exited. She realised that her main issue was uncontrolled, boundless anger. Not just anger directed at Nadia for what she'd done. Juliette was also angry at herself, because she hadn't seen it and she had let it come this far. But in the end, she still wasn't the one who had cheated.

STEPH

Another Wednesday night, another summons, Steph thought as she knocked on the massive door of Dominique's office at the Palais Bourbon.

"Entrez." Dominique's voice on the other end of the door sounded as if she was out for blood.

"Oh, it's you," she said as Steph walked in.

"Expecting someone else?" Steph waited by the door.

"No, I'm sorry, I lost track of time." Dominique rushed over to Steph. "I think I need a hug."

Confused, Steph opened her arms wide. "What's wrong?"

"You might be holding the biggest hypocrite in the Assemblée right now."

"I'm sorry, I didn't quite get that," Steph whispered in Dominique's ear. "Did you say the biggest hottie? Because I already knew that."

Dominique pushed herself away from Steph's chest and looked into her eyes. "We had a big party meeting this afternoon, the last one before recess. Even my father was there, and we all know what that means."

"The leadership means business."

"One of the conclusions of the meeting was that every MLR député is expected to vote against gay marriage in September, even though it will most likely pass. We want to send a clear message to the hundreds of thousands of people protesting it, what with the elections next year."

"Lovely." Steph was torn between supporting Dominique and launching into a tirade, not that she believed in any form of marriage, gay or straight, but this was a simple matter of principle and equality.

"The best means of protest I could come up with was to call you over here and have my way with you on my desk, maybe on some papers with the logo of the party prominently displayed on it."

Steph shook her head. "Did you stand up for it at all?"

Dominique dislodged herself from Steph's embrace. "Of course I did." Her eyes shot fire. "I wasn't the only one, either. We do have some forward-thinking, progressive people in our party. We're not extremists."

"You have time to think about it. The vote isn't until after summer." Steph grabbed Dominique's hand; she couldn't help herself.

"It will be seen as extreme disloyalty to the party's stance and could have an effect on who the leadership decides to support."

"Surely not for you. You're Dominique Laroche and they're nothing without you. They need you more than they need that vote."

"That's one way of looking at it, but politics are, unfortunately, never that simple." Dominique let her head fall against Steph's chest again. "I've had enough of politics for today, anyway."

"Shall we go home?" Steph stroked Dominique's hair and felt nothing but the most compelling desire to make her feel better.

"Where's that?" Dominique chuckled, irony in her voice.

"Let's go to mine." Steph pressed a kiss on the crown of Dominique's head, engulfed by a tenderness completely foreign to her.

"Okay, but I'm not moving in just yet."

———

After Steph had fed Pierrot and given him enough cuddles to make up for being away all day—something she did every evening—she crashed down into her sofa next to Dominique, whose eyes were fixed on the screen of her phone.

"Enough of that." Steph held out her hand ostentatiously. "My house, my rules."

Without protest, Dominique dropped the phone in her palm. "Sometimes, I really wonder what you've done to me and if I've lost my mind completely." The expression on her face was serious enough to cause a light pang of worry to course through Steph. "My path is laid out. If we win the elections, and, you never know, but all evidence points in that direction, what with the Socialists screwing up the way they're doing now, I will become Minister. And then what?" She inched a bit closer to

Steph. "Sometimes, deeply stashed away in here—she pointed at her chest—a tiny glimmer of hope flickers that we'll lose." Her gaze, full of despair, found Steph's. "Of course, that's unspeakable, unthinkable even, but that's how I feel about you."

Steph looked away, fighting against the tears, because for someone so principally dead-set against relationships, she'd landed herself in the most impossible one she could imagine. "What are you saying?" she asked.

"Oh god." Dominique brought her hands to her mouth. "Not what you're thinking right now." She shuffled closer and cupped Steph's cheeks in her palms. "For the life of me, I'm not letting you go."

Yet. "Isn't that incredibly foolish?"

"Oh yes." Dominique's green eyes looked sincere enough. "But I choose you."

Now you do. When it's still easy and sexy, but what will happen when the wolves come out? The thought crossed Steph's mind, and not for the first time, that if she really cared about Dominique Laroche, she should be the one to let her go. But just like politics, it wasn't that simple.

She was in love with her.

CLAIRE

When Claire arrived home on Wednesday evening, after a long, wine-laden dinner with a potential client, she found Margot sitting barefoot in her sofa, legs tucked under her bottom, reading a book.

Margot looked up as she walked in, a giddy smile on her face. "Your key works," she said.

"Clearly." Claire was a bit tipsy. She hadn't eaten any of the carbs on her plate, just a small piece of salmon and some greens —no dessert. If she ever wanted her belly to even remotely resemble Margot's, she knew she'd have to cut back on the wine as well, but she wasn't prepared to go that far just yet. "What are you reading?"

Margot tossed the paperback on the coffee table. "It's a story about lesbians doing drugs and screwing each other over, but it's well-written."

Claire made out the cover, but nothing on the cover of a book could look as good as Margot perched in her sofa. "How was work, darling?" she asked with an affected tone as she approached.

Margot grinned at her. "Fine, sweetie."

"How many lives did you save? Or was it a slow day?" Claire slanted her long body over Margot's, ready to straddle her.

Margot pulled Claire on top of her. "Do you really want to know or are you just making conversation until you kiss me?"

"I know how important communication is at any stage of a relationship because, lately, I have witnessed first-hand how lack of it can destroy everything, even a ten-year partnership." Juliette had been at the dinner with Claire, or at least a shadow of her. She'd sat there nodding and half-smiling at the jokes François, their dinner date and potentially very important client, had made.

When Claire finally kissed Margot, it was more an absent-minded peck than the passionate lip-lock she'd been going for since walking through the door.

"Let's talk, then." Margot smiled up at her, eyes brimming with understanding.

"Juliette is so stubborn. She'd rather suffer through the worst heartbreak of her life than talk to Nadia right now." Claire pushed herself off of Margot's lap and sat down next to her. "I understand it hurts, at first, but Nadia's made it quite clear that it was a mistake and that it hardly changes the real problems they're having." Claire sighed. "On top of that, it's hurting Barbier & Cyr. She should have excused herself from dinner this evening, but obviously she grabs every opportunity

222

for distraction. She's my best friend, and I know that, now more than ever, I have to be there for her, but it's not easy when, for the first time in our professional relationship, we're having a serious disagreement." Claire sighed. "It feels like I'm the only one thinking straight at the firm anymore."

"Come here." Margot held out her arm, offering the crook of her well-shaped shoulder to cuddle up to. Claire eagerly accepted. "You're strong. You can hold the fort for a while." When Margot said it, in that even, self-assured voice, it sounded as if it couldn't be anything but true. "And I'm here whenever you need me."

Claire trailed a finger over Margot's taut stomach. "I know you are." Claire stretched her lips into a wide smile against the fabric of Margot's t-shirt. "How do I get abs like yours?"

Margot's belly shook with giggles. "I thought we were having a serious conversation?"

"This is serious." Claire slipped her fingers underneath the hem of Margot's t-shirt and hoisted it up, exposing her flat stomach.

"I'm Asian, it's easier for me to have a six-pack."

"Really? How so?" Claire was intrigued, but already her mind was wandering off to the moment her lips would meet the skin stretching over their current topic of conversation.

"Because we're genetically more disciplined and we can't drink as much." Margot's abs contracted as she laughed.

"It's not because you're a doctor that I believe everything you say." Claire circled her index finger around Margot's belly button, awakening the pulse between her legs.

"Now that we're having a meaningful conversation, I wanted to ask you something serious."

"Can I stay down here while you ask me or do you have to look into my eyes while I give the answer?"

Margot stroked Claire's hair, her fingers travelling towards her neck. "Are we girlfriends yet?"

The term 'girlfriends' sounded so silly in Claire's ears—she was forty-four years old, for heaven's sake—she couldn't help but chuckle.

"That funny, huh?" A hint of hurt had crept into Margot's voice.

Claire pushed herself up and found Margot's dark eyes. "Yes, you're my girlfriend and I'm your girlfriend." She pulled her close. "I thought you'd never ask."

"Glad to know we're going steady," Margot whispered in her ear.

Claire buried her nose in Margot's long mane of hair. "Remember when you asked me not to break your heart?" She felt Margot's head tilt in a nod against hers. "The same goes for you."

NADIA

Nadia boarded the plane for Barcelona without Juliette by her side. She needed the break, needed to get away from everything —especially the big dinner her family always insisted she attend on the day of the French national holiday—but it was more than a bit painful that her holiday destination was Barcelona.

She and Juliette had so many good memories there, which is why they'd picked it in the first place. *Oh bloody irony.*

It was an early flight and, not used to travelling alone, Nadia hadn't gotten much sleep the night before. She closed her eyes and tried to nap but, just like every night since what seemed like forever—unless she'd drunk at least three glasses of wine— images of leaving Marie Dievart's hotel room, of arriving home to a sleeping Juliette, of facing her the next day at breakfast and, since recently, of the completely stunned look on Juliette's face when it registered what Nadia had done, intertwined in her mind. Thank goodness she was flying business class and champagne would be offered soon enough.

———

The hotel Juliette had booked was every bit as marvellous as Nadia had expected it to be. The room looked out over the Mediterranean, the space in front of the window lined with pillows on which she could sit and gaze out over the horizon.

It was gorgeous and Nadia hadn't felt this lonely in a long time. After years of sharing everything, being there on her own crushed her much more than she could have imagined.

Afraid she'd burst out into tears when asking for a glass of cava or a plate of patatas bravas, a tapas dish Juliette loved so much, she ordered room service and hid inside, trying to tear her mind away from the significant memories she and Juliette had made in this city.

Outside, the sun was already setting, bathing the ocean in orange and yellow tints, and Nadia knew, with a certainty bordering on manic stubbornness, that she would fight. She wasn't sure how yet, but was fairly certain it would require a good amount of patience and sitting through a slew of unavoidable, blame-shifting arguments. In the end it wouldn't matter. She'd get Juliette back.

Over the course of the last year, she had doubted the viability of their relationship, and had indulged in brief moments of imagining a life without Juliette, or, to be more exact, a life without the selfish, entitled person Juliette had turned into. And then Juliette would smile, or offer Nadia a glass of wine with a particularly tender gesture of her hand and that look in her eyes, and Nadia would melt because she'd see the woman she'd first met again, the one who'd swept her off her feet ten years earlier.

———

The story went that Claire and Juliette had entered a dare to create a profile for each other on a lesbian dating website. Nadia had been taking management classes after her shifts because she was in the running to become nursing supervisor at the hospital. Too busy to go out and play the waiting game in a bar, she'd turned to the internet and stumbled across Juliette's ad.

They'd met for the first time at a café in the Rue Montorgueil, under a heater on the terrace, at first watching the endless parade of people walk past, but soon engrossed in anecdotes about their childhoods and teenage years, and Nadia couldn't believe her luck. If she'd known women like Juliette presented themselves on the internet, she would have turned to it much sooner.

She could see the ambition burn in Juliette's eyes when she talked about her business, and it was exactly that fire that spoke to Nadia. Juliette displayed the gentle arrogance of people who were used to getting their way, and Nadia couldn't wait, given the chance, to take her down a notch—to have her beg for mercy when she slipped her fingers in.

She suspected this unmet need was why Juliette was single, because she had everything else going for her. She wasn't just beautiful and successful, but also eloquent and bursting with confidence. Maybe she came across a bit too intimidating for most women, but not for Nadia.

Perhaps what they saw in each other on that first date, that first inkling of recognition, that first sliver of hope at something more, was just a flimsy thread binding them together, ready to snap at any time too much pressure was applied, but they had thrived.

They'd slept together that first night, in Juliette's tiny studio near Invalides, because Nadia couldn't wait to test if her suspicions were true, if this tall, lanky woman who spoke with a quiet voice while everything else about her was so loud and brazen, would surrender to her in the bedroom. And she had, almost exactly in the way—and as easily—Nadia had predicted she would.

Now, from her window on the twelfth floor, Nadia sat overlooking the beach promenade where they might have walked together, reminiscing joyfully about their time together, in Barcelona and Paris and all the other places they had visited. Nadia realised it had been a mistake to come alone. She should have used her time off more usefully, for getting her partner back, for instance.

STEPH

No matter how cruel it sounded, Steph could get used to Dominique's children being away, because she knew full well that a Friday night like this, huddled cosily in Dominique's sofa watching the news while eating spaghetti bolognese prepared by the députée herself, wouldn't come along again any time soon.

A fuzzy warmth rose in Steph at the sight of the tomato sauce stuck to the corner of Dominique's mouth.

"Quel connard," she shouted at the TV and shook her head. President Goffin was saying something about jobs and the retirement age. "I'm not saying politics is all about charisma, but look at him. Three chins? As if two isn't enough."

Steph, who'd never really taken an interest in politics, snickered. This was the sort of political commentary she could get into. Then her mind flashed back to the conversation they'd had earlier that week about Dominique's political future and, eyeing Goffin's tired face on TV, Steph had no doubt the MRL and, particularly, Dominique would win big next year. A sense of urgency took hold of her, as if they were running out of time.

She set her plate to the side and turned to face Dominique in the sofa. "How did you manage to climb the party ranks so quickly while being such a messy eater?"

Dominique looked at her, grinning. "Messy, huh?" She

deposited her plate on the coffee table as well and stared into Steph's eyes for a split second before coming for her. "I'll show you messy." She rubbed her mouth against Steph's cheek. "Now who's messy?" Steph felt Dominique's lips stretch against her chin.

"Politicians are so dirty," Steph said, while allowing Dominique to push her down in the sofa.

"Now you're just asking for it." Dominique looked down at her and Steph saw much more than mischief and desire glint in her eyes. Dominique reached for the remote on the table and switched off the TV, after which she started unbuttoning her blouse.

Lust bubbled in Steph's veins and if all of this was foolish—and she knew it was—it didn't matter anymore because it all fell away as Dominique exposed her chest, slowly lowering the cups of her bra. A deep throb of lust made its way to Steph's clit and she wanted to say the words, no matter how foolish.

"Je t'aime," she whispered, but Dominique didn't hear because she was tossing her bra onto the carpet.

When Dominique draped her naked torso on top of Steph, she knew it was more than lust crawling up her spine, it was more than an unwise longing for what she couldn't have, even though Dominique's lips were already kissing their way up from her neck—and Steph was about to get exactly what she wanted again, at least for the next hour or so.

Dominique's lips landed on hers, gentler than ever before. "It's crazy how much I want you," she said in between breaths. "I swear to god you'll be the end of me." It was the most romantic thing anyone had ever said to Steph.

She wrapped her arms around Dominique's neck and pulled her closer. Their lips met again and Steph could clearly tell the difference with the first time they'd kissed in her studio. Back then, it was just reckless abandon, almost like stealing something, while now, when Dominique's teeth sank softly into her bottom lip, she might as well be etching their marks into her heart.

Their lip-lock intensified, just as the pulse between Steph's legs. When Dominique came up for air, she pinned her gaze on Steph while her hand travelled down and unbuttoned Steph's jeans. Steph helped and jerked the garment off her as best she could.

She couldn't remember it ever being like this. Not a surprise for someone who visited Le Noir and preferred a one-night stand over a second date and, perhaps, this intimate intensity was what she'd been afraid of all along because how could she come back from it? How could she ever recover?

She had no more time to ponder questions like that—questions that had haunted her her entire adult life—because Dominique's finger was already skating along the panel of her panties, making its way beneath it.

Steph cupped Dominique's chin in her palm and, while slipping a finger inside, Dominique canted her head to kiss the side of Steph's hand, electrifying the entire expanse of Steph's skin.

Dominique kept her head tilted, touching her cheek to Steph's hand, while thrusting slowly and with control—such a simple gesture, with such profound consequences.

Steph didn't crave anyone else's fingers inside of her anymore. Feeling Dominique, pushing herself up to meet her thrusting motions, was more than enough to make her dream about foreign notions such as exclusivity and monogamy. Deep down, Steph had always known it could be like this, but the willingness in her soul had always been lacking.

"Aah," she moaned when Dominique's fingers hit a spot that had gone extremely sensitive. "Aaargh." And then hit it again.

Dominique's face was serious, not a hint of a triumphant smile on it, because, it looked like, in the throes of a passion like this, there was no room for any other sentiments than this love they now shared. Steph knew it could only feel this good because it was so serious. It stumped her all the same.

She kept her eyes on Dominique's as she came on her finger-tips, giving herself up completely, a deep tremor reaching her heart straight from her clit.

"Oh fuck," she sighed when her muscles relaxed and she fell deep into the soft pillows of the sofa. "You'll be the end of me, too."

JULIETTE

Nadia was in Barcelona, Claire was holed up with Margot and Steph wasn't replying to her texts, so Juliette, always thrown by public holidays, gave in to Sybille's fifth message inviting her for a drink.

They met at an Irish pub just down the road from Juliette's flat. The défilé in honour of France's national holiday was being broadcast on two flat screen TVs hanging above the bar. While Sybille, always playing the assistant even outside of the office, fetched them a bottle of wine, Juliette focused her attention on one of the screens, looking out for Dominique Laroche who should be in the stands at the arrival, flanked by her conserva-tive party mates.

Were they friends now? She watched Sybille saunter back. She was dressed casually in a pair of too short khaki shorts and a tank top so white Juliette had to blink when she looked straight at it.

As she sat down, Juliette handed her a twenty euro note, not wanting Sybille to pay for the wine.

Sybille waved it away. "Thanks for meeting me." She poured Juliette a generous serving. "I'm glad we can talk outside of the office and without the chance of being interrupted."

Was she really that bold? Juliette just nodded.

"This is not easy for me to say, Juliette." Sybille squirmed in her seat and Juliette braced herself for having to reject, frankly, very direct advances. "I know you and Steph are friends first, but I really feel as if she's gunning for me."

Juliette hid her surprise—or was it disappointment?—by sipping from her wine. "You're worried about Steph?"

Sybille nodded. "Of course I am." She looked at her hands, twirling the stem of her wine glass between her fingers. "Ever since I found out about her and Dominique Laroche, she's been very unkind to me, which I understand, of course, because it landed her in an awkward position, but what choice did I have but to tell you?" When she glanced up, her eyes were big, her lips drawn into a sad scowl.

"I've talked to Steph in no uncertain terms. I've told her to leave you alone." Juliette had to suppress the urge to inch her hand forward and wrap it around Sybille's—in a purely comforting way, of course.

"I really appreciate that, I just—" Sybille cleared her throat. "I wouldn't want any of this to jeopardise my job because, um, I really enjoy working for you."

"Don't worry about Steph." Juliette gave in to her urge, possibly only to feel another human being's skin against hers. "And this is a public holiday. Let's not discuss work matters." Exactly the sort of thing Nadia would say.

Sybille gave her best impression of smiling shyly—she wasn't the sort of person to paint a demure grin on her face, Juliette knew that much.

Juliette topped up their glasses just as a gang of loud middle-aged men walked in. She rolled her eyes at Sybille while retracting her hand. "Let's drink up and get out of here. I have a bottle of divine Pinot Noir at home, if you're interested?"

Sybille nodded eagerly, almost choking as she chucked back her wine.

———

"I figured you'd be spending the holiday with your partner," Juliette said as she uncorked the bottle to let it breathe a bit.

"She's still away." Sybille looked around the flat. "Life's easy when you don't have to work."

Juliette failed to understand this concept completely. "But doesn't she *want* to work? Do something useful with her time?"

Sybille just shrugged, killing off that topic of conversation when asking, "Do you want to watch the parade on TV?"

"Not particularly." Juliette eyed the bottle of wine eagerly and pondered all the times she'd scolded Nadia for drinking too much. Perhaps she'd been the cause of that too. "Oh what the hell, I'm sure it will taste fine like this." She poured liquid into two glasses and passed one to Sybille, their fingers brushing together for a fraction of a second.

"Delicious," Sybille said after having taken a sip. "Nice place, as well."

"Thanks," Juliette mumbled. She wondered what would happen to the flat if she and Nadia were to actually separate. They'd probably sell it, neither one of them wanting to be confronted by the memories it harboured. The mere notion sent a chill up Juliette's spine.

Juliette drank some more because, all things considered, this was not a situation she wanted to be in—downing wine that she'd saved for a special occasion with her assistant, instead of a loved one. The whole situation had a distinct air of inadequacy, exactly how Juliette herself felt as well.

Before she knew it, they'd finished most of the bottle, the pair of them slumped against the backrest of the sofa. No matter how fuzzy her brain had become, Juliette still realised that the only way out of this desperate phase her life had entered, was for her to be forgiving, to be lenient and understanding.

"She cheated on me," Juliette blurted out, staring at the ceiling. "Nadia. That's why she's not here. Why I'm not in Barcelona with her. Why everything is such a mess." She'd crossed the line she'd vowed not to cross the second she'd invited Sybille to her flat, and figured that this revelation wouldn't make much difference to her moral centre anymore.

"I thought as much."

Juliette didn't have the energy left to ask why Sybille's thoughts had ventured in that direction. She sighed, feeling tears well up in the back of her throat, when, suddenly, she felt a hand against hers. It wasn't an accident, because the hand grew more confident, squeezing her fingers, then slipping underneath and cradling them in its palm.

Instead of retracting her hand, Juliette sat up and faced Sybille, who'd brought their hands to her mouth and planted a kiss on one of Juliette's knuckles. Then another, until she sucked Juliette's index finger into her mouth, swirling her tongue around it.

Perhaps, if Sybille hadn't had that unflinching, promising stare, Juliette would have stopped her. Maybe if her demeanour hadn't promised a certain behaviour in bed, Juliette would have stood a chance.

"What do you want to do to me?" Juliette tested her.

Sybille let Juliette's finger slip from her lips and fixed her dark brown eyes on her. "Fuck you," Sybille said, with a hiss Juliette couldn't possibly resist. And then she surrendered.

She let Sybille push her down into the sofa, strip her of her jeans and t-shirt, until she lay staring up at her half-naked, head spinning, judgement gone.

"I need you to talk to me," Juliette said. "I need you to say it."

She watched Sybille hoist her tank top over her head, revealing a body that was twenty years younger than her own, with supple, unblemished skin, and toned muscles flexing underneath.

Sybille didn't say anything, probably the arousal getting the best of her, but Juliette needed something more than a twenty-something undressing in front of her; she always had. Nadia had understood that from the first time they'd met. But this wasn't Nadia. Sybille wasn't a stranger, but she couldn't know what made Juliette tick, not the way Nadia did after ten years together.

Nadia could make her wet with one killer glance. One that said that she saw through Juliette and all her antics. One that stripped her bare without Nadia even touching her.

"Say it," Juliette tried again, as Sybille poured her body over hers, her nipples poking hard through the fabric of her bra.

But, it seemed that, as soon as Juliette had surrendered, there was nothing left of Sybille's bravado. She didn't even come close to a light version of Nadia.

"I want you," Sybille said. "I've wanted you for so long." Her breath was hot on the skin of Juliette's neck and she was panting as though Juliette's hand had already disappeared into her panties, while all they were doing was lying on top of each other half-naked.

If this was going to happen, Juliette would have to lower her expectations, perhaps even take control herself.

"Come on," she whispered in Sybille's ear. "Let's go into the bedroom."

"Okay," Sybille groaned, and slipped off of her.

Juliette led the way, pulling Sybille behind her by the wrist. Juliette stepped out of her knickers before pushing Sybille down onto the mattress and getting rid of her shorts and undies as well.

Eager—and not getting it at all—Sybille yanked Juliette down on top of her, positioning their faces in front of each other.

"I'm going to show you and then I need you to do the same to me," Juliette said while staring deep into Sybille eyes, hoping this would help Sybille get it.

"I've done this before, boss," Sybille smirked, and then Juliette knew it was a lost cause.

Juliette had two options: give Sybille the one-night stand with her boss she wanted, or nip this frolicking session that wasn't going anywhere for her in the bud. It could just be tenderness, a warm body against hers, someone adoring her— all things she'd been missing of late. And Sybille wasn't Nadia. Wasn't that, also, an important point?

"What's wrong?" Sybille asked, her face suddenly so vulnerable, the desire inside of her laid bare in her eyes.

To be wanted like this. Juliette surrendered again. "Nothing." She kissed Sybille, their lips parting, and pressed her pussy against Sybille's thigh.

CLAIRE

Claire had spent the better part of her day off chained to her bed, not something she'd ever expected that piece of furniture to be used for when she had purchased it years ago. Now, she lay with her head on Margot's chest, listening to the pitter-patter of her heart.

"My parents have been asking about you," Margot said, out of the blue.

"Your parents?" Claire talked to her own parents so infrequently, she figured Margot would barely be a blip on their radar.

"We're very close."

"Don't tell me you and your mum kickbox together," Claire joked. Her head bopped up and down with Margot's chuckle.

"I'm serious. We're very open about everything in my family. They'll want to meet you sooner rather than later." Margot's hand trailed along Claire's spine.

"Do they know you tie me up?" Claire was flattered that Margot would already want to introduce her to her parents, but, even by lesbian standards, it was a bit quick.

"We do have the common decency to not talk about what goes on in the bedroom." Claire couldn't see Margot's face, but her voice sounded free of irony.

Claire pushed herself up from her comfortable spot on

Margot's chest to look her in the eyes. "You're serious," she said, when she saw the grave expression on Margot's face.

"I know it's quick, but they know how much I suffered after Inez, and I guess I just want to show them that they can stop worrying now."

"What do you propose?" Claire hadn't done the meet-the-parents thing in years.

"Dinner at their place. Maybe next weekend?"

"Okay, but promise me one thing." Claire pressed her nose against Margot's neck. "When we're there, the four of us all sitting cosily around the dinner table, when your phone or beeper goes off, you won't answer and dash off."

"What? You can't handle some conversation with two very friendly old-age pensioners?" With that, as if to prove Claire's point, Margot's phone beeped.

"For crying out loud." Claire let her head crash on Margot's shoulder. "I dare you to ignore it."

"I'm not on call. It's probably nothing." Margot was already reaching for the device on the bedside table—she could never keep it more than a few feet away from her. She looked at Claire for an instant. "I'm sorry. You must understand that in my line of work—"

Claire shook her head. "It's fine." She couldn't help a smile from forming on her lips. "Of course I understand." She watched Margot as she grabbed her phone and read the message, her face drawing into a worried expression for a fraction of a second.

"What is it?" Claire asked. "Do you have to go?"

"No, it's nothing." Margot placed the phone on the night-stand again.

"Didn't look like nothing to me," Claire teased.

"It was Inez. She starts tomorrow. She says she's 'looking forward to working with me'."

"Oh." Claire sat up and intertwined her fingers with Margot's. "That must be hard. You haven't seen her in how long?" She tried to let the supportive girlfriend get the upper hand over the slightly jealous one.

"I saw her last week at the hospital. Briefly. She was—"

"You saw her?" Jealousy was about to win. "You didn't say." Claire dropped Margot's hand from hers.

"It was just for a minute." Margot reached for Claire's hand again. "I told you. For me, when it's over, it's really over. You can trust me."

"Why didn't you tell me that you saw her?" Claire couldn't help herself. "I thought you were all about openness, you know, raised that way and everything."

"I didn't think it was important enough to mention." Margot gazed into her eyes. "Are we all right?"

"Yes, of course we are," Claire said, but wasn't entirely sure of her statement, not because of her own feelings towards Margot, which were more than clear enough, but because of the paranoia cropping up in her mind.

"Good." Margot brought Claire's hand to her mouth and pressed a kiss on her palm. "Because there's absolutely nothing to worry about."

"I do trust you, you know." Claire had to admit to herself that she hadn't met anyone as trustworthy as Margot in a long time, but she had yet to be introduced to Inez and she couldn't be sure about her motives and aspirations.

NADIA

Nadia booked herself on an earlier flight back to Paris. She'd had enough of her solo Barcelona experience. All she wanted was to go home—not to her temporary guest room at Margot's, but to her and Juliette's home. Maybe she believed it because she desperately wanted to, but she was convinced that beneath the person Juliette had become—Nadia had let her become—the woman she had met ten years ago was in hiding, waiting for her moment to shine again.

Only now, after re-visiting a small but vital piece of their past, did Nadia fully understand how much her sleeping with another woman had hurt Juliette—despite the reasons why and all the other repercussions.

Nadia had claimed another as her own, thus discarding Juliette completely because the one thing that they'd always shared, no matter what, was that connection, that deep understanding of one another, in the bedroom.

Juliette had tried to tell her several times and Nadia had been the one who had refused to listen. She'd told her when she was practically begging her to move back in—"This is who we are, babe," she had said—and she'd told her again after Nadia had confessed to her dalliance with the consultant. Because in their relationship, in matters like this, Nadia was in charge. And when Nadia cheated, she might as well have said that it was all over. Not worth even bothering anymore. Dead.

Nadia had been too angry with Juliette to see. This new version of Juliette who, with the passing of time and the negligence that comes with taking each other for granted for too long, had morphed into someone Nadia hadn't particularly liked anymore.

Nadia had let her slip. She'd disturbed the delicate balance of their relationship, unknowingly assuming that years spent together equalled change. Some things would never change, like Juliette's need for her. Nadia couldn't possibly hold that against her, despite having done so for the past year. It was the main reason why they were together, the thing that linked them more than any other.

Nadia knew this now and, in that respect, despite having been incredibly lonely, this trip had served a purpose. She was going to get her woman back.

When the flight attendant offered her a glass of champagne, Nadia refused, wanting to keep a clear head. When she landed in Paris, four hours earlier than the flight Juliette had booked for the two of them, she inhaled the summer air, confident, for the first time in weeks, that with patience and the acceptance of some hard truths, she could convince Juliette to give their relationship the clean slate it needed—and deserved.

———

It still felt strange to ring the bell to the apartment that half of her own money had bought, but Nadia could hardly use her key and walk in as if everything was normal. She didn't even know if Juliette was home, but she heard stumbling noises on the other side of the door soon enough after the bell had chimed. It took a while before Juliette opened the door to a crack. She looked as if she'd quickly thrown on some clothes, as if she'd been sleeping.

"Hey," Nadia said. "Can we talk?"

"Erm, now?" Juliette said, hesitantly, checking her wrist for a watch that wasn't there.

Nadia arched up her eyebrows. She hadn't really expected to be the most welcome of guests, but at least to be invited into her own home for a few minutes. "Is this a bad time? Were you asleep?"

"Yeah. Sort of," Juliette mumbled, her cheeks as flushed as Nadia had ever seen them.

"Are you all right?" Nadia took a step forward. "Can I just come in for a brief moment? I won't take up too much of your time, I promise, but I really need to say this." She heard noises coming from behind Juliette's back.

"Now really is not a good time," Juliette tried.

"Do you have company?" Nadia looked Juliette over. She didn't appear dressed to have guests in the flat. Unless… Nadia took another step closer and, despite Juliette trying to hold it shut as much as possible, pushed the door open.

She stood face to face with Sybille, half-dressed in a bra and a pair of khaki shorts. Nadia wasn't sure if she felt anything at all. Or maybe it was just shock. She turned back to Juliette.

"In our home?" She looked away and craned her head to scan the hallway for more evidence. "In our own bed?" She glanced at Sybille, who had picked up a top from the living room floor and slipped it over her head. "With your secretary?"

All the hope that had been building inside Nadia since her epiphany in Barcelona, the speech she had prepared in her head during the flight, and her clearly wrongly drawn conclusion that Juliette needed her, transformed into a mute rage that only allowed her to storm out and slam the door behind her, the image of Juliette's perplexed face burned into her brain.

Her suitcase waited for her outside and Nadia grabbed it while stabbing the elevator button furiously. She couldn't get away from their home—now forever tainted—fast enough.

Maybe there really was nothing left to fight for, after all.

EPISODE FOUR

MARGOT

Margot had truly believed she'd been honest about her feelings for Inez belonging to the past, but now that she stood face-to-face with her for the first time in a year for more than a brief minute, she wasn't so sure. She quickly recovered and pushed away the uninvited, random memories that popped up in her brain. If they were going to work together, she'd need to get better at that.

Besides, she was in love with Claire.

"Can we talk some time today?" Inez asked. "Just for a few minutes. To clear the air."

"As far as I'm concerned, there's no air to clear." Did Inez really think she could dash in here with her charm and pretend she never left?

"Come on, Go-Go." There used to be a time when these words combined with a lop-sided grin—and perhaps the sun illuminating a few freckles on Inez' nose—would work wonders on Margot, as if dissolving any stubbornness or opposition to a crazy idea on her part, but that time was long gone. "How about lunch?"

"I'm having lunch with my girlfriend." Margot looked Inez over, hoping her icy stare wouldn't miss its effect. She even found Inez' hair, as well as, basically, her entire presence, offensive. It was too bright, too fiery. Too much.

"Fair enough." The grin didn't disappear from Inez' face. "I know you well enough to take my time with you, Go-Go, and I'm not going anywhere." Inez winked and walked out of the on-call room.

Margot only saw the back of Inez' white coat as she dashed off, but she could easily imagine the smile plastered on her ex' face. She'd soon charm the entire hospital with it.

As she made her way behind Inez, taking smaller steps than usual to keep her distance, her phone buzzed in her pocket.

"Hey, how's it going?" Claire asked.

"Fine." It wasn't really a lie. Margot could have hoped to be completely unaffected by Inez' return, but it had never been a realistic expectation. It would always have stung a little.

"I'm afraid I can't do lunch." Claire sighed, not enquiring further about Inez. "The office is in shambles again."

"What happened?" Margot could not possibly fathom how Barbier & Cyr still turned a profit with all the dramatic shenanigans going on on its office floor, and she probably only knew half of it.

"I'm not sure, but Juliette has finally cracked. She's not coming in today and I have to take some of her meetings."

Margot couldn't help but roll her eyes—Claire couldn't see her anyway. "Okay. I'll try to come over tonight, but I'll check on Nadia first, just in case."

They rang off and Margot glanced at her watch. She didn't have the luxury of time for more lesbian drama. Her first surgery of the day started in exactly seven minutes.

At the other end of the corridor, by the ER nurses station, she spotted Alice, the usually quite stern head nurse, doubled over in laughter, Inez by her side.

It was going to be a long day.

CLAIRE

Claire tried calling Juliette again. She'd only sent her a brief text message that morning, lacking any clarification as to why she couldn't come to work. Claire could probably get most of the information she needed for today's meetings from Sybille, but she hadn't yet shown up either. More than that, she just wanted to make sure Juliette was all right.

After the sixth try, Juliette finally picked up. "Oui," was all she said.

"Jules? What's going on? Are you sick?"

Silence at the other end of the line.

"You're freaking me out." Claire didn't know what to think. "Jules?"

"Can you come over?" Maybe it was a bad connection, but Claire could swear Juliette was sobbing at the other end of it.

"Of course," Claire said, because, in the end, meetings could be rescheduled while friendship could not. "I'll be there soon."

After asking Fred to rearrange her schedule and coordinate with Sybille, when she finally arrived, to postpone Juliette's appointments, Claire walked from the Barbier & Cyr office to Juliette and Nadia's apartment building. It was only a good ten minutes downhill. The weather was sunny and traffic would only be dying down to its summer slump in two weeks, and taking a taxi would have been foolish.

Her mind wandered to two weeks from now. Like every year, she'd be going to her family's summer house in Gordes for a week—about the only time she spent more than two days in a row with her parents and her brother's family. After the key debacle, she'd thought it too soon to ask Margot to join—even if only for a weekend—but now that she was destined to meet Margot's parents in the near future, she might reconsider. Still, she wasn't entirely certain the early stages of their affair could bear the dysfunctions of the Cyr family.

She would wait to see how meeting Margot's parents went

before inviting her to meet Gaston and Léonie Cyr, worried that introducing level-headed, logical Margot to her borderline crazy family would put her girlfriend off.

————

Juliette looked as if she'd drunk a barrel of wine over the long weekend. She opened the door dressed in a robe and slippers, ushering Claire in.

"Jesus, Jules." Claire walked into the darkened living room, the curtains drawn. "Who died?"

"My decency, for one." Juliette crashed down into the sofa, her robe falling open at the chest. She wore nothing underneath. It didn't show anything Claire hadn't seen before, but it still made her feel uncomfortable.

"Tell me." Claire sat down opposite Juliette and scanned her face. Her skin was blotched and her eyes red-rimmed.

"I don't even know where to start." Clearly, Juliette couldn't look Claire in the eyes. "You know how I often give you a hard time about sleeping with Steph that one time years ago?" She briefly glanced up at Claire, before looking away again.

Claire nodded. "Well-deserved on my part."

"I slept with Sybille." It came out as a sigh. "Nadia came home early from Barcelona and as good as caught us in the act."

Claire's mouth fell open. She tried to process the information, but it wouldn't compute in her brain.

"I'm so sorry," Juliette continued. "I've not been myself lately. It's all just been too much. I was drunk and she was here and I wasn't thinking straight." She shook her head. "And Nadia… the look on her face." Juliette swallowed hard. "I'll never forget that look on her face." Unexpectedly, she snickered. "And before you ask, the sex was definitely not worth it. I can't even begin to tell you." She huffed out some air. "All I could think of throughout was Nadia and then, out of the blue, she shows up. How fucking ironic is that?"

Claire still didn't know what to say. She just looked at Juliette in utter surprise. Maybe she should become a doctor's wife and retire from all the drama.

JULIETTE

Juliette had never seen Claire this speechless. "I can control Sybille," she heard herself say. "She has a girlfriend anyway and I certainly won't be going back for more." It was as if she was watching herself act in a play, delivering words that had been prepared for her. "But I fear, after the hard time I was giving Nadia about what she did, I've lost her forever." Juliette thought about the look of perplexed contempt on Nadia's face.

"Jesus Christ." Claire seemed to have found the power of speech again. "I honestly don't know what to say to that."

"You don't have to say anything, but I wanted to tell you as soon as possible, I—" Then the shame returned, engulfing Juliette in ice cold waves. "I'm sorry."

"It's not me you should apologise to, Jules." Claire's voice was soft, almost too gentle for Juliette to bear—definitely much gentler than she deserved. "How you handle Sybille is up to you, as long as it doesn't have any effect on business, but, well, I can hardly judge you on that." She shuffled to the edge of her seat. "But Nadia… was it revenge?"

Juliette couldn't feel more mortified, sitting in her obscured flat with her best friend, debating whether the sex she'd had with her assistant the night before was revenge for what Nadia had done or not. On a Tuesday morning, no less, when they both should have been at work instead.

"It was a big, giant mistake and that's all it was." Juliette remembered how the craving for human contact, for someone to wrap their arms around her, had so easily won out in the end. "There's no place for revenge in a relationship, not if it's a good one." With all the strength she could muster, she straightened her posture and looked Claire directly in the eyes. "I'm sorry for dragging you all the way over here. I was feeling particularly sorry for myself."

"It's me, Jules, you don't have to put up a front for me." The smile on Claire's face made Juliette feel even more guilty.

"I have to, for myself." She rose from the sofa. "What am I going to do? Sit around here all day and mope?" She walked to the window and pulled the curtains open, squinting against the sudden hit of sunlight.

"You should talk to Nadia. Don't wait too long."

Juliette sighed. "I'll try." She leaned against the windowsill. "Come here," she said. "Please."

She watched Claire get up from her seat and head in her direction. Good old Claire. She always looked so composed, so impeccable. Juliette opened her arms wide and waited for her best friend's embrace. She had hurt Claire badly once as well. Not intentionally—they just weren't right for each other as lovers—but nonetheless, she'd caused her pain.

"Next time you need a hug," Claire whispered in her ear, "call me first."

That's when Juliette broke down, at last. She'd cried the night before, but not with heaving, freeing sobs like this. Not on Claire's shoulder. Not in the arms of her best friend.

"I'll take care of things in the office. Go see Nadia. Make it right." It sounded simple—almost doable—when Claire said it, but Juliette knew that, now that the tables had turned again, Nadia wouldn't give her the time of day.

NADIA

"You were dead right about Sybille," Nadia said to Steph. She'd had the entire night to process, a long, sleepless one, tossing and turning in Margot's guest room. She'd have to do something about her living situation as well, make it more permanent. "She got her way already."

Opposite her, Steph narrowed her eyes—it looked more like sharpening her claws. "What do you mean?"

"I booked an earlier flight back from Barcelona, determined to get Juliette back—or to at least have an adult conversation with her for once—only to find Sybille half-naked in our flat. *After* the act." Nadia had tried to wipe the memory of Sybille's sudden appearance behind Juliette from her brain, but the more she tried, the more images of the young, still perfectly-sculpted girl crowded her mind. "I know I have no claims to make, what with what I did, but… in our bed, Steph? She brought her into our home."

Steph shook her head. "I knew it. I fucking knew it." She hunched over the table they were supposed to have lunch at, neither one of them touching their food. "You can't let this come between you and Jules. That's exactly what she wants. Little b —" Steph stopped before pronouncing the word.

"It's not even that, anymore." With every step she'd taken away from their flat, any trace of fighting spirit had left Nadia. "Look at us. There *is* no us anymore. It's all gone too far. We've hurt each other too much. It's ridiculous, really."

"Don't say that, Nadz." Steph pinned her blue eyes on Nadia. "It must hurt, but—"

"It's over." Nadia shoved her sandwich further away from her, feeling queasy at the sight of it. "I'm done assigning blame. I'm done trying to explain myself and, mostly, I think we've hurt each other enough." Dread rose like bile from her stomach. "Sometimes, it just doesn't work out."

"No, no, no…" Steph's voice rose, as if the mere intensity of it could make Nadia change her mind—or any of the events that had led her to this conclusion. "Juliette needs you, Nadz. You must know that."

"She used to." Nadia knew that much, but Juliette hadn't really needed her in years. She'd gone her own way.

"What if you hadn't found her with Sybille." Steph kept

pushing, seemingly much more willing to do battle for their relationship than Juliette and Nadia were.

"But I did, and that's just it." She held up her hands. "Cause and consequence... I might as well have deposited Sybille in our bed myself." Nadia couldn't be sure, but she suspected that Juliette's reasons for bedding her assistant were just as escapist as hers had been when she'd ended up between the sheets with Marie Dievart. "Even if we say stop now—start acting like adults at last—we can't just erase the past." Nadia was hardly so naive to believe that Juliette sleeping with someone else could undo the fact that she had done the exact same thing. "This is a mess we can't untangle, a wound so deep we can't possibly recover from it." Saying the words like that, stating them, made it seem logical and acceptable, but the despair straining in every cell of Nadia's body—causing her actual physical pain—was far from acceptable.

After the conclusion she'd drawn on the flight home, Nadia saw everything that had happened between her and Juliette as her own failure. She should have stood up for them when they still had a chance. Now, it was too late.

"Ten years, Nadz," Steph murmured, as if Nadia needed reminding.

STEPH

Steph felt the demise of her friends' relationship in her bones, like a sharp, cold ache she couldn't shake. She walked back to the office, not even having the energy to be pissed off at Sybille. For a split second, she considered a detour. A quick stop at the Palais Bourbon. She'd welcome a hug from Dominique's arms, but that was just another impossibility amassed along the way.

Fuck it. Steph walked past the street where the Barbier & Cyr office was located and proceeded along the Champs-Élysées, all the way to the Place de la Concorde, and crossed the Seine until she stood outside the Palais Bourbon. She worked for Dominique—as plausible a reason as any to drop by.

"You're not on the schedule," Germaine, Dominique's secretary, said. Steph knew her first name, although Madame Moreau wasn't aware of that.

"I know. I'm so sorry." Steph could be extremely polite, and utterly charming, when she needed to be. "The last thing I want to do is complicate your life, Madame Moreau." She shot her a flirting smile. "I just need three minutes, that's it." Steph canted her head to the left a bit while arching up one eyebrow.

"What's it regarding?" Germaine didn't flinch.

"I wish I could tell you, but, well, with the divorce and everything… it's delicate." Steph tried a conspiratorial tone. "Not really for saying out loud in corridors." She winked at Germaine, hoping to appeal to the conspirator inside of her.

"She's not in." Germaine glanced at her screen. "Lunch with Monsieur Laroche." It was as if her features stiffened when she spoke of Dominique's father. "But you can wait if you want. She should have a few minutes to spare when she gets back."

First hurdle taken. Steph mentally high-fived herself. *And Germaine was a formidable one.*

She'd only just sat down in one of the two visitors chairs when Steph heard footsteps approach, accompanied by what could only be Dominique's laugh, although it sounded very forced and much more high-pitched than usual. Germaine shot up from behind her desk, adjusting her skirt and putting a hand to her stiffly hair-sprayed coiffure.

"Monsieur Laroche," she said. "Quelle surprise."

Steph glanced up and looked straight in the face of the notorious Xavier Laroche.

"Madame Moreau," he said, in a rich, deep baritone of a voice. He hugged Germaine as if she was a long lost family member.

Steph caught Dominique's eye, but she kept her face expressionless and her limbs stiff, not showing any signs of recognition.

The entire space seemed filled with Xavier Laroche's presence. Steph had seen him on TV, but never paid much attention. In real life, though, he simply couldn't be ignored. *That's where Dominique got her effortless charm.*

"And who have we here?" Laroche Senior turned to Steph, who automatically, as if pulled up by invisible strings, rose from her chair.

"Stéphanie Mathis. Barbier & Cyr." She extended her hand and Laroche squeezed it firmly. "Enchantée."

"We have a meeting, Papa." Dominique finally acknowledged Steph's presence.

"All right, all right," he said, broadening his chest, "but you can't blame your retired dad for wanting to visit his old stomping ground." He painted a wide, confident smile on his face. "I'll go browse around." As if Xavier Laroche ever casually browsed around anywhere. "Pleasure to have made your acquaintance, Madame Mathis." He turned to Germaine. "Madame Moreau." He nodded at Dominique's secretary. "Goodbye, darling." He pressed a quick kiss on Dominique's cheek and turned to leave.

Dominique waited to speak until his footsteps had died down to soft thuds—the three of them standing around like frozen cartoon characters. "What can I do for you, Stéphanie?" The harsh tone with which she addressed her cut right through Steph, adding a chill to her already frozen bones.

"You could invite me into your office." Steph tried to keep her voice steady.

"I told her you had a few minutes, Madame Laroche," Germaine interjected. "I hope that's all right."

"Two minutes." Dominique led the way to her office.

Steph felt like a wrongfully scolded child. She followed Dominique into her office and closed the door behind her.

"What the hell are you doing here?" Dominique started. "You can't just barge in here at your convenience."

Any hope of finding comfort in Dominique's presence quickly escaped Steph. "At *my* convenience?" It wasn't so much anger that flared beneath Steph's skin than the gloomy sensation of her needs being completely ignored.

"That was my father." Dominique didn't pay any attention to what Steph said. "Do you have any idea what would happen if he found out?"

"What would happen, Dominique? Really? Would the sky come crashing down? Would French politics be doomed forever? Would the citizens of this country suffer irreparable damage after discovering that their favourite right-wing chick likes to eat pussy?"

Dominique glared at her from behind her desk, a vein throbbing in her neck. "Get out," she said. "I won't be spoken to like that. Not even by you."

"My fucking pleasure." Steph tried to compose herself before exiting Dominique's office, but she was fed up with pretending. She slammed the door behind her and, ignoring Madame Moreau, took a deep breath before finding the gates of the Palais Bourbon.

"Madame Mathis?" She heard Germaine call behind her. "Ça va, Madame Mathis?"

She stood outside, on the sidewalk in front of the building, seething with anger. Dominique had taken enough from her and Stéphanie Mathis was nobody's toy to play with as they saw fit.

JULIETTE

Juliette hadn't seen or spoken to Sybille since she'd asked her to leave after Nadia had slammed the door to their flat. She'd received numerous text messages the day after and let them all go unanswered because what could she possibly have replied?

As expected, Sybille was already there when she arrived at the office on Wednesday morning, a bright smile glued to her face.

"Bonjour, Juliette," she said, and her voice grated on her nerves so much, Juliette wondered if she'd be able to keep on employing her. But, in fairness, the girl had done nothing wrong. She had tried and succeeded—and maybe she shouldn't have—but Juliette could hardly blame her for that. Juliette was the boss and, ultimately, she was responsible.

"Could you come in for a second, please?" Juliette tried to keep her face neutral.

"Bien sûr." Sybille eagerly rose from her chair. "Coffee?"

"That's all right." Not that Juliette couldn't use it, after another sleepless night, but she wanted to get this conversation over and done with.

Sybille followed her into the office, closed the door behind her and sat down.

Juliette cleared her throat, chastising herself for needing to sit through this talk. "I'm sorry for what happened on Monday and asking you to leave so abruptly, but honestly, it was a mistake. I drank too much and it should never have happened." Juliette felt like such a mid-life cliché.

"I'm not sorry," Sybille was quick to say. "Not one bit."

Juliette had feared as much. She proceeded without acknowledging Sybille's feelings and the pleading look in her eyes. "I can't guarantee this won't come out. I had to tell Claire, obviously, but I want you to know this won't affect your position at Barbier & Cyr."

"You know you can trust me, Juliette." Sybille fiddled with her fingers. "I've never told anyone about Stéphanie and Laroche and I won't tell anyone about us."

"I know. I really appreciate that, Sybille." Trying to keep her voice level, Juliette went in for the kill. "But you must understand that what we did on Monday can never happen again."

"And *you* must understand," Sybille leaned forward a bit, "that there are no limits to what I would do for you."

"What about your girlfriend?" Juliette couldn't help herself. Throughout all of this, there had been no mention of Sybille's mysterious, well-off partner.

Sybille just shrugged. "Let *me* worry about that." She didn't look particularly worried about that aspect of her life.

"Just to be clear, Sybille." Juliette couldn't suppress a sigh she hated herself for. "We do understand each other?"

"You're upset, shocked and conflicted. I understand." Sybille brought a finger to her chin. "And I'll be here whenever you need me, and I'll still be here when you get over all of the things you need to get over."

"That's not what I mean—" Juliette stopped mid-sentence, watching Sybille get up and plant her palms on the side of the desk, leaning over so Juliette could get a good look at her ample cleavage.

"But you know what *I* mean." She smiled a smile that could either be interpreted as shy or knowing. Juliette knew exactly which one it was, but she was no push-over—not today and when sober, anyway—and she had to nip this in the bud. Nor did she have any desire to share a bed with her assistant ever again.

"It will not happen again, Sybille."

Sybille straightened her posture and took a few steps in the direction of the door. "Of course not," she said, before turning to open it. Her words conveying one thing, while her tone spoke of an entirely different conviction.

Of all the people Juliette could have slept with. She watched the closed door, suddenly consumed by a deep understanding of why Steph had chosen to sleep with Dominique Laroche. Sometimes it wasn't a choice. Sometimes it was a compulsion, or a mere opportunity.

She called Steph's direct line and asked her to come to her

office immediately. She had to tell her, if she hadn't already heard from Nadia.

As soon as Steph closed the door behind herself, she said, "You have to get rid of her, Jules. If you don't, she *will* destroy you."

Evidently, she already knew.

"Let's not exaggerate, shall we?" Juliette gestured at a chair. "Please, sit."

"I know you don't believe me and you think I have a beef with her over that picture she shot of me, but it's not just that." Steph was adamant. "You're my friend. I care about you and I care about this firm. That girl is bad news. If she doesn't get what she wants, she will take you down."

"What is this? A revenge B-movie?" Juliette was more interested in finding out about Nadia, who Steph had clearly spoken to. "I'll be careful, Steph, I promise." Only now did Juliette notice the wide, dark circles under Steph's eyes and the paler-than-usual complexion of her skin. "Is this keeping you awake at night as well?"

Steph sighed, her body sagging into the chair. "There's you and Nadia, and Dominique and I had a fight, and…" Exasperated, she let her arms fall over the armrests of the chair.

Juliette knew she was being insensitive, but she had no desire to butt into Steph and Dominique's clandestine love life. "What did Nadia say?"

"I'm not doing this, Jules. You're my boss, but you're both my friends and I can't pick sides or convey messages. You're both grown-ups and you can do your own legwork." Steph regarded her with a stern glance for a second. "But obviously, she's shattered by the whole situation. Go see her, Jules. Don't wait."

Juliette wondered what her life had become if she was now taking relationship advice from Steph. Then her phone started ringing, reminding her this was a work place. Juliette picked up.

"Dominique Laroche is here to see Steph." The sarcasm in Sybille's voice was impossible to ignore.

"Your girlfriend's here," Juliette said to Steph.

"What?"

"Laroche. She's here to see you."

Steph shot up out of her chair, hurrying towards the door. "Thanks," she mumbled, in a very un-Steph-like fashion, before exiting Juliette's office, leaving her alone with her thoughts.

STEPH

Steph didn't have a meeting planned with Dominique, but, after their short but hurtful disagreement the day before, she could easily guess why the députée had shown up unannounced at Barbier & Cyr. She went by reception, where she found Dominique waiting for her. Most of the anger she had felt the day before had transformed into the sadness that comes with a blunt reality check.

Without saying anything, Dominique followed Steph to her office. It took a few seconds after Steph had closed the door behind them for her to start speaking. She gestured at a chair, but Dominique remained standing.

"You," she said, glaring at Steph, and shaking her head. "I'm sorry. My father always rubs me up the wrong way." She put a hand to the navy blouse tucked tightly into her light-grey pencil skirt, just under her cleavage. "I'm sorry for asking you to leave. When he's around, I seem to have a bit of a temper."

Steph had wanted to stay angry at Dominique, just to make things easier. "I'm sorry for pronouncing the word 'pussy' in your office, but, in my defence, I'm sure it wasn't the first time." She couldn't help it. That scowl on Dominique's face had to disappear.

The tightness around Dominique's lips slackened. She approached the chair on the other side of Steph's desk while checking her watch. "I really don't have time for this." She looked up at Steph. "And obviously I shouldn't be here, but I guess I just can't stay away." Dominique sat down and glanced at Steph, who stood leaning against the side of her desk, only inches away from Dominique.

The nearness of her morphed Steph's insides into a fire pit, a flaming pool of nothingness where every sense of logic disappeared and left only dirty ashes. It was impossible for her to be strong in Dominique's presence. Her brain knew exactly what needed to be done, because, now that they'd had their first weeks together, situations like the one in Dominique's office would probably become more regular, taxing their... their what? Their love for each other?

"How can something that is such a bad idea, feel so damn good?" Steph asked.

Dominique sat motionless and mute, staring up at her, and in her glance, Steph saw that she felt exactly the same way. Dominique uncrossed her legs and pushed herself up out of the chair, facing Steph at eye-level.

"The smart thing to do, would be to end it," she said, in the voice she used for TV interviews, when she really wanted to leave an impression. She didn't touch Steph, just stood there, occupying most of her personal space.

The fire in Steph's belly turned to a hot, quickly descending, throb.

"Then end it," Steph said. "Walk away." She realised that, because of this, because of the fire and the attraction, they'd barely ever had a real conversation. Dominique hardly knew anything about Steph's life. She didn't know that Steph didn't do this. She kept things casual and easy. She protected herself.

"Who hurt you?" Dominique asked, her face so close, Steph felt her breath pass across her cheeks.

"What?" Steph hadn't seen that question coming. She curled her fingers around the wooden top of her desk.

"Someone must have scarred you pretty good along the way for you to hang out with the likes of me." Dominique started leaning against Steph, their pelvis making contact first. "What do you get out of this, Stéphanie? I ask you to hide, to make up lies about me, to pretend this isn't happening, and you still stick around."

"I see what you're trying to do." A flash of anger crackled through Steph's brain. "You're trying to make me push you away." Steph shook her head, but kept her eyes on Dominique's. "Coward."

"Would I be here if I were a coward?" Dominique pressed her pelvis harder against Steph's. "Maybe you're the coward." She brought her lips to Steph's ear. "Maybe you want to be in the shadows. Maybe you want a relationship that can't really be one, just so you don't have to call it a relationship."

Steph grabbed Dominique by the shoulders and pushed her away from her pulsing body. She wasn't sure if her flesh was throbbing with desire or anger—probably a mixture of both. "Walk away," she said, unsure if she meant it.

"How can I, Stéphanie? We have a meeting tomorrow, remember?"

Steph should have known better than to challenge Dominique. Rising to challenges was basically what she did for a living.

"One week." Steph held up a finger. "One week of only professional contact. You don't text me, you don't summon me, you don't send me pictures of your cleavage." She pushed herself away from the desk. "Then we'll see who comes crawling back."

Dominique chuckled. "Are you breaking up with me, Stéphanie?"

"No, I'm saying *you* can't break up with me."

Dominique took a step closer, tilting her head before finding Steph's cheek with her lips. "You'd make an excellent politician. Do you know that?" she whispered in Steph's ear, before ducking down to grab her briefcase from the floor, turning on her heels, and leaving.

257

Steph didn't really know what had just happened. Had they broken up? Gone on hiatus?

She didn't have time to ponder the questions racing in her mind for too long. She had a briefing to prepare, in which she would explain to her bosses what her brilliant plan was to make Dominique Laroche win the elections unscathed by the news of her divorce. And her secret lesbian lover.

MARGOT

"This weekend, I'll start looking for my own place to live." Nadia scooped a large portion of spaghetti carbonara onto a plate for Margot—clearly fighting heartache with carbs.

"You can stay here as long as you like. I hope you know that." Margot glanced at Claire, who suspiciously eyed the mountain of pasta Nadia had served her. "Claire has given me the key to her flat already, anyway." Margot was desperate to inject some lightness into their dinner conversation, although it really wasn't one of her specialties.

"Moving fast, I see." Nadia sat down. "You'll be booking that U-Haul in no time."

"Are you serious, Nadz?" Claire didn't appear to be in the mood for light conversation. "About finding your own place, not about the U-Haul."

Nadia poured herself a large glass of red wine before she replied. "What choice do I have?"

"Just give it some more time."

The conversation was going in the exact opposite direction than Margot had hoped. She'd had a rough day at work—a rough few days, actually—adjusting to Inez' presence. She'd, wrongly, believed that inviting Claire for dinner with her and Nadia would have brightened the atmosphere. Now, she was tempted to go for another glass of wine as well, despite already having had two—her usual weekday limit—while Nadia was preparing dinner.

"Time for what?" Despite having cooked it, Nadia seemed quite reluctant to eat her dish. She'd been having a lot of liquid dinners, of late. Another conversation Margot dreaded. "Another round of cheating?"

Margot twirled some spaghetti around her fork, drowning out the conversation. If a new element were to find its way into the great Juliette and Nadia saga, she was sure she'd hear about it. Multiple times.

Maybe other people could come home to this after three surgeries, of which one didn't end well, and listen to endless, going-around-in-circles conversation, but Margot wasn't one of those people. Especially now that Inez had returned, to Saint-Vincent of all places, adding even more stress to Margot's life.

Claire seemed like an extension of Juliette, fighting her best friend's battle for her, in Margot's home. All the while, Margot was convinced that Juliette and Nadia wouldn't solve any of their differences as long as they couldn't be in the same room together for at least thirty minutes without fighting.

"Is she going to Steph's birthday party on Saturday?" Nadia asked. This question made Margot tune in again.

"Of course she is," Claire said, before turning to Margot. "I forgot to tell you. Are you on call?"

Secretly, Margot wished she was, because there was no way that party could ever end well. "No, I'm free."

"You'd better tell Juliette not to bring her new girlfriend. Steph hates her," Nadia said.

Here we go again. "Where's the party?" Margot asked, wanting to change the topic.

"L'Univers. Steph's most-frequented hang-out, apart from Les Pêches," Claire said.

A loud, crowded bar in Le Marais was not Margot's favourite place to be on a free Saturday night, but she'd go for Claire's sake.

"Don't forget dinner at my parents on Sunday," she addressed Claire, who had some cheese sticking to her chin.

"Moving even faster," Nadia said, plastering a smile on her lips for the first time that evening. *If that's what it took.*

"I'm not nervous at all," Claire said, reaching for the bottle of wine. "No biggie."

"They'll love you. How can they not?" Margot held out her glass for a refill.

CLAIRE

Under normal circumstances, Claire would have looked forward to a party like the one she was headed towards, but normal seemed far away as she walked into L'Univers on Margot's arm. Nadia and Juliette were barely on speaking terms. Steph had to celebrate her birthday without Dominique, who she clearly cared for, and Claire was having dinner with Margot's parents the next day. Despite that being a positive direction for their relationship to go in, Margot had been more quiet than usual the past week, more lost in thoughts, some sort of darkness brooding in her eyes. Claire couldn't shake the feeling it had something to do with Inez, but she wouldn't bring up the subject as long as Margot didn't.

"This is such a train wreck waiting to happen," Margot whispered in her ear as they made their way to Steph's table. Steph was flanked by Fred and a girl Claire had never seen before, but who seemed to know Steph intimately, the way she draped her arm over Steph's shoulder possessively. *That wouldn't last long.*

After hugging and congratulating Steph and being offered a glass of champagne, they sat down around the table. Claire was glad to get a few moments of respite before Nadia and Juliette arrived, which would surely sour the mood. She eyed Steph, who came across as happy enough, nothing in her demeanour betraying that she was pining for someone who wasn't there— on the contrary. She whispered something in the girl's ear. She had introduced her as Cassandra with a twinkle in her eye

Claire had taken as a well-acted front. This Steph was a far cry from the one who had sat in Juliette's office mere weeks ago, struggling, but unable to contain her feelings for Dominique.

When they'd had a meeting with Laroche earlier that week, it had been pokerfaces all around—usually not the way Claire preferred to conduct business, but in this case she had gladly made an exception.

"Who's that?" Margot asked. "I thought she was seeing that politician."

"Me too," Claire replied, "but—" She was interrupted mid-sentence by Nadia's arrival. Hot on her heels, as if they'd come together, Juliette walked into the café.

And thus the party begins.

Everybody exchanged cheek kisses, even Juliette and Nadia pecked each other on the cheek awkwardly, and then, after Juliette and Nadia had received their glasses of champagne, the silence descended.

"Oh fuck," Margot said, with a twinge of panic in her voice, breaking the silence.

"What is it?" Worried, Claire turned to her, noticing Margot's lips drawn into a stern pout. Around them, chatter broke loose—Juliette was in PR, after all, and being sociable in every circumstance was a big part of her job description. Of Claire's as well, but she was currently transfixed by Margot's reaction to something.

"That redhead over there by the entrance. That's Inez."

Claire scanned the bar until her eyes fell on a tall woman with a fiery mane of curly, shoulder-length hair. She walked towards the bar and ordered drinks from the bartender as if she knew him well. Behind her a man with a full black beard put a hand on her shoulder and whispered something.

"I guess you'd better introduce me then," Claire said, after the first shock had subsided. She'd do battle—the quiet kind, consisting of intimidating stares and possessive hand placement —if she had to.

261

Margot's body had stiffened and Claire curled an arm around her waist. Maybe she should be worried, and she was a bit, but she wasn't going to show Margot.

"Best get it out of the way before this party turns into a complete disaster." Margot had found her steady, stern voice again.

As they made their way to the corner of the bar where Inez had taken up court with the bearded man and a bunch of other people, all of them seemingly standing around her in a circle, as if in the middle of worship, Inez looked in their direction and Claire's eyes met Margot's ex's gaze for the first time. Inez' lips crinkled up into a wide smile and, while Claire had seen pictures of her on the internet and should have been prepared for this moment, the brightness of her smile and the presence that radiated from her just standing there, knocked the wind out of her briefly.

Margot squeezed her hand as they approached, but it did nothing to squash the pangs of worry making their way through Claire's brain.

Inez threw her arms wide, as if she didn't see Margot every day at work and was, only just now, meeting her for the first time again after years of absence.

"Margot," she yelled theatrically. "Quel plaisir."

"You must be Claire." She shot Claire a wink, as if they were in something undefined together, and hugged her like she was a long lost friend.

Inez introduced the bearded man as Manu and a slew of other people whose names Claire barely got. She was too busy gauging Margot's reaction, who, obviously, at some point in her life, had been very friendly with Manu. She seemed to focus her attention on him rather than on Inez, who kept chattering away.

Claire had encountered many a loudmouth through her profession, but Inez was something else. She seemed to suck all of the attention towards her. Not in a bad way, but definitely in an unmistakable one. She was one of those people who were impossible to dislike. Claire wondered if Margot had tied her to bedposts as well.

"We have to get back to our party," Margot said, after a few minutes.

"Is that Nadia?" Inez asked. "I'll come with you to say hello."

Claire hoped it wouldn't be one of those nights where different groups of people blended effortlessly, some individuals leaving the premises feeling as if they had made new friends for life. It was bad enough that Inez was part of Margot's professional life, she didn't need to worm her way into Margot's personal life as well.

They headed back into the direction of Steph's table, Inez and Manu in tow.

NADIA

As if this night isn't stressful enough. Nadia pecked Inez on the cheek, not something she would normally do with colleagues in private situations, but Inez had pressed her lips to Nadia's cheek before Nadia had a chance to do or say anything.

Nadia had no choice but to make introductions, slightly hesitating when it was Juliette's turn, her brain automatically putting the words 'my partner' in her mouth.

Steph, who'd been acting as if Dominique Laroche didn't exist, curling her arm around the girl she'd introduced as Cassandra, whispering things in her ear that made her go all gooey-eyed, shot Inez her flirty smile—a lopsided grin, accompanied by narrowed eyes and a slightly slanted head. This was definitely pre-Laroche Steph on display.

Nadia beckoned Steph and they stood as far apart from the group as their crowded quarters allowed.

"What's gotten into you?" Nadia asked. "Have you and Dominique already progressed to an open relationship?"

"We're on a break," Steph was quick to say. "And I'll be

damned if I just sit around on my, frankly, quite agile hands." She shook her fingers loose as if to prove a point.

"What happened?" Nadia looked around, at the complete shambles around her. Juliette and Claire in the middle of a forced conversation with Margot's ex. Cassandra eyeing Nadia suspiciously. Fred drooling over Manu. She and Juliette had barely exchanged a word, the pain of being in the same place as her while their relationship had turned into undefined nothingness overshadowing everything. And then there was Steph.

"It's just impossible." Steph shrugged. She held out her empty glass of champagne while Margot refilled. "And I prefer things easy."

Nadia had no arguments. If Steph could be willingly coaxed away from the disaster that her affair with Dominique would eventually end up being, she wouldn't stand in the way. She just hadn't expected it to happen so quickly and so easily, as if Laroche had just been a momentary blip on Steph's radar, there for a minute or two, but already fading out. The way Steph downed her drink betrayed a deeper malaise though.

"Happy birthday," Nadia whispered in Steph's ear before kissing her on the cheek again.

"I hope you know there's only one thing I really want for my birthday." Steph pinned her watery eyes on Nadia. Nadia had an inkling of what she was going to say, but didn't have the heart to brush Steph off. "I want you and Jules to give each other another chance. Just one break. Meet each other halfway. Talk. Whatever. Just do something to restore my faith in humanity."

"I'll try." Nadia shot Steph an encouraging smile that didn't really work out, noticing in the process, that her glass was empty again. Good thing she wouldn't be going home alone tonight. She would need someone to support her.

Spurred on by Steph's words, and even more so by the sight of Juliette, who looked as if she was desperately trying to hold on to something but wasn't quite succeeding, Nadia walked over to Juliette.

Claire, who, as a result of Nadia's intervention, would have to engage in solo conversation with Inez, didn't hesitate to give them some privacy. It felt as if all their friends were trying much harder to fix their relationship than they were.

"Please tell me the reason why Steph has her tongue in that girl's ear is because she and Dominique have wisely decided to call it quits," Juliette said, chuckling nervously.

"I think they might have, but I can't give you any guarantees." Nadia nodded in Claire's direction. "How is she holding up?"

"You know Claire, she's not that easily deterred." Juliette's eyes wandered to Inez. "But I can see why she would be worried, though."

"We should talk," Nadia said, unable to look Juliette in the eye. "Maybe tomorrow?" She focused her attention on twirling her glass around in her hands, because the desire to fling an arm around Juliette's shoulders was too big. She wanted to feel her close, smell her skin.

"Yes?" Juliette asked, as if Nadia had thrown her the biggest bone. "Would you?"

Nadia nodded, her throat closing up. She knocked back her drink before continuing. "Shall I come to the flat?" She'd never seen Juliette this small, this broken down, as if her bones had collapsed and shrunk her entire body.

"Please." Juliette shook her head. "I'm so sorry, Nadz." Her hand touched Nadia's side.

"I know," Nadia said, because it was all over Juliette's face. Nadia pondered all it had taken to get them to this point. All the betrayal, the cheating, the wounds they had inflicted on each other. All of that to have a level playing field again. Could they really rebuild something on the ruins they'd created, on everything they'd smashed with blind, brute force? "Around two?" Nadia briefly leaned into Juliette's touch, but she knew that was one mistake they shouldn't make again. She straightened her posture, causing the sad puppy look to return to Juliette's face.

"Sounds good." Juliette looked over at Claire and Inez. "I'd better go rescue Claire from her nemesis."

Nadia nodded and watched Juliette saunter off. If five minutes of conversation in which nothing was said already hurt so much, how would they ever get through the painful stuff?

STEPH

Although well on her way to being blind drunk and increasingly convinced she couldn't care less, Steph was unable to keep her eyes off the door. As if looking at it longingly would make Dominique walk through it somehow. As if she'd suddenly been transported to a world in which MLR's star députée could make an appearance in a gay bar in Le Marais without consequences.

"Je te veux," Cassandra kept whispering in her ear. *I want you.* As if that hadn't been clear since the night before when Steph had ended up at Les Pêches and, quite inebriated after downing a couple of shots, had invited Cassandra to her birthday party. At the time, she'd been convinced she couldn't face it alone.

Steph turned her face towards Cassandra and kissed her full on the lips, more to shut her up than anything else. She felt nothing. Not the usual—pre-Dominique—sense of having conquered someone, of having acquired something she really, really wanted. She certainly didn't feel the desire to undress Cassandra and find out what was hiding underneath, the thrill of discovery chasing up her spine.

"Excuse me for a second." Steph left Cassandra to her own devices and found Fred.

"That Manu is so gorgeous," was the first thing he said.

"Then by all means, go for it," Steph said dryly.

"No need for such enthusiasm, darling." Fred turned to her. "You know we do things differently than the lesbians, not that you're a typical one." He refilled her glass from another bottle that had magically appeared in the ice bucket. "Although you do seem to be off your game a bit of late. And that Cassandra doesn't seem to be doing it for you either. What's going on?"

"I guess I'm getting too old for all of this," Steph slurred.

"Age has nothing to do with it." Fred nudged her in the bicep. "I'll go with you to Les Pêches after the old-timers have left, find you someone you really want."

"I don't think so." She spotted Manu throwing backward glances at Fred. "Go on. You found your mission for the night."

"Should I take him to Le Raidd? Christophe is DJ-ing until closing time, maybe we can make it a threesome…"

There was a time when Steph couldn't get enough of listening to Fred's tales of his open relationship, which seemed so simple and uncomplicated on the surface. She'd been intrigued by it, wanting to learn as much as possible about Fred and Christophe's arrangement, mainly because it was the complete opposite of how everyone else she knew conducted their relationship. But tonight, she couldn't care less.

It was her birthday and the one person she had wanted to celebrate with was sorely missing. Not just because Steph had challenged her to a break, but even more so because Dominique would stand out in L'Univers as much as Steph would at an MLR party congress.

Steph reached for her phone in the back pocket of her jeans. *Not even a text message.* They had exchanged birth dates. Dominique's was in two weeks, and she'd be spending it on a beach on the Côte d'Azur with her children.

She felt two arms curve around her waist from behind and for a split second, a huge smile already spreading across her face, she thought it *was* Dominique. But that was impossible.

"When can we get out of here?" Cassandra whispered in her ear. "I want you more with every minute that passes."

Steph straightened her face and turned around in Cassandra's embrace. "Soon," she said, willing to settle for this girl she would never care about, anything was better than spending her birthday alone, waiting for someone who wouldn't come.

MARGOT

Margot didn't wear her heart on her sleeve and had never told anyone, not a single person on this planet, how much Inez had hurt her. She was a rational, logical person, someone who put much more stock in the brain than in the heart, and the only reason she had held on was because she knew it would pass. With time, the pain would diminish and numb to barely even being there.

The day Inez had left for Africa, Margot had stopped eating. She knew what it would do to her body, but if the food wouldn't go down, it simply wouldn't go down. And they hadn't even officially broken up then. They would try to make it work, somehow, and, despite the rationality her brain forced upon her, Margot had believed it. Because she loved Inez with every fibre of her being. She'd had no choice but to believe it.

They'd talked on Skype—often through bad connections—and made vague plans for a future they wouldn't have. A few weeks later, during which Margot had survived on the odd piece of fruit and a bowl of soup in the evening, Inez had sent her an e-mail telling her it would be better to end it, and, the real kicker, that she'd met someone else.

Margot had immediately ceased all contact, going into protective mode, but it had been too late. In the year and a half they'd been together she'd let Inez past every barrier she'd ever put up, all the way into her soul, until she had become a part of her. She'd revelled in her presence, blossomed into a person she never thought she could be.

When all of that had been brusquely taken away, Margot had felt as if a part of her had been taken as well. As their affair had progressed, Margot had started to believe she could make Inez stay. She wasn't the type of person to ask for something like that out loud, especially because MSF needed people like Inez, but she'd been convinced their bond was strong enough to change Inez' mind.

She'd been wrong.

And now, there she stood, talking to Claire as if it was the most normal thing in the world. Margot could already spot the signs that Claire was getting tipsy—ever widening hand gestures, her voice shooting up louder—and possibly even friendly with Inez. Would they all be going out for dinner next week?

It was bad enough that Margot had to encounter Inez at work every day, reminding her of the heartache she'd, honestly, only just put behind her. But she had Claire now. Kind, caring, mature Claire who wasn't going anywhere soon. Margot couldn't help but wonder if it would be enough to counter the force of nature Inez still seemed to be. Despite saying the words, over and over again—*when I'm done with someone, I'm truly done with them*—Margot knew, deep down, that against Inez and what she had meant to her, Claire didn't really stand a chance.

"I love Steph dearly, but this is the worst birthday party ever," Nadia slurred in her ear. "Don't tell me you disagree." She elbowed Margot in the bicep while tossing her head to the side, in the direction of Claire and Inez, who appeared to be in the middle of a conversation Margot simultaneously wanted to know everything and nothing about.

Margot just drew up her shoulders, realising that by now, she was probably the only sober person in their group—and she had least reason to be. "Can I buy you a whiskey?"

"Why don't I buy you one?" Nadia asked. "I hired her. I owe you." She didn't wait for Margot's reply and dashed off to the bar.

Margot was not usually one to drown her sorrows in alcohol, but this was a very unusual evening. She stood watching

Claire and Inez while waiting for Nadia to return. After a few seconds, Claire found her eyes and shot her a quick smile. Margot smiled back, a feeling of compassion she didn't fully understand rising in her gut. When Inez' gaze landed on her just as Nadia returned with their drinks, something ripped through her, like a knife cutting through her flesh, and Margot couldn't knock back the whiskey soon enough.

"Another?" she asked Nadia.

JULIETTE

Juliette watched the evening unfold. Nadia and Margot had switched to the hard stuff. Steph was pretending not to care about Dominique by hooking up with Cassandra. And Claire and Inez seemed to have found some sort of common ground. Juliette had tried to insert herself into their conversation, but hadn't found anything to contribute—not something she usually had issues with. They were talking about Friedriechshain and Kreuzberg and, frankly, Juliette didn't really have a clue what it was all about.

Six months earlier, when she still believed she was happy and as carefree as could be—even though she was probably too busy to notice how things had started to crumble already—this sort of party would have been a joy. An occasion for all of them to let their hair down and make some silly memories, remembering the night long after it had passed. Now, Juliette wished she could forget about it already.

At least she had an appointment with Nadia tomorrow—she could hardly call it a date. But, judging from the way Nadia was knocking back the whiskeys with Margot, as if it was some sort of competition, her hopes of having a fruitful discussion were starting to fade.

She knew that if she told Nadia off, asked her to take it easy, it would come across as another criticism, so she turned to Steph instead. She looked as if she'd rather be anywhere else than at her own birthday party and, possibly for the first time, Juliette felt sorry for her friend and colleague.

Juliette leaned into Steph's ear. "If those two keep knocking them back that quickly, it will not end well."

"As opposed to how it will all end gloriously and we'll all live happily ever after if they stop drinking, you mean?" Steph's eyes had glazed over. She used to be able to take more than a few glasses of champagne. Then again, she probably had less practice these days, leaving a string of disappointed damsels in her wake when not showing up at Les Pêches. She took another sip of her drink. "I think I'm going to leave."

"Seriously?"

"You and Nadia aren't talking. Margot clearly can't handle seeing her ex again and, to be perfectly honest, it all hurts too much. This is not how I wanted to feel on my birthday." She threw her arms wide, dramatically. "This is not where I wanted to be." She looked over at Cassandra who was refilling her glass from the bottle at the centre of the table. "And that is not the person I want to be with." Steph drank some more. "This has now officially become the worst birthday ever."

Juliette didn't know what to say to that. All she wanted to do was turn to the bottle herself, but someone had to keep a clear head—and get all of these intoxicated people into a taxi.

"Will you be all right getting home?" She hoped the concern she felt for Steph was adequately expressed on her face.

"Oh, I'm not going home. Cassandra lives just around the corner. How great is that? A flat in Le Marais?" Steph chuckled. "She's been dying to get out of here for the past hour anyway." Steph threw her arms around Juliette's neck and kissed her on the cheek. "Take care of your woman, Jules. Give her some aspirin before putting her to bed." With that, she started saying her goodbyes, breaking up the party prematurely. Something Juliette was not sorry for.

Juliette looked over at Nadia. She and Margot had found chairs in the corner, a half-full bottle of whiskey between them.

If they didn't stop soon, Juliette would actually have to follow Steph's advice and put Nadia to bed. She approached them, dragged another chair close and sat down opposite the two of them. They both looked at her as if she was a creature that had miraculously appeared in their presence.

"Don't mind me," Juliette said. "Unless I was the topic of your no doubt fascinating conversation."

"No snark needed," Nadia said.

"We've got plenty of that ourselves." Margot snickered, her eyes so watery Juliette questioned if she could actually still see anything. Obviously, the doctor was a lightweight. Was Claire so enthralled with Inez that she didn't know what was happening? Juliette swivelled around in her chair and called for Claire, who rushed over in a panic.

"I think you should take her home." Juliette couldn't keep the reproach out of her voice.

Claire crouched next to Margot. "Are you all right?" she asked, which was quite possibly the most stupid question she'd ever asked anyone. Seemingly quickly realising the error of her ways, Claire hooked her arm around Margot's elbow. "Come on. Time for some fresh air." She eyed the bottle on the table. "Jesus." Shooting Juliette a worried glance, she pulled Margot up out of her chair.

"Where were you," Juliette hissed, "when this was happening?"

Claire muttered a few I'm-sorrys under her breath and coaxed Margot towards the door.

"What's going on?"

Juliette had only just met Inez, but she had no trouble recognising her voice. She rose and turned to face her. "What the hell are you doing here anyway?"

"Merely a coincidence," Inez said, keeping her cool.

"Oh sure, just like you working at Saint-Vincent is a coincidence, I bet." Juliette was so fed up with everything. With people not taking care of their relationships. With everyone hurting each other. Mostly, she was fed up with herself because, of all the fuck-ups her friends had landed themselves in, she considered her own failure the worst.

The woman she loved more than anything in the world sat blind drunk on a chair in the corner and it was all because of her.

"Think whatever you want," Inez said. "My conscience is clear." Without saying another word, she walked away.

Juliette turned back around to assess the damage the whiskey had done to Nadia. She sat down next to her and gently put a hand on her thigh.

"If it's okay with you, I'm going to take you home. To our flat."

Nadia nodded. It was difficult for Juliette to gauge her presence of mind. She scooped her arm underneath Nadia's armpit and helped her up. "Come on, babe. We're going home."

It almost sounded like the truth.

CLAIRE

By the time the taxi had reached Claire's street, Margot had been fast asleep. Claire had practically had to drag her into the building and the elevator, yanking Margot's clothes off as she half-snoozed through everything. Despite Claire's incessant urging that she'd drink a few glasses of water, Margot had ignored everything she'd said and fallen into bed, out of it within seconds.

Claire had hardly been sober herself, but she'd stuck to champagne while, having been sucked into a conversation with Inez, to her great embarrassment after the fact, about Berlin and its various neighbourhoods and how it had changed so drastically over the years.

Just like Claire, Inez had briefly lived in the city in the nineties and, although Inez had ended up there a few years after Claire had already left, during their conversation they had happened upon mutual acquaintances and hang-outs. Before Claire had had a chance to blink, having lost herself so completely in a conversation with someone who was supposed to be more of an enemy, Steph was saying her goodbyes and she'd found Margot next to a half-empty bottle of whiskey.

Inez was charming, Claire had to give her that. So disarmingly friendly and an excellent conversationalist, speaking to Claire as if she'd known her forever. But Claire was not oblivious to the effect her lengthy talk must have had on Margot. Hence the bottle of whiskey.

After taking some aspirin, she'd put in a load of laundry, emptied the dishwasher and watched the one o'clock news on TV, and Margot still hadn't woken up.

She pattered to the bedroom and opened the door. Margot lay on her back, her mouth slightly open, her chest exposed. She looked so vulnerable, so in need of a hug, so completely different than how she presented herself in everyday life.

Claire sat down on the edge of the bed and gently stroked her arm. "Wake up, sleepy," she said. Her fingers wandered to Margot's belly, where they trailed over her abs before heading upwards, to the swell of her breasts and her dark nipples.

"Taking advantage of me?" Margot's voice sounded as if, instead of just having slept for almost twelve hours, she hadn't had a slumber in days.

"I wouldn't dare." Claire pinched Margot's nipple between her thumb and index finger. "Just trying to cure your hangover."

Margot tried to grab Claire's hand with hers, but it never reached her chest. Instead, she clasped it to her head. "Ouch," she groaned. "What happened?"

"You're Asian. You can't drink like that. You said so yourself." Claire pulled up the duvet to cover Margot's torso, tucking it snugly around her body. "Here's some water." She handed Margot the glass she had refused to drink the night before.

"Oh god, this is not good." Margot tried to sit up, but collapsed back onto the bed. "Where's my phone?"

Always the phone. Claire grabbed it for her from the nightstand. "I doubt you can deal with emergencies today."

"I need to call my parents to cancel dinner. There's no way I can eat roast chicken today." She squinted at the light the screen of her phone threw on her face.

"What will you tell them?" Claire was a little bit relieved at not having to meet the parents just yet.

Margot looked at her quizzically. "The truth. What else?"

"That you can't come to dinner because you have a hangover?" Admitting something like that to her own parents would never occur to Claire. Not in a million years.

"Yes." Margot placed the call. A short, matter-of-fact conversation during which, as far as Claire could tell, no impertinent or nosy questions were asked. *How odd.*

Margot sat up and wisely gulped down the glass of water, handing it back to Claire empty.

"More?" Claire figured they had some things to talk about, but she wasn't sure this was the best time.

Margot nodded and fell back against the pillows. "Bring me some paracetamol as well, please."

Claire tried not to think about the opportunities she had missed because of her chat with Inez. Instead of reminiscing about a past they didn't even share and, truth be told, also taking the chance to get to know Inez better, she could have learned a thing or two about Margot. Claire suspected Margot didn't let her hair down like that very often. Or maybe she wouldn't have if Claire had paid her a bit more attention.

"I'm trying to reconstruct the night," Margot said when Claire returned with a tall glass of water and a strip of pills. "I should probably also apologise because I'm not usually like this."

"I haven't known you that long, but I think I know that." Claire perched next to Margot on the side of the bed and watched her drink. When she'd swallowed two pills and emptied the glass, Claire continued. "Besides, I'm the one who should apologise."

"What did you do?" Margot put the glass on the bedside table and reached for her head again, massaging her temples. "It's all a bit of a blur."

"Let me do that." Claire shuffled closer to Margot. "Sit with your back to me." Margot obliged without protest.

While her fingers caressed Margot's scalp, Claire took a deep breath and said, "I may have gotten along with your ex a bit too well for your comfort."

MARGOT

Margot leaned her back against Claire's chest and, as her fingers travelled through her hair, applying divine pressure to her temples, it started coming back to her. Inez. Manu. The genuine interest Claire seemed to have taken in Inez. She probably believed that was why Margot had hit the bottle, and perhaps that was partially true, but Margot only ever drank like that when the pain was too big to bear.

Inez at the hospital was different from Inez in social situations. Not night and day, but subtle nuances, possibly only gestures, facial expressions and glances that Margot noticed. All the reasons why she had fallen so hard for Inez had come back, crashing over her, and she'd realised that, in a way, she'd been lucky that Inez had left Paris.

"You did seem rather chummy," Margot said. "But really, it was just one of those nights. Too much tension. Too much unhappiness. Too many ghosts from the past." What was she supposed to say? *Perhaps I'm not as over her as I thought I was?* "That feels good." With her hands, she found Claire's thighs behind her, and dug her nails in deep.

"So you're not mad at me?" Claire leaned forward and kissed Margot above the ear.

"Of course not." Margot closed her eyes and wondered why she was digging this hole for herself. She believed in honesty and openness, but she couldn't possibly tell Claire how running into Inez like that had really made her feel. It simply wasn't an option.

She needed Claire now more than ever and the last thing she wanted was to lose her as well. She'd get a grip on her feelings for Inez. She'd take some extra kickboxing classes, and spend even more time with Claire. She'd even transfer to another hospital if she had to. It was not because Inez Larue ignited this old flame in her soul, that she would ever act on it. Besides, Inez had shown much more interest in Claire than in her. Maybe that stung a little as well.

"You were brave, facing her like that." Claire's hands had dipped down to Margot's shoulders, kneading away the knots in her muscles. "Did she have anything interesting to say?" Margot had to ask.

"We got talking about Berlin. We both lived in Prenzlauer-berg before it became fashionable. That's mostly all we talked about."

"Oh." Margot moved away from Claire and turned around to face her. She wanted to forget about Inez. She'd have to see her again the next day at work, keeping up the charade of being good colleagues. "I know another excellent cure for a hang-over." The instant grin on Claire's face was more than enough to numb the worst of her headache.

"And you don't need to be a doctor to administer it." Claire pulled her top over her head. "What I'm trying to say is that I'll be doing the nursing today."

"That works for me." Margot's throat went dry at the sight of Claire's exposed chest. "It's my day off, anyway."

Claire was not a fling, not someone she'd allowed into her bed and heart to forget about Inez, even though, in that moment, it helped. Seeing Claire come for her, feeling her arms wrap around her, and how she pushed Margot down onto the bed, made her forget. As if Claire's touch was the best antidote for the memory of Inez. Relieved, Margot relaxed against the covers as Claire's tongue licked along the skin of her neck. By the time Claire's lips reached Margot's erect nipple, Inez might as well have fallen off the face of the earth.

Margot twirled her fingers through Claire's hair. While her mind was dazed by the effects of her hangover, her body seemed extra-sensitive and every little peck Claire pressed onto her skin, shot through her flesh.

Margot had no recollection of how she had ended up naked in bed, but she was glad they didn't have to go through the routine of removing underwear. She was glad Claire could go straight for the prize.

Under normal circumstances, when Margot was in control, she would have spent a lot of time on Claire already, revelling in the building throb between her legs, but that wasn't necessary today. She wanted Claire's tongue on her clit as soon as possible.

"Please," Margot begged—not really her style either. "I need it now." She coaxed Claire's head down further, but, except when tied with her arms to a bedpost, Claire wasn't that easily controlled.

Claire responded by slowing the pace with which she planted kisses on Margot's skin. She'd reached Margot's belly button and spent much more time there than she probably would have if Margot hadn't said anything. It made Margot's pussy lips pulse harder.

When Claire's lips, at last, skated along the edge of her pubic hair, an image of Inez, out of nowhere, appeared on the back of Margot's eyelids. Despite her bubbly personality in the light of day, in the bedroom, Inez was all darkness. More than anything, she needed to be controlled. It was that darkness that had drawn Margot to her, the contrast between night and day. It all came crashing back now. Images of Inez tied up, hands and feet, a blindfold over her eyes, totally at Margot's mercy. She'd never told Margot that was what she wanted, but Margot knew because such loud bravado needs a place to rest at night.

Claire's lips travelled along her inner thighs, teasing, and when Margot begged again, it wasn't only out of impatience, it was her way of punishing herself. And she needed Claire to not give in yet, to leave her hanging, possibly not make her come at all—definitely not bestow all this unconditional love on her. Margot knew she didn't deserve it.

She tried to push any notion of Inez out of her mind, peering at Claire's short, blonde hair through her eyelids as her head moved between Margot's legs. But Margot needed the tension coiled in her gut to be released. *Need. Need. Need.* She could hardly believe she'd become that kind of person, again.

Claire's tongue flicked lightly over her clit.

"Please, please," Margot pleaded. "Don't—" Then the words died in her throat because Claire acquiesced. She let her tongue dart over Margot's clit again and again, and Margot needed it so much that she came in seconds. An ocean of guilt rolling over her, along with the sensation that she was drowning in her own pleasure.

There was no way she could push back the tears that stung behind her eyes, no way to quench the pain in her soul. Because this thing she had going with Claire, it was a good, promising, by-the-book romance. But Margot knew, even though she had firmly believed the opposite, that she wasn't ready.

STEPH

When Steph returned home early the next morning after a disappointing night of trying to imagine it was Dominique responding so vocally to what her fingers were doing, she found a bottle of Bollinger in front of the door to her flat. A card was attached to the neck of the bottle. It simply said 'Happy birthday'. There was no doubt in Steph's mind it was a present from Dominique. Had she dropped it off herself? Had she been here? Was this a breach of the rule of no personal contact between them for a week? Or just a small gesture because it was, after all, Steph's birthday?

Steph opened the door and held Pierrot in her arms while staring at the bottle. Although she had barely recovered from too much alcohol the night before, she wanted to open it and drink its entire contents. Breakfast of heart-broken champions.

She fed Pierrot and while he ate, she sagged down in the sofa, pulling her phone from her pocket. No messages from Dominique. *Should she?*

"Why the hell not?" she asked Pierrot, who was too busy wolfing down his food to even spike up his ears.

Last night had been miserable and, for Steph, the only person who could have made it better was Dominique. Wasn't that what a partner was for? To make her feel better when she felt this unbelievable, possibly unprecedented, gloominess bloom in her chest. So she gave in because, in the end, what did it matter?

Thanks for the champagne, she texted, not wanting to go over-board. Pierrot had finished eating and pattered over to the sofa, asking for more with a vexed meow. Steph shook her head at him, as if he would understand.

"Come here," she said, patting her lap. Instantly, he jumped on top of her. She buried her face in his soft fur. "Happy bloody birthday to mummy."

The beep of her phone startled her.

Shall I come over for an apéritif?

As fast as she could type, Steph texted back a confirmation.

"That posh lady is coming over again, Pierrot," she said to her cat. "We like her, don't we?" Steph didn't care about the complications of them being together, she just wanted to see Dominique. The desire to see her walk through the door, that confident smirk on her face, trumped any notion of how desperate their situation really was.

She placed Pierrot on his favourite pillow and showered again, despite already having done so at Cassandra's, hid her dirty clothes at the bottom of the laundry basket and slipped into a pair of tight jeans and a tank top, no bra. Then she waited.

––––––

Dominique dropped her purse and a plastic shopping bag to the floor and curled her arms around Steph's neck. "Happy birthday," she whispered in Steph's ear. "I've been going nuts without you."

"I'm sorry about last time," Steph said.

Dominique kissed her hard on the lips. "It doesn't matter."

And it didn't matter. It didn't matter who had broken the foolish rule they'd instated. Nothing mattered, just this moment of reunion, and the pure joy, for the first time since she'd turned thirty-four, rushing through Steph's body.

"Here." Dominique ducked out of Steph's embrace and fished a gift-wrapped box out of the bag she had brought. "For you."

"You got me a present?" Steph eyed her in disbelief.

"Of course." The features of Dominique's face had all gone soft.

Steph tore at the wrapping paper. A black Armani box appeared from underneath. "This better not be a dress," she joked.

"Oops," Dominique replied, and brought her hand to her mouth.

When Steph opened the box she found a black fitted blouse, exactly the kind she would buy herself, although she'd never get Armani when H&M would do.

"It's beautiful." She checked the label inside. "How did you know my size?"

"I've had my hands on you," Dominique moved closer again, "and I checked your closet."

"You went through my stuff?" Steph feigned indignation. "How dare you?"

"I was a little disappointed, you know, hoping to find some more interesting contraptions than just clothes."

"I keep my toys in a box under the bed." Steph took a step closer as well.

"Good to know, but we won't be needing them today." Dominique took the blouse from Steph's hands and draped it over a nearby chair. "Which doesn't mean you won't get another, even more spectacular birthday present very soon." She kissed Steph again, softly this time, their lips parting already. "Before things progress beyond control," Dominique said after breaking their lip-lock. "The kids are coming back from their holiday with Philippe today, so I need to be home by six."

Nothing like a reality check to kill the mood.

"And… I've been thinking," Dominique continued, gesturing to the sofa. "Shall we sit for a moment?"

"Sure." Steph's heart pounded frantically. They walked the few steps to the sofa and sat down.

"You know I'm taking them to my family's house in Juan-les-Pins in August, right?"

Steph nodded, already dreading the time away from Dominique.

"I think you should come with us."

Steph's eyes grew wide. "What? Isn't that crazy?"

"The first week, it will be just us. My parents only arrive a week later, and Lisa and Didier are children, they go to bed at nine and they have all these beach camp activities during the day. We'll have lots of time to spend together."

"But… what will you tell them? Who am I?" Steph's brain tried to process. She couldn't see it.

"A good friend." Dominique sat looking at her, glee glinting in her eyes.

"As your PR advisor I would strongly caution against it."

"But you're not just my PR advisor, are you?" Dominique shuffled closer. "And we bring friends to the house all the time. The children are used to it." She grabbed Steph's hands and cupped them in hers. "You'd have to officially sleep in a separate bedroom, of course, and leave before my parents arrive, but I'd really, really, really like you to come." She gazed deep into Steph's eyes. "Frankly, I've missed you so much over the past five days, I can't imagine being away from you for two entire weeks."

"I want to go," Steph said without thinking. "But you must realise that this can have serious repercussions."

"I don't care." Dominique brought their hands to her mouth and kissed Steph's knuckle. "It won't always be like this, you know. Not if I can help it."

Steph feared Dominique had lost her mind. "Really?" She arched up her eyebrows. *Someone had to keep a clear mind.*

"Society is changing," Dominique said in between pressing her lips to each and everyone of Steph's knuckles. Steph couldn't tell if she was being serious or not; her eyes were already glazing over, nothing but lust portrayed on her face.

"That's why hundreds of thousands of people demonstrate against gay marriage in the streets of Paris every other Sunday," Steph tried. "Because society is changing?"

"Change is always scary—"

Steph was getting worked up. "Stop it, just stop it." She pulled her hands free from Dominique's. "Only two weeks ago you weren't even sure you'd vote for gay marriage and now you what? You want to come out of the closet?"

Dominique pinned her eyes on Steph. "I want two things." She held up two fingers. "I want my children to know that you exist, not that you're my lover, but that you're someone important in my life." She hid one finger. "And I want *you* to know that this doesn't have to be the dead-end street we always thought it would be."

"And you actually believe that?" No matter how hard she tried, skepticism still ruled in Steph's mind.

"I do. I have to. And I hope you know why." She slanted her head to the right a bit. "Because I'm in love with you."

Steph put all conflicts of interests aside and reached for Dominique's hands again. "You're insane and I'm in love with you too."

They kissed, as if it was all really that easy, their lips meeting again and again.

"Promise me you'll think about going on holiday with me," Dominique said after coming up for air.

Steph would have to tell Claire and Juliette, who would not be pleased with it—and she'd already disappointed them so much. And what was all this talk of love? Were they supposed to be exclusive now? Not that Steph wanted to sleep with other people, last night had made that abundantly clear. Should she tell Dominique about Cassandra?

She didn't have worries like this before she fell in love. She pushed them all to the back of her brain and let her lips hover over Dominique's again. "About my other birthday present," she said, and kissed her while pushing her down into the sofa.

NADIA

Nadia could easily take a drink or two, but the pounding inside her skull hinted at having had more than a few. And she hadn't even opened her eyes yet. When she did, to her great astonishment, she recognised her and Juliette's bedroom. *Had they?*

"You're awake." Juliette's voice was low and soft and sounded very considerate.

They must have… Nadia racked her brain and she vaguely

remembered Juliette bringing her here, but after that… nothing. She sat up and faced Juliette who was perched at the end of the bed. How long had she been sitting there?

"I'm sorry, my memory seems to elude me a bit." Nadia looked down at her body. She had worn a dress last night, which she spotted draped over a chair in the corner of the room when she glanced up again. Her chest was bare. She could feel panties clinging to her hips, though.

"You and Margot got hammered on whiskey, while the rest of us were just slumming it with champagne." Was that a smile on Juliette's face? Was this a truce?

"I should never have gone to that party." Nadia looked around for some water. As if reading her mind, Juliette handed her a bottle.

"You had to go, and so did I. Steph's our friend."

Nadia swallowed a few gulps before facing Juliette again. "Look, Jules, I don't mean to be rude, but, did we, you know…"

"All you were good for last night was falling into bed. With Margot being so wasted as well, I thought it better to bring you here instead of her place."

"Oh." Nadia sipped some more water. "Poor Margot, she hardly ever drinks, let alone whiskey."

"I texted Claire, but she hasn't texted back. Which I take as a good sign." Juliette grinned at Nadia, who suddenly realised, still a bit slow in the head, that she was only partially covered by the duvet. She deposited the water bottle on the night stand and pulled the covers up to her chin, feeling out of place in what was still, after all, her flat as well. But Juliette had brought Sybille here and had slept with her in this bed.

Nadia remembered that she'd felt so sorry for Juliette the night before that she had invited herself over for a much-needed conversation, but she was in no fit state to have it.

"What are we going to do, Jules?" Nadia leaned against the headboard of the bed. "I hate this." She glared at Juliette from under her lashes.

"For now, just try to get some more sleep. We'll deal with the rest later."

"Are we even now?" The words just rolled out of Nadia's mouth. "Now that we've both slept with someone else?"

Juliette stood there, looking at her with a perplexed expression on her face. She took a step closer and sat down next to Nadia. "I know you well enough to know you don't believe that."

"You may think it's not that easy, and maybe it isn't, but what if we make it so? What if we just put it all behind us?" Nadia was grasping at straws. She didn't want to go back to Margot's and sleep alone in her guest bedroom. She didn't want to face tomorrow as a single woman. "When I rang the bell last week, I came here to tell you that I was ready to move back in. That I would fight for you and that I, finally, understood what you've been going through and that, in the past year, I failed just as much as you, if not more." She shook her head. "Barcelona without you was horrible. It opened my eyes, babe. I'll do whatever it takes."

"Even after…" Juliette hesitated, reminding Nadia of what she had walked into earlier that week.

"I'm ready to forgive you." Nadia was exhausted, not just physically, but also mentally. The endless bracing herself for another fight had taken its toll on her nerves. She was ready to surrender. She had one more question, though. "Have you slept with her ag—"

"God no." Juliette shook her head fervently. "Never again. It was such a dud. It only made me want you back more."

Nadia locked her eyes on Juliette's and she understood. Between them, it had never been necessary to say it out loud.

"Are you sure? You haven't really thought about this, though? You just woke up with a massive hangover and suddenly—"

Nadia stopped Juliette mid-sentence, holding up her hand. "I don't need to think about it anymore. What good is that going to do me? Really? We've done enough thinking and look where it got us." She pushed herself up a bit more. "I'm willing to forgive, are you?"

Nadia's heartbeat picked up speed. Juliette was so close, all of it felt within grasp again, but one word would be enough for another chasm—or even a complete break-up.

Juliette nodded, with small movements of her chin at first, tears springing from her eyes. The closer she shuffled to Nadia, the more resolute her nods became. "I love you," she said through the tears. "I only want you."

Nadia opened her arms wide and wrapped them around Juliette as she brought her head to her chest. Just to feel her near again, just to touch a finger to her hair. Nothing else mattered.

JULIETTE

"Just like that?" Claire sat opposite Juliette in her office. "You're back together?"

"I understand your skepticism, but you could also just be happy for me." Not that Juliette wasn't skeptical herself—it really couldn't, nor should it, be that easy.

"I am, Jules, truly." Claire brought a hand to her chest. "Glad to know Steph's party was good for something."

"This does raise another issue, though." Juliette slanted her head towards the door of her office. "Sybille."

"Has Nadia demanded—"

"Nadia has no demands to make." Juliette realised blurting out things like that was something she should work at. "I just don't think it's a good idea to keep her as my assistant."

"What do you suggest?" Claire intertwined her fingers and rested her chin on her hands.

"We have two options: ask her to leave or promote her. Both have obvious drawbacks." From a purely professional point of view, Juliette would be sorry to see Sybille go, but she couldn't possibly keep on working with her. "I doubt she'll go away quietly if we terminate her contract, taking into consideration what she knows. But if we promote her so quickly, other employees will be disgruntled."

Claire looked away and stared out of the window for a few seconds. "You don't trust her to keep Laroche's secret?"

Juliette sighed. She could easily predict what Claire was thinking. If only they'd dropped Dominique Laroche as a client. And if only she hadn't slept with her assistant. "I think she has feelings for me."

"Merde."

"I'm sorry, Claire. I know I made a mess of things."

"No need to dwell. We'd better focus our energy on solving this problem." She shifted in her seat. "Do we really want an employee who can't be trusted?"

"I'm not saying she can't be trusted, just that her feelings for me may make her unpredictable. And Laroche is our most high-profile client, we can't take any risks with her."

"She's taking plenty of risks herself." Claire uncrossed her legs and leaned forward. "If her affair with Steph comes out, it's her own damn fault."

"But it will reflect badly on us." Juliette sagged into her chair. "And Steph is one of us."

"Speaking of, maybe we should get her take on this. Like it or not, she's involved."

Juliette nodded. "I'll call her." She dialled Steph's direct line and asked her to come over immediately.

While they waited, Juliette couldn't help herself. "You seemed to get along swimmingly with Margot's ex at the party."

"Let's leave that for another conversation, this one's already complicated enough."

A knock on the door announced Steph's arrival. She sat down and they explained their conundrum.

"Sack her," Steph said without hesitation. Hardly a surprise to Juliette. "You can't possibly give her more responsibility.

She's only your assistant now and look at all the trouble she has already caused."

"That's hardly all Sybille's fault," Juliette said, not hiding the harshness in her voice—and momentarily forgetting her own contribution.

"For once, let's approach this as the adults we all are," Claire said. "This is no time to assign blame." She turned to Steph. "I have to ask this, Steph. What's going on with you and Dominique? Obviously, you were cut up about something last Saturday."

Steph squirmed in her seat. "She has asked me to go to her family's house on the Côte d'Azur in August."

Juliette couldn't speak for several moments. "But… what about that girl? What was her name… Cassandra?"

"We were on a break, figuring some things out…" Clearly, this was a conversation nobody in Juliette's office wanted to have.

"I hope you said no?" Claire looked at Steph expectantly. "To the holiday?"

"I haven't said anything. I mean, I advised her against it but, she's a hard woman to say no to…"

"Obviously," Juliette offered. *Or we wouldn't be in this mess in the first place.*

"She wants to introduce me to her children. It's getting serious."

Juliette had to step in. She was the one who had convinced Claire to keep Laroche as a client, but this farce had to end. "Why were you on a break?" It wasn't a fair question, but none of this was fair on anyone.

"W-what?" There was a dull shimmer of hurt in Steph's eyes.

"Why did you and Laroche decide to go on a break?" Juliette could guess the answer, but she needed Steph to say it out loud, to acknowledge it.

"Because… our relationship has nowhere to go," she stammered, barely getting the words out.

"Exactly." Juliette had to be hard and cold in this moment, even though that was her friend sitting across from her. "So what exactly do you expect to change about that in the future?"

"Jules, come on," Claire said. "That's not fair."

"With all due respect, presently, you're both in some sort of loved-up state and are clearly missing the bigger picture. This has to end. There is only one solution."

"And you're such an expert now?" Steph asked. She rose from her chair, visibly shaken. "You have no right whatsoever to ask me that. You slept with your bloody assistant, something, for the record, I had seen coming from miles away. She just twisted you around her little finger and you didn't even see."

"Stop." Claire stood up as well. "This is ludicrous. This is our place of business, for god's sake, not the set of some soap opera." She took a deep breath. "We all make mistakes and this is no time to judge. We need to do something about this, but we'll need to have a more productive meeting before we decide. Juliette, don't say anything to Sybille about Nadia yet, not until we've figured out how to play this. And Steph, you'd better know what you're doing. We can only protect you and Laroche so much." She looked at the pair of them with a determined glance that wouldn't accept any more objections. "Understood?"

Juliette nodded and pushed herself out of her chair. "I'm sorry," she said to Steph. "I think we could all use a holiday."

MARGOT

Margot caught herself actually looking forward to seeing Inez at work. She quickly pushed the thought away. She'd have to find a way past it, possibly even confide in someone—despite that never having been her way of dealing with trouble. That extra kickboxing class earlier in the morning hadn't helped either.

On her way to see Nadia and ask her if she had a moment to spare for her today, they ran into each other in the ER hallway.

"Fully recovered?" Nadia inquired. Her hair didn't shine as it usually did and her eyes looked rather dull, but it was Monday morning, so it could just be that.

Margot nodded and pulled Nadia aside. "Are you free for lunch?"

"Sure. I wanted to talk to you as well. I have some news." Nadia smiled widely, erasing the remnants of the hangover off her face.

The only news that would cheer Margot up would be the announcement that Inez had decided to leave the hospital. Although Margot wasn't so sure it would cheer her up that much.

"Can we use your office? I'll bring food."

"Sure. I'll see you then." Nadia nodded and went on her way. As she slipped out of Margot's field of vision, someone else cropped up in it. Instantly, her heart beat faster. Margot couldn't stop the memories from coming back.

"Morning," Inez said.

Last week, when seeing Inez at the hospital, Margot hadn't felt this way. Or maybe she hadn't allowed it. Or buried any inkling of it so deep, until it no longer existed. Today that didn't seem to work anymore.

"Hey." Margot steadied herself against the wall, until she tapped into her core strength—those abs that Claire so admired —and stood tall. More bravado than anything else. Did Inez know? Could she tell that she was getting under Margot's skin already? Had it been her plan all along?

"Are you all right, Go-Go?" Inez lifted her arm and touched her fingers to Margot's upper arm. "You look a bit pale."

"Fine," she mumbled. "I'd better get going?" But Margot didn't move.

"Are we still doing that?" Inez tilted her head to the left. "It was great meeting Claire and your friends this weekend. She's quite the catch." Inez winked at her, a grin plastered on her face.

"Sure." Margot had to get out of there. "See you around." She sauntered down the hallway, in a direction she didn't have to go, but carried on nonetheless, as long as it took her away from Inez and offered some temporary relief.

———

"I can't do it." Margot's salad stood untouched on Nadia's desk. "It's driving me mad." Margot was fully aware that Nadia had never seen her in this kind of state. Even when she was still hurting over Inez after their break-up and joined Nadia's hospital, she had never brought any of her inner turmoil to work.

"Inez?" Nadia picked a leaf from her salad before dropping her fork.

"It's too much. I, um, loved her so much and I thought I could cope, but I can't." Margot stared out of the window, avoiding Nadia's gaze.

"I'm so sorry. I should have tried—"

"It's so unfair on Claire." Margot had to vent, let it all out in one go. "It was going so well, until Inez came back. She's been here a week and I'm already falling to pieces."

"It's only normal to experience a shock to your system when someone you cared for pops back up into your life. Just give it some time. You'll get used to having her around. The shock and novelty will wear off. Focus on Claire."

Margot shook her head, nothing but despair coursing through her veins. "You don't understand. I can't. I can't go on a date with Claire tonight feeling like this. I already feel as if I'm cheating on her, betraying her, chipping away at the pureness of what we have between us."

"What are you saying?" Nadia placed her elbows on her desk and leaned forward. Margot couldn't avoid her gaze anymore.

"I thought I was over her. Because she was so far away and I believed I had taken the time to heal. But I'm not. After seeing her at the party on Saturday, everything changed." The first tear broke free. "I know she left me to pursue this dream she'd had since forever and not breaking up with me immediately when she left for Africa was her way of letting me down easy, even though it was never going to be easy. What we had was special from the beginning. And, I may be totally wrong, but I think she came back for me. I think she feels it too."

"Has anything happened between the two of you?" Worry crossed Nadia's face.

"No, of course not. I would never do that to Claire." For once, Margot was too upset to take other people's personal dramas into consideration. And it wasn't because Nadia and Juliette had both cheated that Margot ever would. "But I know it will. I feel it in my bones. I never used to believe in 'the one' and all of that sentimental bullshit, but Inez changed me. As cruel as this may sound, and as gentle, kind, beautiful and smart as Claire is, she pales in comparison." More tears broke free. "I feel so horrible for saying that, you have no idea."

It wasn't that Margot didn't care deeply for Claire, and that she hadn't strongly believed that they could work without having the feeling that she was settling for less—already quite an achievement in Margot's post-Inez world. But Inez had the advantage of time spent with Margot. In a matter of months, she had transformed the insecurity hiding beneath Margot's leather-clad exterior into quiet self-confidence.

It wasn't fair, but it was how it was.

"Are you going to break up with her?" Nadia started fidgeting with a stack of papers on her desk, shuffling them to the side.

"What other choice do I have?" Margot's hands had started trembling and she hoped her beeper wouldn't summon her to an emergency surgery any time soon. She was in no state to work. She should take the rest of the day off and get her act together. She waited for Nadia's reply—perhaps some words of wisdom—but none came.

"I'm very sorry you feel that way. Claire adores you, I know that much."

Margot fished a handkerchief out of her coat pocket and blew her nose. "What's your news?" she asked, looking to change the subject, if only briefly.

"My news can wait." Nadia cleared her throat. "Please don't make any rash decisions, Margot. You may feel like this now, but don't forget that you have grieved for Inez once already. Getting over someone changes things. It won't be the same. You can't just pick up where you left things out of nostalgia."

"If it were nostalgia, I wouldn't be sitting in your office crying my eyes out." With that, the rest of the tears rolled out, moistening Margot's cheeks and leaving black drops of despair on her white coat.

STEPH

I need something on Sybille." Steph paced through Dominique's living room.

"Is this really how you want to spend the forty minutes we have together?" Dominique sat in the sofa, nursing a glass of wine. "My children will be here soon, unless you'd like me to introduce you already."

"I don't understand why you're not taking this more seriously. This girl could damage you." Steph eyed Dominique. "Besides, they're ready to fire her. If I have concrete evidence that she was following me, it may push Claire and Juliette over the edge."

"I have documents of the last owners' meeting, including the names of tenants, although most people who own a flat in the building also live here." Dominique found Steph's eyes. "Do you know what the girl who supposedly lives here is called?"

"No, because she probably doesn't exist. My guess is Sybille

294

made her up as a cover story. She thinks she's so clever, but does she really think we wouldn't check?"

Dominique rose and made her way to the study next to the living room. Steph followed her. She watched Dominique ruffle through a drawer and dig up some papers. "I inherited this apartment ten years ago and, as far as I know, the ownership of the building hasn't changed since. Two units are rented out, but, officially, the tenants haven't changed in the past few years. Obviously, it is possible that someone would sublet or let a family member stay, but I haven't noticed any new faces. Then again, I only moved in a short while ago." She handed a sheet of paper to Steph.

Steph studied the names on the paper, a few of them vaguely rang a bell and she suspected this building to be quite the strong-hold for conservative politicians and their families.

"For obvious reasons, the management takes great pride in discretion. If someone is taking pictures of the front door, I'm certain they'd take an interest."

Steph sighed and waved the sheet of paper around. "This doesn't prove anything."

"Do you need me to come in and testify?" Dominique smiled. "Meanwhile, I can convince your bosses to let you go on holiday with me." She opened her arms. "Come here."

"I realise this is just a tidbit for you, but this is important to me." Steph couldn't hide the frustration in her tone, not that she tried very hard. "Let's see how casually you'll react when a picture of us pops up on the front page of *Le Matin*."

"I couldn't care less what *Le Matin* writes about me."

"Well, I do care. And so will your children, your ex-husband, your party *and* your father."

"I'm sorry." Dominique scrunched her lips together in an apologetic pout. "If I had to worry about every person who might hypothetically be out to get me, I wouldn't get any sleep at night."

"What will you do when it does come out? Deny my very existence?"

"Never, and you know it." Instead of waiting until Steph came to her, Dominique bridged the gap between them. "I invited you to my family's summer house. I told you that I love you and I made it quite clear how I feel about us. What more do you want from me? Do you want me to announce it on the podium of the Assemblée?" She curled her fingers around Steph's wrists.

"No, I want you to take this seriously. Take *me* seriously."

"Oh, but I do, Stéphanie. I do. Just watch me take you seriously." Dominique slipped her fingers from Steph's wrists straight into the waistband of her trousers. With a quick flip, she undid the button, and before Steph had a chance to protest, Dominique had twirled her around so her bottom pressed against the mahogany desk in the middle of her study.

"That's not what I meant," she tried.

"I know." Dominique peered into her eyes before dropping to her knees and pulling Steph's trousers all the way down. The cold air rushing against her pussy lips was quickly replaced by the hot touch of Dominique's tongue. They didn't have much time left.

Bottoming again, Steph thought as Dominique licked along her pussy lips, wriggling her tongue inside of her. *She seemed to be making a habit of that.* Then Dominique's tongue hit her clit again, and Steph stopped thinking. Instead, as Dominique stepped up the pace, hitting the spot she knew Steph liked over and over again, Steph imagined the two of them doing this against a tree in the backyard of Xavier Laroche's villa in Juan-les-Pins. She almost came, but Dominique pulled back.

She rose and looked Steph in the eyes. "Spread wider for me, baby," she urged.

Steph, as if complying to women's orders during sex was all she'd ever done in life, obliged. She opened her legs and let Dominique in.

"You're under my skin now," Dominique said as she thrust two fingers deep inside of Steph. "You're in my blood. You're part of me." Her eyes didn't leave Steph's. "Je t'aime."

Steph came with the same force that had been hitting her so much of late. An unrecognisable surge of relief rushing through her. A wave of something unknown to her—or at least long forgotten—before she'd embarked on this insane affair with Dominique Laroche.

CLAIRE

"I called in a favour at Johnson's. Marc, the CEO, owes me big for convincing our client to drop the lawsuit against them when they represented Maceau Pharma. He'll take on Sybille as his second executive assistant. It's a big step up for her and Marc runs a tight ship. He'll keep her in line."

"Good to know scheming and plotting can still get you promoted in this business," Steph said.

Claire shook her head, indicating this was neither the time nor place for snide remarks. "For what it's worth, I believe you when you say she doesn't actually live at Avenue Foch, but I guess we'll never know."

Juliette didn't say anything. Claire turned to her. "You'll have to give her the news, Jules. And you'll have to make it sound plausible. Tell her she's been headhunted or something." Claire watched Steph bite her lip. "We need to get our stories straight."

"And I'll need to get a new assistant."

"Try to pick someone you'll never be sexually attracted to," Steph offered.

"She won't believe me, of course. She'll see through it," Juliette ignored Steph's remark.

"It doesn't matter as long as you make it sound as good as possible, like a real opportunity. Don't mention Nadia, just make her believe that you can't work with her anymore. That it's too hard."

"At least that won't be a lie," Juliette said.

Claire felt quite pleased with herself for coming up with this elegant solution. More in control than in her personal life, where Margot had cancelled a date two nights in a row—and she hadn't used her key either. Being a doctor's wife was not all it was cracked up to be, then.

"How's the big reunion going?" Steph addressed Juliette. She looked as if she was out for blood. She probably wasn't too happy about the way they were trying to rid Barbier & Cyr of Sybille, but she could at least be happy that she was leaving. Nevertheless, Claire pointed her ears, curious about Juliette and Nadia's magical reconciliation.

"Slowly, but she's moving back in." Music to Claire's ears.

Steph stood up. "I don't care how you do it, just make it work and restore my faith in humanity. You and Nadia being apart is just not right."

"Hey, um, Steph…" Juliette hesitated. "I'm sorry about what I said about you and Dominique the other day. I was out of line. I apologise."

"I understand." Steph leaned against the armrest of the chair she had just risen from. "You're trying to protect your company."

"At your expense."

Claire cleared her throat. She hated to interrupt their moment but she wasn't finished yet. "Look, Steph, it's not our place to forbid you something and to instruct you what to do in your free time, but I've given this more thought and I really don't think it's a good idea for you and Dominique to go on holiday together."

"I know." Steph held up her hands. "I won't go. It's too risky and I've done enough damage." Her bottom lip trembled almost imperceptibly, but Claire noticed.

She tried to put herself in Steph's shoes and tried to imagine what it would feel like if someone asked her not to go on holiday with Margot because it involved too many risks. Any beginning of a new relationship was already so fragile, and to have that kind of pressure added. It must be so hard for Steph.

"Are you going to Gordes?" Steph bravely asked.

"Yep, for the annual Cyr holiday extravaganza." Claire nodded while pouting her lips.

"Are you inviting Margot?" Juliette asked, still seated.

"Do you think she's ready for something like that? My family can be quite full-on, you know what they're like. I don't think there are people on this planet who are more the opposite of her than my mother and my brother."

"Maybe not then." Juliette grinned. "Remember when I met your family at that barbecue, and while happily gnawing on a sausage, your brother asked me how we did it? In front of your parents. Your father nearly had a heart attack."

"And my mother didn't even bat an eyelid." Claire snickered. She considered cutting her holiday short and returning to Paris earlier to spend some time off with Margot.

Juliette rose as well. She walked to the door, Steph following her. "I'll take care of Sybille today."

Claire nodded and hoped for the best.

MARGOT

Margot waited for Inez in the changing room. Her own shift had ended an hour earlier, but she'd stuck around because she had to ask. Since her talk with Nadia, she'd been avoiding everyone as best she could, Inez being the only one she couldn't help but encounter several times a day. She hadn't been able to face Claire and had stayed late at the hospital two nights in a row, pretending—to herself included—that it was necessary. Now, she couldn't bear it anymore.

Inez walked in with a colleague in tow. She nodded at Margot, but stayed engaged in conversation with Anna the anaesthesiologist, who'd just come into the changing room to fetch something from her bag. Within minutes, she rushed out, leaving Margot alone with Inez.

"Can we talk?" she asked.

Inez sat down on the wooden bench in front of the lockers and regarded her from below. "Are you all right, Go-Go? You still look so pale. That hangover should really have passed by now." She shot Margot one of her trademark smiles and it cut straight through every armour Margot had ever put up, straight into her heart.

"I'm serious." Margot sat down on the bench as well, but left at least two feet between them.

"Of course." Inez swung one leg over the bench so she faced Margot fully. "Shoot."

"Why did you come back?" With all the courage she could muster, Margot stared Inez straight in the face.

"Ah, the million dollar question." Inez shuffled a little closer. Before she replied, she wiped the grin of her lips. "I came back because it was a mistake to leave in the first place." She drew a deep breath. "Not only because the things I've seen will still give me nightmares ten years from now, but because I should never have left you." She swatted a stray ginger curl away from her face. "There was no one else, Go-Go. I just told you that to make it easier, so you could move on."

"What?" Margot's heart felt as though it was being pierced by a hundred daggers at once. "You lied to me?"

"I did. I had to. Because I know you." Inez briefly looked away. "I knew you would have waited for me while I was chasing my idealistic dreams and, in hindsight, it's my second biggest regret. Leaving you being my first."

Margot was still processing the part of there not having been someone else. The nights she'd lain awake imagining that other woman. The torture she'd put herself through over nothing.

"You wouldn't have met someone like Claire if I hadn't set you free to live your life, Go-Go. And, as sorry as I am for the mistakes that I've made, and I've made plenty, I'm glad that you're happy." She gave a small chuckle. "And before you ask, yes, it was my initial plan to join Saint-Vincent and sweep you off your feet. I wanted you back more than anything, but I respect what you have with Claire and I have no one to blame for that except myself."

"I *was* happy with Claire. She's amazing." Margot's voice trembled as she continued. "Until you walked into that bar last Saturday and brought it all back." The tears came. Tears for being convinced that she'd been replaced by someone better, or at least more convenient, as soon as Inez had touched foreign soil. Tears for Claire who didn't deserve this. Tears for all the time they had wasted. "What we had, you and I, was magic. A once in a lifetime thing." Margot wasn't sure Inez could make out what came from her mouth in between sobs and heaves. "I thought I was over you. I would have been if you hadn't come back." She wiped her cheeks with the back of her hand. "Now look at me."

"I'm so sorry." Inez inched closer still. "Oh god, I am." She put her hands on Margot's thigh, making Margot shiver in her skin. "I was foolish, reckless, and so so stupid."

Inez' breath was near. It was the only sound Margot heard apart from her own sniffles. Never a woman of many words, Margot didn't have any left. In some twisted way, she'd believed this conversation would have made her feel better. But she'd never felt so bad, because not only was she getting hurt all over again, Claire's happiness was at stake as well.

"I forgave you for leaving, because you wanted to help people who needed it most, but I'll never forgive you for lying to me."

"Go-Go." If Inez came any closer, she'd be on Margot's lap. Her fingers dug deep into Margot's thigh muscles. "After what you've just told me, you must know that I will fight for you."

Margot found Inez' eyes. They were filled with tears as well. Despite what she'd just said about never being able to forgive her, she found herself slanting her head and leaning in. Because this was how it had always been between them. This constant pull towards each other, stronger than any resolve Margot had ever had.

The kiss was as much a shock to her system as seeing Inez again had been. At least, when she'd first walked into Inez during that orchestrated stroll down the hospital corridor alongside Nadia, Margot had been armed. She'd been prepared and had shut herself off. Now she opened up, lips first, and let Inez in again, even though it was probably the biggest mistake of her life.

The kiss was soft and tender and instantly recognisable. It changed everything.

"I still love you, Go-Go," Inez said, their lips still almost touching. "I will always love you."

Margot wanted to hate herself for what she said next, for such an obvious display of weakness and betrayal towards Claire. "I love you too."

It was complicated and difficult and painful, but it was, also, as deadly simple as that.

JULIETTE

"Close the door behind you, please." Juliette was nervous and she knew it showed. She watched Sybille shut the door and sit down in the chair opposite her desk. The chair she'd sat in every morning for a chat when she brought her coffee, until they'd slept together.

Sybille looked impeccable again, dressed for a board meeting in a navy Chanel suit and crisp white blouse. Maybe she really did have a wealthy girlfriend, because Barbier & Cyr surely didn't pay her enough that she could afford to buy designer suits.

"I have great news." Juliette stretched her lips the furthest they would go, into one of the most fake smiles she'd ever managed.

"You want an encore?" Sybille half-grinned, her eyes sparkling.

This was exactly the reason why she had to leave the company.

"No." Juliette's tone was firm, her nerves quickly dissolving. "But you are a wanted woman."

"Really?" Sybille arched up her eyebrows.

"Marc Dujardin, the CEO of Johnson PR wants to hire you. I have the proposal here." Juliette slid a folder over her desk in Sybille's direction. "It's a very attractive package."

Sybille eyed the papers, but didn't reach for them. "Funny that," she said.

Juliette should have known she wouldn't have made it easy on her. "Please, have a look." She made an inviting gesture towards the folder with her hand.

"So this is how you try to get rid of me. I bet you'll make me sign a confidentiality agreement as well." She simply uncrossed and crossed her legs again, not making any moves towards opening the folder. "I would have expected more honesty from someone who has fucked me."

Something I deeply regret. Juliette smiled away her uncomfortableness. Her job was not to make this into a verbal sparring match. She just needed to handle this as gracefully as possible. "Fine. Let's be honest. You can't be my assistant anymore, but, instead of ending your contract—because you *are* still in your trial period—we've lined this up for you. I made a mistake. I shouldn't have slept with you."

"And this is your bribe…" Sybille sat there nodding, as if she knew every little secret of the universe. "And your way of keeping me quiet about Dominique Laroche." She looked out of the window for a split second, before her eyes landed back on Juliette, a harsh coldness glinting in them. "How generous."

Sybille was made out of ambition, and it burned much

brighter in people like her than any inkling of feelings she might actually have for Juliette. She would take the deal.

"I guess I have no choice." She started to lean forward a little bit. "Even though I know very well that I'm not the first junior member of staff to end up in bed with someone from management. And look where that got them…" She narrowed her eyes. "I guess I learned the valuable lesson that PR is never a fair game."

Juliette wanted to point out all the differences between Sybille and Steph, but wisely held her tongue. "I'm sorry it had to go this way."

"I bet." Sybille finally grabbed the folder from Juliette's desk and leafed through it. Juliette saw her eyes widen slightly as she speed-read through it—probably when she saw the proposed salary, which was a twenty-five percent bump from what Barbier & Cyr paid her. Claire had done a good job in making this an offer Sybille couldn't refuse.

"I'll take it," she said. "Where do I sign?"

Juliette presented her with the necessary papers. "Johnson PR is lucky to have you."

Sybille scribbled her signature on a few dotted lines, put the pen Juliette provided her with down, and stood up. "I'm glad you think so." She exited Juliette's office without saying another word.

Relieved, Juliette sagged into her chair, happy to have that ordeal behind her.

MARGOT

Margot didn't use her key when she went to see Claire. It wouldn't have been right.

"Hey stranger," Claire said. "Who are you again?" She leaned against the front door frame and slanted her head. "And what can I do for you?" A wide smile played on her lips. *She had no idea.*

Margot couldn't possibly play along this time. "Can I come in?" She tried to make her voice sound light and carefree, but she knew she failed miserably.

"Of course." Claire grabbed a fistful of the fabric of Margot's t-shirt and yanked her inside. "I haven't seen you in days, doctor. I want to eat you alive." Obviously Claire's attention was not focused on the gravitas in Margot's voice.

When Claire pulled Margot close for a kiss, Margot's body went rigid. "I, uh, we need to talk."

With a look of stunned hurt on her face, Claire took a step back. "We do?"

Margot could not recall a time in her life when she'd felt this utterly useless. The fact that she'd been hurt so badly herself didn't make it easier. "Let's sit." She gestured at the sofa.

"Just tell me." Claire stood there, arms crossed over her chest, as if she already knew.

"I'm so sorry." Afraid her knees would buckle, Margot needed to lean against something. She shuffled closer to a hallway cabinet. "But I can't do this. I really, truly believed I could, otherwise I would never have let it come this far, but I was wrong."

"What are you talking about?" Impatience and brooding anger seeped from Claire's voice.

"I still love her. Inez. She…" The speech Margot had carefully prepared slipped from her mind at the sight of Claire's crumpling face. Margot rushed over to her. "I'm so sorry." If she said she was sorry one more time she'd have to slap herself.

"Don't touch me," Claire said and took another step back. She glared at Margot, grinding her teeth. "I don't understand. The other day…" As if the news just hit her, she sought support against the nearby wall.

"You don't deserve this, I know. This is all on me. You are an amazing woman, the only one who—"

"Clearly not amazing enough to match up to your bloody wonderful ex." Tears started leaking from Claire's eyes. "I'm in

305

love with you, for heaven's sake. I haven't felt like this about anybody in years and now you stand there and tell me that it's over? Because Inez Larue came back from curing sick children in the desert and you simply can't resist her?" She blew air through her nostrils in quick puffs. "I—" She tapped her chest and just shook her head.

Not even saying goodbye to Inez at the airport when she'd left for Rwanda had felt as dreadful as this, as if she were taking away someone's life force.

"What can I do?" Claire asked. "There must be something I can do." She wiped the tears from her cheeks, as if preparing to do battle. "I'm not losing you, not like this."

Margot couldn't hold the tears back either. She leaned against the wall as well, mirroring Claire's position.

"If you need some time, I can give you time. I mean, I've waited long enough for someone like you to come along… or, have you? Are you back together with her?"

Margot shook her head. "No, we talked and… we kissed."

"You can't let her do this to us." Claire grabbed Margot by the t-shirt again. "I thought you were strong."

"I'm not." Defeated, Margot shook her head, tears running down her cheeks, staining her t-shirt. "Not when it comes to her."

"Not even for me?" Claire's voice broke, along with Margot's heart, in a thousand pieces.

"I wish I was." It wasn't a lie. "Maybe I need time, I don't know. All I know is that this is not fair on you. I can't string you along like that. I'm not just going to get back together with her but… it's too much. I see her every day and, sometimes, just looking at her feels like betraying you."

"She broke your heart."

"I know," Margot said. *And now I've broken yours.*

"Go. Please. Go." Claire started sinking through her knees, a sniffling mess against the wall.

"I'll call Nadia and Juliette. I'll ask them to come over."

306

"No," Claire shook her head. "You've done enough."

"Okay." Margot couldn't do anything but leave Claire in the state she was in—the state she'd put her in—and deposit her key on the hallway cabinet on the way out.

NADIA

Nadia could say she'd give Juliette another chance all she wanted, but she wouldn't know if she had actually meant it until they took the leap. Juliette had done her bit by firing Sybille, not something Nadia had insisted upon—although it helped—but more an act of goodwill.

She showed up at their flat with another suitcase full of clothes that had made their way to Margot's over the weeks they'd spent apart. Every time the front door opened though, a flash of panic shot through her. A pang of fear of finding Sybille standing behind Juliette in the hallway again. A recurring surge of the dread she'd felt when she'd come to tell Juliette about Marie Dievart.

Whereas before their life together had always been relatively trouble-free, now they had a joint past that was worrisome. And of course it was foolish to believe that one act of betrayal could just erase the other, but what other choice did they have but forgiveness? If they truly wanted to put this behind them, they had to at least try.

Nadia was scared, however, because she knew, more than anything, that this would be their last chance. If this failed, they were done. And above all that, she knew that she had to take the lead. Not only when they decided to sleep together again— which could well happen tonight—but also in their slow conversations about what it would take to heal and move on.

"I opened a bottle of wine," Juliette said, after Nadia had entered the flat, they'd greeted each other with a still awkward peck on the cheek, and Nadia had deposited her suitcase in the bedroom.

"Maybe we should try without wine, babe." Nadia stood a bit forlornly in the living room. *God, she wanted a glass of wine so badly.*

"Seriously?" Juliette eyed her with skeptical curiosity in her glance.

Nadia nodded. "It's one change I feel compelled to make. At least tonight."

"Okay." Juliette sat down in the sofa. Nadia took the seat next to her.

"It feels so good to be back." She extended her arm and touched Juliette's thigh. The last time they'd sat in the living room together, Juliette had made a play for her. Advances Nadia had had no choice but to reject.

Juliette found Nadia's hand with hers. "Good to have you back."

The scene was tender and awkward at the same time. Nadia was bursting with good intentions, but simultaneously, it felt as if she didn't know how to kiss her partner anymore—or if it would even be an appropriate thing to do.

Juliette turned to her, found her eyes. "I need to say this, okay?"

Nadia nodded, gripping Juliette's hand tighter.

"What happened with Sybille was madness. I was lonely and hurt and, honestly, it could not have meant less. When it came down to it, there was nothing between us. Not a spark."

Nadia could tell by the look In Juliette's eyes that she spoke the truth. "I know. It was just a shock seeing her here, especially because of what I had come to say."

"What had you come to say?" Hope flickered in Juliette's glance.

Nadia took a deep breath. "That I was wrong to blame it all on you. That about sums it up."

"I wasn't here. For a long time, while eating dinner with you, or while watching TV, my head was elsewhere. It's only normal that we drifted apart, but, as usual, I was waiting for you to fix it all."

"That's what I should have done. It's my—"

"No." Juliette stopped her, shaking her head. "We can try to assign blame all we want. Divide it neatly amongst the two of us. Maybe it will even make us feel better, but we must look at the future, not dwell on the past."

Nadia was impressed with Juliette's positive, forward-thinking outlook. In the past year, assigning blame had been one of her favourite hobbies. "I've missed you so much, babe. Not just these past few weeks. I've missed you for months." She tugged at Juliette's arm, pulling her closer. "I've missed this." She cupped Juliette's chin in her palms and drew her near for a kiss.

"Take me like you did the very first time." Juliette's eyes smouldered with desire, with the need to erase and go back. To undo things. Perhaps she had been thinking back at their first encounter as well. At the significance and the innocence of that first date.

"I could try," Nadia gasped. "But we have ten years between us now." She hoisted Juliette on top of her. "Back then…" She slid her hand underneath Juliette's blouse, in search of the cup of her bra. While her fingers roamed across Juliette's skin, Nadia kept her eyes on Juliette's until she squeezed a rock-hard nipple between her thumb and index finger. "…I didn't know how crazy this could make you." Juliette's breath caught in her throat, her muscles flexing. "And this." Nadia slanted her head and inched closer until her teeth hovered over Juliette's earlobe. She bit down while simultaneously pinching Juliette's nipple again.

Nadia could only guess at the wetness spreading between Juliette's legs, but for years, this had been the only foreplay she'd needed. Tonight, it wouldn't be like that, though. Tonight was about reacquaintance, recommitting and remembering the good things between them. Trying to find that joint frequency again. It couldn't be frantic like all the times they'd tried to resurrect their relationship with a quick frenzy of thrusting fingers in between mind games.

"Come on," Nadia loosened the grip of her teeth on Juliette's ear and whispered. "I hope you don't have a busy day tomorrow because I plan to keep you up all night."

Then Nadia's phone started ringing. She ignored it as long as she could, until it started ringing again, along with Juliette's.

CLAIRE

While Claire waited for Juliette to arrive, she drank vodka straight from the bottle, desperately trying to numb the acute pain in her soul. She'd asked Juliette to come alone because the last thing she wanted was to stare Juliette and Nadia's magical reunion in the face. They were probably kidding themselves as much as she had fooled herself.

Most of her thoughts were occupied by images of Doctor Inez Larue. Why else would she have invested so much of her time last Saturday into a conversation with Claire, if not to stab her in the back royally after? It wasn't that Margot had confessed to having kissed Inez that hurt the most either—it was the simple fact that she loved Inez more than Claire. *It's too much*, she had said.

Words that were etched in Claire's memory forever.

Claire jumped when the bell rang. For an instant she hoped it was Margot who had come back to tell her she'd made a big mistake.

Juliette wrapped her arms around Claire the second she walked in. "I'm so sorry," she said. "I truly believed she was one of the good ones."

"She was," Claire said, strangely devoid of tears now.

They sat down and Claire drank more vodka before speaking. "I love her. I haven't said that about anyone in a very long time, but I love her. How bloody ironic is that?" She shook her head. "And I can't fight for her because I can't possibly compete with what she had with Inez. But fuck, it hurts." She took another swig. "She was a good one. Too good. That damned doctor without borders, though… The things I want to do to her."

"You can, you know. You can fight for her." Juliette said it with such passion and Claire wanted to believe it so desperately, but she'd seen the look in Margot's eyes. "What are they going to do? Pick up where they left things? Margot doesn't strike me as the kind of person who would do that, regardless of any leftover feelings she may have." She reached out her hand, demanding the bottle. "Give me that." She sipped from it and made a face. "That's ghastly." She handed the bottle back. "I've told you this before. You're a catch, and you're not the one who broke Margot's heart before."

"If I'm such a catch, why does everyone I ever really care about end up leaving me?" Claire slouched in the sofa and drank more.

"You're not referring to me, are you?" Juliette poked her elbow in Claire's ribs. "We were two big bottoms. What were we ever going to do with each other?" She held out her hand again. "And look at us now. Still best friends after all these years."

"Years you've spent with someone who loves you by your side." Claire didn't want to go back to having friends with benefits to meet her sexual needs. Now that she'd had a taste of what it was like to fall in love again, she was no longer interested in casual flings. She wasn't like Steph, protecting her heart at great cost to her love life. She'd never been like that. She'd just been selective, until Margot had entered the scene.

"As you well know, it's not all sunshine and roses." Juliette sipped from the bottle again before giving it back to Claire.

"I think we should tell Steph to go on holiday with Dominique." Claire was starting to feel the effects of the booze. She hadn't had dinner—expecting to have a meal with Margot.

"What?" Juliette turned to her. "Where's that coming from?"

"No offence, but out of the three of us, she's the one happiest in love. Who are we to ask her to not enjoy that? This rare and precious thing called love. She'd be a fool to listen to us in the first place." Claire grabbed her phone from the armrest of the sofa. "I'm going to text her so she can start making arrangements."

"Why don't you sleep on that?" Juliette covered Claire's hand with hers, palming the phone.

"Sleep? I don't think I'll be sleeping tonight." Claire yanked the phone from Juliette's hand. "They're in love. Steph never falls in love. Let her have it."

Claire started typing and showed the message to Juliette before sending it.

Please, go on holiday with Dominique. If you love her, then be with her. Nothing is more important than love. Not politics, and especially not PR.

"You're the one who wanted to keep Dominique as a client," Claire said while Juliette read the words on the screen of her phone.

"Not so our staff could go to the south of France with her."

"Jules, come on. This is important." Claire felt the tears sting behind her eyes again. "At least one of us miserable cunts at Barbier & Cyr deserves to be happy." She shook her head. "You had to fire your bloody assistant this week because you slept with her, for crying out loud. With all that stupid business at work, the only thing that kept me sane was knowing that I'd see Margot at night. That's what love is, what it does. Why we need it." The tears broke through. Claire put her phone on the coffee table, the message unsent.

Juliette reached for it and touched the screen a few times. "Sent," she said. She inched closer and wrapped her arm around Claire's shoulder. "Do you have any mixers for that vodka?"

"It's pure or nothing," Claire sulked. "Thanks for coming."

Juliette chuckled. "You're almost as stubborn as me."

"I'm glad you and Nadia are trying again." The last wave of tears started to dry, but the sense of loss that had settled in Claire's gut the instant Margot had walked out stayed. Too tired to hold the bottle, Claire set it on the coffee table.

"It's not easy, but we'll see."

"Remember a few weeks ago when you and Nadia were fucking like rabbits and you unceremoniously told me that the sex was earth-shattering?" Claire could have sworn she felt something sting on the skin of her wrists. "Margot blew my mind… and to think she might be doing the exact same thing to Inez perhaps even as we speak. Maybe she was waiting on the back of her motorbike downstairs."

"You mustn't think like that." Juliette reached for the bottle. "And, yes, I know I sound like a hypocrite. Just like I know me saying that doesn't make any difference to how you feel or think."

"Lovers come and go, but you're always here, Jules." Claire turned to her friend. "You can be a real bitch sometimes, but you're the best friend I've ever had."

"Ditto, minus the bitch part." Juliette took a large swig of the vodka, coughing loudly as she pushed the bottle away from her.

Maybe their promiscuous friend Steph, while absolutely not looking for it, had found true love, while Claire, who had been much more receptive to the idea, and had had a taste of it briefly as well, was actually the one who wasn't cut out for it.

Maybe Claire should try going to Les Pêches on her own this weekend. The mere thought of it made her nauseous.

STEPH

Steph showed Dominique Claire's message. She wondered what had triggered it, but she could either spend her time trying to find out why Claire had changed her mind, or planning a trip to the Côte d'Azur.

"Permission from the boss lady," Dominique said. "I feel so validated. A bit like winning an election." She sat reading e-mails on her laptop, her back against the armrest of the sofa, her feet propped up on Steph's lap.

Of course, having Claire's blessing didn't change the fact that they would be taking a risk. Steph realised this all too well, which is why she had decided, well before Claire had asked her, not to go. But tonight was their last night together before Dominique left for two weeks, leaving behind a big well of nothingness for Steph to drown in.

"Don't look so excited." Dominique drew up her leg and nudged Steph in the thigh with her big toe.

"You know I want to go, but I still think it's an insane idea."

Dominique put her laptop on the floor and folded her legs underneath her bottom, facing Steph. "It's perfectly containable. I wouldn't have proposed it if it were to put me at risk. We just won't be able to leave the grounds together, but frankly, I see no need for that." She shot Steph her sexy smirk. "The children and I fly out on Saturday, so you should book a flight for Sunday. Rent a car at the airport and drive down. Easy."

"How many times will I be hiding in your bathroom though?"

"You worry too much, Stéphanie. Lisa and Didier get so excited when we go to Juan-les-Pins, they'll barely even notice you're there."

"That makes me feel so much better. Thanks." Because, if she was really honest with herself, Steph knew that if they played it smart and were careful, no one would find out that Dominique Laroche had brought her lesbian lover to her family's summer house. It was mainly the secretive aspect of it that didn't sit well with her, once again—the constant reminder of the impossibility of their affair.

"They do sleepovers at other people's houses… so we'll have the whole place to ourselves. Swimming pool. Jacuzzi. No clothes…" Dominique inched closer, her mouth hovering over Steph's ear. "Just you and me and the stars in the sky."

"If you put it like that." Steph was melting again, her entire core turning into gooey liquid for this woman with whom, when she thought about it, she had nothing in common.

"We'll have time to chat, endless hours in the sun, excellent wine… and I'll get to see you in a bikini." Dominique's lips all but touched Steph's ear now. "Or without."

"Fine." Steph turned, looking Dominique straight in the eyes. "But if you think you're going to top me every night, you're terribly mistaken."

Dominique stretched her lips into a wide smile. "I have no idea what that means, but it sounds kinky."

"Don't play dumb with me." Steph rose from her seat and started pushing Dominique down. "I'm about done bottoming for you." She wasn't though, not by a long shot.

"About that box under your bed." Dominique wrapped her arms around Steph's neck. "Does it contain… what's it called… a strap-on? I'd love to try that."

"I bet," Steph said before shutting Dominique up by kissing her, while the mere thought of it made her go dizzy. In her imagination, she wasn't the one strapping it on either.

She'd book her flight first thing tomorrow.

EPISODE FIVE

STEPH

"You're not using it on me," Steph said in a low voice. She looked at Dominique who held the toy in her hand, eyeing it quizzically. "That's just not something I do."

"Then why did you bring it?" Dominique glanced at her.

Steph was bone-tired and feeling out of place. They sat in Dominique's bedroom, connected to Steph's room for the week by a bathroom. The house was big and white and stunning, about twenty times the size of Steph's studio near Père Lachaise. The view, although already obscured by darkness by the time Steph had arrived in her rental car, was spectacular and all it did was reinforce the feeling that she shouldn't have come.

"To, you know—" She tilted her head and arched up her eyebrows, unsure of which words were allowed to be used in the house. Dominique had assured her the children were out like lights in the garden bedrooms—so they could jump into the pool as soon as they woke up—and fully briefed that there would be a guest for breakfast.

Dominique chuckled. "If you think you're going to fuck me

with this thing, you've come a long way for nothing." She cast the dildo aside and shuffled closer to Steph.

"Your loss." Steph kept a brave face. "I'll have you know I'm quite the expert and I've never had any complaints."

"Oh, I'm sure." Dominique painted a coy grin on her face. "But I simply have no desire for a fake penis inside of me." She grabbed hold of Steph's hand and lifted it to her mouth. "I'll make do with these." She kissed the tips of Steph's index and middle finger.

"That's what you think it is? A fake penis?" Steph was not ready to surrender just yet.

"Come on, sweetie, you know what I mean." Dominique wrapped her lips around Steph's index finger and sucked it deep into her mouth.

As much as Steph wanted to flop down onto the bed with Dominique and engage in the activities she'd been dreaming of all the way over here—the promises that had enticed her to take this trip—it all felt off.

Dominique didn't seem to notice, though. She looked relaxed and glorious, her casual white top contrasting already with the deeper colour of her skin, seemingly having tanned overnight. She rose and stood in front of Steph, slipping Steph's fingers from her mouth and sliding them under the elasticated waistband of her linen shorts. Wet heat radiated on Steph's fingers and, just like that—again—she acquiesced. It wasn't as if she had anywhere to run, except to her own room, which wasn't even hers, on the other side of the bathroom.

Dominique bent at the waist until her lips found Steph's ear. "Fuck me with your fingers, Stéphanie." Her tongue flicked over Steph's earlobe for an instant, her fingers still curled around Steph's wrist. "I've been wet all day, waiting for you."

Then it stopped being a matter of acquiescing altogether. With her free hand, Steph tugged Dominique's shorts down, panties included.

Dominique smiled at her while wrestling her legs out of her

shorts and spreading wide. She scooted forward a bit, pushing Steph on the bed, so she could plant her knees next to Steph's thighs.

Barely unpacked and still wearing her travel clothes— although, she suspected, not for much longer—Steph slid two fingers inside of Dominique's moist pussy, and it all fell away. Steph curved her free arm around Dominique's waist for support, and fucked her the way she'd asked her to. She hadn't lied about being sufficiently lubricated either.

If this is the only woman I ever sink my fingers into again, Steph caught herself thinking, while digging deep inside of Dominique, curling her fingers, finding that spot, she might actually be able to live with that. Dominique crawled further onto the bed, pushing Steph onto her back in the process, until her pussy was positioned right above Steph's mouth. Steph knew what to do.

Dominique lowered herself until Steph's tongue connected with her clit, while Steph's fingers kept on thrusting inside. Steph looked up through her eyelashes, at this woman who had changed everything about her. Not just the fact that she rarely came back for seconds, let alone thirds and trips to the Côte d'Azur, but also that, apparently, she now enjoyed this sort of lovemaking—the kind where she wasn't solely in charge. Dominique had her by the heart and by the crotch. And Steph knew full well that, before her holiday was over, Dominique would have used the toy on her. It was why she'd brought it.

"Oh, babe," Dominique moaned, and it was the use of pet names that, quite possibly, got to Steph the most. The intimacy it implied. How it deepened their connection.

"I'm—" Dominique collapsed on top of her and Steph's fingers slipped out with the forward movement of Dominique's pelvis. "See," Dominique said, her hair a tangled mess across Steph's face, her limbs sprawled across her body. "Your fingers are more than enough."

NADIA

"Let's go to bed," Juliette said, freeing herself from Nadia's embrace.

"Okay." Nadia's heart started thundering in her chest. Margot and Claire's break-up had changed the course of her and Juliette's reunion considerably. Juliette had stayed late at Claire's every evening, not making it home at all on two occasions. It had bought Nadia some time, given her a clearer view on what had happened.

She refused to sleep in their bed—the thought of Juliette and Sybille being together in it too much of a reminder of everything that had gone wrong. With Juliette barely coming home, it hadn't been an issue. They had seemed to fall into a mellower version of the routine they'd perfected before everything had crumbled. No sex. Only running into each other for brief moments. Hardly taking the time to talk—simply because there was none.

Nadia had accompanied Juliette to Claire's a few times, and she'd seen with her own eyes how unfit their friend was to be alone at night. Nadia had never seen Claire, who looked like she'd taken up the habit of emptying a bottle of vodka every evening, in such a state.

They sat up and Nadia switched off the TV. It was only nine o'clock, not their usual time for bed, but she knew what Juliette was saying. *It was time.*

"Will she be all right?" The only 'she' Nadia and Juliette referred to lately was Claire, so there was no room for confusion. "All alone on the road like that?"

"I can hardly hold her hand through her holiday." Juliette looked at Nadia. "Or is that selfish of me?"

"God no, babe." Nadia had been impressed with Juliette's incessant care for her best friend. "You've done plenty."

"Come on." Juliette pushed herself out of the sofa and extended her hand. "Time for *us* now. At last."

Nadia allowed Juliette to pull her out of the sofa and lead her to the hallway. She halted when they reached their bedroom door, tugging at Juliette's wrist.

"Right, sorry." Shame crossed Juliette's face. "Guest room it is."

Not the best sensation to start the rekindling of their love life with. All these things that stood between them now. Could they just fuck them away?

Maybe they should start by getting a new bed. Every time Nadia ventured into the room to fetch some clothes or jewellery, the current one stood there like a giant reminder of their failure. Ironically, it was after waking up in that same bed that Nadia had proposed to bury the hatchet. A hangover will do that to you—will make you forget temporarily only to slap you in the face with it ten times harder later. Not that she regretted the decision she had made that day, but that bed, that would have to go, no matter the memories they'd made in it themselves.

"It's okay." Nadia pulled Juliette closer, coaxing her towards the guest room. "It's not important where it happens." Nadia could say that all she wanted, straight face and everything, but she knew it was a lie. And in unguarded moments, she did compare grief. She'd had a one-night stand that Juliette hadn't even noticed, while Juliette had let Sybille fuck her in their bed. Perhaps Nadia wouldn't even have known if she hadn't come home early that day, but she had come to the flat for a good reason. And she *did* know.

"I'm sorry," Juliette said, again, waiting for Nadia to make the next move—also, again.

"Take your clothes off." Nadia stood back and watched Juliette. "Slowly."

She looked just as beautiful doing it as the first time Nadia had asked her. Ten years older, with shorter hair and a few more wrinkles, but just as gorgeous and ready to surrender as then. But if Juliette expected this to be a copy of their first night together, she'd quickly have to modify her expectations. Try as they might, it would never be the same again.

Nadia waited until Juliette stood naked in front of her. She eyed her from underneath her lashes. Juliette always looked so pale next to her own nut-brown skin, so delicate. "Now undress me." Noticing the surprise in Juliette's eyes, she shot her the beginning of a smile. Perhaps Nadia was overcompensating, throwing Juliette off to keep her attention at all times, to make a point. Unlike Sybille, she was not a girl in her early twenties, either. Not just because she hardly still had the body of one, but because she knew what she was doing.

Juliette's hands reached for the buttons of her blouse. Looking into Nadia's eyes, she undid them one by one, her fingers brushing against Nadia's skin.

"Faster," Nadia whispered, surprised by the raggedness of her own breath. She was usually able to control herself much better. By the time she stepped out of her underwear, Juliette freeing it from around her ankles, her exposed clit was throbbing wildly and her nipples couldn't point upwards more.

"Come here." She beckoned Juliette. Wrapping her arms around her, their breasts meeting, she said, "You're going to make me come twice before I even touch you. Tongue only the first time. You can use your fingers the second time around."

This scenario couldn't be further removed from their first time, when Nadia had coaxed several orgasms from Juliette, one from barely even looking at her the way she knew how, before she'd even allowed Juliette to touch her.

Juliette looked her in the eyes, biting her bottom lip, and nodded. She grabbed Nadia by the wrists and yanked her towards the bed, swivelling them around so she could push Nadia down onto the covers.

"I love you," Juliette said after laying her warm body on top of Nadia's. She pressed her lips to Nadia's and kissed her. The way heat crashed through her flesh at the mere touch of Juliette's lips, Nadia figured the first orgasm wouldn't take very long. Especially if she kept envisioning what she'd make Juliette do to reach her own first climax.

"Lick me," Nadia whispered in her partner's ear. "Now." It wasn't as much a command as the sheer need coursing through Nadia's body finding a way out.

Juliette smiled down at her with that lopsided grin of hers. God, those lips. If there was one body part of Juliette that was irreplaceable it was her upper lip. The curve of it. The way one side was fuller than the other and how it made her look so irresistible even when she pouted.

"Brace yourself, babe," Juliette said.

And Nadia did. Her muscles contracted as Juliette's tongue travelled over her body, her lips nipping their way down her skin, only briefly stopping at Nadia's nipples, because so much urgency filled the air by then—mainly in the shape of Nadia's hands pushing Juliette's head down.

When Juliette dragged the tip of her tongue along Nadia's pulsing pussy lips, Nadia's muscles tensed further. So much tension had built up in her flesh the last few weeks—and she'd hardly been in the mood to tend to herself. Still sticking to her almost-no-booze rule—except when visiting Claire, then it was impossible—her head was clear, her body reacting more keenly to Juliette's touch.

Juliette pushed her tongue inside of Nadia, before licking upwards again, stopping at her clit. She sucked Nadia's swollen bud between her lips, time and time again, before unleashing her tongue.

All around Nadia, the walls seemed to cave in. A black hole swallowed her for a few seconds, before releasing her into a bubble of sheer joy. The tingle spread through her flesh, tears stinging behind her eyes, as her muscles relaxed and she fell back onto the bed.

Juliette was smart. She didn't give Nadia time to recover. Pushing herself up, her fingers already roaming around Nadia's soaked pussy lips, she said, "Look at me, babe."

HARPER BLISS

Nadia opened her eyes and looked into Juliette's angelic face, her chin glistening with juices. It was the only time of the day when Juliette's face could be described as angelic—when she did this. When she let go of everything and gave herself to Nadia.

Juliette locked her gaze on Nadia as she let three fingers slip inside, spreading her wide from the get-go.

Nadia huffed out a blast of air—pure relief bursting from her lungs—but held Juliette's gaze. She didn't have to say it this time. Juliette was already fucking her. Three fingers delved inside of her, going wide, thrusting deep. It seemed that, with every stroke, another layer of hurt dissolved, and Nadia was glad she'd taken that first, deceptively simple step to reconciliation. Hadn't Juliette said it once when they were shagging like bunnies to forget there issues? *This is who we are.* Juliette had held the right end of the stick many more times than Nadia had given her credit for.

"Yes, oh yes," she said, still staring into Juliette's face, which didn't look so angelic anymore. Her eyes were narrowed to slits, and those lips, oh goodness—Juliette thrust deeper, deeper than Nadia thought she could go, and the sensation crashed through Nadia's entire body as if she'd taken some sort of instant pleasure drug. Hit after hit pounded through her veins, quickly saturating her blood.

Out of breath, the back of her head met the pillow, as Juliette let her fingers slip out. She kissed her way back up Nadia's torso, until she reached Nadia's face, a triumphant grin playing on her lips.

"And to think I was worried about this," Nadia said. She pulled Juliette closer and wrapped her arms around her. "That we almost walked away from this." Nadia's cheeks were wet with tears, her heart full of love. She planted a kiss on Juliette's tousled hair, before finding her ear. "I need you to lie on your back for me, babe."

Juliette broke away from their embrace and looked down at Nadia, biting her lip. She complied instantly.

"Spread your legs and touch yourself. I want to see," Nadia instructed. She pushed herself up and positioned herself at the other end of the bed to get a better view. "Make yourself come for me."

Juliette's legs fell apart, both of her hands reaching between her upper thighs. Her eyes were wild, her lips crooked, and, as she started tracing her fingers across her pussy lips, she was still, after all this time, the most beautiful woman Nadia had ever seen.

CLAIRE

Claire made a detour before steering her car towards the motorway. She couldn't leave on holiday before she'd seen her, before she'd asked. She found a parking space near the hospital's entrance and hoped she wouldn't run into Margot in the corridors. Or Nadia, for that matter. She didn't feel like explaining herself, she just wanted to confront Inez. She stalked through the hallway to the on-call room where she'd met Margot a few times, praying that she wouldn't find the two of them together, sitting across from each other, not touching but as good as all over each other, the way she and Margot had been.

"Claire?"

Fuck. It was Nadia's voice. Claire supposed it would have been too easy to just walk in and find Inez. She didn't even know if she was working today. She turned around. "Yes."

"What are you doing here?" Nadia had that look of compassion on her face again, as if she understood everything Claire was going through. And perhaps she did, but she didn't feel her pain. Didn't feel that bitter sting of rejection that only seemed to intensify as the days progressed.

"I'm looking for Inez. I need to speak with her. Is she here?"

"Yes, but—"

"Please, Nadz, five minutes, then I'll be out of your way." She dropped her hands to her sides. "Please." Claire didn't have to try to make it sound heartfelt. The state her heart was in was plastered all over her face—she saw it every time she looked in the mirror.

"Okay." Nadia nodded. "You know where my office is, right?"

"Yes." Claire guessed Nadia felt guilty. After all, she'd set her and Margot up, after which she had hired Inez—the consequences of that staring her straight in the face.

"Wait there. I'll ask her to meet you there as soon as possible."

"Thanks." Claire turned on her heels and quickly made her way to Nadia's office before she could change her mind—and before she ran into Margot in the hallways. Claire wouldn't be able to handle that particular confrontation, she knew that much.

If she ever had an emergency, she'd be sure to never come to this bloody hospital, where doctors got hired because of their family connections instead of their skills. Not that she suspected that Inez lacked skills, obviously being a model human being and all that.

She didn't have to wait long before the door to Nadia's office opened, and, without knocking, Inez walked in.

Claire was well aware of the dark circles under her eyes, the pallid complexion of her skin because of too much vodka and not enough sleep. She suspected it stood in stark contrast to Inez' radiant appearance, ginger hair tucked into a neat ponytail, her skin as clear as day. Claire didn't know what to say now that she stood face-to-face with Inez, the person who had taken it all from her.

"I'm so sorry, Claire," Inez said. "Why don't we sit for a minute." She gestured at the two chairs across from Nadia's desk.

Claire's legs shook as she padded to the chair. She'd hoped

for a brave stance, a stern voice and hands that didn't tremble the way hers were doing. Already emotionally exhausted, just by looking at Inez, she fell into the chair.

"Are you and Margot—" Saying her name was enough to elicit a tear to spring from Claire's eyes.

"Look, Claire…" Inez sat down in the chair next to Claire's and turned it towards her. She put a hand on Claire's arm.

"Don't touch me." Claire held up her palms. "Just…" She shook her head. "Don't."

"I didn't mean for Margot to break up with you." She actually sounded as if she meant what she was saying.

"Then why the hell did you come back for her? Do you think I can't put two and two together?" All the anger that had been building inside of her came out. "Are you bloody happy now?"

"I understand you're angry." Inez kept her voice calm. After the things she must have seen, a scorned lover was probably nothing for her. A bit of a nuisance, maybe, but nothing she couldn't cope with. "If I was in your shoes, I'd be angry too. But you must believe me. Neither I, nor Margot, set out to hurt you."

"Oh really." Because, fuck, it hurt. "Next you'll be telling me you're not sleeping together, either. And that you didn't come back for her, to this very hospital."

"We're not together. You know Margot. She's devastated by this."

Claire narrowed her eyes. "She is?"

Inez puffed out some air. "What do you think?"

"I don't know what to fucking think. All I know is that we were happy, then as soon as you came along, she dumped me."

"I'm sorry." Inez didn't say anything else. Was the great, heroic doctor at a loss for words as well? Did she not get exactly what she had bargained for? It didn't change anything for Claire.

"Yeah, well, so am I." Claire rose from her chair. The most she could take from this meeting was that Inez and Margot hadn't fallen into each other's arms… yet. It was only a matter of time. "Thanks for nothing, doc." Claire walked to the door and shut it behind her with a loud bang. She stormed out of the hospital as quickly as she could, found her car and sat behind the steering wheel for about thirty seconds before the tears came. She banged her fist on the dashboard, but all it did was leave her with a sore knuckle. Maybe a few days with her family would do her good. As if.

MARGOT

"Claire came to see me." Margot had just arrived at the hospital for the graveyard shift, had literally just slipped into her white coat, when Inez sprung the news on her in the changing room. Her stomach did another one of those flips it had been doing quite frequently the past week.

"What did she say?" Margot crashed with her back against the lockers, the image of Claire crumbling in front of her still fresh in her mind.

"What do you think, Go-Go?" Inez stared her down. "She came to wish us the best of luck." Frustration seemed to seep from every pore of Inez' skin.

"What did you say to her?"

Inez took a few steps closer. "That I was sorry you broke her heart." She paused. "And that, in the end, it had probably all been for nothing anyway."

"Lay off." If it had been possible, Margot would have pushed herself further into the lockers. Since that heartbreaking scene at Claire's apartment, Margot had barely been able to be in the same room as Inez. She'd thought she was doing the right thing, but all she had ended up feeling was pure guilt.

"It's true though, isn't it?" Inez backed off a little, sitting down on the bench in front of the lockers. "You kiss me. You break up with your girlfriend for me. Then you avoid me like the plague. What am I supposed to think?"

"Don't start." Margot didn't want to have this discussion here. "You're the one who ruined us in the first place." And she was the one who had ruined Claire.

"Yes, I made a mistake. A big one." Inez rose, shuffling closer to Margot again. "And you know how dreadfully sorry I am about that. About hurting you like that." Her green eyes found Margot's. "And I'll give you all the time you need. I hope you know that." She swallowed hard. "But it kills me that you won't talk to me, that you're shutting me out." A finger brushed against Margot's hand. "That you're swapping shifts to avoid me."

"I know." Margot sighed. "I just hadn't expected that hurting someone the way I hurt Claire would have such an effect on me." Margot retracted her hand to no longer feel Inez' touch. "You did that to me and still had the nerve to come back."

"Because I love you, more than anything and anyone in this world."

"That's bullshit, Inez. If you did, you wouldn't have left. You would have stayed for me."

"If you wanted me to stay so badly, you should have asked. You made it seem as if I was doing the world a big favour by joining MSF, as if it was a sacrifice you would easily make."

Margot shook her head. "Don't turn this around on me." She padded to the right a bit, out of Inez' personal space. "Either way, that's water under the bridge now."

"Come on, Go-Go. We have to talk about this stuff." Inez sat down again. "I'm off tomorrow. Come to mine after your shift. Just for a talk."

"I can't. Not yet." She looked at Inez, at how beautiful she was, even just after a shift—and after facing the wrath of Claire. "Maybe this weekend. Okay?"

"I'm going to hold you to that." Inez' voice had grown soft, barely a whisper.

"I'd best get going." Margot threw Inez one last, quick glance before exiting the changing room.

STEPH

"Children are exhausting," Steph said, watching Dominique as she sat down next to her on a bench in the garden.

"And thanks to you, they're exhausted." Dominique shot her a smile. "I think, by the time you have to leave, they'll love you just as much as I do."

Children are also easy, Steph thought. Meeting Lisa and Didier had been uncomplicated. They weren't interested in where she came from or what she was doing at their grandfather's house. They only cared about how much she played with them, how high she could throw them in the swimming pool, and how long she could hold her breath under water.

"Big words, *Maman*." Steph smiled back at Dominique. She seemed to tan so easily. The only thing Steph had to show for a day in the sun was a couple of painful, red patches on her back and shoulders.

"Don't call me that." Dominique banged her heel into Steph's shin. "Exactly how tired are you?"

"What? You want to bang the nanny now?" Spending the entire day with Lisa and Didier hadn't left a lot of time for the two of them. Dominique was a different person with her children, when all the sexual innuendo between her and Steph fell away.

"Why don't I pour us a large glass of wine and we drink it in the jacuzzi?"

"You mean out here?" The children's bedrooms opened straight onto the pool.

"We could just talk, you know." Dominique let her foot fall against Steph's leg again, but softer this time. "We have the luxury of time this week. Besides, I'd like to ask you a few things."

"Sure." Steph hoped the jacuzzi was strong enough to force some new life into her tired muscles. "A conversation with a politician. I look forward to it."

Dominique leaned forward and kissed her on the nose. "Hop on in. I'll be right there."

Still in her bathing suit, Steph walked over to the jacuzzi and let herself slip in, finding a spot where a jet could massage her back. Dominique returned with a bottle of rosé and a plastic ice bag to keep it cool.

"What?" Steph asked, after Dominique had poured them both a generous glass and sat opposite her, their legs intertwined under water. She looked at Steph with a soft glint in her eyes.

"I'm already dreading the moment you'll have to leave." Was she getting sentimental? Steph was discovering unknown sides of Dominique a mile a minute. But she felt it too, and she'd only just arrived. The awkwardness of the first night had dissolved quickly and, after today, Steph wanted to stay for at least another month—although the children would have broken her physically by then.

"Let's make the most of the time we have." Steph was surprised by how philosophical her words sounded.

"Can I ask you an intimate question?" Dominique took her wine glass from the side of the pool and drank while waiting for Steph's reply.

"Be my guest." Steph grabbed her glass as well. The wine was cool against her tongue, its taste tender and fruity.

"I watched you with Didier and Lisa today, all day, really, and I realised I don't know very much about you. I mean, your body has become quite familiar, but Stéphanie Mathis, the person, is still a bit of a mystery." Dominique caught Steph's leg between hers under water.

"What would you like to know?" They spoke differently to each other here. Not feeling the effects of the pressure of time so much. Not blindly wanting to grab each other every second before one of them would have to rush off. Steph, also, didn't feel the need to reply to every question Dominique asked with a sparring quip—the way she often did when they were in Paris.

Dominique bit her lip before asking the question that, obviously, had been on her mind a while. "How many women have you been with?"

Steph looked away, into the darkness to her right, for an instant. She wasn't ashamed of her lifestyle, she simply didn't have a clue. "I don't know, fifty maybe, or a hundred. It's hard to keep track of these things sometimes." She scanned Dominique's face, only half-lit up by a garden lamp, looking for signs of disapproval.

"Mmm." Dominique retreated behind her pokerface. "How about since we met?"

Steph puffed some air through her nostrils. "Two. You and this girl I went home with on my birthday, because you weren't there." Steph regretted Cassandra—and conveniently forgot about her visit to Le Noir—because of how empty it had made her feel. "And we were on a break."

Dominique sucked both of her lips into her mouth and nodded. "Okay. I appreciate your honesty. Always have."

"Does it, huh, bother you?" A small surge of panic rushed through Steph.

"A little, I won't lie, but I have no claims to make." Dominique dropped Steph's leg from the under-water grip she'd been holding it in.

"If it's any consolation, it didn't mean anything." She took a quick sip. "I'm not one to declare my love easily, but, well, you know."

"Remember that day I came to your office, the day we decided to go on that break?" Dominique deposited her glass on the side of the jacuzzi, focusing her full attention on Steph. "The question I asked you that triggered the whole thing?"

Steph nodded. Of course she did.

"Do you mind if I ask you again?" Dominique pushed

herself to the edge of the mosaic bench, closer to Steph. "You can say no if you want. It won't change anything. Not this time."

Steph took a deep breath and nodded again. "There was this girl, obviously…" She got rid of her glass as well and her limbs met Dominique's in the water. "My second year of college. Her name was Laurence. We became friends, then more. I'd had girl crushes before, but with her, it was different. I could see it, you know. Could see the two of us doing all sorts of grown-up things together. I loved her. And she loved me too." It was a long time ago, but the memory still stung—it always would. "We were inseparable for a year, until one day, we met this guy who was a year above us. Ivan. I liked him and the three of us had a lot of fun together, until she left me for him." Steph felt Dominique slip closer under water, her palms on her thighs. "It hurt so much that I told myself that if this was how it was going to be every time I loved someone, I'd do things differently from then on. And I did."

"That's it?" Dominique's face was close to hers, drops of water falling from her hair. "Your first girlfriend hurt you and you believed everyone else would do the same?"

"She didn't just hurt me. She fucking ripped my heart out. She wasn't just my girlfriend, she was also my best friend. And I had to watch them go around campus together for the rest of my college career."

"But these things happen, babe. You bounce back from them."

"I bounced back, many times."

"I don't mean it like that." Dominique practically sat between Steph's legs.

"I *know* what you mean. I had crushes after Laurence. Girls I really liked, but I just never let it go further. I just couldn't face the prospect of someone doing that to me again." Steph cocked her head to the side. "And, well, I've never experienced a lack of women who were up for the sort of good time I was after."

"All the hearts you've broken." Dominique's arms curled around Steph's back.

"Nuh-uh. I'm always honest and clear about my intentions."

"And now?" Dominique slanted her head towards Steph's ear. "You've gone and fallen in love with a straight girl all over again."

"I'd hardly call you straight, chérie." Steph was surprised that Dominique's last comment didn't rub her up the wrong way. She planted a kiss on her cheek. "All that repressed lesbianism you need to get out. It makes you more of a dyke than me—at least in the bedroom."

"I have a confession of my own to make." Dominique broke free from their embrace and looked Steph in the eyes. "I told Philippe about you, about us."

Steph's eyes grew wide.

"I had to, because of the children. I thought he had a right to know that they were going to meet their mother's lesbian lover."

"You actually told another human being? This must be getting serious." Steph pulled Dominique close again.

"I've introduced you to my children, it doesn't get more serious than that." She pinned her gaze on Steph's. "And I'm glad I did."

Not bad for a doomed relationship, Steph thought. She'd only gone and got herself a girlfriend.

JULIETTE

When Juliette turned her key in the lock of their front door, she was surprised to find it unlocked. At four in the afternoon on a Tuesday?

"Hello," she shouted.

"Babe?" Nadia's voice beamed from inside the flat. A few seconds later she appeared in the hallway. "What are you doing home so early?"

"I could ask the same of you," Juliette said, although it was clear as day what Nadia was doing. Half of her face was covered in flour and she wore the large white apron she hadn't put on in months.

"I wanted to surprise you," Nadia pouted. "I figured I'd have the place to myself for the next couple of hours."

"What are you making?" The return of homely Nadia filled Juliette with a warm glow. She stepped closer and wiped some flour off her partner's nose.

"Homemade ravioli with parsley sauce." Nadia curved her arms around Juliette's waist. "What's your excuse to skive?"

"It's very quiet in the office and I'm expecting a delivery, which was meant to be a surprise for you."

"A surprise?" Nadia arched up her eyebrows. "Tell me, tell me, tell me."

"See, this is why I wanted it delivered when you weren't around. You're too nosy." She put her hands on Nadia's arms. "Is Saint-Vincent not crumbling without your presence?"

"I've decided to be more French about these things and take up at least half of the hours they make me work on weekends. You know, spend some more time with my lady." She started walking backwards, dragging Juliette with her in her embrace.

"You mean fatten me up with luscious home-cooked meals?" Juliette let Nadia drag her into the kitchen. When she reached the fridge, she leaned against it with her back and pulled Juliette close for a kiss. Something smelled great and the aroma, Nadia's warm welcome and the prospect of a long evening at home together, easily made Juliette forget about the mistakes they had made.

"As much as I would like to stand here and kiss you for a few hours, I must roll out the pasta before it gets too hard." Nadia released Juliette, swatted her on the backside, and padded to the countertop.

"Would you like some wine?" Juliette asked, an automatic

question so engrained in her daily life she still forgot that Nadia was trying to kick the habit of—at least—a bottle a day.

"I'm fine, but you go ahead, babe." Nadia shot her a wink. Juliette could never have dreamed that their reunion would go this easily. Granted, they were still somewhat walking on eggshells, taking extra care not to say anything offensive, a reflex that would certainly wear off sooner rather than later, but still, this picture of domestic bliss she had just walked in on was not what she had expected at all.

"That's okay." Juliette grabbed a bottle of water from the fridge and leaned against the window sill, watching Nadia work.

"Have you heard from Claire?" Nadia asked, while rolling out the dough.

"Yes, she has arrived safe and well and her family is driving her nuts already."

"When she comes back, you can take some time off before things pick up again in September, right?" Nadia looked up from the countertop. "Should we go somewhere? Just the two of us?"

Juliette remembered what had happened the last time they had planned a trip. "Sure." They were interrupted by the chime of the bell. "Ah, that must be for me." She walked into the hallway and turned to Nadia. "You stay here, okay?"

"Yeah right." Nadia wiped her hands on a towel and followed Juliette to the front door.

"LPM delivery," a man said. Behind him stood another man, stabilising a mattress and three large cardboard boxes. "Installation included." Juliette turned around, curious to see Nadia's reaction. It was supposed to be all ready and installed—the old, soiled bed safely removed—by the time Nadia came back from the hospital.

"You got us a new bed?" Her mouth fell open as she stepped aside for the two men.

"Yep," was all Juliette said, still unsure of how Nadia felt about it.

"I guess we can't sleep in the guest room forever." A smile started tugging at Nadia's lips. She grabbed Juliette by the fabric of her blouse and pulled her close. "Can't wait to break it in," she said, before kissing her on the lips.

CLAIRE

"How's the single life treating you," Sam asked. Claire had always gotten on fine with her brother, until he'd had children —three of them. Claire loved Emma and Léa, the five-year-old twins and Nathan, their two-year-old brother, but, about six months after the twins were born, she started wondering if she would ever get her brother back.

From the moment they'd been born, all of Claire's conversations with her brother had been absorbed by news of the girls. *They did this and then that. They'd both been sick. They can walk now. Have you seen how cute they are?* Also, when she and her brother were not alone, he actually spoke in baby talk and, to her horror, Claire had started doing the same.

There was nothing more effective to make siblings grow apart than one of them having children while the other remained childless. As if procreating was the most important aspect of life, and an existence that didn't even consider children was a mere waste of time. As much as Claire loved her nieces and her nephew, she loved her own child-free life just as much. Apart from the current bout of heartbreak she was battling.

"Don't ask," she said.

"Why not?" Sam looked at her expectantly. They had the house to themselves for a blissful few hours. Their parents had taken the kids to a new playground near Marseille and Sam's wife had tagged along, not wanting to leave the grandparents alone with the burden of keeping an eye on three rowdy toddlers.

Claire wondered how Margot would have reacted to the chaos in the house. She couldn't believe she had actually considered bringing her here. Their relationship had been much too young to even broach the topic of children, but Claire simply couldn't imagine someone like Margot as a mother.

"Because." She and her brother had always had an easy, effortless sibling relationship, banding together against the explosions of anger and misunderstanding in the Cyr house. It had become clear to Claire from a young age that her parents loved each other despite having not many things in common, resulting in frequent volatile moments. But, as a child, it wasn't always easy to distinguish loud-voiced banter from a full-fledged fight.

"Because? Come on, Claire, it's me, your little brother." Maybe years ago, she would have been able to find comfort with her brother, and perhaps this was his way of trying to make up for their one-sided conversations of the past five years, but Juliette felt more like her family now. And Steph and Nadia.

"I met someone. It didn't work out. Back to square one." Claire tried to keep the pain out of her voice, tried to make Margot sound insignificant.

"I can see it in your face, you know. This woman hurt you." If he continued like this, Claire would be reduced to tears again within seconds.

"Don't pretend we're still close and you care more than you do, Sam. Besides, I'm a big girl. I can manage," she snapped. She remembered when she'd first told him she fancied girls. He was in his late teens and, probably imagining all sorts of things due to hormone overload, his eyes had grown wide as saucers, but he'd always, always been supportive.

"Wow, she must have gotten to you good." He put a hand on her arm.

"Oh, fuck." The tears were coming already. "I'm sorry. I

shouldn't have said that." Claire looked at him and realised there *was* comfort in being with her family, no matter where life had taken them.

"Tell me about her," Sam insisted. He always did.

"No, I can't. It's still too fresh, too raw." She looked at him in despair.

"Hey," he said, while reaching for his phone. "I read about this app for lesbians. For hook-ups with people in the neighbourhood. It's August, there must be some ladies of your persuasion around on vacation."

Claire let out a weak giggle. "Thanks, Sam, but that's really not necessary."

"Come on, sis. You need to rebound. Get her out of your system. Have a holiday fling." He painted that smile on his face —the same one Claire used for getting her way.

"This is a family holiday." She shot him a fake grin.

"So? Do you think mum and dad will mind if you don't come back one night? You're forty-four, sis. You *are* a big girl."

"I don't even know why we're wasting time discussing this."

"Because we're on holiday and it's mandatory to have fun." He held out his palm. "Give me your phone, I'll install it for you and then you can still see what you do with it. Just so you have the option."

Claire kept her phone close by—because someone might just call to apologise—and it lay on the table next to her glass of wine. "Never put your phone so close to your drink," Margot had once said. "It's asking for trouble." She slid the phone over to Sam.

"See if you can find any Asian women on there," she said, without thinking. "How do you know about these things anyway?" She tried to change the subject quickly.

"Asian, huh?" Sam looked at her while palming her phone. "I didn't know you'd developed a taste for the Orient." He rested his eyes on her. It was almost like looking in a mirror.

"Neither did I." She watched Sam fiddle with her phone.

"I know when we went last year it was a bit of a dud, but I hear there's a new bar in Marseille. Why don't we check it out? Maybe tomorrow?" Sam asked.

"Why the sudden interest in my love life?" Claire swallowed a large gulp of wine.

Sam glanced up at her again. "I've always taken an interest." He sighed. "You've had a sad scowl plastered on your face since you arrived. I'm just trying to help my sister, I guess."

The tears started stinging again. Claire caught one with her thumb before it tumbled down, her emotions all over the place. "Do you really think they're going to let you into a lesbian bar?"

He nodded enthusiastically. "I read about this place. It's supposed to be really laid-back and dude-friendly."

"Are we going for you or for me?" Claire asked, a grin forming on her lips.

"Ha ha, very funny," he said while handing her phone back. "I've used the first picture I could find as your profile pic. You're such a stunner, sis. Don't be surprised if this thing starts going off immediately."

Claire looked at her phone, shook her head, and drank again.

MARGOT

Margot looked at herself in the mirror and hated what she saw. She couldn't find peace, not after what she'd done. Not that she had expected to fall right back into Inez' arms after breaking up with Claire, but the guilt that had wrapped around her heart the second she'd left Claire's flat had all but paralysed her. Inez wasn't the problem. Inez was still Inez, confident, loud and utterly gorgeous. But this person looking back at her, was that really Margot de Hay?

She pulled her top over her head and glanced at her abs. They'd gotten more pronounced because she had to go to kickboxing class every morning, just to find some sort of release. And she was barely eating. Claire would have gone nuts over them. Inez as well, for that matter.

Stepping out of her pants, she recognised the heat that rose inside of her again. She quickly unhooked her bra and wriggled out of her panties. As outwardly morose as the whole breaking-up with Claire for Inez business had left her, the thirst inside of her could only be quenched by one thing. And kickboxing was not doing the trick.

She walked to her nightstand and unearthed a vibrator. No frills—like her—just a sturdy, quality piece of equipment that never let her down, that did the trick without her having to lose herself in fantasies. Mechanical and quick. Just what she needed.

Because fantasies would force her to choose, and Margot had already made her choice. Only, every time the moment arrived, in that split second she gave her subconscious free reign over her mind, she wasn't so sure she'd made the right one. Hurting someone else was never going to be easy, especially someone as dear to her as Claire, but it seemed to be destroying her. Margot liked matters to be clean cut and right now, everything was such a mess. Everyone involved had gotten hurt.

Relieved that, at least, she had her flat to herself again, Margot reclined on the bed. While spreading her legs, she turned the bottom of the vibrator to switch it on. The buzzing sound alone was enough to make her clit throb. This was what she did now, every night before bed. She could hardly call it touching herself, because it was only the plastic that made contact with her clit for a few minutes of mindless relief.

The back of her head sank into the pillow as she brought both of her hands between her spread legs. With one, she pulled her pussy lips apart, while the other wielded the toy. The first touch of it against her clit sent a shudder up her spine, true to the tried and tested scenario. She tried to clear her mind as best she could while she let the vibrator hover over her clit, teasing herself. It was important not to think of anything as it touched down.

As she pressed it against her, the vibrations tickling her clit, she focused on her body, on how her abs contracted, and the air floating around her pussy lips. It worked—it always did. It was just a matter of failsafe mechanics. Just as the hum of the vibrator was foreplay, the touch of it sealed the deal. It shot through her in quick spasms, tugging at her soul. And in that moment of short but complete surrender, a new image filled her mind. Claire with her hands in Inez' ginger hair, kissing her.

Margot moaned as the climax glowed inside of her, fading out quickly—this was not about orgasms with a powerful after-glow, just temporary relief. The image stuck with her as she dropped the toy next to her on the bed. It was punishment, of course. Her subconscious berating her, because, really, how would two complete bottoms like Inez and Claire ever get off together? They weren't going to tie themselves up, were they? Margot allowed herself a little snicker at the thought—a highly needed one.

Then the gloom returned. Untrue to her nature, she didn't get up to wash the toy, but slipped under the covers instead. Claire would be away for a few more days and, before she returned, Margot needed to find out. She'd take Inez up on her offer and meet her for a date. How else could she really discover if she'd done the right thing?

STEPH

"How many people have *you* slept with?" Steph had been waiting for the right moment to drop that question. The children had been carted off to a friend's house for a sleepover—a favour Dominique would only have to return once Steph had left—and she knew tonight would be the night Dominique would be reaching for the toy Steph had packed. Not only because it was inevitable, but because she'd been hinting at it all afternoon.

"Best lube up, babe," she had said every time she refilled Steph's glass of wine.

"Top up?" she asked now, an unambiguous grin smeared on her face.

Steph smiled back, nodded, and waited for Dominique to refill her glass and reclaim her seat at the end of the lounge chair Steph sat in. She went back to massaging Steph's calf, which had gotten hurt after an unfortunate dive into the pool while playing catch with Didier.

"Three," Dominique said, before tilting her head back and gulping down more wine. They only had two nights left together and it was starting to sting.

Steph's mouth fell open. "Three?"

"Makes you look like a bit of a slut, doesn't it?" Dominique pinched her little toe.

"But… only three?" Steph shook her head. "No way."

"It's true." Dominique lightly ran her fingertips over Steph's shin. "Luc, my first boyfriend. We broke up just before I entered university. Then there was Murielle." She slanted her head and glanced at Steph through hooded eyelids.

Steph nodded. She knew all about Murielle. If she hadn't found out about Murielle, she probably wouldn't be sitting here.

"Then I met Philippe. We married. I never strayed." She reached for her glass again. "My life has always been so busy with work and politics, then the kids came along…"

"Did you and Philippe have a satisfying—"

"You want to discuss my marriage now?" Steph felt Dominique tense. She'd never really stopped to think how much the divorce must have hurt Dominique. She knew she'd been the rebound person, neither one of them having expected it to last this long. "I'm sorry." She took a deep breath. "We did—"

"We don't have to talk about it," Steph was quick to say. Conversations like this made her nervous anyway.

"It's fine, and only fair." Her hands rested on Steph's knee. "Philippe and I did okay. Nothing too spectacular happened towards the end. Only logical, I guess, since he was cheating. It was, um, very different than how things are with you now."

Steph opened her arms wide. "Well, I *am* a woman."

"That you are." Dominique's hand traveled upwards, to the crotch of Steph's bikini bottoms. "It didn't stop you from bringing a fake penis, though."

"How many times." Steph sighed. "It is not a fake penis, simply a means to an end."

"Shaped like a penis," Dominique continued, two of her fingers pressing down on the fabric of Steph's bikini.

"If you want to use it on me, you'd better pipe down." Steph's breath caught in her throat when Dominique's finger brushed against her clit.

"So, just to be clear, I *can* fuck you with it now?" Dominique's finger kept circling.

"As if you don't know."

"I'm not used to being with women, Stéphanie. You say one thing and mean another... Good thing I have a lot of political experience." Her finger slipped under the panel of Steph's bikini. "Jesus. You're so wet again, babe. I'm starting to think you suffer from a serious condition. You could get dehydrated."

Steph stopped listening to Dominique's teasing words. The only other woman who'd ever fucked her like that was Laurence, near the tail end of their relationship, when her trust had been the deepest—just before it had been betrayed.

Dominique let her finger slip from underneath Steph's bikini bottoms and started tugging at them. "Just so you know, I suffer from a condition as well, possibly incurable." She slid her legs from underneath Steph's and crouched down to rid Steph of her bikini. "I can't get enough of this." She straddled the end of the lounge chair and shuffled forward until her thighs rested underneath Steph's knees. "Come a little closer," she said, before leaning forward and finding Steph's pussy lips with her mouth.

Steph slid forward, her pelvis thrust high on Dominique's thighs, her pussy glued to Dominique's lips. She couldn't stop thinking about how it would be when Dominique entered her with the strap-on. She hadn't surrendered like that in more than ten years. Would it all end in heartbreak again?

Dominique pushed her tongue deep into Steph's pussy, and Steph couldn't wait any longer.

"Do it now," she said. "Put it on and fuck me now."

Dominique let her tongue slip from Steph's pulsing pussy. "Are you serious?"

"Yes," Steph urged, already moving her legs off of Dominique.

"Okay, but stay here. Don't move." Dominique manoeuvred herself from underneath Steph.

"What? You want to do it here?"

"Uh-huh." Dominique nodded. "Don't worry, I'll bring everything." She rushed inside. After they'd waved the kids off she'd put the toy ostentatiously on the middle of Steph's bed, so she'd see what she had on her mind when she went to change. Subtlety was hardly ever a conservative politician's strong suit.

It took a little while before Dominique re-emerged. Did she even know how to attach all the bits right? She was a smart woman, she would figure it out.

She wore a long blouse when she walked out of the house, the toy sticking out between the flaps of fabric at the bottom. She'd brought the bottle of lube Steph had packed as well, and a blanket, which she spread out on the patch of lawn next to Steph's chair.

She kneeled next to Steph. "I know I have a big mouth and I'm terribly bossy, but you do want this, don't you? I wouldn't want to talk you into something you don't really want." It was moments like this that floored Steph the most. When

Dominique showed her true, loving, caring colours. When she made sure Steph knew that their affair wasn't just a rebound fling. That it was more than acquiring as much sexual gratification in a short period of time as possible. More than an experiment.

"I do," Steph said. "I want you."

Dominique rose from her crouching position and extended her hand to Steph. Steph took it and let Dominique wrap her arms around her. She felt the toy against her legs and desire spread through her like wildfire. This was so much more than all the flings she had amassed over the years put together. Dominique kissed her while her hands found the lock of Steph's bikini top and unhooked it. Steph stood completely naked in the garden of Xavier Laroche's summer house, his daughter fully strapped-on in front of her. The irony of the moment didn't escape her.

Steph opened the sides of Dominique's blouse, which she hadn't bothered to button up, and looked at her lover. She etched the sight into her memory as one of the hottest things she'd ever seen.

"Let's lie down," Dominique said. A solemn note had crept into her voice. This was a big deal for her as well. She shrugged off the blouse before laying down.

Only three people? Four with herself included. Steph lowered herself onto the blanket. A light, late-afternoon breeze chased over her skin. It wasn't even dark yet. She guessed them doing this in the bright light of day could be perceived as symbolic as well.

Dominique flanked her, her lips on Steph's neck, kissing her way down. Steph felt the toy press against her thigh. The feel of it made her pussy lips throb even more. She may have slept with a lot of different people since Laurence, but she'd never surrendered like this. Not since then.

Dominique pushed herself up and lowered her body back down on top of Steph's, the toy now pushing against Steph's inner thighs. Dominique stared down at her, nothing but tenderness in her eyes, before finding Steph's mouth with her lips. Steph let her hands drift down across Dominique's back and clutched her tightly around the waist.

"I'm ready," she whispered in Dominique's ear. "Fuck me."

Dominique planted her palms on the blanket next to Steph's head and stretched her elbows. "Yeah?" she asked.

Steph nodded, every cell in her body thrumming with anticipation.

Dominique shifted her weight backwards until she sat on her knees in between Steph's spread legs. She reached for the bottle of lube that rested near the edge of the blanket and squirted some in her hands before applying it generously to the toy. For a woman who'd only had sex with a man the past twenty years, she sure looked like she knew what she was doing. Had she prepared for this? Steph made a mental note to ask her later.

When Dominique let her lubed up fingers flutter against Steph's wet pussy lips, a shiver ran up her spine. Before crawling closer, Dominique rubbed the excess lube over the length of the silicone, letting the shaft disappear and reappear in her fist. Steph had to swallow a lump of lust out of her throat at the sight of it. *Le Matin* would have a field day if this ever came out. Dominique Laroche strapping it on in the backyard of Xavier's house, stroking a silicone cock before entering her secret lesbian lover's pussy with it, all in the clear light of day. Maybe it wouldn't be such a bad thing if it came out—not like this, of course, but in a more decent way. Maybe then, they'd stand a chance.

Steph let the thought evaporate in her mind. She shouldn't think like that. And anyway, Dominique was coming for her now, inching closer, taking position.

She let the slippery tip of the dildo glide up and down Steph's pussy lips, briefly brushing it against her clit. If the hot

HARPER BLISS

flicker of pleasure it sent through Steph's flesh was anything to go by, Steph was in for the climax of her life.

Dominique looked up from between Steph's legs and found her eyes again. Her lips were parted, her stare intense and Steph wondered if the députée would ever really be able to walk away from this. She held the toy in one hand and guided the tip to Steph's opening, slipping it in gently.

Instantly, Steph felt herself open up wider than she could remember. Her breath hitched in her throat, a quiet calm spreading through her muscles. She needed to relax to take this, to take in Dominique.

Dominique slowly inched more of the toy inside of Steph, filling her so much already. She brought her weight forward again and repositioned her hands next to Steph's cheeks, changing the angle of penetration, suddenly, seemingly, filling Steph completely.

"Oh god," Steph cried out, staring up into Dominique's face. Her features were focused, her teeth sunk into her bottom lip. She moved again, thrusting even deeper into Steph, who felt her pussy walls spread as wide as they'd ever had.

Dominique held herself completely still for an instant. "Okay?" she asked.

"Good god, yes," Steph heard herself groan, her voice seemingly having fled her body.

Dominique started moving inside of her, slowly at first, with tiny movements of her hips, but it felt like the world around Steph was changing already. As if the position of the sun shifted and the sky swirled around her, puffy white clouds carrying her. She spread her legs wider, inviting Dominique inside of her deeper, as deep as she could go, as much part of her as she could be.

Steph closed her eyes and let herself be carried away further.

"Je t'aime," Dominique whispered, over and over again. Her thrusts came quicker, touching Steph everywhere at once so it seemed, ripping through her body, pounding in her veins.

When Steph opened her eyes and looked into the teary brightness of Dominique's eyes, she knew that was it. A storm rose in her blood and carried atoms of pure pleasure through her veins, prickling her flesh. She lay wide open for Dominique and for the climax she was bestowing on her—and all the rest. The love, the companionship, the sheer fun they had when they were together.

Steph dug her nails into the flesh of Dominique's back as she came, her breath stalling, her muscles flexing, her body dissolving underneath the wave of pleasure.

Panting, she released her grip on Dominique, who took it as a sign to retract, gently sliding the toy from Steph's stretched pussy lips.

Steph couldn't speak, only watch as Dominique loosened the straps and manoeuvred herself out of the contraption of strings as quickly as possibly, before folding her body over Steph's again, covering her.

"What is this between us?" she whispered in Steph's ear. "What have you done to me?"

Steph couldn't say, she only knew that Dominique had done the exact same thing to her.

NADIA

"Spending the summer in Paris is hardly a punishment," Juliette said. They'd met at the Place des Vosges after work for an al fresco dinner on one of the terraces along the square.

"Fair enough." Nadia reached for another oyster. "It's gorgeous." She eyed Juliette's glass of wine with envy. She'd, again, opted to abstain, but the lowering evening sun, the balmy Paris air and, most of all, the oysters, begged for a glass of wine as accompaniment.

The past few days had been dreamlike. The calm of August in Paris had relaxed them both, and with Claire and Steph on holiday, distractions were few and far between. They'd broken in the new bed successfully, chasing away as much of the ghost of Sybille as possible, and spent their evenings together like this. Nadia was grateful for this grace period, but she knew it wouldn't last. The real test was yet to come.

"Can I ask you a question that might be too serious for an evening like this?" Juliette asked before sipping from her glass.

"Of course." Nadia sighed. "But, babe, I think I'm going to order a glass of wine. I was born in France, half of my blood's composition is made up of wine."

Juliette opened her palms to the sky. "Be my guest."

"You don't mind?" Nadia looked around for a waiter.

"I never asked you to stop drinking. That was your own choice." Juliette grabbed an oyster from the tray and sucked it out of its shell expertly.

A waiter appeared and Nadia ordered a glass of rosé. She hardly ever ordered wine by the glass. Usually she'd at least drink a carafe, most nights a bottle.

"I guess I thought it would help." She sagged back into her chair, feeling more relaxed already at the prospect of some alcohol coming her way. "What did you want to ask me?"

"At the risk of sounding like I'm conducting a job interview." Juliette gave a small chuckle. "But where do you see us, say, five years from now?"

"Gosh." Nadia was glad her wine arrived, so she could have a second to ponder Juliette's question. She swallowed a heavenly gulp, soon followed by another. "Do you need the answer straight away or can I think about it?" Was Juliette trying to say something by asking this? They'd only just got back together.

"We've spent the past ten years building a career. Barbier & Cyr is doing better than ever and you have the top job in your hospital. I guess I'm just wondering what's next…"

Nadia exhaled, relieved that Juliette was, rather typically, talking about work.

"Other people have children and go through the stages of raising them, but we don't have that in our lives. We have each other…" Juliette reached for her glass and sipped. "And our dramas and the home we've built, but, I don't know, what comes after that?"

Was Juliette asking her if this was it? They'd decided against having children a few years after they'd met, both having been much too focused on work—as well as not displaying any signs of suffering from a ticking biological clock, although it should have been ticking loud and clear by then. Juliette would be turning forty-five at the end of the year, some sort of midlife crisis could be a possibility.

Nadia was at a loss for words. Were they, perhaps, not skipping a few steps after their reunion? "What's brought this on?" Nadia emptied her wine glass in a few gulps and started looking around for the waiter again. Juliette could use a refill as well. They should just get a bottle.

"The way I see it, we've had our relationship crisis. We've chosen each other, again. I know I want to spend the rest of my life with you, Nadz. But what will that life be like?"

"Hey." Nadia caught the waiter's attention. "If same-sex marriage gets approved in a few weeks we can always get hitched." It was a joke. Nadia knew Juliette didn't believe in a piece of paper to validate a relationship. She ordered two more glasses of wine—Juliette was drinking white while she had opted for rosé—and another tray of oysters.

"And then we'll each wear a ring on our finger, but everything else will be the same."

"What are you saying, babe? You want to adopt a child to stave off a midlife crisis?" She found Juliette's ankle underneath the table and caught it between her legs. Nadia had proposed once, a few years after Belgium had legalised gay marriage. They'd gone to Brussels for the weekend and had ended up in a lesbian bar. They'd struck up a conversation with a local couple who'd just got married. Afterwards, when walking back to their hotel over the Grand Place, Nadia had turned to Juliette and said, "Maybe we should just do it, Jules. Will you marry me?"

Juliette had burst out laughing and taken it as much more of a joke than Nadia had meant it. It had triggered a whole discussion on the merit of marriage and Juliette had carefully laid out all the reasons why she didn't believe in it.

"Romance is walking past the grandeur of these buildings with you, babe," Juliette had said. "Not tying you to me legally, as if we own each other. It's choosing to crawl into bed with you every single night because I want to, not because it's written down in a *carnet de mariage*."

Nadia had understood, but she wouldn't have minded becoming Juliette's wife in the least.

"No, just that we should consider making some changes in our lives," Juliette said.

The waiter placed their fresh glasses of wine on the table.

"Like what?" A nervous fear crept up on Nadia. Had Juliette not just said that she wanted to spend the rest of her life with Nadia? That she'd chosen her all over again?

"I don't know." Juliette shook her head. "But it's worth thinking about."

Nadia nodded. "Sure, babe." She scanned Juliette's face. Her features were serious, not a hint of irony in them. Perhaps, they had grown apart in more ways than they had realised.

CLAIRE

"Headache, dear?" Claire's mother addressed her as if she, herself, never touched a drop of alcohol. She also seemed to bang the lid of the sugar pot back down much harder than was necessary.

Thank goodness Steph was arriving today and they'd be driving back to Paris together after lunch. One more meal, Claire repeated to herself. One more meal.

"Morning." Sam's voice didn't betray any signs of the shots they had done the night before. Of course, he'd offered to drive and had slowed down his alcohol intake before heading back to the house. "How are things, sis?" He shot her a fat wink.

"She seems to be feeling somewhat under the weather. I wonder why," their mother said before Claire had a chance to reply.

They'd visited the bar in Marseille Sam had looked up. It had been half-empty and if, by any chance, any of the ladies present had sent signals of interest in Claire's direction, she had been too drunk—and still too heartbroken—to notice. In fact, Claire's main memory of the night was asking Sam to pull over on the way back so she could throw up on the grassy kerb.

"Tante Claire, you must come watch me jump in the pool. I've been practicing all morning." Léa stormed towards the table, her sister in tow. Claire tried very hard not to grab her head. She'd let Steph drive to Lyon, and she wouldn't drink a drop tonight—or ever again.

"Later, honey," Sam intervened. "Tante Claire is not feeling very well."

Claire did remember that she'd told Sam all about Margot, because how could she possibly hold it in? He'd kept scanning the app he'd installed on her phone. "Looking for Asian women," he kept saying, until she'd caved in and told him about Inez' return.

"What a stone cold bitch." Sam, just like their mother, was never one to mince his words. He wouldn't last a week in PR. "And that Margot, I know it must hurt, sis, but she doesn't deserve you." It was easy for him to say. With his perfect family, living only a few miles from their mother and father so they could witness on a daily basis how by-the-book, at least, their son's life was.

The pain of losing Margot combined with the pressure, irrational or not, she always felt when under her mother's scrutiny, had simply been too much to bear. So Claire had kept on drinking, vodka at first, then chased down by tequila shots. Until it had all spasmed its way up again, leaving Claire heaving by the roadside, a broken version of herself.

"You know how you sometimes take a nap after lunch, sweetie." Claire looked into Léa's pleading eyes. "Tante Claire needs to have one of those after breakfast today." She touched the girl's arm briefly before she pattered away, her sister in tow again. She should see more of them. Family was important. She'd bonded with her brother over, of all things, this painful break-up. But first, she needed to go back to bed and forget some more.

"No wonder," her mother said, not waiting until the girl was out of earshot—and always gunning for a fight, it seemed. "I heard the car drive up. What time was it?" She nudged her husband in the ribs. "It woke your father up as well. Not that I regret that, as he was snoring so loudly—"

"Just leave her be, Léonie," her father said, looking up briefly from his newspaper, finding Claire's eyes and blinking. "And me as well, while you're at it."

"I'm just going to go…" Claire didn't finish her sentence, just headed back inside.

"I'll keep the kids as quiet as possible," Sam said, a tender smile on his lips. A smile that broke Claire apart even more.

What would that dinner at Margot's parents have been like? And what about her sister who lived in the suburbs? Was Margot tightening a pair of handcuffs around Inez' wrists right now? Or were they working the weekend shift at Saint-Vincent's ER together? No matter which direction Claire's mind wandered in, she couldn't win. She lay down on her bed, closed her eyes and tried not to think of anything.

———

"Drive safely, darling." Claire's mother opened her arms for a hug, tears brimming in the corner of her eyes. As if all the

354

emotions they couldn't express during a week together had to be crammed into that one moment of goodbye.

Claire accepted the hug, but her muscles remained rigid, the curve of her arms around her mother's shoulders forced.

She watched Steph shake her father's hand and she was glad she didn't have to go through this alone. If Claire was sick of anything, it was of being alone. Of driving up here alone, of facing her family alone, of waking up alone.

After kissing her nieces and nephew goodbye and whispering a muffled thank-you in Sam's ear, she led the way into the city, where Steph deposited her rental car.

"How was your holiday?" she asked, as soon as she slid into the passenger seat of her car, ready to be distracted by Steph's tales and, at the same time, dreading to be confronted with any sign of love in Steph's voice. But they had miles and miles of motorway between them and Paris. And a night in Lyon. If only it were enough.

MARGOT

Margot parked her motorcycle along the Canal Saint-Martin. The place buzzed with the excitement of a sunny summer Paris afternoon, but Margot didn't have eyes for the people strolling past, for the joggers and how the sun left its mark on the water with a million fractured rays reflecting back on its surface. She counted the house numbers until she found number fifty-six and rang the bell to the top floor flat.

"Oui," Inez said through the intercom, the electronic connection making it sound sultry. Or maybe that's how she wanted to come across. Maybe she knew why Margot had come. She'd be a fool if she didn't.

The building had no lift, but Margot easily climbed the stairs to the fourth floor. She had plenty of energy to burn.

When she reached the flat, Inez stood leaning in the door

frame, wearing an oversized shirt and ultra-short jeans shorts. "Hey," she said, smiling from ear to ear.

"Nice neighbourhood," Margot said, not interested in small talk. She had only come here for one purpose. To find out if they still had that spark. If it had survived what Inez had done to her.

Inez invited Margot in. Her place was small and sparsely decorated, exactly how Margot would expect the home of a returning ER doctor to look. The most important feature of her apartment was that it was a ten-minute walk from Saint-Vincent. Margot understood. If her parents hadn't given her the Saint-Germain-des-Prés flat, this would probably be how she would live as well.

"Are you…" Margot watched Inez' eyes wander to the bulge in her jeans.

Margot nodded and inched closer to Inez.

"Never one to waste time." Inez' eyes narrowed while her hand reached for Margot's crotch, but Margot swatted it away.

"Wait for it." She pushed Inez against the wall nearest to the sofa. "You know better."

Inez chewed on her lip and nodded.

Margot took a step back and started unbuttoning Inez' shirt. She wore nothing underneath. They both knew why she was here. While her hands cupped Inez' breasts, her lips touched Inez' mouth. It was only the second time they'd kissed after Inez had come back—the first time since Margot had broken up with Claire. Wet heat throbbed beneath Margot's jeans, beneath what she was packing.

Inez' hands delved into Margot's hair, pulling her close. "Fuck, I've missed you, Go-Go," she said, when they broke apart. "I want you so much."

Margot had every intention of giving her exactly what she wanted. Her hands drifted down to the button of Inez' shorts. "Take it off," she said, after flipping the button open. "All the way." She gave Inez room to wiggle out of her shorts and underwear and stripped off her own t-shirt in the process.

Margot had decided against wearing a bra as well. What would have been the point?

When she kissed Inez this time, she made sure to press her pelvis hard against Inez', making sure she could feel every last inch of what she had stowed away beneath her trousers. Margot grabbed Inez by the wrist and brought her fingers to her face. She let them slip between her lips and sucked them deep into her mouth, before letting them slide out and letting them hover against Inez' lips. "Make them wet," Margot said, her knees buckling at the sight of Inez' eyes. They burned as brightly as her hair did in the afternoon sun.

Inez sucked two of her own fingers into her mouth, letting them glide out with a loud smack of her lips.

In response, Margot painted a crooked grin on her lips. "Are they wet enough?" she asked.

Breathless, Inez nodded. Margot still had her fingers curled around Inez' wrist and pulled her hand down between her legs. "Finger yourself," Margot said, her own breath starting to hitch in her throat. She kept her fingers around Inez' wrist and guided her hand until Inez' fingertips reached her entrance. Margot let her own fingers skate along Inez' pussy lips to make sure she was moist enough. "Now," she said, while unbuttoning her jeans with her free hand.

Inez' eyes went wide as she glued them to Margot's toy. Margot stepped back and enjoyed the show. She grabbed the dildo in her fist and rubbed her palm along its length while Inez fingered herself as best she could in the position she was in, lower back against the wall, legs bent, shoulders hunched.

She didn't say it out loud, but Margot could read it in her glance. "Fuck me," it screamed. "This is not enough."

Margot shuffled closer and stilled Inez' hand with her own. "On your knees," she breathed into Inez' ear.

Inez couldn't kneel fast enough. She dropped down, her hands already cupping Margot's bottom. Margot looked down at her, at how she opened her mouth for the toy, let the tip of her tongue slip across the head.

"The deeper you take it, the deeper I'll fuck you with it." Out of nowhere, just as Inez looked up into her eyes, Margot wondered how Claire would react to a scene like this. Would she like it? Margot didn't know her well enough yet. *Yet?*

Inez' lips slid over the shaft of Margot's strapped-on dildo, taking it in her mouth deeper every time her head cocked up and down. Not a surprise to Margot at all. Inez was still Inez. But was *she* still the same person as well?

"That's enough," Margot said. She waited until Inez let the toy slip from her mouth and offered her a hand to get up. Inez took it and hoisted herself up. Her lips looked puffed up, the fire in her eyes blazing with a hunger Margot could barely remember ever seeing. She led Inez to the sofa and, once there, spun her around so her backside faced Margot. "Bend over." She let her fingers roam across Inez' spine, who looked back at her, her lips forming an 'o'. *Oh yes.*

Inez toppled her torso over the armrest of the sofa, her bottom up in the air, her legs spread. Margot's heartbeat tightened to a quick drum in her chest. She stepped closer, until the tip of the toy touched Inez' flesh. She couldn't leave her hanging like this any longer, she had to give it to her now.

She dragged the tip along Inez' soaked pussy lips once, before thrusting deep, her fingers curled around the base of the dildo.

"Jesus," Inez cried out. "Oh sweet Jesus." Did she do this for anyone else in the jungle? She'd said there'd been no other girlfriend, but she must have had sex. They had so much to talk about. So much pain to explore further.

Margot increased the speed of her strokes, burrowing deep inside of Inez, her glance focused on the red of her hair— somehow glad she didn't have to look her in the eyes. Didn't have to see Inez surrender.

Inez bucked herself back against Margot, the curve of her

behind brushing against Margot's pubic hair as she fucked her. Margot curled her arm around Inez' thighs and found her clit. She just held her finger there so Inez' clit could brush against it as she shot forward to the rhythm of Margot's thrusts.

"Oh god, I'm coming," Inez hissed, and before, it would have been enough for Margot. She would have been right there with her, her own clit finding its own release against the silicone base of the toy, but not today. The disconnect between them was too big. Whatever Margot had hoped to find, it was gone.

Inez' body sagged into the sofa, her muscles relaxing as Margot withdrew. She stepped out of her jeans because she needed to get the strap-on off her, couldn't face the feel of it against her skin anymore.

By the time Margot had discarded the toy, Inez had turned around, her backside leaning against the armrest now. "No one makes me come like you do, Go-Go. No one." Again, it made Margot wonder about other people in Inez' life, but she didn't ask. Inez reached out her hand. Margot took it and let herself be pulled close.

"Shall I do you or are you good?" she asked, her cheek against the hot skin of Margot's belly.

"I'm good," Margot lied, because, in that moment, she had no interest in Inez' fingers inside of her.

JULIETTE

While it was true that Juliette had never asked Nadia to stop drinking, nor expected it, the speed at which Nadia was knocking back the wine of late, made her regret that she'd never explicitly demanded it.

They'd spent a nice enough Sunday outside, going to the market and eating ice-cream in the Parc Monceau. But from where she sat at the dinner table, Juliette could see the first thunder clouds loom through the window.

Juliette looked away from the window as Nadia manoeuvred to refill her glass. She held her hand above the opening, indicating she'd had enough—hoping her sated state would rub off on Nadia. It didn't.

"Babe," Nadia said after she'd taken a sip. "What did you mean the other day when you said we should consider making some changes in our lives?"

Juliette sighed. "I don't know." She shoved her empty glass to the middle of the table. "I guess I'm afraid that, if we're not careful, we'll go right back to where we were before."

"How could we ever go back?" Nadia rested her dark eyes on Juliette. "We'll never be the same people again."

"I'm not so sure of that." Juliette grabbed the near-empty bottle of wine and moved it to her side of the table.

Nadia arched up her eyebrows. "Are you serious?"

"Deadly." Juliette could hardly not say anything just to keep the peace. She'd done enough of that.

"What? I can't have a glass of wine on Sunday?" Nadia's naked foot found Juliette's ankle underneath the table. She always did that.

"I think you have a tendency to mistake a glass for an entire bottle." Juliette tapped a fingernail against the belly of the wine bottle.

"I didn't drink all of that on my own."

"No, but you seem to be increasing your units steadily by the day."

"Only because you freaked me out by talking about change and not saying what you really meant." Underneath the table, Nadia retracted her foot.

"And that's your answer?" Juliette glanced at Nadia's glass. "Instead of just asking me?"

"I did ask and all you gave me was vagueness. What am I supposed to do with that?" Nadia sagged back in her seat. "We seem so fragile still, as if something's missing and I don't know how to fill that void."

Tightness coiled in Juliette's gut. "What we miss between us now is the trust we once had. It will take time."

"And change… apparently." Nadia looked away briefly. "I have plenty of time on offer, Jules, but I am who I am."

"I didn't mean you had to change, babe. We just need to be vigilant."

"The way you said it, the other day, you made it sound as if the prospect of your life with me wasn't enough."

"No, no, that's not what I meant… On the contrary. I love the thought of waking up next to you for the rest of my days. I was just pondering the choices we've made in the past… thinking about whether they're still valid."

"This is exactly what I'm talking about. If you could say what you mean instead of wrapping everything in vagueness. From where I'm sitting, you may either be talking about our choice to live in the city, or, I don't know, be hinting at wanting an open relationship or something."

"What?" Juliette's eyes grew wide. "Where did you get that?"

"From having to guess." Nadia took another sip of wine. "In the position we're in, after what our relationship is trying to recover from, our lines of communication should be wide open, but instead you speak in riddles."

"Okay." Juliette straightened her posture. "I do not want an open relationship and I love living in the city."

"I know, I was just giving examples of what's going through my head." Nadia sucked her bottom lip into her mouth. It made her look extra vulnerable.

Juliette didn't really know how to broach the subject, which was why she'd been dilly-dallying around it. "Today in the park, when we were at the playground, I just, I don't know… I second-guessed some of the choices I have made." She watched Nadia grow speechless, but continued. "Other people our age, when they close their office door behind them in the evening, they have this other life that waits for them at home." Afraid of

Nadia's reaction, she couldn't immediately bring herself to say it.

"You mean they have children?" Nadia said it for her.

Juliette brought her hands to her head. "I don't know what's going on with me lately." She rested her chin on the palm of one hand. "We live in this bubble of work, too much wine in the evening, and the same old places we go to in the weekend… and I was always okay with that. We built our careers instead of a family life." She snickered. "I mean, most of the time, I even wondered why people put themselves through that, you know. Sacrifice their time and their job to pick up the kids from school, but I guess that, now, I'm starting to see why they do it." That near-empty bottle of wine suddenly seemed appealing. "What do I have to show for?"

Nadia reached for her glass and swallowed back its contents. "I have to say, babe, I was expecting a speech on me drinking too much—again. I know I have." Nadia caught Juliette's glance. "But I wasn't expecting this."

"With all that's happened between us, I had a lot of time to think and I came to the dreadful conclusion that, with you out of the equation, I have nothing." Desperate, Juliette extended her arm over the table. Nadia instantly grabbed hold of her hand.

Nadia shook her head. "But I'm still here." She squeezed Juliette's palm between her fingers. "And you have the firm, your friends, and my family, for that matter. You *have* a full life."

"What if it's not enough, though?" Juliette ran her fingers over Nadia's wrist. "What if I need more?"

"Are you saying you want children? Because, well, nothing is impossible, but we're no spring chickens, and we kind of made that decision a while ago."

"I just… I've been shaken to the core." Juliette dug her nails into Nadia's flesh a little, for support. "I slept with a girl in her twenties, for crying out loud. My bloody assistant." She made tiny left-to-right movements with her chin. "What's next? A Porsche?"

"We don't have a garage, babe," Nadia said dryly. "They cost a fortune in Paris."

Juliette burst out in a nervous giggle. "God, I know." She tugged at Nadia's arm, pulling her across the table. "Maybe we should just get a cat."

"Maybe a dog as well." Nadia allowed herself to be hoisted up, her face inching closer to Juliette's across the tabletop. "But seriously, Jules. I need you to know I'm not dismissing you. If this is how you feel, we need to address it. Think about it."

"So, you're not… automatically opposed to the idea?" Juliette rose from her chair, meeting Nadia half-way.

"If the *idea* equals your happiness, of course not."

"I don't know what exactly lies ahead for us, babe," Juliette said, her lips already hovering over Nadia's mouth, "but I do know for certain you and I are going to make it."

Nadia nodded and pressed a kiss on Juliette's mouth.

STEPH

"Thank you for sending me that text," Steph said to Claire over a glass of chilled white wine. "My time with Dominique in Juan-les-Pins was nothing short of amazing." Steph thought back at their goodbye. It had been restrained and decent, for the children's sake, but on the inside, it had torn her up completely to drive away from that house.

"Sorry for practically forbidding you to go in the first place." Claire didn't look as if she had a night of moderate drinking in mind. They sat on the terrace of what seemed like a very lesbian-friendly bar in Lyon.

She looked Claire straight in the eyes. "I let her fuck me with a strap-on, you know."

Claire nearly spit out the gulp of wine she was swirling around in her mouth. "Jesus christ, Steph."

"I know, it's shocking." A warm glow tumbled down Steph's flesh at the memory of that night on the lawn. And the night after in her room. "I'm a bottom now."

Claire started laughing. "And hell has frozen over." She narrowed her eyes. "Do you remember that night we got together?"

Steph took a sip from her drink. That had happened so many girls ago. In another lifetime, really. "As if it was yesterday."

"Sure." Claire slanted her head. "Do you think we could have ever worked out if, well, if I hadn't been your boss."

Steph pursed her lips before speaking. "First of all, I was twenty-four years old and suffering from the worst heartbreak of my life. Second, you only went for a drink with me that night because you were still hung-up on Jules and you couldn't stomach that she was moving in with Nadia. And third, I'm sure the sex was great and all, but I wasn't really looking for anything steady back then."

Claire nudged Steph in the ribs. "I knew you didn't remember."

"I'm not proud of it, okay?" Steph held up her hands. "When your girlfriend asks you how many women you've been with and you don't really know, that's kind of an embarrassing moment." Steph had tried counting again, numerous times while lazing by the pool, but she always lost count around 2010 —a particularly busy year.

"Girlfriend, huh?" Claire glanced at her sideways. "I have to hand it to you, Steph, you sure know how to pick them."

"What can I say?" Steph refilled their glasses from the bottle in the ice-bucket next to their table. "I'm a sucker for punish-ment." It was good to see Claire smile, to have this moment with her. "Don't turn around, okay? But there's this chick who's been staring at you for the past fifteen minutes. She's hot. If it were me—"

Steph witnessed how Claire's face dropped. "No. I'm not interested."

"Okay. Your call." Steph received the message loud and clear.

"My brother installed this app on my phone. I mean, as if…"

Steph eyed Claire's phone, her interest piqued. She had never really relied on technology to get the sort of thing she was after.

"Margot is not someone I'm just going to get over by hooking up with a stranger," Claire continued. Steph respected the silence that came after her last statement. "I only want something similar to what I had with her. Something meaning-ful." She curled her fingers around the belly of her wine glass before finding Steph's eyes. "I don't know how she did it, but she got me. She really understood what I wanted."

Steph could safely say she'd never seen her friend and boss this heartbroken. "Hey, you know I'm well-connected, right? I can make stuff happen to the lovely doctor without borders."

"That's very nice of you, Steph, but the only thing I need is a time machine so I can send us back in time. So I can live happily ever after with Margot as if Inez Larue never existed."

"Would you take her back? If she realised she made the mistake of her life and begged you for forgiveness?" Steph scanned Claire's face.

"In a heartbeat," Claire said without hesitation. "In a fucking flash." She reached for her jeans pocket and fished out a handkerchief, dragged it over the bottom of her nose. "But *they*'re probably living happily ever after now."

"I don't see it, though." Steph found Claire's knee under the table and gave it a squeeze. "I simply can't envision Margot going back to her ex like that. She just… doesn't strike me as the type."

"That's what Jules said, but guess what? She did." The handkerchief made an appearance again. "Fuck, I dread going back to Paris."

"I'll drive slowly." Steph drank and glanced at the woman a few tables down from them. Before Dominique, she would have prolonged the eye-contact, walked to the ladies' room slowly and looked back just before heading inside. She didn't miss it one bit.

"Can I ask you a very personal question?" Claire asked.

"Anything you want." Steph focused her attention fully back on Claire.

"Have you ever..." Was she starting to blush? "Tied someone up, you know, like really dominated them?" Claire averted her gaze and stared into her wine glass briefly.

"Yeah, sure. Quite a few times actually." Steph waited patiently for Claire to look at her again.

"That's what Margot did. And she didn't joke about it either." She pinned her eyes on Steph. They were watery and small. "It was so thrilling to completely relinquish control like that. I never experienced anything like it before."

Steph couldn't suppress a smile. "Now there's something I *do* see Margot doing." She imagined what would have happened if Margot had accepted her advances that first night they met. It seemed so long ago, her mind couldn't even go there anymore. "You'll find love again, Claire. It may not seem like it right now, but another person who seems just right will come along."

Claire shook her head. "Not someone like her." She emptied the last of the wine into her glass unceremoniously. Steph couldn't hold it against her.

MARGOT

"Hey you." Inez walked into the hospital changing room wearing a big grin on her face, coming straight for Margot. "Such a pity you couldn't stay yesterday."

Margot had invented a dinner date with her parents, so as not to have to linger at Inez' flat. Not that everything was so cut-and-dried in her mind. Now that Inez shot her that glorious smile, and had that knowing twinkle in her eye, it took Margot back again to that time in her life when she'd been the happiest.

Still, her mind kept wandering back to the thought that Claire was coming back from holiday today, and that she should maybe go and see her. Old and new feelings were doing battle inside of her, and if she knew only one thing very clearly, it was that it wasn't fair on either of them.

It hadn't been fair on Inez to barge into her place and have her like that, implying much more than Margot had actually been willing to give. And it wouldn't be fair on Claire to show up at her doorstep again, not after the obvious pain Margot had caused her the last time she had done that.

"Will you come over tonight?" Inez' nose nuzzled the skin of Margot's neck. Did she not remember that Margot wasn't really one for public displays of affection in the work place? Of course, personality-wise, Margot hadn't been very consistent lately.

"I'm sorry, I can't. Not tonight." Hadn't she fooled everyone enough? Including herself?

"If you tell me you can't one more time, I will spontaneously combust, Go-Go." Inez pulled back a little. "At least have lunch with me. We need to talk."

Before Margot had a chance to reply, both their beepers went off. They shared a glance and sped out of the changing room.

———

As it turned out, neither Margot nor Inez had had time for lunch, and Margot found herself hovering outside of Nadia's door. She seemed like the only person she could confide in.

"Got a minute?" Margot asked, after knocking and sneaking her head in the door.

Nadia looked up from her computer screen. "Of course."

Margot sat down and pondered how many times she'd sat

in this chair discussing non-hospital business in the past few months. She really needed to get a grip on herself.

"What's on your mind?" Nadia asked, tilting her head slightly.

"What's not?" Margot sighed. "I'm such a mess." There had been a time when Margot wouldn't have dreamed of uttering these words to another human being.

"Just a heads-up, I have to attend a meeting with the board in ten minutes." Nadia glanced at the wall clock to her left. "But if you'd like, you're welcome to join Jules and me for dinner tonight."

"Juliette hates me after what I did to Claire."

Nadia shook her head. "That is absolutely not true. Claire's her best friend, but—"

"It's all right." Margot started getting up. "I shouldn't be coming in here in the middle of the work day, anyway."

"Margot, wait." Nadia shoved her chair back. "Please, come over tonight. Trust me, Juliette doesn't hate you and, if anything, at least give her a chance to prove that."

"Okay." Desperate for some friendly company, Margot gave in.

"Just don't bring Inez," Nadia said, a smile on her lips.

Margot was speechless and headed to the door in silence.

"Lame joke," Nadia was quick to say. "My bad."

But Margot knew she deserved it.

———

When Margot rang Juliette and Nadia's bell, a bottle of Saint-Émilion in her hand, she wondered how she'd gone from wanting five quick minutes to vent with Nadia to a full-blown dinner with the pair of them.

"Bonsoir." Juliette answered the door and pecked Margot on the cheeks warmly. Maybe Margot had been imagining things, after all. "Come in. Nadia's in the kitchen." Margot remembered the first time she'd come to dinner here—and considered how much everything had changed since then.

Juliette poured all three of them a glass from the bottle Margot had brought and invited Margot to sit.

"Just to quickly clear the air between us," she said, crossing one leg over the other. "I know you never meant to hurt Claire and I'm sorry things turned out the way they have."

"We're good?" It made Margot sound as if she was in a gangster movie.

"Of course." She scooted to the edge of her chair. "And, if you don't mind, I'm going to need you to do me a favour," she whispered. "Nadia's birthday is approaching fast and I—"

They were interrupted by the chime of the bell.

"Can you get that, babe?" Nadia shouted from the kitchen. "It's probably the delivery from Le Gourmand. Check if everything's there."

Margot leaned back in her chair. What was that about Nadia's birthday? Was Juliette planning a surprise and expecting Margot to attend? That wouldn't be awkward at all. And what was that noise in the hallway? That didn't sound like a delivery.

"Straight from the road, *les amies*." Margot recognised Steph's voice. "Dropping off your neighbour here and we thought we'd check in with our favourite non-dramatic couple. See if you're still together and such."

Margot's chest tightened. Did she say 'we'?

"Salut," a familiar voice said. "I hope we're not interrupting anything romantic." Footsteps approached and Margot shot up out of the sofa. *Fuck.*

"Claire, wait." Margot heard Juliette say. "We have company." But it was too late, because there they stood. Face to face. In the same living room where they had first met.

"I should probably go," Margot mumbled. Nadia had come out of the kitchen and the five of them stood frozen in time for an instant.

"No, that's all right," Claire said, her voice broken. "We shouldn't have barged in like that. I'll go."

"There's plenty of food for everyone," Nadia offered. "You know me, I always make too much."

Margot glanced at Claire. Her skin was nut-brown, contrasting with her blonde hair. She looked tired though, with dark circles under her eyes. "Stay," Margot said. "Please." She started making her way to the hallway, past a perplexed Steph and Juliette.

Nadia came behind her when she'd almost reached the door. "You don't have to do this." She planted her hand on the doorknob. "I know it's awkward, but it will have to happen once…"

"No, it's too hard. For both of us." Margot put her hand over Nadia's on the handle.

"Can we talk for a minute?" Claire's voice crackled behind them. "It won't take long."

Nadia nodded and rushed back into the living room, leaving them alone.

"I hope you had a good holiday," Margot said, not knowing what else to say.

"I didn't." Claire inched closer, leaning her upper body against the wall—just like she'd done that night when Margot had gone to break up with her. "I just… I need to know, Margot."

Margot shook her head. "We're not back together." Although Inez would beg to differ.

CLAIRE

"You're not?" Hope flared like fireworks in Claire's veins.

Margot shook her head. She looked rattled—just as rattled as Claire felt. "We should talk." She fiddled with her fingers. "Soon."

"We should?" They were talking now. Why couldn't Margot say what she had to say.

"In private," Margot said, as if reading Claire's mind.

"I guess I'd better not stop by the hospital." Claire had to call upon a lot of willpower not to rush over to where Margot was standing and pull her close. Kiss her. Could she really have changed her mind? Was that why she wanted to talk?

"Maybe not." Confidence started creeping back into Margot's voice. She looked as if she was regaining control. "How about tomorrow evening?"

"Why don't you stay? You were here first." Claire suddenly didn't want her to go, wanted to bask in her presence—no matter how awkward—a while longer.

Margot pursed her lips before speaking. "It's not a good idea."

"Fine. Tomorrow." Despite herself, Claire inched closer. "Just…" The words died in her throat.

"Yes?" Was that hope flickering in Margot's eyes? Or pity?

"Tomorrow. Come to mine." Claire wasn't sure she could face going back to Margot's flat.

"Okay." Margot nodded solemnly. "See you then." Her voice had gone so soft, it almost felt like a caress.

I miss you, Claire wanted to say. *Stay.* But Margot was turning the handle already, slipping through the small crack the edge of the door created with the wall.

Claire stood staring at the door for a few seconds longer after Margot had left. It had been oddly less painful than she'd imagined an impromptu meeting between them would be—hopeful, almost.

"Are you all right?" Juliette came up behind her.

Claire sucked in a deep breath before turning around. "No."

"I'm sorry, if we'd known you'd be stopping by—"

"It's okay." Claire looked her friend in the eyes. "Just give me a hug, will you?"

Juliette wrapped her arms around Claire and, although she tried not to, Claire couldn't help but pretend it was Margot holding her.

"She brought an excellent bottle of red," Juliette whispered in her ear. "Come on, I've poured you a glass already."

As they headed into the living room, Claire glanced at Nadia and Steph sitting there, while Juliette still had a hand on her shoulder, and she realised this was her other—her chosen—family.

"Let's eat," Nadia said and rose from her seat, squeezing Claire's shoulder as she passed her on the way to the kitchen. "I've made my mother's world famous merguez tajine."

"How dare you serve sausages to a bunch of lesbians," Steph said.

"You certainly seem to have taken a shine to them," Claire said, shooting Steph a crooked grin. "From what you've told me."

"Please elaborate." Juliette grabbed the bottle of wine from the coffee table and carried it with her to the dining table.

"Gosh, there really is no such thing as privacy with you ladies, is there?" Steph sat down and winked at Claire.

Claire took a seat next to her and she guessed that, no matter what happened with Margot, her friends would get her through.

STEPH

"Happy birthday," Steph said to the image of Dominique on her laptop screen.

"I wish you were still here," Dominique replied while sticking out her bottom lip.

"For an elaborate birthday dinner with your parents? Sure, sounds like fun."

"The kids miss you. Didier can't stop talking about how you taught him to dive into the pool headfirst and Lisa keeps telling her grandmother about how pretty our visitor was. I can only agree, of course, but if she keeps this up, she'll be spilling the beans before I ever have a chance." Dominique sent her a lopsided smile. "Did you get me a present?"

"Of course. I'll give it to you when you get back." Steph was counting the days until she could watch Dominique unwrap her present—and then use it on her.

"How about you give me something I want today?" On the screen, Dominique squinted and pouted her lips.

"I would if I could, but you're too far away." Steph fell asleep to the image of an all strapped-on Dominique every night.

"Come on, Stéphanie, this is the year 2014. Do I really need to tell you about all the technology we have at our disposal?"

Steph sunk her teeth into her bottom lip. "Do you mean Skype sex?"

Although not a hundred percent clear on the screen due to the nature of their connection, Steph could see determination build in Dominique's glance. "Yes."

"But," she protested, "I have Pierrot here on the bed with me."

"Really?" Dominique shook her head. "The things that poor animal must have seen."

Steph bent sideways to where Pierrot rested, oblivious to the conversation she was having, and kissed him on the head. "He's the best pussy I ever met."

"Oh yeah?" When Steph glanced back at the screen, she saw Dominique had started to unbutton her shirt. It looked a lot like the one she'd worn to cover herself up that afternoon in the garden.

"Well, huh—" Steph's throat went dry at the sight of Dominique trailing her fingertip along the edge of her bra cups.

"Best grab a toy from that box underneath your bed, sweetie. You're going to need it," Dominique said.

Automatically, Steph coaxed Pierrot off the bed and reached underneath, unearthing a brand new black dildo she'd bought when she had purchased Dominique's present.

"Classy." Dominique nodded her approval, her hands behind her back, the cups of her bra sagging down as she unhooked it. She let her bra drop and sucked a finger deep into her mouth before bringing it to her right nipple and encircling it. "Push your laptop back a bit. I want to see you. All of you."

Steph did as she was told—again. She shuffled backwards on the bed, checking the angle of the camera, and hitched her t-shirt over her head. She wasn't wearing a bra.

"I have such a thing for tan lines." Dominique's voice sounded a bit raspier. She repositioned her own laptop so Steph had a full view of her body.

Apparently, she had already disposed of her underwear—or simply hadn't been wearing any—because she was completely naked on the screen. *The screenshots Steph could take.* She didn't, though. Instead, she manoeuvred herself out of her shorts and mirrored Dominique's naked image. She spread her legs and leaned back against the pillows.

"Put it in your mouth," Dominique instructed, her fingers roaming across her skin. "Make sure it's wet enough."

Steph couldn't keep her eyes off Dominique's glistening pussy on the screen. Entranced, she brought the black dildo to her lips and let her tongue slip over the tip.

"Suck on it," Dominique said, with a voice Steph barely recognised. Her fingers had reached her pussy and she spread her nether lips wide with her index and middle finger.

Steph imagined that, instead of sliding the dildo into her own mouth, she was guiding it between Dominique's pussy lips.

"Tease yourself with it until you're wet enough." Dominique's voice was no more than a few puffs of ragged breath. She had started rubbing a fingertip over her clit, all of her exposed to the camera and to Steph.

Steph dragged the tip of the dildo over her throbbing pussy lips, ready to receive.

"When you slip it in, imagine it's me fucking you with it."

Steph momentarily closed her eyes as she slid the head of the toy inside of herself slowly, cutting off her breath.

"How does that feel? Talk to me, babe." When Steph looked at the screen again, she saw that the movements of Dominique's fingers were becoming more frantic. With one hand, she pulled her lips apart, while a finger of her other hand skated along her clit in an ever quickening pace.

"You're fucking me," Steph heard herself say. She eased the dildo in deeper. "It feels so good when you fuck me."

"More," Dominique said. "Faster."

Without giving it any second thoughts, Steph gave in. She plunged the toy deep inside of her. Next to the image of Dominique, who was straining to keep her head from falling back, she saw herself reflected in a small square in the corner. A black dildo buried inside of her, her own hand coaxing it in and out.

"I'm going to come," Dominique said. "I can't—" A brief silence descended on Steph's bedroom, just the sound of the silicone toy disappearing inside of her. "Oh fuck." Dominique let her hands fall to her side. "Come for me, sweetheart," she said. "Do it for me."

As if it had really always been that easy, a quick climax tore through Steph, the sound of Dominique's voice enough to send her on her way. She felt the walls of her pussy clench around the dildo, and the subsequent ripple shudder through her muscles, as if Dominique was actually there. Her head had fallen back into the pillows, the toy still half inside of her.

"God, you're hot, even when you're six hundred miles away." Dominique's voice brought her back to life. Steph pushed herself up out of the pillows and looked straight into Dominique's face. She'd repositioned the laptop and her naked body was hidden from view. "Somehow, it makes me sad we couldn't tape this."

Steph chuckled. "You're crazy."

"If you mean crazy about you, then I agree." Dominique

winked. "I can't wait to make you do that when I'm actually in the room with you."

The mere thought of it sent a brand new shiver of lust up Steph's spine. "Soon," she said.

NADIA

"I'll be forty-two years old in less than three weeks," Nadia said. "You'll be forty-five this year." She was just stating the obvious, but someone had to do it.

"Speaking of." Juliette appeared in the doorframe connecting their bedroom to the bathroom. She didn't look a day over thirty-five, her skin shiny from the moisturiser she'd just applied, her long legs disappearing into a pair of black panties. "What would you like to do for your birthday? I'd like to start planning."

"You know I don't like a big fuss, and it's not a milestone birthday, anyway. Something intimate. Maybe we could go away, just the two of us?"

"Hm, yes." Juliette didn't look convinced. "But don't you want to celebrate with your friends?"

"Remember the last birthday party we attended?" Nadia threw back the sheets from the bed.

"I certainly do, but I'm surprised you have any memories of it." Juliette shot her a wink. "I'll be right back. Just brushing my teeth."

Nadia slid onto the bed and pulled the sheets over her legs. She knew Juliette would want to throw her a party. She also knew how to meet her halfway. And part of her was still reluctant to book a trip—even a short weekend getaway.

She waited until Juliette was nicely tucked under the covers with her, her head resting in the crook of Nadia's shoulder, to pick up their conversation again. "We can do it here. A small dinner party with only people I know, no hangers-on. And no exes who turn up unexpectedly."

"Does that include family?" Juliette's jaw moved against Nadia's skin as she spoke.

"No, let's keep it separate. You know my mother, she'll invite us over for a big meal on the day anyway."

"We'll have to be very specific to Steph about the no-hangers on bit."

"She and Dominique are good now, aren't they?"

"One day they are, the next day, they might not be. Who knows what will happen between now and then."

"She looked so happy the other day, though."

"Yes, because she'd just returned from fantasy-land. Once Laroche is back in Paris, it's back to reality."

"Hey." Nadia pushed herself up. "We should invite Dominique as well. I've seen her on the news, but I've never met her. I'd like to see her and Steph together. They seem to be getting quite serious."

"Really?" Juliette pressed herself up as well, finding Nadia's eyes. "You want to invite Dominique Laroche to your intimate birthday party?"

"Correction." She held up a finger. "I want to invite my good friend Steph's significant other to my party." The sheets fell off them, exposing their bare upper bodies. "It's only normal."

"She's my client."

"It's my birthday."

"Okay, okay." Juliette acquiesced very easily. "We don't want a repeat of Steph's party." Juliette put her hand on Nadia's thigh. "But, no matter if they're together by then, Margot can't bring Inez."

"She would never do that." Nadia put her hand over Juliette's. "God, I hope Margot and Claire are back on speaking terms by then. I want them both there, but, more than anything, I don't want any tension."

"We're getting too old for all this drama." Juliette's fingers started digging into Nadia's flesh.

"Well, we're not exactly guilt-free in that department, babe. The anguish we put them through. The hours of their time they had to sacrifice to processing." Nadia chuckled.

"And look at us now." Juliette's fingers crawled upwards, her eyes locking on Nadia's.

"Yeah." Nadia nodded. Did Juliette still think it was this easy? So easy that she'd started thinking about children, had started re-thinking the very foundations of their life together.

Juliette's other hand found Nadia's wrist. "Did you know that Margot tied Claire to the bed?"

"What? No." A tingle crept up Nadia's spine.

"Claire loved it." Juliette curled her fingers tighter around Nadia's wrist. "She's like you, you know. Margot."

"Is she now?" Nadia let her body slip down onto the mattress.

"But not tonight." Juliette, still holding on to Nadia's wrist with one hand, hoisted herself on top of Nadia, and grabbed her other wrist with her other hand, joining both of them above Nadia's head.

"We'll see about that." Nadia didn't need a lot of muscle power to push Juliette's hands up and manoeuvre herself out of the position she'd been put in. "I thought you knew better by now." With a few small movements of her hips, Nadia threw Juliette off her, and flipped her own body over, so she was on top.

Juliette grinned up at her. "It was worth a try."

MARGOT

Margot waited for Inez outside of the hospital doors. She was seeing Claire tonight and, before that, she hoped to find some sort of clarity—although she had no idea how. It seemed so hard to find the old her in the mess her mind had become. The old Margot who would know what to do. Who would automatically dismiss the idea of having feelings for two different people at the same time. How had this even happened to someone like her?

She nodded at a nurse walking past her on her way home. It was Alice, the one who'd never really warmed up to Margot's ways but always appeared to burst into a wide grin whenever Inez walked past the nurses station. Inez had that effect on people—Margot included. But Claire turning up at Nadia and Juliette's the other night, that had *really* thrown her. The obvious hurt on display on her face. The longing in her glance.

In the end, Margot hadn't confided in anyone, had kept it all to herself, as usual.

"Hey." Inez hooked an arm around Margot's elbow. "Sorry to keep you waiting." They'd barely had a moment to talk, the ER overrun by casualties from a pile-up on the périphérique. Did Inez think they were back together? "Want to grab some dinner or head straight back to mine? It's so easy to live just around the corner, Go-Go. You should rent out your flat, collect the money, and move in with me."

Margot let Inez' arm drop as she stretched her own.

"Relax, I'm just joking." Inez put a hand on Margot's neck and squeezed softly. "You seem more uptight than usual. How about an apéritif?"

"Yes, please." There was a time when Margot would have automatically said no. She had to drive. She had to work tomorrow. She had to—there was always a good reason. But tonight, she was meeting Claire. And she needed to have a difficult conversation with Inez first. She could hardly keep on stringing them both along. She'd take a taxi and leave her bike in the hospital's parking lot.

"Come on, there's this new place along the canal. This neighbourhood has changed so much since I left." Inez guided them around a few corners until they reached the canal. They crossed the bridge and halted at a café with a terrace overlooking the water. From her seat, Margot could see Inez' building. The memory of what they had done there, both bitter and sweet, still very much alive in her mind.

"Whiskey, no ice," Margot said to the waiter, not even bothering to look at the menu he had placed on the table.

"Wow," Inez said, while browsing the drinks list. "I'll go for something lighter, if you don't mind." She glanced up at the waiter. "A dirty martini, please."

They handed back the menus and, as soon as the waiter had disappeared inside, Inez turned to Margot. "Should I be worried, Go-Go? I don't remember you drinking like that."

"I've changed," Margot snapped. Damn, she should get her stress levels under control. When she looked at herself in the mirror, she recognised the long, black hair. The almond-shaped eyes and the sparse smile she used in daily life. But how she felt underneath that familiar exterior, that was all new. She *had* changed—but not necessarily for the better. "I'm sorry." She held up her hands.

"Talk to me." Inez never was one to draw things out, nor to keep them under wraps. "Out with it," she said. "And be honest with me. We've wasted enough time."

And whose fault was that? Margot sighed, wishing she'd already had her whiskey to get some liquid courage inside of her. "Honestly?" She looked at Inez, as if asking for permission to speak the truth. "I don't know if I want to be with you or with Claire, and it's driving me crazy." She could no longer look at Inez after saying that.

"At least you're honest." Inez' voice had lost some of its sparkle already.

The waiter came back outside and served their drinks. They both sipped—Margot fighting the urge to knock all of it back in one go.

"I'm sorry. It's how I feel."

"At least I'm not completely out of the picture yet." From behind her martini glass, Inez shot her a weak smile.

"I loved you to pieces, but you left. I grieved for so long, and then I met Claire… and she changed things for me. For the first time in months, I could feel things again. And then, *bam*, you're back." Margot shook her head. "Now, I don't know anything anymore."

"I'm sorry you feel that way… that I made you feel that way." Inez drained the rest of her glass. "Obviously, I'm not the best person to advise you on this." Putting her glass down, she twisted in her chair. "But know this, Go-Go." Her voice went all soft again. "If you choose me, I'm here. All the way. No reservations. I fully realise what I let go when I left. I love you and I want to be with you. I came back for you."

"I know." Margot nodded, but it didn't make things easier. She couldn't help but wonder if, in affairs of the heart, it shouldn't be simpler. More obvious, at least. *I wish you hadn't come back*, she wanted to say. Then she wouldn't be feeling this way. Then, it would be obvious. But, deep down, she couldn't help but be glad that Inez had come back.

She glanced at her watch. "I think I'm going to go."

"I hate to see you like this," Inez said, putting her palm on Margot's arm.

"Yeah." Margot shrugged herself free, not feeling comfortable with the physical contact. "Me too." She stood up and left, feeling sorry for herself.

JULIETTE

Juliette met Claire and Steph for a drink at Le Comptoir and everything almost felt normal again. Except that Claire didn't seem to have benefited from her holiday at all, and Steph appeared to have enjoyed hers a bit too much—heading for certain disappointment, Juliette thought, although she was trying to work on no longer having automatic negative assumptions like that. And then there was the turmoil in her own head.

Claire looked up from her phone. "I just got an e-mail from Marc Dujardin. He says Sybille has been a godsend and asks if we have any other valuable employees we'd like to usher his way."

"I request a change of subject this instant," Steph was quick to say. "I don't want to hear about her, talk about her and, least of all, think about her."

"I agree with Steph." Juliette didn't waste time thinking about Sybille anymore. She was a part of her past now. A mistake. One that had left a stain, but she preferred to focus on the present. "You should both keep the Friday after September first free. We'll be having a small dinner party for Nadia's birthday."

"Small? That's not your style, Jules?" Steph joked.

"So small, in fact," Juliette continued, "that you can bring Dominique, if you want." She watched both of their jaws drop.

"For real?" Steph sat up. "How can I, though?"

"It'll just be us." Juliette turned to Claire briefly. "And Margot." She drew her lips into an apologetic smile. "Nadia would like to meet Dominique, and it seems like a good occasion."

"I'll pass along the invitation," Steph said.

"How official." A small grin tugged at Claire's lips. Juliette was glad she at least attempted a smile.

"We'll see." Steph leaned back in her chair.

Juliette eyed her for a few seconds before asking the question that had really been on her mind. Steph's hair looked as if she, at the same time, never went to a hairdresser and had just come back from one. Most of all, Steph always came across entirely relaxed and at peace with the world. A sort of nonchalance Juliette had always somewhat envied, and had always suspected came from living a no-strings-attached life. But there she sat. She was deeply involved with someone now. She was in love and, yet, her demeanour appeared the same. She exuded the same air of not knowing where life would take her next, and not particularly caring. Steph didn't look at all like a person who had just spent an entire week with her secret lover's children.

"Before you know it, you'll be a stepmother." Juliette pinned her glance on Steph, not wanting to miss a fraction of a second of her reaction.

"Wow." She lifted up her hands. "Take it easy, Jules."

"What was it like, though?" Juliette refilled their glasses of wine.

Claire held her hand over hers. "I'm meeting Margot after this. I need to keep a clear head."

"They're great kids. Really wonderful." Steph grabbed her full glass from the table and sagged back into her chair. "They're at a really funny age, always asking questions and saying silly things."

"Did they not wonder about you?" Juliette noticed how Steph's lazy smile faded a bit.

"I'm just a friend of their mother." She shrugged. "Their mind doesn't go there. They asked a lot of questions about me, of course. Lisa even asked me if I had a husband." Steph snickered. "Not in a million years, I told her."

"How old are they?" Claire asked. "Emma and Léa are five now and Nathan is two and they're all bloody exhausting."

"We all know how *you* feel about children, Claire," Juliette said.

"How *I* feel?" Claire brought a hand to her chest. "Last time I checked, dear Jules, we both shared the sentiment that we were not cut out for them."

Juliette could almost feel the heat of Claire's stare on her cheeks. "Maybe I changed my mind."

"They're six and—" Steph started to say.

"Hold on." Claire sat up straight in her chair and leaned her torso in Juliette's direction. "Could you say that again, please?"

Juliette lifted her shoulders. "Nadia and I have been talking about it." It wasn't exactly the truth—they'd barely skirted around the subject a few times—but Juliette wanted to get her friends' take on it.

"We go away for a week and you and Nadia start talking about having kids?" Claire rolled her eyes. "Jules, come on. After what you've just been through… isn't it more like a reaction, a reflex to somehow change the instability of your relationship?"

Juliette looked over at Steph, but she seemed to be staying out of this one.

"Look, I'm not saying we'll be running to the sperm bank next week. It's just something that's been on my mind." She locked her gaze on Claire defiantly. "Take Olivier from Connu… He owns his own company and he's a single dad, even. Adopted David when he was forty-three."

Claire sighed. "I'm just shocked, Jules. I'm not trying to say that what you're experiencing is invalid. I mean, all of our clocks are ticking."

"You and Nadia would make great parents," Steph interjected. "Hell, I'd want you to adopt me." A smile slipped across Steph's lips. "But I'm just as shocked as Claire, Jules. Whenever the conversation has landed on children in the past, you were always the one making the most vocal arguments against having them. They take over your entire life. They drain you of all of your energy. They put a strain on your relationship." She shook her head. "I'm just repeating what I heard you say."

"Maybe I've changed my mind." Juliette was hesitant to express the profoundness of the change inside of her. "Look at Dominique. If all goes well, she'll be a minister in the next cabinet."

"It's different for straight people, though," Steph said. "For most of them, their life isn't complete when they haven't procreated. When they haven't followed the exact same pattern as their parents and grandparents. They don't have to question the biology. They just do it." Steph sipped from her wine and found Juliette's eyes. "I'm quite certain that one of the reasons Lisa and Didier were so ecstatic on holiday, was because they got to spend uninterrupted time with their mother. And for Dominique, it's a constant guilt trip. She loves them to bits and they're well cared for, but she's not the best example here."

Claire pushed her chair back. "I'd love to stay for the rest of this conversation, but I have to go."

Steph rose as well and opened her arms wide. "Come here." Claire stepped into Steph's hug. From where Juliette was sitting, her body seemed tense. Juliette was sorry she'd hijacked the conversation. They should have used their time to prepare Claire for meeting Margot. But what could they possibly have said?

Juliette stood up and squeezed Claire's hand. "Don't let her break you all over again. Tell her she'll have me to deal with if she does."

Claire shot her a weak smile and went on her way.

"I'm worried about her," Juliette said as soon as Claire was out of earshot. "How was she on the ride back?"

"A big mess," Steph said. "She's still so in love with Margot and she'd take her back in a heartbeat."

"Love, eh?" Juliette looked at her watch. "I promised Nadia I'd take care of dinner."

"Just remember, Jules…" Steph poured the last of the bottle into her glass. "No more after work drinks once you adopt that baby."

"And who says that's a bad thing?" Juliette drained her glass and kissed Steph goodbye. "Let me know if Dominique can make it to Nadia's birthday in a timely fashion, please."

"Yes, boss." Steph touched two fingers to her temple and saluted her.

CLAIRE

"You broke me," Claire said, not caring how overly dramatic it sounded. To her, it was the truth. "You broke me into a thousand little pieces and the worst part is, sitting across from you now, looking at you, trying to figure out what's going on inside your head, I still want you so much."

Margot had asked for something stronger when Claire had offered her wine. Claire had poured her vodka, the same brand she'd found comfort in after Margot had ripped her heart to pieces. The sight of it now—after too much of it for days—made her nauseous. Claire stuck to wine, sipping it slowly while watching Margot. She looked like she'd been drinking already —like she was falling apart as much as Claire was.

"I wish I could sit here and say that breaking up with you was a mistake, but that would be a lie. I had to break up with you—and, unfortunately, hurt you in the process—because of Inez. Because of what she made me feel."

Claire remembered the words Juliette had uttered as she'd left Le Comptoir earlier. *Don't let her break you all over again.* Margot was the one who had instigated this talk, had wanted to meet in private. Claire already knew the reason why they'd broken up. Had Margot come to ask for permission to take things further with Inez, or something equally twisted? Claire let Margot continue uninterrupted though, as if she couldn't help but hang on every word she said.

"But, I've come to realise that what Inez made me feel, has not changed a thing about how I feel for you." She reached for the glass of vodka, sipped and pulled a face. "I know I broke you. Fuck, I know. But I broke myself in the process as well."

Claire wanted to listen attentively, but every word Margot said started to sting a little more. "What are you trying to say? Either you're with her or you're with me. I thought this was all so simple." *Simple comme bonjour.* "You were with me. She came back. You dumped me. The way I see it, things really can't be clearer." A ball of fury came loose inside of Claire's chest. "And if you've come to ask for forgiveness, excuse my bluntness, but you can stick it up your backside."

"I haven't come for absolution, Claire. I—" Margot seemed

to have trouble finding her words. "I didn't break up with you because I wanted to get back together with Inez. I did it because—"

"Have you slept with her?" A red mist descended on Claire's brain.

"I—I don't think that's relevant to this conversation."

"Are you fucking kidding me?" Claire shook her head. "I'm beginning to think I had you all wrong from the start. All along, I believed you were this person with super morals, someone with integrity and purity, someone who, no matter the circumstances, would always do the right thing." A tear dripped out of the corner of Claire's eye. "Someone who wouldn't hurt me, because you knew what that felt like. It made you careful and more principled. I loved that about you." Claire wiped the tear from her cheek, frustrated that she hadn't been able to keep it from raining down. "And look at you now. There's nothing left of that person." Claire straightened her shoulders. "But hey, my bad just the same. I wanted to believe that someone like you would exist and sweep me off my feet. I wanted the illusion so fucking badly, and you had me fooled." She huffed out a breath. "But not anymore." Surprised by her sudden strength, Claire sat up. "I take it back. What I said earlier about still wanting you." She stared straight into Margot's black eyes. "I don't want you anymore. Go be with Inez. Tie her to your fucking bed for all I care."

"Claire—" Margot's voice broke. "I didn't come here…" All subsequent words stayed stuck in her throat as her eyes filled with tears.

The sight of her, crumbling in the sofa, felt as if someone had found the plug and let all the air out of Claire's short-lived bravado. But she could hardly say she was sorry now. Instead, she refilled Margot's glass, adding more vodka and a splash of orange juice. "Drink," she said.

Claire watched Margot sip, her hand shaking heavily as she brought the glass to her lips.

"It's not easy to explain," Margot said, before drinking again. "And yes, I slept with her, but—" She knocked back the rest of the vodka in one big greedy gulp, her shoulders shivering when she put the glass back down. "I still love you. That's as simple as I can put it, although it's much more complicated than that. But I still love you."

Despite those being the exact words Claire had wanted to hear, she was more perplexed than touched by them. Confused, Claire rose from her seat. "I'll get us some water." She sauntered to the kitchen and splashed some cold water on her face before grabbing a bottle of Perrier from the fridge. She took a deep breath and tried to re-enter the living room with a steady, confident gait.

She poured them both a glass of water, sat down and said, "Explain it to me."

MARGOT

Once again, this was not going according to the plan Margot had made in her head. Had she really thought she could just waltz into Claire's apartment and tell her about her struggle with her feelings for her, as well as for Inez? If she kept this up, she'd end up with neither one of them. It would be exactly what she deserved.

She chucked down the water Claire had poured, as if it could undo the cloudiness in her brain. Again, she knew better. Margot de Hay always knew better, always did the right thing, always had everyone's back. As if she was immune to making mistakes and had somehow bypassed the most fundamental of human flaws—the ability to hurt other people.

To top it off, Margot was not a talker. She could deliver a diagnosis to a patient because she'd been trained to do so, but this, this trying to put into words what was going on in her heart, it seemed as impossible as all of this having a happy outcome.

"Would you consider giving me a second chance?" It was direct, perhaps rude, but in that moment, it was the only way for Margot to say it.

Margot watched Claire's jaw slacken. Was that a glint of hope shimmering in the darkness of her eyes?

"You've got some nerve," Claire mumbled. "I have to give you that."

The fact that Claire didn't give an immediate negative response brought Margot some much needed clarity. "When I broke up with you, it was not my intention to get back with Inez. But I couldn't be with you anymore, face you on a daily basis while struggling so much with seeing her again. It simply wasn't right, Claire. It undermined us, devalued what we had together and that was the last thing I wanted."

Claire shook her head. "How about, instead of turning up here to deposit your key on my hallway cabinet—it's still there, by the way—you had tried talking to me? You had opened up to me and told me what her return did to you?"

"It would never have been the same." Something inside Margot crumpled again, the way it had done when she'd witnessed how Claire had collapsed against the wall—when she had realised that nothing would ever be the same between them again, either way.

"And it is now?" Claire gave a huff.

"I guess I—" Margot looked into Claire's eyes and knew she had lost her. It made her scramble for words again. "I need you to understand why I did it."

"And I need you to understand this." Claire shuffled nervously in her seat. "I sat here for days waiting for you to return, hoping you'd magically appear in my doorway to undo what had happened, to admit that you had made a mistake and to beg me to take you back." Her face tensed. "But even now, sitting across from me, having come back, you can't even admit that you made a mistake."

"I'm—" Margot tried to say, but Claire talked over her.

"I would rather suffer for months from this ridiculous heartache for a person who turned out to be someone entirely different than I thought, than give you another chance, and have you rip me to pieces again. I'm done, *Go-Go*. When it comes to heartbreak, I don't go back for seconds. Unlike you."

Margot wondered what had happened to her. How she had ended up sitting across from a person she loved saying things like that to her. In that split second of Claire still having her eyes on her, her glance full of contempt, and the instant she looked away, Margot realised there was only one solution. She had to break all ties with Inez. Not go back to pretending she didn't exist anymore, but move on. Untangle herself from this mess and start anew.

She *would* end up with neither one of them, but Claire deserved better and Inez... Inez was the past. She'd known it after she'd gone to her flat that Sunday afternoon, on the way down, taking the stairs two-by-two to get out of there faster— running away from everything Inez stood for.

"I understand." Margot swallowed away a lump in her throat. "I'm so sorry and, yes, it *was* a mistake."

With the tiny bit of energy still left in her muscles, she rose from her seat and walked over to where Claire was sitting, crouching down beside her. "I truly hope you get over this quickly." While planting a hand on Claire's knee, she couldn't keep the tears from breaking free. "I'm so sorry I had to do this to you. Believe me, I will never forgive myself." Slanting her upper body, she pressed a kiss on Claire's cheekbone. "I was foolish to let you go." *Had Inez not said the exact same words to her?*

Margot pushed herself up, cast one last glance at Claire, who just sat there, stunned again, seemingly unable to speak anymore. Wiping away most of her tears, she turned around and made for the door.

She couldn't leave the country because of her father's weak health, but she could move to a suburb, like her sister, or a city close by. She was a good surgeon with an excellent reputation. Nadia would give her a cracking recommendation. She could easily get a job at another hospital. Leave this mess behind.

STEPH

Steph couldn't believe she had actually counted down the hours. This time last year, she had made the most of summertime in Paris by strolling along the quays at Paris Plages, eyeing skimpily dressed girls—or scanning for prey, as Fred called it. This year, she found herself drawn more to spending time with Juliette and Nadia, absorbing their new-found happiness, than going on a binge with Fred.

Dominique's plane would land in forty-five minutes. For obvious reasons, Steph couldn't turn up at the airport arrivals hall and surprise her—not that she hadn't considered it.

While she had feared that their holiday together would have been just another reality check, what with two small children running around the house and Steph feeling rather out of place, it had turned out to be the opposite. In fact, on her way back, Steph had found her reality vastly transformed. She didn't get that crushing feeling in her gut anymore when Dominique spoke of the future. Steph had even talked about Didier and Lisa with her friends. The truth was that, despite barely recognising what her own life had become, she revelled in the unexpected joy of it.

Ten years ago, when Laurence had ditched her, Steph had never set out to become the resident heartbreaker of the Parisian lesbian scene. She had just chosen to actively avoid any form of commitment. In the depths of her soul, she had never wanted to hop from fling to fling, let alone craved the loneliness that came with it, but it had all been collateral damage.

In the end, what the girls at Les Pêches—and even her friends—didn't see, was that she was the kind of person who needed years to recover from a break-up. Maybe it was a medical condition, an illness even, that made her suffer from the end of love so much more than anyone she knew.

In that respect, Dominique had been a safe bet. Because, in theory as well as in practice, it simply couldn't work. And now, somehow, it did. Maybe because Steph had finally shed the last sad remnants of her relationship with Laurence. Or maybe, quite simply, because Dominique was the single most irresistible woman Steph had come across in years. Perhaps even because for every person on earth there are only a few matches out there, and Dominique was one of hers, happening to cross her path when she was most receptive to it.

Steph could try to explain it all she wanted, but the simple truth was that she had fallen in love.

She glanced at her watch again. Only fifteen minutes. She grabbed her phone to check the Charles De Gaulle website to see if any delays were announced. The four fifteen flight from Nice was still scheduled to arrive on time. Dominique had told her that Philippe was picking the children up at the airport, giving her a ride as well. Philippe, who now knew about Steph's existence. Would she dare ask him to drop her at Steph's place? No, too complicated for Lisa and Didier.

Steph refreshed the website again. A green rectangle lit up next to Dominique's flight. *Landed.* A tingle spread from her stomach to her limbs. This was love now, and all her defences were down.

Steph's phone beeped, causing her heart to thump against her ribs.

Meet me at mine in an hour? Tu me manques trop.

Steph texted back, showered, dressed in jeans and a tank top, waited fifteen more minutes, and went on her way, practically skipping all the way to the Métro.

———

"C'est qui?" Dominique joked as she opened her front door to a crack.

A huge smile split Steph's lips as her eyes landed on a stripe of Dominique's tan face. She pushed the door open wide and stepped straight into Dominique's embrace.

"Whatever will we do if I become Minister of Foreign Affairs?" Dominique whispered in Steph's ear as she pulled her closer.

"I'll march on the Élysée and claim it's discrimination. A ploy to keep us apart," Steph whispered back.

"I wouldn't expect any less of you." Dominique tilted her head back and scanned Steph's face. "It's good to see you, Stéphanie."

"How good?" Steph asked.

Dominique didn't reply with words, instead she hoisted Steph's tank top over her head, dragged down the cups of her bra, and enclosed her lips over one of Steph's nipples.

Steph trailed her fingers through Dominique's sun-bleached hair—now more salt than pepper—as a shudder of desire ran across the expanse of her skin.

"Before I top you again," Dominique said when she came up for air. "I need to tell you something." A big grin was plastered across her face.

Steph arched up her eyebrows in expectation.

"When the Assemblée reconvenes in September, I'm voting for same-sex marriage."

Something inside of Steph melted. "In that case." She tugged at Dominique's t-shirt, wanting her closer. "You can top me all night long."

EPISODE SIX

NADIA

"You're running away?" Nadia asked. "Because of her?" She shook her head.

"I have no choice." Margot sat across from her, fidgeting with the sleeve of her scrubs, avoiding Nadia's eyes.

"Why do you have to be so goddamned stubborn?"

This made Margot look up. "Excuse me?"

"You believed so strongly that you didn't have a choice but to break up with Claire when Inez returned." Nadia started counting on her fingers. "That was mistake number one." She added a second finger. "And now you *have* to leave Saint-Vincent because of her?" Nadia looked her friend in the eyes. "The way I see it, you've been making horrible decisions ever since she came back." She held up her hands. "It's understandable, but it has to stop, Margot. Come on."

"I've made such a mess—"

Nadia didn't let her speak. She knew full well she was expressing her concern for Margot through anger, but perhaps that was what she needed. "When something goes wrong in surgery, do you run away?"

"Of course not, but that's not a good comparison."

"This is life. Sometimes it sucks. Deal with it, for crying out loud." Most of all, Nadia didn't want Margot to leave. "Yes, you messed up. We all do. It doesn't mean it can't be fixed."

"I agree with everything you say, Nadz. I do. I'm a coward, but for me, it's the only way."

"Bullshit." Nadia slammed her fist on the desk with a bit more force than she had anticipated. "And don't for one minute think I will ever accept your resignation. You're staying."

"With all due respect." Margot straightened her back. "You have no say in this. I'll go straight to the board. And we both know they have the real power in this place."

The words stalled in Nadia's throat for a split second. She relaxed back into her chair. "So that's what this is all about."

"I'm sorry." Margot's shoulders sagged again. "I shouldn't have said that."

Nadia pursed her lips together. "No, it's fine. Because you're right." *My hands were tied,* she wanted to say, but after what Juliette had told her about what Margot did to Claire in the bedroom, she considered it a poor choice of words. "I should have fought harder. I would have, if I had known this was going to be the outcome." *And I had never expected you to crumble like this,* Nadia wanted to add.

"The simple fact is that I can't work side by side with her every day. I just can't do it. I tried, but—" Despair glinted in Margot's eyes.

"I understand, but there could be alternative solutions. Have you asked Inez? Maybe she—"

"I'm not asking her to leave because I can't handle having her here," Margot said quickly.

"If you won't, I *will*." Nadia made her voice sound stern. "I mean it."

Margot glared at her from under her lashes. "Don't you dare."

"Then beat me to it." Nadia couldn't be more serious and

she hoped it came across successfully. "I'm not losing you to her. This hospital is not letting go of one of its best surgeons because of some fickle doctor without borders. No way."

"Dream on, Nadz. Do you really think asking Inez to leave will work?"

"If she loves you as much as she claims she does, it should. She came back, tried to get you back, and failed—and destroyed your life in the process. If anyone should take a step back, it should be her. She's a smart woman, she should be able to grasp that."

"It's not just Inez, though. I broke Claire's heart and I can't live with that. Not in this city where everything reminds me of her."

"Oh, and you think it's going to be easier somewhere else, where you're all alone and starting from scratch? Hey, at least you'll be able to double up on your mysterious, broken-hearted chick game. A lot of women really go for that. It'll work like a charm."

This time, it was Margot's turn to be too perplexed to reply. But Nadia wasn't done yet.

"You hit rock bottom… so what? We all have at some point, but guess what other people do? They get back up again and fix things." Nadia bent over her desk for effect. "If you leave town, you can scrap me right off your friends' list."

"In that case." Margot pushed herself out of her chair, her eyes narrow and her lips drawn into a thin slit. "Who needs a friend like you?"

"Sit down, I'm not done."

"Maybe you're not, but I am." Margot headed for the door.

"Why don't you try fighting for Claire. We both know she still loves you."

That stopped Margot in her tracks. She turned around and leaned with her back against the wall. "Claire and I are over." Her voice trembled when she said it.

"Everything is always so black and white with you. Do you

even realise there's an entire grayscale in between the extremes where you choose to live your life?"

"We all make our own choices." Margot caught a tear dripping from the corner of her eye. "I've made mine." She spun around and exited Nadia's office.

When Nadia banged her fist on the desk this time it hit the wood with a loud bang—and all the force she had intended to put in it.

CLAIRE

"Give me your phone," Steph said.

"Why?" Claire looked at her friend over the rim of her cosmopolitan glass.

"Because I'm stepping in." Steph held out her hand. "Have you opened that app your brother installed at all?"

"Yes." It wasn't a lie. Claire had started it up a few times and found a flurry of messages from strangers she wasn't the least bit interested in, only resulting in her shutting down the app as soon as she had fired it up. "I'm still not interested."

"That's exactly why I'm stepping in." Steph was still holding out her hand, palm upwards.

"What? You need your fix?" Claire covered her phone with her own hand, keeping it safe. "Now that you've found monogamy you want to live vicariously through me?"

"Yes, Claire, that's exactly what I want." Steph rolled her eyes and dropped her hand.

"Is Dominique coming to Nadia's party next week?" Claire changed the subject.

Steph nodded with slow movements of her head. "Yep. If nothing unexpected happens, she'll be there."

"She'd better not RSVP positively and dare to not turn up. You know what Jules is like." Claire grinned at Steph. It was so much easier talking about other people.

"Have you noticed something strange about Jules lately?

Either she's seriously overcompensating or she's up to something… And all this talk about children." Steph rolled her eyes again.

"She's still in crisis mode, plugging holes at breakneck speed. It's how she is. I'm sure it will all settle down soon enough." Claire knew Juliette well enough to see through her current antics.

"Do you think they'll be all right in the end?" Steph sipped from her beer, resting her eyes on Claire.

"I do. I really do." Saying it made Claire remember that first night when Nadia had moved out and Margot had turned up on her motorcycle at Le Comptoir—like a knight in shining, motorised armour, saving someone else's relationship. She pushed the thought away and focused her attention on Steph again.

"Thank goodness for that." Steph checked the liquid level of her beer. "Another?"

"Why the hell not?" Claire drained the rest of her cosmo and signalled Tony that they'd be having the same again.

"It's not all doom and gloom, Claire." A twinkle shone in Steph's eyes. "Against MLR instructions, Dominique is voting for gay marriage in the Assemblée nationale." Steph couldn't hide the pride in her voice, as if she were single-handedly responsible for turning a conservative députée. Perhaps she was.

"That's bold. Then again, she can hardly vote against it in the afternoon and step into bed with you in the evening. I fully realise politics is a hypocritical business, but that would be a bit much."

"I know." Steph nodded. "It just means a lot to me."

Tony arrived with their fresh drinks.

"It's not as if her vote will matter," Steph continued. "The Socialists have got this one in the bag, anyway. But as a symbolic gesture, it counts."

"Let's drink to that." Claire raised her glass. "A few more of these and I'll let you have a crack at my phone, work the old Steph magic." It wasn't even that much of a joke.

"I'm your friend, right? One of your best," Steph said.

"You know you are." Claire wondered where she was going with this.

"And you trust me?" The glance Steph shot her was both hopeful and a little mocking.

"Well, not as far as I can throw you, but to have my best interests at heart… yes, I do." Claire giggled.

"Then let me arrange *one* date." She cocked her head to the left and shot Claire her most sultry smile. "The woman of your dreams may be walking along this very street as we speak. Who knows? Look at *me*, Claire. Do you think I ever expected to fall in love—really in love—with one of our clients? Sometimes, it just happens when you least expect it. And I know you're still hung up on Margot. I know she was special and all that, but she's not the only special woman out there, I promise." She arched up her eyebrows suggestively. "I should know, right?"

"Are you saying I should take advantage of your experience with the ladies?" Claire took a large gulp of her drink.

"That's exactly what I'm saying." Steph held out her hand again. "Full transparency. I won't contact anyone without asking your permission first."

Claire eyed her phone. She wasn't drunk, but the first hints of a buzz numbed her brain a little, made her feel less apprehensive—and perhaps a bit more sorry for herself as well. "Deal," she said, while slipping her phone in Steph's direction. She could always cancel if she didn't feel like it in the end. And if she were truly honest with herself, it beat another night home alone with a bottle of vodka.

"Great." Steph's eyes twinkled. "And don't act as if you're all new to this either, Claire. Jules and Nadz met on the internet, and I know how the story goes." She winked at Claire.

"That was ten years ago."

"My point exactly. Do you have any idea how many more

women have found their way to apps like this by now? It's pussy galore."

"Oh christ." Claire shook her head, but she was secretly glad that someone like Steph had her back. She watched Steph fiddle with her phone in silence and drank some more.

"How about this one?" Steph held up the phone and showed her a picture of a blonde woman with blue eyes—about as much the opposite of Margot as anyone could be.

"No. Isn't there someone a bit more, uh, exotic on there?"

"Hold on." Steph focused on the phone again. "I'm just going through the messages you've already received. You got a new one about an hour ago from this woman…" She touched the screen twice and turned it around so Claire could see.

"I guess." Claire looked at the picture of a woman with tan skin, huge blue eyes and ruffled half-long dark-brown hair.

"You *guess*? She's a fucking stunner." Steph shook her head.

"Are there any other pictures of her?" Claire didn't wait for Steph's reply and swiped the screen of her phone, hoping to find more images of the woman. The next one showed her in full profile. She wasn't very tall but wore that leather jacket and those Ray-Bans well. Not bad.

"Can I reply?" Steph asked, her voice almost a stutter because of the excitement in it.

"What will you say? Does the thing have any more information on her?"

"Not a lot, but let's find out. Let's chit-chat."

Claire watched Steph type something. "Now we wait," she said. "Let's leave it on for notifications. Or do you want to totally slut it up and contact multiple prospects at once?"

"Prospects?" Claire took another sip from her cosmo.

"What a rush." Steph beamed a smile at her. "And she hasn't even texted back yet."

Now it was Claire's time to roll her eyes. "Let's have another because you're not leaving me alone with this."

"I'm going to have to leave you alone with her at some point. You know that, right?" Steph chuckled.

Claire looked around for Tony.

————

Claire had just put her feet up and settled in the sofa for the ten o'clock news when her phone buzzed. She and Steph had ended up having two more drinks, waiting for the 'prospect' to reply, to no avail.

The message read:

Hey, just got off work. Thanks for your reply.

A workaholic? Shifts? Claire was curious—and definitely tipsy enough to not have any reservations about what she was doing.

A fellow workaholic?

She typed. Maybe her game was a bit off. Where was Steph when she needed her. Her phone beeped again a second later.

Perhaps… want to discuss further over a drink? These phone keyboards are so annoying.

Claire's thoughts exactly… Regarding the keyboard, she wasn't so sure about the drink. She checked the woman's picture again. She really was rather hot.

You'll have to give me your name first. I'm Claire.

Nice to meet you (virtually), Claire. My name is Sarah and I'm sorry for being so forward. ;-/

Maybe she should ask for her e-mail address so they could correspond first. *Correspond?* Claire shook her head. She should just go for it. She had, after all, nothing to lose.

How about Le Comptoir on avenue Mac-Mahon tomorrow evening? Or are you working?

At least, if she met this stranger at Le Comptoir she'd feel sort of on home turf. And she could ask Steph to drop by if she needed rescuing.

Free as a bird. 7.30?

Sounds good.

Claire already felt a bit stumped for words and this was supposed to be the easy part. She'd have to ask Steph for advice tomorrow. What would she wear? Should she even be doing this? Claire's phone beeped twice in quick succession.

I look forward to meeting you, Claire. Sweet dreams.

P.S. At the risk of sounding corny, you have such beautiful eyes in your profile pic.

Flattery already? It made her glow a little on the inside. But which profile picture was Sarah referring to? Claire hadn't even checked it since her brother had set it up. She went into the settings and looked at a much younger, much healthier version of herself. *Damn you, Sam,* she muttered under her breath. It looked like Sarah was in for a bit of a disappointment. But what could she do? Take a selfie on the spot? Confess that she was one of those people who uses old pictures on the internet? Or worse, tell this perfect stranger that her brother had installed the app and her friend had instigated the conversation?

Not so bad yourself. ;-)

Claire typed and put her phone aside. She was glad she was drunk, otherwise she wouldn't be getting any sleep at all.

STEPH

"I think you should meet Philippe before the vote," Dominique said.

Steph was barely awake, but Dominique, as usual on a weekday, was already up and about, freshly washed and dressed, ready to go.

It was a bit much to take on an empty stomach. "What?"

"Now that he knows, he wants to meet you." Dominique perched on the edge of the bed. "It's only fair."

"Fair?" Steph rubbed her eyes and pushed herself up. Glancing up at Dominique, she figured there was nothing she wouldn't do for her, but still, having shied away from relationships for years had allowed her to avoid all sorts of occasions for awkwardness like the one Dominique was suggesting now.

"You've spent time with his children. It's natural that he wants to get to know you. I basically bombarded him with the news before I left for Juan-les-Pins. He's had some time to process now. He's a modern man. By which I mean he's not like my father."

"What about Lisa and Didier?" Steph hoisted herself up a bit more, covering her entire body with the sheet—not convinced this was a conversation to be had with naked body parts on display.

"We've talked about it. They're too young. Either they'll grasp it of their own accord—perhaps Lisa will soon—or we'll tell them later."

"Don't they need clarity or something? For things to be explained and made clear."

"They do, but I'm thinking this might just be a bit too

confusing for them right now. They're only just coming to grips with the divorce. It's all a bit much."

"Whatever I can do to help." Steph reached out her hand, waiting for Dominique to put hers in it. "What was his reaction when you told him you'd gone back to pussy, by the way?"

"I didn't really give him a whole lot of opportunity to react at the time, but I presume he must have been quite shocked. It would be easier for him if he could put a face to the name Stéphanie Mathis. Make it more concrete and graspable."

"Set it up and I'll be there." Steph tugged at Dominique's arm. "It's such a shame you've already put all this effort in getting dressed."

"Why's that?" Dominique shot her a crooked grin while shaking her head.

"Because you're going to have to do it all over again after this." Steph cradled her hands around Dominique's neck and pulled her close for a kiss.

"No, no, I'm already running late," Dominique protested. "I really don't have time."

"It's the only currency you have with me, baby," Steph whispered. "Besides, you wiped me out so completely last night, I didn't get a chance to do what I had planned."

"That's okay, really. It always needs to be so quid pro quo with you lesbians. It's not—"

Steph brought her fingers to Dominique's lips. "It's not political, babe. The more you go on about it, the less time we have left." Steph felt Dominique's lips stretch into a smile against her fingers. She knew she wouldn't be able to resist. She never could. One of the main reasons why they were in this situation, discussing meeting her ex-husband and telling her children. And, if anything, it had convinced Dominique to go against the MLR's conservative directive to vote against same-sex marriage. Steph hadn't felt this loved in years.

"I guess an emergency meeting with my PR advisor is as

good a reason as any to be late. It is August after all. The country's basically asleep."

"A good politician always has an excuse." Steph pulled Dominique on top of her, crumpling her pristine blouse in the process. "And you're the best."

"What did you have in mind for breakfast, Stéphanie?" Dominique smiled down at her, causing pangs of lust to crash through Steph's flesh at high velocity.

"Some juice, I guess." Steph pulled her close for a kiss. Dominique's lips tasted of lipstick and Steph already anticipated the moment she'd look at herself in the mirror later, her mouth smeared with traces of Dominique's make-up, evidence of their love clinging to her skin.

Steph started coaxing Dominique's body off of her. As much as she had come to enjoy Dominique being on top, she wouldn't be this morning.

"I'll let you take your own clothes off to minimise the damage," Steph said, once she sat on her knees—stark naked—on the bed. "But remember, the clock is ticking." She tapped an imaginary watch on her wrist.

Dominique seemingly could not get her blouse off fast enough. Steph knew it wasn't because she had a meeting to go to after, but because she couldn't wait for Steph to touch her the way she'd promised. So much had changed between them and Steph's insecurities had started to evaporate. Because when Dominique looked at her with that unmistakable glimmer of longing in her glance, Steph knew that she was loved.

She waited for Dominique to get fully undressed and stretch herself out on the bed, like the pillow princess she all but was.

"Give it to me, baby," Dominique joked, trying to sound like a rapper on the radio.

It coaxed a wave of laughter mixed with endearment to swirl inside of Steph. "I'd best shut you up." She draped her body over Dominique's.

Their kiss was instantly deep—instantly touching Steph in

that spot deep down where pleasure ignites. When Steph broke the lip lock and started kissing her way down Dominique's neck, Dominique tugged her head upwards and stared into her eyes.

"Thank you," she said. "I know it's not easy being with me." But in that moment, it felt like a breeze for Steph.

"Thank me later," she said. "After this." With that, she let her glance drop to Dominique's body. It wasn't perfect like the bodies of so many other women Steph had bedded, not kept toned by hours in the gym, not free of a bit of padding around the hips, but this was Dominique's body. Steph always made a point of kissing the crooked stretch mark on her side and that dimple on her thigh. It was these little marks that made her different, made her stand out from the other, meaningless ones that had come before.

Steph kissed a quick, moist path down Dominique's skin, not wanting to linger too long. She had her own job to get to as well. But, as always, she took the time to savour the moment when Dominique spread wide for her. It never got old. A constantly renewed invitation for Steph to enter.

Steph didn't waste time on gentle kisses on Dominique's inner thighs, instead she pushed her nose in Dominique's neatly trimmed pubic hair and let her tongue twist around until Dominique's muscles tensed. With broad strokes, she licked up and down, just to make her pussy wet enough. She wanted— needed—to be inside. To feel her there. Craved the intimacy of it.

"Oh, baby," Dominique groaned as Steph let her tongue circle around her clit one last time. Steph pushed herself up from between Dominique's legs, let her eyes roam across her glistening pussy lips, before taking position next to Dominique's outstretched body.

Her gaze now on Dominique's face, her body glued to her side, she let her fingers dance along Dominique's opening. She pushed two fingers inside before Dominique had a chance to beg, her body going rigid again, tension coiling in every muscle.

Steph tried to look into Dominique's eyes but they had fallen shut. Her face, when on the way to ecstasy, was wondrous enough. Mouth half-open, tiny wrinkles crinkling on her temples, her head tossed back into the pillows, exposing her neck. Steph didn't need anything else but to know that the reason why Dominique was experiencing this intense pleasure was all because of her.

Leaning on one elbow, she drove her fingers deep inside. Two for a few minutes, but quickly adding another, spreading her wide, feeling as much of her as possible, locating that spot inside of her.

When Dominique's eyes shot open, Steph knew she had found it. She felt a smile slip across her lips as she applied more pressure with one finger, while keeping a small thrusting motion with her other fingers.

"Jesus, babe…" Dominique pinned her eyes on Steph while the walls of her pussy clamped themselves around Steph's fingers with forceful spams. Dominique's one hand had found a muscle on the back of Steph's shoulder, her nails scratching hard. Steph would wear any wounds as badges of honour.

Steph kept moving, only tiny flicks of her fingers needed now, judging by how crazy they seemed to drive Dominique, how they contorted her face into a mask of abandon and joy.

Then the contractions around Steph's fingers became more pronounced and she felt a gush of warm liquid pool around her wrist.

"Oh fuck." Dominique sounded shocked and only briefly let herself fall back into the pillows before pushing herself up. "What—what happened?"

Steph let her fingers slip from Dominique's pussy and stared at the puddle of wetness between her legs in disbelief. No matter how ridiculous, a burst of pride swelled in her chest. "Looks like you came, babe," she said. "A bit more than usual."

She turned her face back to Dominique and looked into her stunned eyes.

"That has never happened—" Dominique shook her head. "I can't really describe it. I've never—"

"It's okay." Steph pushed her down and kissed her on the lips. "You're a squirter, there's no shame in that." Her body convulsed with giggles as she poured it over Dominique's sweaty flesh.

"How the hell am I supposed to contribute to governing this country after that?" Dominique whispered in her ear. "This is almost a matter of national security."

"Maybe you should call in sick," Steph said. "Tell Madame Moreau you're doing extensive research on gay marriage, more particularly the lesbian kind and the physical effects of two women getting to know each other better." She kissed Dominique on the nose. "Or just tell her the truth and say your apartment has flooded."

JULIETTE

Juliette looked over the résumés the agency had sent her. She automatically discarded all females that even remotely resembled Nadia or Sybille. Ideally, she'd hire a man as her new assistant, just like Claire, who had lucked out with Fred. Then another matter crossed her mind. Perhaps, instead of looking for a new assistant, she should spend her time training a junior, someone who could truly take over from her when she was absent—if she was really serious about cutting down her hours. Someone she could trust to step in on her behalf. Someone like Steph.

Either way, she'd still need an assistant. She made a mental note to discuss this with Claire later, after she and Nadia had had more time to evaluate their life and the choices they had made. For better or for worse, her short break-up with Nadia had changed her. Opened her eyes. After fourteen years of working sixty hour weeks—in a country that somehow prided itself on promoting thirty-five hour work weeks, even when the economy was going down the drain—and investing all her time in building Barbier & Cyr the way other people devoted their life to raising children, Juliette had had enough.

Maybe she was lucky to experience a high level of job satisfaction and to be her own boss but, truth be told, the way things at the firm had taken a turn for the dramatic of late, had made her question everything. Had made her focus on what really mattered. She had driven Nadia in the arms of the neurosurgeon. She had attached more importance to her clients' needs than to her own wife's. Worst of all, she'd come to think of it as normal.

The true breaking point had been the look in Nadia's eyes when she'd turned up at their place *that night.* When her own partner had displayed nothing but contempt and disgust for her, even for a brief moment in their long history together, that had crushed her. In the end, it didn't even matter whose fault it was. They'd gone off the rails, somehow—because of the years they had loved each other—had gotten back on, but Juliette was no longer pleased with the direction the train was headed in. More work. More clients. More drama.

She needed something else. Not more of the same, but a drastic change. In the quiet moments of August at Barbier & Cyr, Juliette had taken the time to think. To just let it all wash over her. The guilt. The pain she'd caused. What she believed was missing. She wouldn't be dashing off to an adoption agency and start filling in papers, but she would consider her options.

She shoved the résumés to the side and got up to fetch her own cup of coffee. Outside of her office, Sybille's desk was empty and, in that unguarded moment, Juliette couldn't help but wonder how she was really doing. For all she knew, Claire could be making up the news of her success at Marc Dujardin's firm—just to keep the peace.

Juliette found simple satisfaction in making her own coffee, even in answering her own phone and managing her calendar. It reminded her of the time when Barbier & Cyr consisted of just her and Claire. Two friends with a dream. With the same goal. Profit before personal happiness. Had they been too ruthless? Too selfish? Attached too much importance to the wrong things?

Perhaps Claire was right. Maybe Juliette *was* suffering from an early midlife crisis. But she wasn't interested in a sports car, nor in trading in Nadia for a younger model—because look how that had turned out.

She had other, more profound, matters on her mind.

NADIA

"We need Dievart," Doctor Andres said, "and we need her now."

"Surely there are other—" Nadia tried to protest.

"She's the best and she's close-by. I'll contact her myself. I need another pair of extremely skilled hands for this surgery, Nadia." He stood shuffling from one foot to the other in her office, making his case. "I don't see what the problem is? We've invited her to Saint-Vincent before. I know she wasn't able to save the patient, but her chances were slim going in. Doctor Dievart really was our last resort then, but you can't hold that against her."

"I don't." Nadia held up her hands. If only the doctor standing in front of her knew where else Doctor Dievart's hands had ventured. "I know she's the best and I trust your judgement. Set it up." She tried hard to suppress the sigh that came with accepting the doctor's request.

Doctor Andres pushed his glasses up the bridge of his nose while almost bowing reverently. "Thank you." He gave her the thumbs-up and rushed out of her office.

He'd be trying to get Doctor Marie Dievart to Saint-Vincent

for surgery the day after tomorrow. Nadia checked her calendar to see if she could take the day off, but she had a budget meeting scheduled with too many other parties to cancel.

The hospital was big enough to stay out of her way. At any rate, she'd have to tell Juliette. She reached for her phone and dialled Juliette's number—unable to completely drum out the memory of Sybille answering Juliette's phone.

Juliette picked up after the first ring.

"Still quiet, huh?" Nadia said.

"I was just about to call you. Guess what?" Juliette sounded excited.

"What?" It bought Nadia some time before having to deliver the news.

"Claire's going on a date tonight." Juliette's voice nearly exploded through the speaker of her phone.

"Really? With Margot?" Nadia had spotted Margot earlier in the hallway and she hadn't come across as if things were looking up—in fact they had avoided each other expertly.

"No, silly. With this woman from a dating app. Apparently they were chatting last night."

"Well, I'll be damned."

"Hey, remember how we met? You just never know…" Juliette's voice trailed off on the other end of the line. "I'm just happy she won't be sitting home alone sulking for once. They're meeting at Le Comptoir after work and Steph will be there, discreetly having a drink, to break things up if needed."

"Another busy day at the office, I see," Nadia joked.

"It's August. The only month of the year we have time for drama."

Speaking of, Nadia thought. "Listen, babe, I need to tell you something."

"Sure." Juliette sounded so carefree. Nadia hated to spoil her mood.

"There's no easy way to say this. The hospital needs a neuro-surgical consult from Marie Dievart. She's coming here the day after tomorrow." Nadia took a deep breath. It wasn't so much the fact that Marie Dievart would physically be there, but how much she reminded Nadia of what she had allowed to happen that night.

Silence on the other end of the line. Nadia waited patiently.

"Oh," was all Juliette said after a few empty seconds.

"I probably won't even have to see her, but I wanted you to know."

"Okay." Another icy silence.

"I'm sorry. There's just no other way." Nadia's voice grew high-pitched.

"I understand, babe. It's work."

"Yes. Yes, it is."

"I have to go now. I do have some meetings scheduled." All the excitement seemed to have drained from Juliette's voice.

"Sure. Wish Claire good luck from me. And, babe, I love you." Nadia rested her forehead in the palm of her hand.

"Me too." Juliette hung up, but Nadia stayed immobile for an instant, the beep of the phone ringing in her ear.

CLAIRE

At Le Comptoir, Claire made sure she had a table with a view. From the corner of her eye, she could see Steph, who sat a few tables down from her. They had agreed that, when Steph needed to step in and rescue Claire from a disastrous date, Claire would drop her purse. If she didn't give any signs of acute boredom and being in need of urgent saving within half an hour, Steph would leave and let her pursue the mysterious Sarah in peace—without lookers-on. Claire was nervous enough already, she didn't need Steph's scrutinising, expert glance on her for the entire evening.

She'd ordered a cosmo and sipped from it eagerly, while wondering if Margot leaving her had actually caused her to lose her mind. But Steph and Juliette had encouraged her all day long. Telling her this was an excellent first step to recovery—while Claire wasn't even entirely sure Margot was someone she wanted to recover from. By the time her watch read seven-thirty Claire was getting started on her third drink of the night.

Her phone buzzed, and she half-hoped it was Sarah cancelling.

A message from Steph appeared on the screen of her phone:

Take it easy, thirsty tiger.

Claire looked in Steph's direction, who shot her a stern scowl. With her fingers, she made the universal 'slow down' sign. Claire responded with a mere shrug.

"Claire?" A voice beamed next to her.

Claire looked into the face of a minuscule but very attractive woman. "Yes." She shot up out of her chair and extended her hand. "In the flesh."

"I'm Sarah." Claire witnessed how Sarah looked over at Steph. What an excellent start to a semi-blind date. Sarah sat down. "What are you drinking?"

"Cosmo." Claire sat back down and waved Tony over while suppressing the urge to drop her purse already, just to save herself from imminent humiliation.

"I'll have the same," Sarah said to Tony.

Tony nodded and headed back inside, leaving them alone. Despite having just dated Margot, Claire felt so out of practice. How old was this girl sitting across from her, anyway? She looked about twenty-five.

"I—" They both started talking at the same time, then burst out in an awkward giggle.

"You go first," Sarah said while making a cute gesture with her hand. She was probably just as nervous as Claire.

Claire cleared her throat. "I'm sorry if I don't look like the spitting image of my picture. My brother put it on—"

"You look just fine. Really," Sarah said quickly, offering a smile in the process.

Maybe this could be fun, after all. Without thinking, Claire glanced over at Steph.

"Back-up plan?" Sarah asked.

Claire shot her an apologetic grin. "Sorry. I don't usually do this. I guess I needed some moral support."

"Believe it or not, I understand."

"Do you also have a friend hanging around?" Claire asked while scanning the terrace, but Tony, who was carrying over Sarah's cosmo, blocked her view.

"No, but I understand the impulse." Sarah nodded at Tony as he placed her drink on the table. "Let me guess…" She cocked her head and let her eyes linger on Claire's face. "You recently ended a long-term relationship and you thought you'd give new technology a try?"

"Close." Claire drew her lips into a thin strip and held up two fingers. "But I promise to not be one of those first dates who goes on about her ex the entire evening."

When Sarah sipped from her cosmo, she kept her eyes on Claire the entire time.

"I usually know better than to ask a lady about her age," Claire started to say—because she had to know if she'd be chatting up a girl in her twenties.

Sarah shrugged before replying. "Don't worry, I'm legal." She shot Claire a wink. "Only a bit vertically challenged which takes about fifteen years off my actual age." Putting a hand on her chest, she bowed, and said, "I know I don't look a day over twenty, but I'm actually thirty-six."

While they both drank, Claire felt something fizz in the air between them. But would someone as tiny as that be able to tie her up? She erased the thought from her mind immediately and looked over at Steph, giving her a slight nod. There was no need for her to stick around because, in that moment, Claire couldn't have been more convinced that this date would have a happy ending. She signalled Tony for another round.

Over two more cosmopolitans Claire found out that Sarah worked as an IT consultant, had lived in Paris for ten years, had been single for the past year—navigating the pitfalls of the single lesbian scene quite unsuccessfully—and had been on a slew of rather catastrophic dates.

"Until now, it seems," she said, flashing Claire a smile that could not be misunderstood.

And perhaps it was that smile, and what it implied, or how it, somehow, emphasised what Claire was missing, but instead of lifting her up—and solidifying the good outcome of this first date—it broke her a little. The first crack in the armour she'd so expertly worn all night. By then, she was also quite drunk, her head swimming, her mind unable to escape recurring thoughts of Margot and how she'd looked at Claire on their first date—the interrupted one. The one after which she'd been convinced they could never work out together. She should have trusted her instincts. Why didn't she do that anymore?

She looked away from Sarah, not returning—or even acknowledging—the compliment. Sarah's company was entertaining enough, her smile seductive and her eyes glinting with the promise of more, but she wasn't Margot.

"Claire? Are you all right?" Sarah asked.

Claire shook her head and pinned her glance on Sarah. "I'm sorry. You are truly wonderful but I can't do this." She started looking around for Tony to ask for the check—and because she couldn't keep her eyes on Sarah and the vexed expression on her face for more than a split second. "I apologise for wasting your time."

"W-was it something I said?" Sarah slid to the edge of her chair, slanting her upper body over the table.

"God no." Claire started slurring her words, the alcohol suddenly hitting her with full force. "She ruined me and she's a fucking doctor... how ironic is that?" Claire shrugged. "I guess it would have been more ironic if she was a heart surgeon, what with breaking mine and all..." A loud cackle made its way out of Claire's throat.

Sarah scraped the feet of her chair over the ground while pushing it backwards. "Let me get you a taxi."

"I've got it." Out of nowhere, Steph appeared next to their table. "I'm so sorry about this." Claire heard Steph say to Sarah. "She, um, hasn't been herself lately."

"Where did you come from?" Claire asked Steph.

"The way you were knocking them back, I figured you'd need a ride home."

"But Steph, you don't have a car." Claire chuckled loudly at this.

Without anyone having asked, Tony deposited a cup of coffee and a carafe of water on the table.

From her seat, Claire watched Steph exchange a few muffled words with Sarah, who proceeded to walk away without saying goodbye. Steph sat down in Sarah's chair.

"Drink up," Steph commanded. "You really need to get your act together, Claire. I know it hurts, but come on." Her eyes rested on Claire and her lips were drawn into a serious, very un-Steph-like pout. "Have some self-respect."

MARGOT

"Were you even going to tell me?" Inez had Margot cornered in the changing room after her evening shift. "Or were you just going to sneak off?"

"What?" Clearly, Nadia had executed her threat and talked to Inez. "She had no right to tell you."

Inez rolled her eyes. "After everything, you were just going to run? That's not like you, Go-Go. You're a fighter."

"And you're the one who's going to teach me about the virtues of sticking around? Give me a break." Margot didn't have the energy to change out of her scrubs. She just stood there, looking at Inez, wishing she'd disappear into thin air.

"No, I'm the one who's going to leave." Inez took a deep breath. "But I had really expected you to have the balls to just be honest with me."

"What are you talking about? You're leaving?"

"Sit down for a minute, please." Inez crashed down on the wooden bench, a pleading look in her eyes.

Mostly because her legs were trembling so hard, Margot sat down next to her.

"I'm not a monster who wants you back no matter the cost," Inez started. "I've disrupted your life twice. Once when I left and all over again when I came back. I should be the one to go. I did this."

"But—" Margot couldn't immediately think of any objections.

"I know you don't want me back. You may not be able to admit it, not after the price you paid for thinking that you did, but I get the message loud and clear." Inez swallowed hard. "It's done. My letter of resignation is sitting on Nadia's desk as we speak."

"But, where will you go?" Despite being touched by Inez' gesture, an unexpected sadness crept up on Margot.

"There are quite a few hospitals in this city. I'm sure I'll find one that will have me." Inez looked down at her hands. "I'm so sorry for coming back here and destroying your relationship, for waltzing in and thinking I could just have you back. It was selfish and foolish and incredibly disrespectful." She sucked in a breath. "Your family needs you here, Go-Go. Saint-Vincent needs you."

"I've made such a mess." Margot realised she was beginning to sound like a broken record.

"No." Inez shuffled closer and put her hand on Margot's knee. "I'm the one who messed up. Listen to me." She dug her nails into Margot's scrubs. "Fight for her. You're not that easy to get over. I should know."

"Claire has told me in no uncertain terms that she doesn't want me anymore." Because this was all well and good, this display of remorse way after the fact, but it didn't change the look of pure disdain that Claire had shot her when Margot had gone to see her last.

"You'd be surprised to learn what people say and do when they're hurt." Inez smiled at her—a dimmed-down version of her million dollar smile. She bumped her shoulder into Margot's. "And she'd be a fool not to give you another chance."

Margot just shook her head. *Maybe the old her.*

"I know you better than most people. The minute you stop expecting from yourself to be at least twice as perfect as everyone else, I know you'll be all right." She slung her arm over Margot's shoulder. "Nobody's perfect. Not even you." Pulling Margot closer, Inez broke into a chuckle. "And least of all me."

"God, it's not funny," Margot said, desperate for the release that came with a bout of laughter.

"Maybe not, but what else are we going to do? Sit around and cry all night?"

"When are you leaving?" Margot freed herself from Inez' embrace and turned to look her in the eyes.

"Next week." Inez swung one leg over the bench and faced Margot. "And I'm going to miss your grumpy face like crazy."

Margot couldn't suppress a giggle at that remark. "This will sound so fucked-up, but thank you."

Inez pinned her green eyes on Margot, her lips lightly parted, already splitting into a grin. She leaned closer and, instead of curving her lips into a smile, she pressed a kiss on Margot's lips. "I'll never forget our last time, Go-Go. I'll never forget you."

A tear ran down Margot's cheek, but she didn't brush it away.

"What did I say about crying all night long?" With her thumb, Inez caught Margot's tear.

JULIETTE

After Nadia's call announcing Marie Dievart's visit, Juliette didn't feel like planning Nadia's birthday party anymore. Perhaps it wasn't fair, but at least Juliette had stressed—repeatedly—that her night of straying with Sybille had been completely unsatisfactory.

She'd bought a new bed, and erased the memory from their life as best she could. Nadia, on the other hand, had never made any specific confessions about her night with the neurosurgeon being something she desperately wanted to forget about. For all Juliette knew, she conjured up images of the dexterous doctor when they were in bed together. And now, she was allowing her to consult at the hospital again. Wasn't she supposed to be the boss? And was there really only one neurosurgeon as gifted as her in the region?

So, she waited for Nadia to walk through the door that evening, ready to ask the question. By the time Nadia made it home though, Juliette was so revved up, her mind so saturated with images of Nadia and the other woman, her tone could, perhaps, have been a bit less accusing.

"Show me what she did to you?" Juliette said as soon as Nadia had put her purse down. "I need to know."

"What?" Nadia sat down next to her. "Is this about Dievart?"

Juliette rolled her eyes, fully aware of the row she was creating, but utterly unable to stop herself. "Who else?"

"Babe, come on. I hope you know I wouldn't have her at Saint-Vincent if I had any other choice."

"What is your job exactly at that hospital? I mean, first they make you hire someone who destroys my best friend's life, and now, you're bringing back the woman you cheated on me with.

From where I'm sitting, it looks like you're having some authority issues, *babe*. Unless you *want* her to come back." As the words exited her mouth, Juliette knew she was making a big mistake—that she was just lashing out—but she still couldn't stop herself.

"Silly me for thinking we were past this," Nadia said with a sigh. "If I had known you wouldn't be able to handle it, I would have just let her come and go without you even being aware of it. It wouldn't have changed a thing, because that night with her —that drunken, regrettable night—meant nothing. We've been over this."

"We haven't, though." All the muscles in Juliette's body tensed. "My dalliance with Sybille, *that* was nothing. I didn't come, didn't derive the slightest pleasure from it. Basically, I only slept with her because you and I had broken up... because you slept with the surgeon."

"Really?" Nadia's eyes narrowed. "Do you really want to say that to me right now? This is really what's on your mind? Because if it is, we *do* have a big problem."

"Just tell me. I need to know." Juliette didn't know when to stop. It was the story of her life.

"Yes." Nadia pinned her dark eyes on Juliette. "If you really want to know. Yes, I had an orgasm, possibly even two. I don't really remember. But you know what? It doesn't make a difference if I remember or not, because it doesn't fucking matter." She blew out a large puff of air. "You need to let this go, Jules. You really need to. If you can't..." She shrugged. "Well, then I don't know..."

Juliette's muscles collapsed. "I'm sorry. Just, you saying her name, it brought it all back."

"Actually." Nadia dragged the tip of her tongue over her teeth. "You may have a point."

"What do you mean?" Panic coiled in Juliette's stomach.

"I'm going to show you." Nadia's eyes grew even darker. "You need to be shown."

"But…" Juliette knew her protest was futile. She had voiced her paranoia, now it was Nadia's turn.

"Get up." Nadia set the example and pushed her chair back. "Don't make me wait for it."

The panic in Juliette's gut quickly transformed into pure lust. One look from Nadia was still all it took. The point Nadia was trying to make came across perfectly. She rose from her seat and awaited further instructions. To her surprise, Nadia gently slid an arm around her neck, finding Juliette's ear with her lips.

"I'm going to fuck you the way *we* fuck. Not how Marie fucked me and certainly not how Sybille fucked you. This is us. There's no room for others in our bed. They're history. We made it through, babe. You and me. Understood?"

Almost piously, Juliette bowed her head and nodded.

"Come on." Nadia pressed a kiss on her cheekbone and coaxed her to the bedroom.

Juliette's blood thumped with excitement. She'd caught a whiff of it in Nadia's glance. *The way we fuck*, she'd said. It could only mean one thing in a situation like this. Punishment.

"Take off your clothes and get on all fours." Nadia's voice was close, lurking behind Juliette, giving orders from the shadows of their bedroom.

Juliette slipped out of her work attire—a loose linen suit because of the mild temperature outside and the relaxed atmosphere at work. Her clothes fell to the ground, crinkling in a beige pool of fabric. Instantly, the expanse of her skin was transformed into a plain of goosebumps. Nadia hadn't punished her in months—the right occasion had been hard to find.

Naked, Juliette crawled onto the bed, facing away from Nadia. She only heard—and felt—her in the room. A dip in the mattress when she joined Juliette on the bed, the tell-tale nervous cough escaping from her throat as she prepared. Juliette could probably predict, second-by-second, what would happen next. Then again, Nadia had surprised her lately and she was right: they weren't the same people anymore.

The air around Juliette stirred as Nadia inched closer and ran two fingers over the flesh of her bottom.

"Your ass is a work of art, babe," Nadia hissed. "And it's all mine."

Although expected but still catching Juliette off-guard, the first stroke landed hard just below her buttock, on the delicate patch of skin connecting ass and thigh. A trickle of juice freed itself from between Juliette's already aching pussy lips.

Slap. Another one hit her a little higher, but harder with the fingertips. Juliette steadied herself, engaging her core muscles to keep her posture rigid and receive the blows better. Nadia followed up with a quick caress before trailing her hand to Juliette's other buttock.

Juliette's clit throbbed, blood pooling in her pussy lips, beating hard in her veins. She hadn't expected the next three blows to rain down hard on her cheek, administered, she suspected, with the wrist held tight. Nadia's fingertips landed so close to her engorged lips and more moisture ran down her inner thighs.

"Do you think that's enough, babe?" Nadia's voice was a low hum, all the kindness stripped from it, but for Juliette, for someone who knew her the way she did, it was still there.

Juliette shook her head. "No."

"I didn't think so either." Nadia let her fingertips trail over the most painful patches, pressing down hard where it hurt the most. Then, in a flash, her palm connected with Juliette's right buttock again. Juliette caught the shock in her elbows, her body pushing forward slightly. Blood roared in her ears, lust drowning everything out. It was just Nadia's hand on her behind, over and over again. Not too hard to make her cry, but hard enough to make her feel. To let her know that this was them.

After a short explosion of slaps, only interrupted by the

sound of Nadia sucking in her breath, preparing for the next one, Juliette felt something warm and wet on her behind. Her pussy was a moist mess and Nadia was kissing her way down there, both of her hands now caressing Juliette's cheeks, erasing the hurt.

Juliette all but crashed through her elbows when Nadia's tongue connected with her swollen pussy lips, then trailed higher, and higher still. While her tongue stayed there, Juliette felt Nadia's finger trace a wet line to her pussy.

"I will fuck you now, Jules. The way only *I* fuck you." With that, Nadia thrust deep, her tongue back between Juliette's butt cheeks. Relentless from the start, Nadia burrowed down with fast, swift movements—in and out, quick and deep, from an angle Juliette wasn't that accustomed to. Nadia's tongue there added extra stimulation and before Juliette had a chance to repent—to think about anything else but pure pleasure—Nadia had her teetering on the edge.

"I'm going to come," she moaned.

Apparently, this was the sign for Nadia to thrust her tongue deep while her fingers delved even further inside of Juliette. Every cell in Juliette's body exploded into fireworks, burst after burst of ecstasy filling her blood. This time, she did crash through her elbows, her face buried in the sheets, her bottom high in the air.

Nadia slowly slid out her fingers and planted one last kiss on her butt cheek before draping her body over Juliette's, finding her ear with her lips. "Now you know," she said. "There's only you."

And Juliette did.

CLAIRE

"Good god, Jules. I made such an ass of myself." Claire eyed Juliette, who couldn't seem to find a comfortable position to sit in. "Would you sit still, please? You're ruining my drama."

"Sorry, I just, huh—" A blush crept up her cheeks. "I'm a bit sore this morning."

"Oh christ," Claire groaned. "Please don't give me details."

"Fine, I'll just say I deserved it." Juliette painted a forced smile on her face.

Claire sighed with exasperation. "To have Steph, of all people, tell you to pull it together and have some self-respect. It's not something one easily forgets."

"Speaking of…" Juliette drummed her fingertips on the top of her desk. "We should consider promoting her this year."

"We should?"

"Yes. There's no one like her in this company. Someone with her charm and effortless communication skills. She's smart and more than capable. And she's proven herself over and over again."

"Erm… aren't you forgetting that she's currently shagging our biggest client?" Claire asked.

"No thanks to you, who only brought them closer together by encouraging them to go on holiday together."

"Hey, we all deserve some happiness in our lives, Jules. And they contained that beautifully. Promoting her is something entirely different. It will make it look as though, when you fuck the right person, it's a recipe for success."

"Seriously? I slept with Sybille and we fired her."

Claire wiggled her finger in the air. "Oh no, we didn't. She got the promotion of a lifetime."

"At least she doesn't work here anymore. And it's not as if it's common knowledge that Steph and Laroche are together. No one knows."

"Where is this coming from, anyway? Why the sudden desire to promote her?"

"Apart from the fact that she deserves it, I'd like to work less hours." Juliette bit the inside of her lip, as if what she was saying was only tentative.

"Ah… are we back to having babies now?" Claire knew Juliette well enough to at least try to talk her out of this.

"That's only part of it. We work too hard, Claire. Our personal lives suffer."

"Mine doesn't." Claire momentarily pursed her lips together. "And time spent at the office doesn't necessarily equal working, what with what's been going on here lately."

"It's August. It's normal." Juliette pulled up her shoulders.

"Are you saying we're at different stages in our lives, Jules? Are you breaking up with me professionally?" Claire joked. She knew work had taken its toll on Juliette and Nadia's relationship and handing over some responsibilities to Steph was actually not a bad move. The baby thing didn't sit right with her though.

"I love this company and I love you, Claire," Juliette continued. "I love working with you. But this life of always being available, of checking e-mail first thing in the morning and right before I close my eyes at night, of lying awake trying to solve a client's problem, of carrying the responsibility for our employees, it's not what I want anymore." She shook her head. "I almost lost Nadia and not having to go through that again comes first now."

"Are we talking partnership? Name on the door and everything?" *Barbier, Cyr & Mathis.* Claire rolled around the words in her head.

"It's worth thinking about, but let's not take too long. September, and the craziness that comes with it, is right around the corner."

"Okay. I'll give it some thought and get back to you." She slanted her head. "As long as you know that this firm still needs you, and that, honestly…" Claire weighed her words before proceeding. "I don't see you pushing a stroller through the streets of Paris. I just don't see it."

Juliette chuckled. "I hardly see it either, but it's just one of many things going through my head right now."

Relieved, Claire relaxed in her chair. "Whatever it takes."

"Was your date really such a disaster?" Juliette planted her elbows on the desk.

"You wouldn't believe it… it went fine up to a certain point, and then I just cracked." She pulled her lips into an apologetic smirk. "Too many cosmos." She remembered how Steph had picked up the pieces, taken her home and tucked her into bed— and given her a much-needed speech. Come to think of it, Claire wouldn't have a problem at all welcoming her to the management of Barbier & Cyr. Despite what had happened with Dominique, she trusted Steph with her life.

Juliette leaned a bit more over her desk, taking on a conspir-atorial tone. "You didn't get this from me, okay? But I hear a certain doctor without borders is leaving Saint-Vincent."

Claire's eyes grew wide. "What?"

"Nadia told me she resigned yesterday. She's out of there by next week."

"And you're only telling me this now?" A uncontrollable urge to punch the air ripped through Claire's muscles—despite having told Margot that she was done with her.

"Nadia and I had our own drama last night. That doctor she slept with is coming back for a consultation. She only told me about Inez this morning at breakfast."

So that's why your bottom's sore, Claire thought, but didn't waste any energy on saying it out loud. Her brain was too busy processing the information. "What happened?"

"I haven't gotten to the bottom of it yet." Juliette grimaced. "But I thought you should know."

"Shit," Claire said, while sinking her teeth into her bottom lip. "*La salope* is leaving. I can't believe it." She instantly recog-nised the tingle sprouting in her stomach as hope.

STEPH

Steph glanced at Philippe. With his mousy mouth and thinning hair, he wasn't that particularly good-looking—but what did she know? Dominique must have seen something in him if she married him and had two children with him. What she didn't get was why he would have cheated on her, but she'd never had much insight in the thought process of straight men. Sometimes, one tried to get chummy with her, because he believed he and Steph were the same—which couldn't be further from the truth.

He was on the phone, saying goodnight to the children, who were spending the night at his parents. So they could have this meeting. Just the three of them. Very cosy. Steph hated every minute of having to be here.

Philippe handed the phone to Dominique so she could say her part to Lisa and Didier. "Another beer?" he asked.

Steph shook her head. She was only halfway through this one. Was he nervous as well? Perhaps it was difficult—or, at the very least quite peculiar—to meet your ex-wife's girlfriend.

Steph looked around, at the house where Dominique and Philippe had spent most of their life together. She felt as if she'd been dropped into a picture of a bourgeois lifestyle magazine, if such a thing even existed.

"They're all ready for bed." Dominique gave Philippe his mobile back and sat down at the kitchen table. What must it be like for her? Did she feel in any way mortified? It wouldn't be her style and, either way, even if she did, nothing in her demeanour would ever give it away.

They still seemed to have a familiarity about them, punctured by a snide remark here and there, uttered in a tone that could be a tad friendlier. Seeing Philippe and Dominique together like that was such an advertisement for people not to get married.

"Okay." Dominique cleared her throat. "Thanks for having

us over, Philippe." Why did she even say that? This was still her house as well. Steph refused to get worked up about things like that though, mostly because it was none of her business and also because such practicalities gave her a massive headache.

"I've had some time to adjust to the idea." He twirled his beer bottle around between his fingers. "If you're happy, I'm happy. My only concern is the children."

Were they asking for his blessing now? Why was Dominique being so meek with him?

"I've decided to vote in favour of gay marriage in the Assemblée next week, against the MLR's instructions. It may cause a bit of a stir, but it shouldn't be anything too disrupting. The real news will be about the bill, not about an MLR party member voting against expectations. I'm working on some other party members and I think I have at least two more on my side."

"You're not just a party member, Domi. You're Xavier Laroche's daughter. Every step you take is scrutinised, and if not now, then at least it will be a big deal in the lead-up to next year's elections."

Domi? Was that what he called her? Did she call him Phi-Phi? Steph didn't understand why she had to be here. This was a discussion between parents, about the welfare of their children. She was fond of Lisa and Didier, but she had no say in the matter.

"You're right, but that's months away. By then, I will have told them." Dominique shot Steph a tender glance.

"Not to be the devil's advocate here, but can you even run?" He brought his beer bottle to his thin lips and took a small sip.

"Why not? Because I believe in the fundamental right for everyone to get married? I honestly believe it can only work in my advantage. Lots of voters are—"

"I don't mean that. I mean, uh, when it comes out. What's the plan?"

Steph had avoided that dreaded question since Dominique

had come back from holiday, not wanting to burst the bubble they'd been in since Juan-les-Pins. Her ears perked up now though.

"I don't mean for it to come out. We're discreet." Dominique started fidgeting with her necklace.

"But, this is serious, right? You've introduced her to our children. You're sitting in my kitchen. We wouldn't be having this conversation if this wasn't serious... Surely, you must have a long-term plan." His voice shot up a bit. Dominique tugged harder on her jewellery. "And you, Stéphanie. Can you live like this?"

Steph hadn't expected that question. She suddenly liked him a bit more. He was almost defending her. How chivalrous. Maybe he was just a nice guy. "I have no choice."

"Of course you do. Everyone always has a choice." He slammed his beer down on the table top, apparently surprising himself with the force of it as well.

"Philippe, come on. That's not why we're here. It's also not for you to worry about." Dominique's voice sounded tight, clipped.

"Of course it is. If, for some reason, this comes out tomorrow, it will be all over the news and the children will see. You can't keep it a secret forever."

"I don't intend to." Dominique caught Steph's glance. "But it's going to have to happen in phases. You're the first to know. Papa will be next. And the children. Then the leadership. This doesn't necessarily have to be an all-round disaster."

"You must really have it bad if you believe that." Steph didn't really want to, but she agreed with Dominique's ex-husband.

"The world is not black and white. Things are changing. Look at Belgium. They had a gay Prime Minister."

"Tssss," Philippe hissed. "Sure, but that's Belgium. And he was a Socialist."

"MLR is not the far-right, Philippe. Maybe we need some-

430

thing like this. Something to connect a large group of discon-
nected voters to us."

"While alienating people who have voted MLR forever."

Dominique shook her head. "There aren't a lot of choices
here. This is my life."

"I know. I know." Philippe, who sat next to Dominique, put
a hand on her shoulder. "I trust you to do right thing, Domi.
You've always had such a knack for that."

Steph was slightly bewildered by this sudden display of
affection. She tried to imagine she was somewhere else, but this
was her life as well now. Ex-husbands. Right-wing party politics. Election strategy. Children. A tiny part of her wished she
was at Les Pêches, doing shots with Melanie. Or Le Noir. God,
she'd have to tell Dominique about that as well. Would she have
to be vetted? She hoped not because there was no way anyone
could ever conclude Stéphanie Mathis was fit to be a politician's
wife.

She sat there and watched Dominique and Philippe drift
further into a political discussion about right-wing versus left-
wing values, and she caught herself not caring. She fell in love,
but this, this was not what she had signed up for.

Still, she knew she wouldn't walk away. One glance at
Dominique, at the fire in her eyes and the determined movements of her hands, was enough to make her stay.

MARGOT

Margot slipped the envelope underneath Nadia's office door,
glared at the white paper triangle sticking out for a second,
crouched back down and pocketed it. What was she? Twelve
years old? She sure felt like it of late. She sucked in a breath and
knocked on the door. No reply. All this agony over nothing all
the time.

"Looking for me?" Nadia was just rounding the corner and
walking towards her in the hallway.

Margot nodded. Perhaps, in all of this, and despite their fight, Nadia had been her only true ally.

"That better not be..." Nadia pinned her eyes on the envelope.

"No, no." Margot extended her arm and handed it to Nadia. "Open it, please." She watched Nadia fold the paper open and extract the card. A crooked grin slipped across her lips as she read.

"Hey, you never left so you're still at the top of my list." Nadia inched closer.

"So you really do have a friends' list?" Margot allowed herself a smile as well.

"You mean you don't?" Nadia reached for the handle of the door. "Come in for a minute."

Margot followed Nadia inside and didn't wait for Nadia to turn around and face her. It was easier that way. "I'm sorry for what I said. I could give you a list of excuses, but, no matter how I felt at the time, I shouldn't have said the things I said. I value your friendship enormously and, frankly, without you I probably would have lost it even more." Margot swallowed a lump out of her throat. "And thank you for talking to Inez. You know I like to fight my own battles, but I had given up on that one. It was a mistake." A tear ran down her cheek, but she didn't mind this time. "Thank you for having my back."

Nadia clasped a hand to her chest. "God, what a relief. I thought you'd be furious with me for months... but I told Inez because then, at least, there'd be a chance you'd be around for me to witness your anger."

"I, uh, never thought she'd be so gracious about it."

"She's not a bad person and she cares about you... what was she going to do?" Nadia leaned her bottom against the arm rest of a visitor chair.

"Looks like you know her better than I do."

"Ever heard of tunnel vision, doctor de Hay? And gosh, you're stubborn. Not the best of combinations, you know."

Nadia tapped the card against her thigh. "And hey, after what you did for me…"

"I'm glad I'm staying." *And that I have a friend like you*, Margot wanted to say, but she'd about reached her dose of sentiment for the day.

"Come here." Nadia pushed herself up and opened her arms wide.

Awkwardly, Margot stepped into her hug, but once there, once her chin rested on Nadia's shoulder, it freed her of a little bit of the sadness that had nestled beneath her stomach, and she threw her arms around Nadia's waist and held her tight.

"Now let's talk about the consequences," Nadia whispered in her ear. "And by that I mean a woman named Claire Cyr."

They let go, Margot slightly reeling from the tenderness bestowed on her. She eyed Nadia and shook her head. "She said some things… All spot on and well-deserved on my part."

"Maybe, but Inez leaving changes everything." Nadia perched on the arm rest again. "God, Juliette told me she went on this disastrous date—"

"Claire's dating?" Nadia might as well just have sucker-punched her in the gut.

"No, not really." Nadia blinked twice and scratched her face. "I mean, she went on this one blind date Steph set up for her, but she got totally drunk because she's not over you." Nadia straightened her back. "Trust me, nothing happened and she won't be going on any more dates. She wants *you*, Margot. It's so obvious."

"I just… don't know if I can handle another outburst like the last one. I hurt her and now there's all this anger between us, this resentment. I blew it. I have no idea how to approach her." Margot sighed. "I can hardly write her a card."

"It worked on me." Nadia shot her a soft smile. "Listen, my birthday is next Monday and we're having a small gathering on Friday. You have to come, I mean, you're at the top of my list, Margot. I can't celebrate without you."

433

"And that won't be awkward at all… I don't want to ruin your party."

"Hey, even Dominique Laroche is coming… I'm sure I can handle some initial tension between you and Claire."

"Seriously?" Margot's eyebrows shot up.

"If two people as unsuited for each other as Steph and Dominique can make it, I have faith that you and Claire who, let's face it, are made for one another, can at least have a civilised conversation for my birthday." Nadia held up her hands, as if saying it like that was all it took.

"Of course I won't miss your party, Nadz. I wouldn't dream of it." A fresh set of nerves was already starting to tingle in Margot's stomach.

"Good." Nadia nodded. "It should be an interesting evening."

JULIETTE

"What time's the vote?" Juliette looked into Steph's strained face.

"It starts at three. They're broadcasting it live on Deux."

Juliette checked her watch. They had thirty minutes to give Steph the day of her life. "We can watch it together later—"

"That's not what I meant," Steph said quickly. "We have work to—"

"This is a big deal." Juliette didn't let her finish. "And Dominique is our client. I like to think that if it wasn't for Barbier & Cyr, she'd be voting against same-sex marriage today."

"Her vote isn't of great importance, though." Steph looked as if she was barely holding it together, fumbling with the sleeves of her blazer, crossing and uncrossing her legs.

"Are you all right, Steph?" Claire asked. "Because we have some news for you, but perhaps you're not in the right state of mind to receive it."

"What?" Steph glanced at Claire skittishly. "No more personal dramas, please. I really think I've had enough."

"This is business," Juliette said. At least for Steph and Claire it would be. "I want to work less hours. Spend more time with Nadia. Re-evaluate my life." *And possibly surprise the pair of you in the process*, Juliette thought. "As a consequence, Claire and I would like to ask you to take up more responsibilities at Barbier & Cyr. To gradually move into a more managerial role and, who knows, eventually become a partner." Juliette scanned Steph's face. She just sat there, her features frozen.

"That is if you're not planning to become a stay-at-home step-mom, of course." Claire broke the silence.

"You're—you're promoting me?" Steph twisted her head, looking from Juliette to Claire and back again. "After all that has happened?"

Juliette nodded. "Yes, because you deserve it, Steph. I, for one, can no longer judge you on who you decide to sleep with, but more than that, you've proven yourself above and beyond."

"And you're our friend," Claire added. "We trust you to have our and our firm's best interests at heart."

"You're the only one who saw through Sybille's dirty game," Juliette said, a fresh but unexpected dose of shame flaring in her mind.

"And you made an MLR députée stand up for our rights," Claire said.

"The vote hasn't even started yet." Steph tensed again.

"Is that why you're so nervous? Do you think she's going to change her mind?" Juliette asked.

"No. Yes. I don't know." Steph buried her head in her hands. "I'm so proud of her, but I'm also scared for her, you know?"

"If anyone can handle herself, it's Dominique." Claire rose from her chair and put a hand on Steph's shoulder.

"So, what do you say, Stéphanie?" Juliette pinned her gaze on Steph. "Do you take the job? Before you say yes, it does mean you'll be working more closely with me." She pulled her lips into a comic pout. "And we both know I can be an insufferable bitch sometimes."

"Fuck yes." Steph put her hand on Claire's and looked Juliette straight in the eyes. "Thank you for the vote of confidence. I won't let you down."

"I know you won't. Otherwise you wouldn't be sitting here right now." Juliette stood up and extended her hand to shake on it. She'd stashed a few bottles of Veuve in the pantry fridge, but she and Claire had decided to wait to pop them until after the vote.

"This calls for an impromptu office party," Claire said. "Switch on your TV, Jules. I'll ask Fred to call everyone in."

Claire exited Juliette's office, giving her a brief moment alone with Steph.

"Thank you for not firing me when, uh, well, you know," Steph said, her face more relaxed.

"Despite some of the things I've said, I never stopped believing in you. You're one of us. You're family."

"I guess that makes you my tough-love auntie," Steph said while getting up. "Come on, auntie. Let's hug it out."

Juliette made her way from behind her desk and gladly accepted Steph's hug, not a doubt in her mind that she had made the right decision.

"Hey, if all goes well, you can pop the question to Nadia tonight," Steph joked when they released each other.

"Ha ha, very funny," Juliette said quickly. "Dominique is coming on Friday, right?" She swiftly changed the subject.

"She sure is." Steph's eyes glinted with pride.

Juliette found the remote control and switched on the TV.

CLAIRE

Claire re-entered Juliette's office carrying two bottles of champagne. "Sorry, couldn't wait," she said.

Juliette rolled her eyes while Steph looked on in surprise.

"Has it started yet?" Fred knocked on the open door.

"Come in, everyone," Juliette said. "Work has been suspended for the rest of the day."

If Claire hadn't been in the same room as Juliette, she would never have believed she'd actually spoken those words. But, whether they believed in the institution of marriage or not—and Claire knew full well how Juliette thought about it, having sat through many of her rants against it—today's vote was important. Barbier & Cyr was founded by two lesbian women, and they'd just promoted a third. This was a huge deal for all of them.

Claire waited until Fred had deposited enough glasses on the coffee table in Juliette's office to pop the first bottle. To her chagrin, most of her co-workers—Steph and Juliette included—refused to drink until the vote had actually passed. Claire didn't have the patience. She retreated to the furthest corner and sipped because, in her own way, she had reason to celebrate.

Inez Larue was leaving Saint-Vincent. She didn't know exactly what it meant yet, what the direct consequences on her life would be, but just the fact that she was leaving was enough cause for a little burst of joy to course through her every time she thought about it—and she had done so often since Juliette had shared the news.

Juliette's office went quiet as the president of the Assemblée announced the vote.

"A bill granting same-sex couples the right to marry…" Claire heard the man say. Steph had positioned herself right in front of the TV.

"Turn it up," Fred said and Juliette instantly obliged.

"Will all those in favour please raise their hand," the man on the screen said.

A joint rush of tension swept through Juliette's office. Only three of them in there knew the truth about Dominique Laroche. For how much longer, though?

As far as Claire could see, a great deal more députés raised their hand than not. The camera zoomed in on the MLR députés and there sat Dominique. Her arm stretched rigidly, her face stern. In that particular wing of the room, most hands had remained lowered.

Claire watched as Juliette curved an arm around Steph's neck. The office broke out in a cheer for her—for their client. When the députés who were against the bill were called to raise their hands, a loud boo noise resounded in unison. But it didn't matter anymore. The bill had passed. A tear ran down Claire's cheek. Then another. As if weeks of emotions were trying to make their way out in that cathartic moment.

And if Claire knew anything in that instant of pure happiness that came with administrative acceptance of what was, basically, her human right, it was that she had to at least instigate a conversation with Margot.

Steph walked over to her, looking as if the weight of the world had been lifted off her shoulders, and clinked the rim of her glass against Claire's.

"You'd better let her fuck you with the biggest strap-on she can find tonight," Claire said, bursting into laughter, not bothering to wipe the tears from her cheeks.

"And you better make sure that, let's say three years from now, Dominique and I can attend your wedding, you know, when you marry a certain doctor who has a penchant for leather."

Claire was too stunned to reply.

"I'm not saying that just for shock-value, boss," Steph said. "I'm saying it because you're my friend and you're miserable without her. Because it needs to be said."

"It's not that simple," Claire heard herself say, going into automatic—and typical—instant defense mode.

"Of course it is," Steph said. "Do you know what *is* complicated? That woman on that TV over there raising her hand for us, for me." Steph's voice broke a little. "Love won today. Remember that."

Then Steph's phone started ringing. By the look on her face, Claire could tell it was Dominique. Steph was right. She was the last person Claire had ever expected to hear those words from, but it didn't make them less true.

She looked around her. Everyone was hugging and breaking out into spontaneous toasts about the power of love. Would Margot be watching this? Perhaps on a TV in the hospital with Nadia? Did Claire even know who Margot really was anymore? Because, yes, three hundred and twenty-nine députés might have just voted that love is love, but what was the love she felt for Margot actually based on?

Perhaps there was only one way to find out.

STEPH

"My boss instructed me to let you fuck me with whichever size strap-on you want," Steph said into Dominique's smiling face. "And she said that after she gave me a promotion."

"They promoted you because I voted for same-sex marriage?" Dominique kept one eye on her phone, which kept buzzing on the table. "Gosh, these lesbian-owned firms…" She shook her head and pulled Steph close. "Congratulations, sweetheart." She'd barely spoken the words before her teeth sank into Steph's earlobe.

"I'm so proud of you," Steph whispered. And she was. Pure euphoria had rushed through her veins on the way to Dominique's apartment. So much so that, on the Métro, she had wondered if people could deduce her level of happiness from the way her skin glowed, and from that smile that seemed etched on her lips forever.

But now, as they stood in their embrace, Dominique's ringing phone a loud reminder of the consequences—because despite the Marriage-for-All bill passing being the headline news, any journalist worth his or her salt would be desperate for a quote from one of MLR's three rebels, and Dominique was still the poster child—Steph's rush soon petered out into a deflated anti-climactic sensation because, as ever, the question remained: now what?

Because yes, lesbian couples could now get married, but Dominique still couldn't come out. The effects of the care-free seven days they had spent together in Juan-les-Pins had worn off—along with the budding confidence Steph had regarding their viability as a couple. Steph was touched by the stand Dominique had taken, but where would they go from here?

"What's wrong?" Dominique asked, when Steph didn't respond to her advances.

But Steph didn't want to bring it up again, not tonight. "Have you heard from your father?" she asked, instead.

"No. Knowing him, he'll wrap himself in silence for a while, expecting me to make the first move. To make it up to him. Because, of course, he's going to take this as a personal affront." Dominique reached for her phone. "But look at this." She scrolled through a few messages and showed Steph the screen. "From my mother."

I raised you well. As your mother, I could not be more proud.

"How sweet." Steph hadn't even told her own mother about Dominique yet. She didn't even know if it was allowed. "Is she a secret Socialist?"

"God no," Dominique said with a huff, as if anything was better than that. "But we share some liberal views."

"I'd love to meet her some day," Steph said without thinking.

"You will, darling. You will." Dominique drew her face into the same expression she had used when raising her hand to vote. Steph didn't know if it was a well-worn mask or a show of determination. She chose to believe the latter.

"How much time have you got?"

Dominique checked her watch. "They want me on the

evening news. I'll be appearing next to Goffin. How's that for getting one over on the Socialists?"

"And here I was thinking you'd voted with your heart."

"I did." Dominique stepped closer. "But this makes it doubly sweet. And I strongly believe that, in the end, MLR will benefit—"

Steph stopped Dominique mid-sentence by kissing her. She wasn't so naive to believe that Dominique had voted against her party's instructions solely out of the goodness of her heart— and based on her feelings for another woman. This was as much politics as anything else she did. But Steph would already have to sit through a TV interview later tonight, in which Dominique would recite all the reasons why she'd voted for the bill, while the only reason that truly mattered would be hiding in the shadows of her own living room.

"I have an hour," Dominique whispered when they broke free from the kiss. "Let's celebrate."

Against Steph's expectations, Dominique pulled her towards the bedroom, where she undressed her slowly—as opposed to the frenzy of the living room quickie Steph had anticipated.

"I won't be using any toys tonight, sweetheart," she said. "I want to feel you."

And then Steph felt it too, because this was the real Dominique. The woman she'd fallen so hard for. The woman only she knew. Not the calculated politician, the divorcee looking for PR advice, or the daughter of Xavier Laroche, but a woman who, with one glance—with one bat of her eyelashes, really—made Steph believe, beyond a shadow of a doubt, that she was the only thing she wanted in life. That all the rest could go to hell.

After they'd both stripped off their clothes and lain down on the bed together, Dominique stared down at Steph for a long moment. For a woman of many words, she said it best without.

Every time Steph stretched her neck to kiss her, Dominique

441

pulled back, a sly smile playing on her lips. "Wait for it," she said.

But Steph had waited long enough and instead of following Dominique's orders, she threw her off of her, spread Dominique's legs with her knee and let her hand wander down. When her fingers found the wetness between Dominique's legs, a cloud of desire enveloped her, and she lost herself—again.

NADIA

"Are you thinking about taking the plunge?" Nadia's mother asked. "Now that you can?" The news had dominated the conversation at Nadia's birthday dinner with her parents. They had even eaten dessert while watching the evening news, not a common practice in the Abadi household—Juliette and Nadia both sunken into a deep silence when Dominique appeared on screen.

"You know we're not really that way inclined," Nadia said quickly, to keep Juliette from having to say it in front of her parents.

"Sure, but perhaps that was mostly out of necessity. Because it wasn't an option anyway." Apparently, she wasn't going to let it go so easily.

"We could have done the whole civil union thing years ago if we'd wanted to," Juliette said. "But it's just not for us." Under the table, she squeezed Nadia's knee.

"I don't want to be a cliché, but I only have one daughter. Don't tell your brother, but being mother of the groom just isn't the same."

"Arrête," Nadia's father said. "Don't listen to her, chérie. She's having one of her episodes. I don't particularly believe in marriage either." This remark cost him a slap on the head from his wife.

"Why don't you get off your lazy married behind and pour us another cognac. It's your only daughter's birthday. Behave."

Nadia had always admired her parents' marriage. After more than forty-five years together, their love seemed as strong as ever. She knew it stood in stark contrast to Juliette's parents, whose marriage had fallen apart when Juliette was fifteen. The divorce hadn't gone very smoothly either—but still decidedly smoother than the process of accepting that they had produced a lesbian daughter. Juliette had cut all ties with her parents before she'd even met Nadia, and Nadia had never been introduced to them—only heard about them in unflattering terms.

She also knew it was one of the many reasons why Juliette would never marry her. Because, at a young and impressionable age, she'd witnessed first-hand that a piece of paper doesn't mean anything.

Doing as he was told, Nadia's dad poured them more drinks. "Good boy," her mother joked, and play-punched him in the bicep.

"This is the sort of stuff I've had to put up with for years," he said, while planting a kiss on his wife's hair.

"I feel for you," Juliette chuckled. "These Abadi women are not easy to live with." Juliette squeezed Nadia's knee under the table again. "But what can we do? We love them anyway."

Nadia's mother winked at her. Nadia hadn't really given her an update on the state of her relationship, but she hoped it came across sufficiently that she and Juliette were doing much better than the last time they had visited together.

"And who knows, maybe we'll make grandparents out of you yet," Juliette said.

Nadia looked at her in disbelief. How much had she actually drunk? Was it that last cognac that had tipped her over the edge?

Both her mother and her father appeared as speechless as Nadia, shuffling in their seats, twirling their fingers around their glass.

"It's just something we've been tentatively talking about," Nadia said. "Very tentatively." She shot Juliette a stern glance.

"Whatever you decide, we support you either way," her mother said while resting her eyes on Juliette.

"Thank you," Juliette said, looking away from Nadia.

"I think we'd best get going." Nadia started pushing her chair back. "It might be my birthday, but it's still a school night." She ruffled her hand through Juliette's hair. "Come on, you."

"I've wrapped up some leftovers, chérie," Nadia's mother said, making it clear Nadia should follow her to the kitchen to take possession of them.

"Don't mind Jules, Mum. I think it's an early midlife crisis or something."

Her mother rested her behind against the countertop. "Is everything okay between you two now?"

"Yes. It is. We're good." Nadia hadn't given her mother all the details. In fact, she'd barely mentioned that she had moved out of their flat for a few weeks. "And hey, congratulations to you, Madame Abadi. After all, it was you who was suffering in the delivery room forty-two years ago. All I did was make my way out successfully."

"Best day of my life, darling." Her mother opened her arms wide. While she embraced her, Nadia felt a twinge of guilt because she let her professional life get in the way of visits home too much. It was only a thirty-minute ride. She should cherish the fact that she and her parents had such a good relationship, unlike Juliette, whose mother and father might as well be dead to her. "And just so you know, I'm more than up to becoming a grandmother."

"Don't you start as well." Nadia mock-wrestled herself free from her mother's hug.

"Is she just saying things or is there some truth to it?" A profound glimmer of hope shone in her mother's eye—a glint Nadia had never seen twinkle in Juliette's eyes whenever she spoke of children.

"Don't hold your horses. She's just acting out mostly."

"How about you, though?"

How about her? Nadia had had her world rocked just as much as Juliette had, yet she wasn't the type to go full-speed in a new direction as a reflex. She was forty-two years old today. Despite promising Juliette that she wouldn't automatically dismiss the idea, Nadia could hardly stand there—in front of her own mother—and confess to having suddenly become host to a huge maternal instinct.

"If this discussion gets anywhere near serious, you'll be the first to know." Nadia stepped closer to her mother again, suddenly in need of another hug.

"I'm just happy you've recovered from whatever was going on between the two of you."

"Nadz," Juliette called from the living room.

"Thanks for dinner, Mamy." Nadia gave her mother's frame one last squeeze and headed back into the other room where Juliette waited for her.

JULIETTE

"I'm sorry, babe," Juliette said when she woke up in the back seat of the cab as it slowed to take their exit on the périphérique. "It's your birthday, you should be the one slouching half-drunk in a taxi."

"Don't worry about it." Nadia shot her a sly smile. "I believe I owe you in that department."

"You're my wife, you don't owe me anything." Across the leather of the seat, Juliette's hand found Nadia's.

"Now that we legally could be wives, you can't just call me that anymore." Nadia intertwined her fingers with Juliette's.

Juliette sat up a bit straighter, scooting closer, cradling Nadia's hand in her lap. "Oops." She lifted Nadia's hand to chin-level. "Well then, I will at least fulfil my *partner*-ly duties when we get home." She sucked one of Nadia's fingers in her mouth.

"It's not a duty, Jules." Nadia all but retracted her hand.

Juliette let Nadia's finger slip from her mouth and turned to her. The taxi had reached their street, but stood still in traffic, the sound of its blinker tick-tocking like a clock. "It was a joke." She didn't let go of Nadia's hand. "What's the matter?"

Nadia sighed before speaking. "I wish you wouldn't just blurt out statements about having children in front of my parents. Not before we've properly discussed it. It's not something to take lightly. I know for a fact that Mamy will be awake all night thinking about it, even though she'll never admit to it."

"And by that, do you mean you'll be up all night fretting about it as well?"

The taxi came to a halt in front of their building. Juliette paid the driver and they got out.

Nadia waited until they were in the lift, a small coffin-sized space that forced them to stand close to each other, to reply. "I have no need to worry about your child wish, Jules. Because I've been your *partner* for ten years and I know you. You need a new thought to occupy your mind for a while—so it doesn't have to linger on the mistakes you've made."

The elevator ground to a halt with a light bump. Nadia got out first and unlocked the front door, giving Juliette ample time to think before responding. Juliette sucked in a deep breath, but it didn't diminish the sensation of being totally misunderstood by the one person who should get her—who claimed to know her so well.

"The mistakes *I* made?" If Nadia—and Claire and Steph, for that matter—were right about one thing, it was that their relationship was still much too fragile after the reconciliation for Juliette's thoughts to venture in the direction of having children. But what? All three of them suddenly had periscopic insight into her brain? Into her desires?

"Let's sit down for a minute." Nadia wore her calm face, the one that, in situations like this, had the potential to drive Juliette right over the edge. Nadia was always the unflappable, reasonable one, making Juliette look like a loony in the process. And Juliette knew that, in that simple sentence, a whole other meaning lay implied. What Nadia really wanted to say was: *let's take a moment before you go off the deep end again and say things you'll regret.*

Fury rising in her gut—because Juliette knew that, at least about this, Nadia was right—Juliette sat down. It was late. She'd had too much to drink. All she wanted to do was go to bed and sleep it off.

Nadia waited for Juliette to speak, which, on top of the anger already flaring inside of her, made Juliette's blood boil even more. She sat watching Nadia, their eyes meeting only briefly—because Juliette had to look away when she watched Nadia look at her and imagined what she might be thinking.

"I love you, Jules," Nadia said, out of the blue. "Even though you have a temper and despite being a control freak, it's the one thing you can't control. I know it drives you nuts. I know that, right at this moment, you're sitting there feeling like the world is against you, like *I* am against you. But I'm not. I'm always with you. And over the years, I've come to understand where your anger stems from. I know who you are, babe. I know you."

"But—" Juliette couldn't speak through the tears that had started streaming down her cheeks, through the lump in her throat the size of her heart.

Nadia crouched beside her and put a hand on her knee. "It's okay. You don't have to say anything. I know." Nadia rose and reached out her hand. "Come on, let's go to bed."

"But it's your birthday," Juliette managed to say in between sobs.

"So? All I wanted was to spend it with you. I got my wish."

Juliette took Nadia's hand and pulled herself up out of the sofa. Her mind was numbed because of the crying, but Juliette was alert enough to remember the surprise she had prepared for Nadia's birthday party. A warm glow, almost cutting straight through the hurt, spread through her at the thought of it.

MARGOT

"It was a pleasure working with you, doctor de Hay," Inez said. Margot knew she'd said her goodbyes to the rest of the staff already. This was their moment.

"Do you want to go for a drink?" Margot felt uncomfortable doing this in the hospital changing room.

"No." Inez shook her head. "This is it, Go-Go. I can't."

Margot nodded her understanding. "Thank you for—"

"Don't thank me for ruining your life, please." A sad smile crept along Inez' lips.

Still, after all that had happened, Margot wanted to step in and kiss it into a happy smile. Instead, she huffed out a chuckle. "You know me, always too polite."

"Oh sure." Inez' face lit up a bit. "And always overflowing with words."

When Margot didn't reply—because she didn't know what to say—Inez continued. "I'm sorry. I really am."

"I know." Margot did step closer this time. She searched for Inez' hands with hers and curled her fingers in a tight grip around them. "You will always be important to me."

Inez slanted her head to the right a bit. "If only I'd handled things differently, we could have been friends by now."

"No. We could never be friends. There's too much between us."

"Too much unfriendliness?" Inez grinned.

"I wouldn't call it that." Margot lifted one hand to Inez' face and let the back of her index finger skate along her ex-girlfriend's cheek while looking into her green eyes. Her finger gravitated towards Inez' lips, but Margot corrected its path before she got too mesmerised by Inez' presence again. Inez

Larue, the one woman she couldn't resist. The woman she'd given it all up for.

Inez caught Margot's caressing hand with hers and pressed it to her cheek on a sharp intake of breath. "There's no one like you, Go-Go." She swallowed before continuing. "And I truly, wholeheartedly, hope that you and Claire get back together. I saw it when she came here to confront me. She loves you. She loves you like I did. Like I *do*."

Margot inched closer, as close as she could go, and kissed Inez on the lips. One last kiss. A touch with at least a few good emotions attached to it, to erase all the painful ones that came before. "I'll try," she said, as she pulled back, and stepped away from Inez forever.

Inez had packed up her locker earlier and headed for the door. Before disappearing through it, she turned around one more time. Her ginger hair hung loose and wild around her head; her eyes were moist. She didn't say anything, just looked at Margot, but Margot knew what she wanted to express.

One blink of her eyes, and Inez was gone. The thud of the door as she closed it behind her echoing through the room, like the memory of her face, of that last look, etching itself into Margot's brain forever.

Although Margot had promised herself not to burst into tears anymore, especially at work, her eyes filled with moisture, big drops raining down her cheeks in wide tracks. Because with Inez, a part of herself had walked out of that door. The part that had crushed her upon Inez' return. The part of her that loved so unconditionally, it destroyed lives.

She would need to consider her options of how to get back into Claire's good graces. And she knew it would take time. The slow approach. She needed time to get back to herself again as well, to feel like herself again, because this person she'd become over the past month—the too sensitive sides of her personality on full display—had to be reined in. Maybe not as much as before, but enough to make her feel human again.

CLAIRE

"Jules, relax. It's just us." Claire didn't know what Juliette was so up in arms about. "You're not even doing all of the cooking yourself."

"You can't very well expect me to present Dominique Laroche with one of my country home dishes."

"You're a good cook, Jules. No one expects restaurant quality. Is that why you're so nervous? Because Dominique is coming?"

"God no." Juliette shook her head, but didn't elaborate further.

"Do you want to talk about it?" Claire tried.

"No. I want to, but it's a surprise." Juliette chewed the inside of her cheek.

"You haven't adopted a child behind everyone's back, have you?" Claire joked.

Juliette burst out laughing. "Ah, mon dieu. No, of course not." She made a gesture with her hand that signalled she didn't want to discuss the surprise she had planned further.

"Has Margot confirmed her presence?" Because if anyone should be nervous about tonight's party, it was Claire.

"Yep, so try to behave, will you. No crying in my hallway tonight." Juliette said it with a smirk that made Claire forgive her for the remark instantly.

"I wouldn't dream of it." Claire scanned Juliette's face. What was she up to?

"Inez left the hospital already, you know. Said her goodbyes earlier this week."

Claire's heartbeat picked up speed again. "I'm sure deep down she's a lovely person, but good riddance."

"Have you spoken to Margot at all since you heard about Inez' departure?"

Claire drew her lips into a pout and shook her head. "No, I, uh, have been busy with work."

"Oh please." Of course, Juliette saw straight through her. "You're scared."

"Of course I'm bloody scared. The woman broke my heart."

"I know. I'm sorry." Juliette paced to the window of Claire's office and perched against the windowsill. "Are you waiting for her to make the first move?"

"I guess." *At the party you're throwing for your partner*, Claire thought, but was wise enough not to say out loud. "I said some really hurtful things to her the last time I saw her. Practically chased her out of my flat. I really thought we were done after that. Which is why I let Steph convince me to go on that stupid blind date. That poor woman…" Claire just stared in front of her for an instant. "But now that Inez is leaving… and then Steph said some things again. I don't know, Jules."

"No drama in my hallway, either." Juliette raised a finger while cocking her head.

"Don't ask too much of me, Jules. I'm only human." Claire put a hand to her chest. Beneath, her heart was still thundering away.

"God, it'll be so strange to actually see Steph with another woman. Someone she's actually with, as opposed to someone she just picked up. In all the years I've known her, it will be the first time."

"It's going to be one hell of a party." Claire rose from her chair. "Why don't we let the ship be managed by our new assistant manager for the rest of the afternoon? Let's get out of here, Jules. Have a drink at Le Comptoir to take the edge off."

"Oh no. I absolutely cannot be tipsy before this party starts. Out of the question." She started pacing again. "Besides, I have some things to arrange." With that, she walked to the door and opened it. "I'll see you tonight. Seven-thirty sharp." She closed the door and was gone.

Claire checked her watch. It was only four, but there was no way she'd be getting any more work done, what with the thought of seeing Margot again gnawing on her mind. She dialled Steph's direct line and invited her for a drink instead.

NADIA

Juliette tucked the same strand of hair behind her ear for the hundredth time, in between running from the kitchen to the living room, and practically measuring the spacing between the cutlery and the plates on the table—crouching down until her eyes were level with the surface, squinting like a scientist in a lab.

"Babe," Nadia said, but Juliette didn't seem to hear. She put a bit more urgency in her voice when she spoke the second time. "Jules, come here."

Nadia leaned her backside against the armrest of the sofa as she watched Juliette hesitate between obedience and more mania. "Come on." Nadia waved her fingers in her own direction.

"I'm sorry. I just need to adjust these spoons—" She glanced over at Nadia, tugging at her fingertips.

"Fuck the spoons." Nadia held her arms wide. "It's my party and I want a hug from you."

Juliette checked her wristwatch. "The party hasn't started yet."

If Nadia didn't know any better—and if they weren't expecting their friends to arrive in ten minutes—she'd bet Juliette was gunning for another spanking.

"All the more reason to stop freaking out and get yourself over here." The tone Nadia used this time around wasn't one Juliette would ignore.

Juliette headed in her direction, her lips drawn into a defiant pout. "I just want everything to be perfect for you." She grabbed Nadia's hands and looked her in the eyes.

"I think, in this instance, you're mistaking me for you, babe." Nadia pulled Juliette closer. "Because for me, everything is already more than perfect." Nadia kissed Juliette on the forehead. "I wish you'd just relax."

Juliette took a deep breath. "I will," she said, but Nadia could feel the tension in her muscles—and the tell-tale deepening of the line bracketing the right side of her mouth.

"We've thrown dozens of parties like this, Jules. What's so important about this one that it has you all worked up?"

Juliette shrugged. "It's the first one since we got back together."

"Oh babe." Nadia tugged her even closer, wrapping her arms around Juliette. She wished she could sneak inside Juliette's brain and erase a few of the useless worries she carried around with her all the time. "It'll be just fine."

The doorbell interrupted their hug. Nadia felt her partner tense in her arms and wished Juliette had accepted some of the wine Nadia had poured earlier, just to relax a little.

"Showtime," Juliette muttered nervously and sauntered to the hallway.

Nadia hoped that, despite her inexplicable case of jitters, Juliette would be able to enjoy the party. It wasn't as if she'd prepared the meal all by herself—and that Nadia wasn't around to help her.

Juliette re-entered the living room with Steph and Dominique in tow. Nadia recognised her from TV, and that image in the newspaper that had shown her raising her hand proudly in the Assemblée, not a flicker of doubt on her face. Perhaps it was foolish, but she felt strangely honoured to have Dominique Laroche attend her birthday party.

"Happy birthday, Nadz." Steph's eyes sparkled. "Nadia. Dominique. And vice versa." She threw her hands around in an agitated fashion.

"Thank you very much for inviting me into your home." Dominique widened her arms and placed her hands on Nadia's shoulders. "Et joyeux anniversaire." The députée pecked Nadia on both cheeks, giving her frame a firm squeeze in the process.

"Enchantée," Nadia said, and she really was slightly enchanted by the star power Dominique exuded.

The bell rang again. Their friends knew to arrive on time for a party that Juliette had planned. Juliette got the door while Nadia invited Steph and her girlfriend—it felt so strange to think of, first of all, Steph having one and, secondly, referring to Dominique Laroche that way—to sit.

Claire walked in, looking marginally better than the last time Nadia had seen her, although, when they embraced, through the scent of freshly brushed teeth, Nadia could smell a faint whiff of alcohol on her breath. Claire greeted Dominique casually, pecking her on the cheeks as if she were an old friend.

The four of them sat around the coffee table while Juliette poured champagne. Nadia caught her glancing at the clock, quite possibly inwardly cursing Margot for being a few minutes late—but Margot worked the ER and being late could never be held against her.

"We might as well—" Juliette started to say, when the chime of the bell cut through the chatter in the living room. "Please excuse me."

Nadia could see Claire stiffen. Steph, who sat next to her, patted her on the thigh. Claire quickly took a sip of champagne without waiting for Juliette's welcome speech.

Nadia rose when Margot, who was hiding behind her familiar mask of steel, walked into the living room. She hugged her and introduced her to Dominique. Margot kissed Claire furtively on the cheek, barely touching her, and when she sat down next to Nadia, the atmosphere in the room had noticeably changed.

Nadia had hoped Claire and Margot would have met up prior to this evening to at least clear the air, but Juliette had told her that Claire expected Margot to make the first move and Nadia knew Margot was—as per usual—taking her time.

"Thank you all for coming," she said while raising her glass. She let her eyes roam across all of their faces. Steph basked in

Dominique's presence, she sat more upright, more aware of herself maybe, and an edginess had worked its way into her gestures, undoing her usual nonchalance. She was nervous about bringing Dominique here, Nadia could tell, but she looked happy.

Nadia didn't know Dominique and, therefore, couldn't tell if the pride in her glance came from stepping out with her girl-friend, or if it was just how she carried herself through life.

Already, Claire couldn't keep her eyes off Margot. Her gaze appeared unfocused though, as if, either she was ready to burst into tears at any moment, or she'd knocked back more than a few before arriving. Quite possibly both.

Margot didn't move a muscle, her face unreadable. Nadia knew she would mellow—or that she would at least try. God, she was glad she hadn't allowed her to leave Saint-Vincent, that she had spoken to Inez behind Margot's back and against her wish. The stoic doctor had, despite falling apart, become one of her best friends.

Then there was Juliette who, now that she had a glass of champagne in her hand, seemed to relax a little. She allowed the strand of hair she'd been battling with earlier to fall onto her cheek, and her lips were drawn into an easy smile. From the start, and despite falling hard for her, Nadia had known that Juliette Barbier would never be an easy person to love. Nadia loved her all the more for it.

She let her gaze dart around the room and a smile slid along her lips. For all the tension in the room, and all the heartbreak that had caused it, these people were her life. She found Juli-ette's eyes and clinked the rim of her glass against hers.

"Thank you," she said.

MARGOT

Margot hadn't seen Claire since that evening she'd walked out on her. It seemed that, since then, everything had changed all over again. Although Nadia had only briefly mentioned it, the thought had been stuck in her mind ever since: Claire had gone on a date. No matter the fact that Nadia had clearly stated it had been a disaster, Claire had taken conscious steps to set up a rendez-vous with another woman. Margot could hardly hold it against her—after all, she had slept with Inez—but it stung just the same.

"Shall we eat?" Juliette said and, automatically, Margot stood up. She was the first to leave her seat, towering over the other women awkwardly.

"I'm starving." Claire rose quickly, taking a step towards Margot, as if coming to her rescue. Her eyes were a bit watery when they landed on Margot's. "Do you need help, Jules?" Claire looked away from her, and even that hurt. Claire didn't wait for Juliette's answer and headed towards the kitchen.

"Are there assigned places?" Steph asked Nadia with a chuckle.

"Probably, but just sit where you want," Nadia replied.

The following minutes passed in a rumble of scratching chair feet and plates clattering against plates as Juliette and Claire deposited starters on the table. Margot hadn't really paid much attention, but with the couples drifting towards sitting together naturally, she found herself seated next to Claire once they'd all taken their place.

"Before we start eating," Claire said, successfully ignoring—or, at least so it seemed to Margot—the fact that she was sitting next to her ex, their elbows practically touching. "Let's toast to Dominique, who stood up for us this week."

"Hear, hear." Juliette raised her glass and all the others followed suit.

"No need to thank me, it was more a symbolic gesture, really," Dominique said. "And well, this one has her own ways of persuading me to go against my party." She poked Steph in the bicep.

"I'll make a Socialist out of you yet," Steph said.

Dominique turned to her. "There are limits to dirty talk, sweetheart. You know what happens when you push them."

"Oooh," Claire cooed next to Margot, making her break out into a cold sweat.

———

After finishing the starter, as Margot helped clear the plates, she could feel Claire come up behind her in the kitchen. She turned around. It was just the two of them. Perhaps orchestrated by Claire or perhaps pure coincidence.

"I heard she left." Claire's voice was low and still full of reproach.

I heard you went on a date, Margot wanted to say, but the time for unfair comments had long passed. She just nodded, thrown by Claire's presence in the small quarters of the kitchen.

"Were you going to let me know at all?"

This question knocked Margot off guard. "Clearly, you already know."

"Right." Claire nodded sternly while arching up her eyebrows.

"I'm sorry." Margot knew she had to regroup quickly.

"Please don't tell me you're sad to see her go." A bitter grin crept along Claire's face.

"Claire, I, uh, I want to talk to you. Explain things better, if you'll let me." Margot heard her voice waver. "Only, last time, you made it quite clear that you—"

"Stop. Just stop." Claire held up her hands and shook her head. "This—" She let her hands slide through the air between them, from Margot's head until they pointed at her toes. "—is not the woman I fell for. This grovelling, weak mess." She inched closer. "You're going to have to try a little harder. I can't do anything with a bunch of meek apologies." She threw Margot one last glance, before turning around and leaving the kitchen.

457

Margot found support against the sink, folding her fingers around the counter.

"Hey." Juliette's face appeared in the doorframe. "I hate to interrupt, but I need to get the mains out."

"Of course. Sure." Margot straightened her posture.

"Wait up," Juliette said, grabbing Margot by the wrist. "Some unsolicited advice, if you don't mind." She fixed her eyes on Margot. "Just be yourself and she'll come crawling back in no time." She confirmed her statement with a swift nod of the head.

As Margot exited the kitchen, she wondered where she'd left herself—if she'd left with Inez, again.

When she approached the dining table and saw Claire sitting there, her eyes resting coolly on Margot as she inched closer, one arm slung back on Margot's empty chair, she knew she'd better find her lost self quickly.

JULIETTE

"Don't we usually have coffee with the birthday cake, Jules?" Steph asked as Juliette deposited fresh champagne glasses on the table.

"Yes, but today will be unusual." Nerves crept up her spine as she walked to the fridge to fetch the bottle she'd saved for this moment. She popped the cork with a bang, causing a frisson of excitement to ripple though the room.

After distributing the glasses, Juliette cleared her throat. *Fuck. This was it.* She'd memorised the speech, rehearsed it countless times in her head. She could do this.

Five pairs of eyes stared at her expectantly.

"I would like to propose a toast to this gorgeous woman sitting here." She put a hand on Nadia's shoulder. "Whose birthday we're celebrating today, and who I am lucky enough to call my partner of ten years." Gosh, was this all not too formal? "You all know that the last three months have been the most challenging of our relationship, but here we are. On the other end of this crisis that, quite frankly, ripped me apart." She could already feel the first tear burning behind her eyes. "It made me realise that without her, without you, babe," Juliette turned to Nadia, "I'm only half the woman I can be." She took strength from the sweet smile Nadia sent her way. Everyone was silent, despite Juliette having expected a few wisecracks from Steph and Claire at this point. "You know me better than anyone. Put up with all my bitchy moods. Make me a better person." A lone tear slid down Juliette's cheek. "You understand me and accept me for who I am and I love you with everything I have." Juliette swallowed a lump out of her throat. "So, without further ado." Juliette let her hand slip from Nadia's shoulder and slid it into her back pocket. "I would like to ask you…" She produced a red velvet box from her pocket and held it in front of her. She'd practiced this bit in front of the mirror. Falling on one knee, she opened the box. "If you would do me the unspeakable honour of becoming my wife."

The room had been silent before, but now it seemed frozen in a stunned sort of quiet, time standing still. Juliette watched Nadia's jaw slacken, her fingers covering her open mouth.

Hot tears streaked Juliette's cheeks as she looked up at Nadia, her heart hammering furiously beneath her chest.

"Mon dieu," Nadia exclaimed. "Are you? Is this?" Her eyes widened as she rose from her chair. "Yes," she screamed then. "A thousand times yes." She crouched next to Juliette and looked her in the eyes. "Yes." Nadia planted her palms on Juliette's cheeks and drew her close for a kiss. It was sloppy, their lips soaked with tears. "I love you." Nadia rubbed a bit of wetness off of Juliette's cheekbone with her thumb. "And I can't believe it."

Juliette lifted the ring from its cushion in the box. "Give me your hand, babe."

Nadia's fingers trembled as she raised her hand. Juliette had to steady it with her own to slip the ring over her finger.

Having spent the past few minutes in a bubble of just her and Nadia, Juliette slowly became aware of other sounds again. Chairs screeching. Hands clapping. Noses running.

"Jesus christ, Jules. You nearly gave me a heart attack." Claire stood beside her, towering over her—Juliette was still down on one knee. "For someone who doesn't believe in marriage, you sure made a statement."

Juliette rose, holding on to Nadia's hand. She had wanted to do this in front of their friends, had wanted to make that statement.

"Congratulations," Claire said, and hugged them both.

Juliette looked over at Nadia, who still appeared rather perplexed by the turn of events. She pulled her close. "I believe in us," she whispered in her ear. "I believe in you and me."

"You've just turned me into a hopeless romantic." Steph approached them, her eyes wet with tears. "I'm so happy for the pair of you." Dominique came up behind her.

"Thank you," Juliette said to the députée. "Without what you did, I wouldn't have been able to do this." More hugs were exchanged and congratulations offered.

"Félicitations." Margot was last in line, her voice destroyed by emotion.

Juliette held her tight for a minute. "Love is love," she whispered in Margot's ear. "And she loves you." Juliette felt her own throat swell again, a new wave of tears gathering behind her eyes.

"Please grab your glasses," Nadia said, their hands still intertwined. "I'd like to say something as well." She wrapped her fingers a bit more tightly around Juliette's. Dominique offered them both their glasses, and all six of them stood around the dining table.

"If I can stop sniffling, that is," Nadia said.

Juliette squeezed her hand for support. She had the same problem, but she was done with making speeches for the night.

"My lovely Jules." Nadia turned her body so she half-faced

Juliette. "To say that you've blindsided me with this, would be an understatement." Her voice sounded drenched with love. Giggles erupted around them. "But, that being said, I can't wait to become your wife. The day I say 'I do' to you will be the proudest of my life." The last words barely made it out of her throat.

Juliette stared into Nadia's face, at the emotion on display, her moist brown eyes and her lips alternately being tugged into a smile and a grimace because of all the crying. She put her champagne glass on the table and threw her arms around Nadia —her fiancée.

"Oh jesus, if this is anything to go by, imagine what a sob fest the wedding will be," Steph said, followed by an offended, "Ouch."

"You're ruining the moment." Juliette recognised Dominique's voice.

"Sod the speeches." Nadia pulled herself free from Juliette's hug. "Let's celebrate." She raised her glass and looked around the room. "To all of us."

Juliette quickly grabbed her glass off the table and held it high. "And to love," she added. "If I, with all my faults and shortcomings, can snatch a woman like Nadia, there's hope for all of us." She smiled at the sight of her friends, halting the roaming of her glance at Claire. *And none of us would be standing here, celebrating my engagement, if it hadn't been for forgiveness,* she wanted to say to her best friend. But she knew, that, just as had been the case with herself, Claire would find her own way out.

CLAIRE

After they'd all sat down again and Nadia had cut the birthday cake—a rather anti-climactic event after all that had come before—Claire found herself mere inches away from Margot again. She'd been struck by the visible display of emotions on

461

Margot's face at the proposal and Claire was sorry she'd been so hard on her earlier.

Because Claire felt it too. The jubilant presence of love in the room. It stared her in the face. Twice. Her best friend had just proposed to the love of her life while Steph and her secret lover had witnessed it. Dominique had planted a slew of spontaneous kisses on every patch of Steph's skin she could find after the speeches, while Nadia and Juliette had fallen into embrace after embrace. All the while, she and Margot had barely managed a timid smile, had scarcely looked at each other.

Claire knew she had every right to be angry, after the break-up and Margot's pathetic performance at her flat the other week. But now, surrounded by all this love, by the evidence of what a simple bout of forgiveness could achieve—although Claire was far from convinced it was all that simple—a layer of hardness had started to peel away. And then there was the additional fact that Inez had left.

Clearly, Margot was a mess. But wasn't the simple fact that she was in such a state of disarray evidence of how deeply she loved? She had told Claire, from the very beginning, that she'd been hurt and needed to go slow. She hadn't asked for Inez to come back. Nobody would ever wish to be so thrown off kilter. She'd clearly handled it wrong, but what if this *was* their second chance?

Looking straight ahead, trying to tune back into the conversation briefly, Claire put her hand on Margot's knee under the table. Underneath her fingers, she felt Margot's muscles harden. Instantly, it sent a jolt of electricity into her bloodstream. She took a deep breath and turned to Margot.

"Love won," she said, digging her fingers deeper into Margot's jeans. "Let's talk." Claire felt how her hand was being covered by Margot's, their fingers intertwining.

"Please excuse us for a moment." Margot shoved her chair back and rose. Because of their hands being conjoined, Claire had to follow her example and scrambled out of her chair.

"Of course," Juliette said.

Claire barely caught the quick wink Juliette shot her before Margot dragged her through the hallway into Nadia and Juliette's guest room. Margot closed the door behind them and let go of Claire's hand.

"I—" Claire started saying.

"No." Margot had her hands on her hips, staring at her with a look that set Claire's insides on fire. "My turn to talk."

Claire just nodded and sat down on the edge of the bed, allowing Margot to tower over her.

"I was ready to leave. After our last talk, I was going to pack up and skip town. Leave this mess, everything, behind. A coward move, I know." She let her hands slide from her hips, as though in defeat. "When I looked in the mirror, I didn't recognise myself, and, in the end, I'm glad the decision wasn't left solely up to me. Nadia talked to Inez and Inez decided that she should be the one to leave, not me. The point is, I was ready to forsake myself. To give it all up." She clenched her fists into tight balls. "I am not a coward, Claire. But there I was." Shaking her head, she pinned her eyes on Claire. "And you know why?" Margot swallowed something out of her throat. "Because what Nadia said to me the other day was true. I am more principled than others. I always try to do better, achieve more, be—" She interrupted herself with a chuckle. "—more pure and honest than anyone else… and for what?" Scoffing at herself, she stepped forward and crashed down next to Claire on the bed. "I can sit here and try to tell myself I lost myself because of love, because I loved too much and it hurt too much, but if that's the case, it's only because I let it." She turned to Claire and held out her hand. Claire put hers on top of it.

"This is me asking for a second chance, again," Margot said. "But this time, I'm asking for the right reasons."

Claire sucked her bottom lip into her mouth. She knew that she would never get back the Margot she fell in love with, because the person sitting next to her was not the woman she had met a few months ago. This was a stripped bare, torn down version of Margot, with her arms and heart wide open. As if Claire was meeting the real Margot de Hay for the very first time.

"As I said," Claire managed to squeeze through the thickness in her throat. "Love won. And I love you." She ran her fingers up Margot's wrist. "And I can hardly say no after witnessing the most romantic proposal ever." She clasped her other hand to her chest. "For me anyway, because I know Juliette through and through, and that…" She pointed a thumb in the direction of the hallway. "I don't even have words to describe the sheer impossibility of it in my mind, but here we are. I was there to see it with my own two eyes." She got up from the bed and yanked Margot up with her. "My answer is yes, but I do have conditions."

"Of course." Margot drew her lips into a lopsided grin.

"I don't know how this evening will end, but if and when we end up in bed together—be it tonight, tomorrow or next week—you give up control to me." She inched closer to Margot. "I think it's time you learned to surrender."

Margot chuckled. "Really?"

"Oh yes." Claire nodded and threw her arms around Margot's neck. "And I will use those handcuffs you bought."

"Is there any room for negotiation?" Margot's arms curved around Claire's waist.

"None whatsoever." Claire stared into the blackness of Margot's eyes, happy to not have to waste any more energy—and hung-over mornings—on getting over her.

"We'll see." Margot tilted her head and leaned in.

When Claire kissed her she knew she'd made the right call. And when their lips opened and their tongues met, and weeks of pent-up lust and anger and frustration uncoiled in her stomach, she wiped the slate clean. Because, love may have won, but without forgiveness—and second chances—she wouldn't be standing in Margot's embrace, thinking of ways to try and make her submit.

STEPH

They had retreated back to the sitting area with a bottle of cognac and Steph sat watching Dominique chat with Nadia, who was showing off her engagement ring, when Margot and Claire re-emerged, hand in hand.

"Hallelujah," Steph shouted. "There must be something in the air tonight."

In response, Margot and Claire just smiled at each other sheepishly.

"It's your move, babe," she said to Dominique. "Bonne chance, if you want to upstage a proposal and a long-awaited reunion."

"That's hardly fair, Steph," Juliette said. "Clearly, Dominique's big gesture is that she's here with us tonight, after having raised her hand so defiantly during the vote on Monday. What more do you want?"

"Fine. The oldies have it." Steph admitted defeat. "I guess we won't be stopping at Les Pêches tonight."

Margot and Claire joined them in the sofa, practically sitting on top of each other. Was everyone happy now? Steph sipped from her cognac and glanced around, her eyes, as always, automatically halting at Dominique. Sure, it was wonderful that Juliette and Nadia were getting hitched and that Claire had succumbed to the power of love and had decided to give Margot another chance. But, basically, these two outcomes might as well have been written in the stars. The most astonishing fact was that she and Dominique were attending their first social function together, that they sat here, as a couple, amongst Steph's friends.

"Come here," Steph gestured at Dominique, feeling the effects of hard liquor after wine and champagne.

Nadia cocked her head as Dominique squeezed herself into the sofa next to Steph, a big smile on her face.

Steph snuck her arm behind Dominique's back and tugged her close. "I'm so glad you're here," she whispered in her ear.

"Oh, look at our Stéphanie," Claire joked. "She's gone all lovey-dovey on us."

"I wouldn't worry too much," Dominique said, leaning into Steph's embrace. "She's clearly drunk."

"Drunk on love," Steph heard herself say, her words beginning to slur. The others burst out laughing.

"What's that, sweetheart?" Dominique asked. "Is that your phone vibrating or did you bring something from your toy box?" She tucked her hand between their touching thighs.

"Not even I would bring a vibrator to a birthday party." Steph fished her phone out of her pocket and checked the screen. "Oh christ, what does she want?" She looked up and stared into Juliette and Nadia's overjoyed faces. This was not the time to mention Sybille's name. Whatever it was, she would deal with it later. It was after midnight. She was drunk. Her friends had just gotten engaged.

On a cabinet behind where Juliette was sitting, another phone lit up while emitting a loud beep.

"That's mine," Juliette said. "I'll just turn it off." She rose from her seat, giving Nadia's shoulder a squeeze. "Or perhaps word has gotten out already." She shot them all a grin before sauntering off to fetch her phone.

Steph witnessed Juliette's features stiffen as she glanced at the screen. "It's from Sybille," she said, apparently not having any qualms about mentioning her former assistant's name in her home.

How strange. Steph looked away from Juliette and dug her phone out of her pocket again.

"Are you all right, babe?" she heard Nadia ask Juliette, but Steph's eyes were glued to her own phone's screen, a text message from Sybille flickering on it.

466

Just a heads-up, as a courtesy from 1 PR professional to another…
this will be Le Matin's headline tomorrow.

Fear and anger raged inside of Steph as she clicked on the image Sybille had included in the message. *Le Matin*'s bright red heading appeared on top, underneath, in bold black letters, the newspaper's weekend edition headline read:

THE REAL REASON WHY DOMINIQUE LAROCHE VOTED FOR SAME-SEX MARRIAGE

The headline was positioned on top of a collage of pictures of Steph leaving and arriving at Dominique's Avenue Foch address, including the first one Sybille had delivered to Juliette, alongside the picture of Dominique in the Assemblée with her arm stretched firmly.

Steph's stomach dropped at the sight of herself on the front page of this rag, but immediately, instinctively, she thought that a few grainy pictures wouldn't prove anything, unless…

A second message from Sybille arrived.

And in case you're wondering, yes, the 'sources close to' = me. ;-)

Steph looked up, at Juliette's ashen face.

"Cette salope," Juliette said.

"What's going on?" Dominique asked. "Bad news?"

Steph took a deep breath. Her head was swimming, but the shock of seeing herself on the front page of *Le Matin* had, at least, sobered her up. She passed her phone to Dominique, the image of *Le Matin* displayed in full screen mode.

"Putain," Dominique said. She turned to Steph, panic in her eyes. Then something else took over. Perhaps because she was a politician, or perhaps even because, on some subconscious level she'd been expecting this, Dominique's glance turned from frantic dread into cold steel in a split second.

"What?" Nadia had gotten up as well, rushing to a perplexed Juliette's side.

"It's out," Juliette said. "It will be all over the news tomorrow."

"What?" Nadia appeared none the wiser.

Dominique shot up out of the sofa. "That Stéphanie and I are together." Her voice was calm and collected.

"Are you kidding me?" Claire chimed in. Dominique handed her the phone.

"Are you sure this is real? Not some practical joke?" Nadia asked, her eyes on Juliette's phone.

"I've seen enough of these mock-ups to know this is the real thing," Dominique replied.

"This is no joke, babe," Juliette said. "This is revenge."

"I hate to do this to you tonight." Dominique took charge. "But let's make some coffee and get to work." She turned to Steph. "Life as you know it, has just ended, babe."

THE END (FOR NOW…)

468

ABOUT THE AUTHOR

Harper Bliss is a best-selling lesbian romance author. Among her most-loved books are the highly dramatic French Kissing and the often thought-provoking Pink Bean series.

Harper lived in Hong Kong for seven years, travelled the world for a bit, and has now settled in the Belgian countryside with her wife, Caroline, and her photogenic cat, Dolly Purrton.

Harper loves hearing from readers and you can reach her at the email address below.

www.harperbliss.com
harper@harperbliss.com

Printed in Great Britain
by Amazon

44984600R10270